To Trevor
my beloved husband
and to all those who survived
the East End blitz

Book One
1920

Chapter One

It was September 1920 and the shadows were thick against the gleam of street-lamps. The moon swam high above London's East End. It looked like a pallid pea in a soup-laden sky. In number six Solomon Street well-built Clara Cuttings let her freshly dolly-dyed curtains fall into place. The ambulance had driven away from number twelve and there was nothing further to be seen.

Clara pushed her dark tousled hair out of her attractively slanted eyes, and tut-tutted as she went back to her bed. It was the couch in her downstairs front room. Horse hair sprouted through the splits in the brown Rexine.

The broken springs creaked under her rounded, night-gowned vest- and bloomer-covered weight, but she was used to it. All in all the couch was comfortable enough, even though the room itself was cold. Still it was a nice room, clean and well-polished and with some decent bits and bobs around. The couch itself had been all right, handsome when first bought even though priced very cheap. George still said it was his favourite bit of furniture. He used it a lot. That's how young Rosie had come to be born.

Clara smirked in the gloom, looking towards the white blur on the wall opposite – which was all she could see of her husband's Army picture. He had been so young, and thank Gawd, arrived home safe at the end of the war. And she and the twins had been there waiting. The boss had given him a lower-rated job on the railway where he'd been apprenticed. Even though his original place had been taken, he became a fitter's mate, earned two pounds one and sixpence a week, and what with Clara's cleaning jobs, they did very well. After all, lots of Tommies came home from the war to find no job at all. George was aware of his good fortune. Always made the best of things did George, dear ol' boy.

In her mind's eye she thought of how he had looked in his uniform. He'd been a handsome sod, little and perfect. She was sure that Mademoiselle from Armentières would have died for him given the chance – she, Clara Webb that was, would have. Still felt the same. Even more so when you came to think of it.

She began talking to the smiling soldier photograph. She usually did when he, George himself, was not there.

'You're a dirty old devil, Georgy Porgy,' she whispered. 'Like your share of oats you do. You hot-arse little sod! This couch was your idea, eh? No wonder the springs got broke. Wouldn't be put off, would yer? Thank Gawd.'

Her smile faded as her mind went back to the ambulance she had just seen, sliding round the corner like an evil mystery box on wheels. Hospitals! They took you to hospital to die, everyone knew that.

'Poor ol' Jack,' Clara said aloud. 'And poor little cow Kathy what's started before her time. Not a chance there, what a horrible shame. My Gawd! Why do rotten sad things always happen to the good 'uns in the world?'

She pulled the ex-Army blanket over her head and was still unable to sleep. She kept thinking of how she had first met Jack London and his wife Kathy. They were quite new to the street, moving in from a rented room in slovenly down-at-heel Dawlish Close that was way along the High Road.

Right at the start, the word had flown, from the clean and decent top end of Solomon Street to the far more scruffy Feathers end, that the new 'uns were posh – and actually buying! Buying a house? Unheard of! They must be really daft devils cutting off the chance to do a moonlight flit. Everyone should be free to do a runner if things went wrong.

'Wot I wanner know,' loud-mouthed Em Bede told the world, 'is wot's the likes of them doing down Solomon Street anyway?'

This thought was pretty general, except where Clara Cuttings was concerned. Clara believed the best of everyone –

until she learned differently of course, and even then it had to be at first hand.

The Londons were treated with suspicion at first. However, they were open and friendly without being fawning. Indeed, in Jack's case, it was quite the reverse. He was a large fair-haired man who looked as though he could take care of himself very well. His eyes were piercing blue and very direct. One could tell that he could be stern, even unforgiving, and a tough 'un to boot. As different from chalk to cheese against his wife. Kathy London was little and dainty, warm and sweet.

The Londons had grown on people and become very well-liked. Of course Clara Cuttings' taking Kathy under her ample wing so firmly, had helped. In a short space of time everyone knew all there was to know about them.

Jack's young sister Marion was a nice 'un too. When she came visiting, which she did when she could, good old Solomon Street seemed a little bit warmer somehow. The girl was tall and lovely-looking. She dressed smart and had a sort of ladylike air, and she talked real nice. Her smile lit up her face and sparkled in little silvery lights in her eyes.

Jack adored her. Like her, work-wise, he was a go-er. Just missing out on the Army, he'd scrimped and saved, slogged and slaved from schooldays. He had worked for Mr Minchin the window-cleaner. In the beginning it was a common sight, seeing Jack running alongside the furiously pedalling Mr Minchin all the way to the rounds. He knew what he needed most right from the start, and was soon cycling happily alongside his employer. Then Marion got a place in Drews. Posh office job it was, too. Unheard of – especially for a kid just out of school. Talk about luck! But Jack wasn't jealous; he had a job and his beloved bike and that was enough.

When Mr Minchin's age finally forced him to give up, Jack took over. The window-cleaner had even let the lad buy the ladder cheap. From that day Jack had ridden for miles, toiling and working his fingers to the bone. He had extended the round, choosing the largest and best-paying windows wherever he could, and of course he had shops. All the time he was saving to marry Kathy, and of course to better himself. A bloke had nothing if he didn't have self-pride.

5

Once married, and living in one room, Jack began to have bigger ideas. Always mindful of his well-educated parents, how decent they had been, how his father's dearest wish had been to buy his own home, tragically never fulfilled. Jack had determined that he and Kathy would indeed have a place of their own. It needed only to be small and inexpensive to start with, a stepping stone, that was all. And from then on, he and Kathy, and any children that might come along, would take steady steps upwards on the ladder of life.

He had learned at his mother's knee that one must always have dignity and pride. And she had been wont to say, 'My dear boy, remember this. It is no sin to be poor. However, it is a terrible sin to be *seen* to be poor. The world assesses people on how they present themselves. So put on a quietly successful face, and act the part. Above all, remember it is hardest to climb uphill, and easy to roll down. Climb, Jack, and be proud!'

Kathy, bless her, had agreed wholeheartedly. Happy to go along with everything he said, agreeing that their children would be brought up as little ladies and gentlemen. Not like the rough and ready types usually found in orphans' homes. This had been their own cruel fate. Kathy had explained all this to Clara – how she had willingly taken in sewing, working long hours by gaslight to help make her and Jack's dream come true.

Once they had saved a deposit, Kathy confided, it was she who had chosen good old number twelve. The bells of St Christopher's Church had been ringing on the evening that she and Jack had come to view, and that had been it! The acoustics made them sound particularly clear and sweet in Solomon Street.

'I am so happy to have such a dear little house, Clara,' Kathy had said once in her soft breathless way. 'Jack wanted to save more, to do better perhaps, but that room was so terrible and the woman, well!' She shivered and pulled a face that said it all. Then she smiled, 'I love this place – and of course having you as my best friend makes it all quite perfect. Oh yes, Clara, we are so lucky!'

'Weren't no luck,' Clara had replied stoutly, thinking how very young and nice Kathy was. 'Just plain hard work on both your parts, I'd say. Good on yer, gel!'

Clara came back to the present and peered through the gloom at her husband's picture again.

'Of course, George,' she muttered, 'ol' Jack's blooming lucky that there's people rich enough to afford to have their windows cleaned! They don't have to sit out on their top window-sills – what could crumble and drop orf at any minute – like I do. But still, I wouldn't change places with 'em.'

She slept, but it seemed no time at all before she was up and at it again.

Outside, early dawn crept down Solomon Street like a thief in rags. Dark shadows in alleyways gave way and sulkily dissolved. East End sparrows, as brisk and as bright as Eastenders themselves, chirruped and began their busy day.

In her muddly but clean and homely kitchen, which was warmed by the old kitchen range, Clara finished slicing doorsteps of bread and jam. She wrapped one sandwich in each of five newspaper parcels, then she purposefully straightened her hessian apron. Her boots clumped over brown linoleum. Work-hardened hands pulled open the dark green painted door, then she yelled upstairs.

'For the third time, if yer don't move your backsides, I'll be up there! D'yer hear me?'

'Mum!' ten-year-old Sid moaned and thumped Dicky, his stick-thin brother in the ribs. Dicky, just seven, opened his mouth, blinked, then snored in an exaggerated way.

'Coming!' Peg, Sid's twin, tried to sound awake, but rolled over and closed her eyes. Five-year-old Betsy, who had been tightly curled up against her, moved over an inch. This squeezed three-year-old Rosie even tighter against the wall.

'Ow!' Rosie whined. 'O-o-w!'

'You're squashing 'er,' Peg said indignantly as she sat up.

'Well? Wot shall I do then?' Betsy snapped. 'Shove her out of the soddin' bed?'

'D'yer hear me?' The roar from downstairs was like a trumpet-call from hell. Four young Cuttings leapt into action, Rosie twisting like an eel to take up position in the middle of the bed.

Minutes later, Clara's near-black, up-slanting eyes almost disappeared as she smiled at her brood. They sat, shining, at table. Each with a bowl of porridge before them.

7

'Well,' she said, 'I hope as how I don't find no tide-marks round your necks. Still, you ain't a bad bunch, and quick off the mark, I'll give yer that.'

'And you're the cat's whiskers, Mum,' Sid said with his mouth full.

'Stop your flannelling,' Clara told him, trying to hide the fact that he was her favourite. Sid was her firstborn, beating young Peg by a full half-hour. 'An' the way you're shovelling that lot down yer makes me wonder how you'd manage if you lived in the Shattery slums.'

'If I lived in the slums, Mum,' the irrepressible Sid replied quickly, 'I'd come a-begging at your door.'

'Fat lot of good that'd do you,' Clara jeered. She looked fondly at her eldest daughter. 'I'm off soon, Peg, so you look after things proper, understand? Oh, and don't forget to cut Dad's evening paper into squares for the lav.'

'Why can't we be like the knights of old?' Sid asked cockily and began to sing, 'In days of old when knights were bold, before paper was invented, they wiped their arse on blades of grass and rode away contented.'

'You can stop that row!' Clara told him over the shrieks of laughter from round the table. 'And you just watch them Frazer perishers. If any of 'em try to bully our Dicky again I want yer to bash 'em bandy. All right?'

'Gawd's truth, Mum,' Sid said aggrieved, 'I didn't fink I needed telling.'

'Think, Sid. T-H-I-N-K. Don't be so blooming common!'

Sid's roguish face crinkled up in his usual cheeky smile. 'All right, Mum. I'll be all posh like what you are.'

He ducked, but she clumped him one just the same.

'Ouch!' Sid yelled, but his eyes were dancing.

Peg, Dicky and Betsy all laughed even harder and bounced up and down on their chairs. Sid now openly joined in and that's how their dad found them.

George Cuttings, regular night-worker at the railway yard, grinned as he walked into the kitchen. He was small and whippet-thin with a merry face, fine fair hair and twinkling grey eyes. He liked his kids. He told the world at large that they were as nice a bunch as a bloke could wish for. The girls were as fair as him. The boys as dark-haired as their mum. As

8

for Clara, his big, tough, very handsome 'trouble and strife' –
well, he wouldn't be without her. She was as staunch as an
oak, steady and loyal, and there wasn't a man on God's earth
who'd dare try to mess with either her or her kin.

George's grin was very like Sid's as he remembered how
Clara had stomped up to the office, demanding to see Jessop
the foreman. Jessop had been scathing about people like him
who'd had tribes of kids and couldn't afford to keep them.
Gawd! That had got back to Clara and there'd been hell to
pay.

'Had a good night, George?' Clara asked as he took his
place at table. She ladled thick porridge onto a dinner-plate,
plonked it in front of him, then poured him a cup of tea from a
large brown pot. She added a little milk and plenty of sugar.

'So-so,' he told her in his sunny, easygoing way. 'And
you?'

'Not bad, but I keep thinking of poor young Kath. They
took her in last night. Emergency, it was. I hope as how the
young 'un gets born and makes it, but it'll be touch and go.
And ...' Her face became sad, her lips trembled, 'And ...'

'I know,' he told her. 'It's all right, matey, I know.'

'She'd have been nine by now, our little Violet. I still don't
know why fate chose her to take the diphtheria an' die. It's
times like this when – Gawd! George, why am I carrying on
so?'

'Because we loved her, and because life can be a shit sometimes, old girl. I hope as how poor ol' Jack—'

'Jack?!' Clara was herself again and swelled up to twice her
size. 'Poor Jack? Don't yer mean *poor Kathy*? There never
was more'n a 'aporth of her, and she wants this baby more
than anything else on earth.' She looked round at her brood –
the boys kicking each other under the table, the girls intent on
their food. They were dressed in their everyday clothes, all of
which were either too large or too small, but even so were
scrupulously clean.

Sid had string instead of laces in his boots – he'd spent the
penny Clara had given him for a new pair on bull's-eyes, and
got a wallop for his pains – and his short baggy grey trousers
hung too low in spite of the braces he wore. His face shone
with the recent scrubbing with cold water and carbolic soap.

9

His hair, like that of his brothers and sisters, was washed and nit-free. Clara saw to that! And they were all, every one, open-faced, bright-eyed and good-humoured.

'Little demonts, all of 'em,' Clara said in a rare moment of softness, 'an' they keep me on me toes, I can tell yer. But I wouldn't be without 'em, would you?'

'No.' George had been bolting down his porridge and gulping his tea, then he held out his cup for more. Clara obliged, and as before, spooning in three lots of sugar. He stirred it long and hard, pretending not to see Betsy's expectant face.

'Dad!' She was aggrieved. 'Dad?'

He grinned, relented, and carefully poured hot sweet tea in his saucer and held it out to her. She drank it, slurping loudly.

'I did hear as how Ethel Jacobs who lost her job, still can't get anything new,' Clara remarked then.

'Can't lose *your* job, can you, old girl?' George teased.

'Not even if I tried,' she replied, and looked smug. 'There's them as what don't like getting on their knees, and there's them as don't mind. I'm just thankful as how I don't mind. Now, George, hurry up! The boys have left that bed nice an' warm. If you tuck in now, you'll be off in no time. An' don't worry about Rosie. I've done her lunch, made her a school parcel like the others. She likes to pretend she's the same as they are. Mind you, she mightn't get up till I come back and rake her out. Proper little lazybones she is.'

Once George had gone to the bed the boys had left vacant, Clara told her brood in no uncertain terms not to make a noise, and not to be late for school and to, 'For Gawd's sake leave Rosie where she is.' After that she donned George's cloth cap, grabbed up her bucket, scrubbing brush and other cleaning things and clumped off down Solomon Street. She had a long walk to do.

After scrubbing doorsteps and whitening steps in the posh area of Hainault Road, Clara made her way back to Steadmans the bakers on the corner of Solomon Street. She was the first to arrive and waited patiently at the back door. In a while she was joined by ratty Ethel Jacobs, Em Bede and others. Of course Florrie Jessop, foreman's wife, bought fresh stuff. Snobby cow!

The back door opened and smiling Basil Steadman came out. Round and rosy, pink and fat, he and his wife Lucy looked and were in manner uncannily alike. Their daughter, Angela, whom they called their 'littel Angel' was a caricature of them both, her features a faintly flattened distortion of theirs, and her eyes were strange. Even so, Angel had a kind of loveliness for she smiled readily. People tended to push aside the fact that the little girl was strange. The Steadmans were her devoted slaves.

'Gawd 'elp us!' Basil teased Clara. 'Ain't we just early birds this morning? What can I do for yew?'

'Three 'aporth,' Clara said importantly. 'Mixed.'

She held out a clean brown paper carrier bag.

'Right you are, Mrs Cuttings.' A plentiful helping of stale bread and cakes found their way into the bag.

'Ta,' Clara said, 'but I asked for three a'porth! Gawd, I got kippers at two a penny yesterday and here you are hanging on to stale stuff like it's the crown jewels.'

'What a one yew are,' Basil chortled, but one look at Clara's face cut him short. A ragged-edged round of currant scone went into the bag. Two pennies were offered, a half-penny change was received and carefully placed in Clara's shabby purse.

'Ta ever so,' she said.

Pleased with herself, Clara made her way home, then frowned as number six came into view. A man was standing on her doorstep, big and dark-haired and the spitting image of herself. Amazingly, it was her twin brother whom she hadn't seen for quite a while. A sailor, his skin mahogany brown, he was holding a sleeping baby in his arms.

'Steve!' What a surprise! And what have you got there?'

'My kid.'

'Gawd help us! I didn't know. Don't stand there. Go on in!'

Steven Webb put a free hand through the letter box and pulled the string stretched across it and attached to the latch. It clicked back and the door opened. The lino-covered passage was narrow and dark in spite of yellow wallpaper, but you could smell Mansion furniture polish, and kitchen-range warmth. Number six enclosed you in a homely comforting way rather than choked. Brass stair-rods gleamed against the

11

brown lino they held in place. A couple of framed Pears Soap prints of beautiful children hung in full view.

Clara took off George's cap and put it on the ancient hall-stand that held a man's shiny black mac, a worn working jacket, a woolly scarf, two children's blazers that had seen better days, and in pride of place, the best piece of clothing in the house. A throw-out from a posh establishment up Hainault way, it was a girl's navy-blue coat that had served Peg in good stead, then Betsy, and would, when the weather worsened, cover young Rosie. She would grow into it, of course, just as Peg had all those years ago.

'In the kitchen, Steve,' Clara told him. 'I'll make you a cuppa in two shakes, and I've got some nice scones. Add a bit of marge an' some of me homemade plum jam and they'll be fit for a king. George's upstairs and Rosie's probably crept in with him by now if I know her. Gawd, what a one you are, surprising me like this.'

'Look Clar,' he said gruffly as he sat on one of the kitchen chairs, 'I ain't a one for going round the 'ouses. I need your help.'

· 'Get away with yer,' she teased. 'I wouldn't 'ave guessed.'

'This kid's mine, Clar. She's mine fair and square, but her ma's buggered off and I'm due back on ship in less than twenty-four hours. I'll be away a while and—'

'You want me and George to take her on. So her mum's gorn off, eh? Well, I never did!' Clara sat herself down in George's armchair by the range and held out her arms. ''Ere, give her to me.'

The baby, still sleeping, changed hands.

'I'll pay for her keep.'

'No need, Steve. One more mouth won't make no difference. What's her name?'

'Burza.' He spelt it out.

'What?'

'Her mother, Kiffa, is a sort of gipsy. She registered the birth though, and done everything right like I told her to.' His voice flattened, held misery; his eyes told their own sorry tale. 'She reckoned as how she loved me once, but it turns out that me and my little 'un ain't enough. We ain't her own sort, you see.'

12

'A gipsy? And what a funny name. Gawd 'elp us!'

'She's real lovely, Clar, but wild with it, if you know what I mean. But I thought, hoped that when the little 'un was born she'd settle down. Then, out of the blue, she was forgiven by the old woman who they look on as a sort of queen – or witch. Old cow!'

'Forgiven?' Clara's eyes opened wide with astonishment. 'Crikey! Forgiven? What on earth for?'

'Taking me on, living our sort of a life, you know, under an actual roof. Lovely cottage we had. Small and old, but ... Anyway, Kiffa was given a choice. Me and our kid, or to go on with her own kind. She – she waited till I got shore leave before doing the runner, I'll give her that. But she didn't even take a last look at young Burza here.'

'Well, I never did! A woman what leaves her baby is worse than an animal.' Clara was filled with deep and utter contempt. Then, seeing her brother's chagrin, she calmed down, adding, 'Still, what's done is done. My brood will look on this little bread-snapper like our own.'

'Shouldn't you wake George up an' ask?' Steve said anxiously. 'I know he's been at it all night, but – I mean, just to make sure? I'll send money ...'

'Do that – if you can,' she replied briskly. 'Though what it buys will be shared by all the kids. There'll be no differences made. All right?'

'Wouldn't have it any other way, Clar.'

'An' don't worry about my ol' man. George's like me where kids are concerned, and your'n will be something special.' Her expression softened, then a comforting smile lit up her face. 'Don't worry about anything, Steve. Where's her clothes, by the way?'

'She's got them on. I reckon she'd be playing in the fields stark naked all summer if her mum had stayed.'

'What a carry on!' Clara replied, still smiling as she managed to act casual. Inwardly she was outraged and thinking, Blooming gippos! Out loud she told him, 'Well, never fear. We'll soon sort it all out.' She looked down at Burza. 'Poor little mite. 'Ere, you make the tea, Steve. Baby's warm an' cosy and well away. Cor, ain't she got a good head of hair? Luverly!'

Steve Webb stood up. 'It's all official, Clar. She's registered Burza Webb.' He looked sheepish. 'I know you, how big-hearted you are, so I told them like it had all been arranged. The authorities know she's staying here in Solomon Street. I knew you wouldn't let me down.'

'Would I ever, Steve? Don't look all het up. What a chump you are.'

He stood up. 'I won't hang about for no cuppa, if you don't mind. I'm finding all this a bit 'ard, if you know what I mean.'

Clara was now rocking Burza to and fro, her eyes gentle. 'You get along then, eh. And Steve?'

'Yes?'

'Good luck and Gawd bless yer.'

'Thanks, mate,' he said and walked out of number six, a big ox of a man with sorrow in his soul.

Steve strode along Solomon Street, his world ended. He still adored his Kiffa, named after a bright Libran star, so she said. Bright, yes, he could drown in her huge glowing eyes. She had a fire and majesty about her, for all she barely reached his shoulder. He loved the wild tangle of her hair and the way she swung her hips as she walked. To hold her was like trying to hold a ray of midday sun. She belonged to the open spaces, especially at this time of the year. Autumn was in full blast, and sending running fire across the countryside. She'd certainly never settle down in a place like Solomon Street, but he'd hoped the cottage in the country would do.

Now, Steve thought miserably, his baby would be brought up here, in the kind of place where he himself had been born. He stared ahead, to where the alleyway flanking the Four Feathers stank of human urine. Talk about rough end of the stick! How the hell could one narrow bloody road hold such differently cared-for sets of domiciles? At least Clar lived at the decent end, where people got down to brass tacks and bloodywell tried! Still, good bad or indifferent it was all Solomon Street. Everything around here, he thought, was grey. As grey as that chap's face. The bloke passing him by looked the way he, Steve, actually felt.

Then he dismissed the fellow from his mind and strode off round the corner.

*

14

Jack London's mind was on earlier events and he swore long and soft, remembering Matron. The hook-nosed woman hadn't given a tinker's cuss about anyone's finer feelings. Least of all his. And now, after the hours of fear and worry and interminable waiting, he had been all but turfed out of the hospital – still without having been allowed to see Kathy.

Matron, dominant, big-boned, as starchy as her huge winged hat, had stared over his head as though he was polluting her carbolic-y castle. He had felt, as she had so clearly intended, like a nothing and a nobody. Demoralised, he had stood before her, stammering like a kid, trying to explain that he needed to continue to stay near. That he was desperate to hang on because Kathy would know! Would sense his dismissal and be distressed.

Matron, cod-eyed, had been deaf to his entreaties. Had looked him up and down, not trying to hide her contempt of a man who was so obviously working-class. She had pulled herself up to her full height.

'Mr London, the crisis is over. Your wife is resting now and the doctor has ordered that she must not be disturbed. Visiting hours are from two to four. Doctors' rounds are due shortly. I must ask you to leave.'

Ask? It had been an order! With not a nerve left in his body, he had obeyed.

Now, returning from the telephone booth having contacted his sister Marion, Jack looked round and saw his street as Matron would. Its soot-begrimed two-up and two-downers with a bakery on one corner, the general stores opposite and the Four Feathers pub at the far end. Oh yes, the 'Fevvers'. The sozzled row coming from that dump on weekend nights was fit to wake the dead. It certainly drowned out the sound of Kathy's beloved church bells.

Jack curled his fingers into fists until his knuckled gleamed white through his skin. Suddenly he wanted to go mad and punch the guts out of God. Yes, the Almighty that Kathy loved so much. But then, Kathy loved everything and everyone. She even loved bloody shabby lousy rotten Solomon Street. He had been so proud of the place, his special space, his and Kathy's own small personal unit in the world – until now.

15

He looked around and saw and felt and smelled all that was Solomon Street. He looked at the light that was reminiscent of the fag end of winter, at the houses that were slate grey to almost black with soot, at the cobbles and uneven kerbs, the rubbish-festooned drains. He was more aware of the stench of cats' urine than ever before. And of the odour of frying kippers, or sprats.

Towards the Feathers end there was the pitch where the fishman placed his barrow for two hours a day. Sundays he was there with winkles and shrimps. People came to him from everywhere. His prices were cheap, he was an affable, jocular man. He swilled down the cobbles as regular as clockwork. Even so, though long gone, there was the raw fishy stink that not even Steadmans freshly-baked bread could dispel.

In spite of bravely hanging curtains, white or the varying shades of orange and yellow of dolly-dyes, Jack could almost feel the air of desolation. He could practically reach out and touch the cloying sense of poverty. And there was something else. Something too terrible to contemplate. Something that made his stomach drop to his boots and his heart feel like a grinding machine working, sending waves up to his throat. Fear. He was deathly afraid.

That night Jack London's daughter was born.

Two days later his wife died.

In number six Solomon Street Clara Cuttings ran her fingers through baby Burza's shiny black curls and mourned for pretty young Kathy and for the newborn who, like Burza, faced life with no mum.

Just then Burza's thickly lashed brown eyes opened wide, and she looked up into Clara's face. She cooed, a tiny breath of sound, then her lips uptilted and she smiled.

'My Gawd,' Clara said softly. 'What a sweetheart you are, and what a little beauty you're going to be. Don't you worry, little 'un, you've got me. You'll always have ol' Clara Cuttings an' her crew on your side. You belong to us now, and nothing and no one's ever going to take you away.'

Chapter Two

Daylight was dying. A bitter wind was blowing. He could work no more. Without something to do he had time to think. Thinking was terrible. Remembering was worse. It was hell on earth. Jack London grew steadily more enraged. Anger was his only defence against fate that had sent him such mind-numbing grief. He was like a Spanish bull, cut to ribbons, but still trying to fight against impossible odds.

He sat full square on his bike, his window-cleaner's bucket swinging crazily from the handlebars. His ladder hung like a long dark hyphen between him and the kerb of the High Road. He was on the way home, back to Solomon Street, where he knew that his sister would start on him all over again. To the devil with it all, he thought. There's nothing left without Kath. He groaned, low and deep, thinking, My poor precious Kath who actually loved our place!

Solomon Street, he had been apt to think in the beginning, was a nice street opposed to the not so nice. Meaning of course the Shattery area, Matson Street and beyond. That was where poverty proper shrugged its shoulders and got on with breeding ghetto crime. Where gang-fights broke out, knives flew, spiked knuckle-dusters flashed, and language fit to sear the ears of God flayed the smokeladen air.

It was common knowledge that the police recognised certain 'criminal areas'. King's Cross held thieves, Hackney was swamped with cat burglars, Stepney had its con-men, some big-time, but mostly small-time, the Shattery area gang wars, Matson for pros, and Bethnal Green and Whitechapel for villains pure and simple. It said a great deal that the Shattery

Estate and Matson Street, minute areas, constituted a category all of their own. They held the dregs.

Against them Solomon Street was a decent sort of place – poor but honest, penurious but clean. Of course it had its fair share of drinking and gambling, its would-be boxers, and its petty thieves at the Feathers end, but nonetheless it shone against the Shattery Estate and Matson Street. Even so, and in spite of Kathy's glowing vision of the place, Solomon Street had its mannerisms.

Local children had a certain way of speaking. 'Luverly, innit?' 'Git art of it.' 'Sod orf.' 'Me muvver an' me farver could beat your'n at anyfink hany day.'

Jack frowned ferociously, remembering how that particular gem had been snarled at him at school. It had happened the day after he had fully realised he was an orphan. He had retaliated of course, with a swift punch on the other brat's long nose, shouting through his tears, 'My father would have had yours put in a cage years ago, monkey-face.'

It hadn't helped much. Kids could be cruel. Bloody awful at times. It was then that he had made an oath. The day would come when he would beat them at their own game. He would show them all that a Home kid could and would cock a snook at the odds, no matter how great they were. That a chap had to have faith in himself, and never take no for an answer. It had been an uphill climb though. Especially since it was his young sister, Marion, who had been the one blessed with brains. But he was good with his hands. He had guts and determination, and above all he had his pride. He even had pride in the lovely home that Kathy had made him. This in spite of some of the neighbours and their foul-tongued, snotty-nosed brats.

Jack pushed the thought of his near neighbour, Clara Cuttings, out of his mind. Kathy had adored the woman and, grudgingly, he quite liked her. Her children were good-humoured, very nice youngsters with no real harm in them. But locals didn't really matter, would never enter into the equation. It was sufficient that he and Kathy had lived by certain standards. They had agreed that their children would never be set in a common, uncouth mould. They'd be true Eastenders, yes, like the vast majority who were the salt of the earth, the very best. His nippers would be brought up to know the difference between right and wrong, how to speak and act. Yet they must be proud, and never ashamed of their circumstances. In fact, to be as unlike the rotten windfall apples as the round and rosy fruit on the tree.

He stopped his bike outside number twelve, unwilling to go in. His house gleamed under the adjacent street-lamp, its paintwork white, its letter box and doorknocker shining like gold because of regular polishing with Brasso. The shadow of the potted aspidistra in the downstairs front window gleamed through white lace curtains. It looked for all the world like a round head with lots of leafy hair. At least, that was what Kathy thought.

Ye gods! he thought, remembering how Kathy had called the damned thing 'Aspy'. She'd given it a name and acted as though she believed it understood!

'And whatever you do, Jack,' she had said in her enchantingly husky voice, 'remember to wipe his leaves with a damp cloth. He's a truly gorgeous specimen and deserves loving care.'

'You're far more gorgeous,' he had teased, not caring that he sounded so daft, 'and you will always have every inch of my loving care.'

'Nowadays,' she had given her breathless little laugh, 'I'm as round and full-blown as the bowl Aspy's standing in. And as for green hair!'

'Our baby will have hair the colour of the moon, Kathy, and be a little sweetheart, just like you.'

'He'll be a boy and have buttery-gold curls, just like yours. He'll be as handsome as—'

'I don't give a damn,' he'd told her roughly, 'just so long as I have you ...'

'Oh God!' Jack groaned, coming back to the present. 'Oh my God!'

Grey-faced he went inside his house and shut the door. Now Marion's going to play the same old tune, he thought bleakly. Christ, how is it that young sisters can be such pests?

They were sitting in the kitchen that seemed too small for Jack's size. The range was black and shining. The white elephants marching in pairs across the overmantel glowed, as did the tall blue glass vases that flanked the small brass central clock. Jack's face was even more ashen.

'You shouldn't have made me keep it,' he told her quietly. 'You should have let me go through with the adoption plans.'

'Don't be wicked!' Marion's blue eyes were twin brilliants,

19

she was so upset. 'We know what it's like to be without parents. We must try to make things up to your baby, just as Clara is for her niece Burza. It's very, very sad not to have a mother, Jack.'

'It's equally sad,' he replied bitterly, 'not to have a wife.'

'It wasn't the baby's fault.'

Jack looked at Marion straight. 'Wasn't it?'

'You're to stop thinking like that!' Marion held the baby close to her heart. 'You were her beginning. You and Kathy. It was Kathy's heart that caused all the trouble and let her down in the end. You mustn't lay the blame at the baby's door. I can't and won't allow you to do that.'

'It was the cause of—'

'She was what Kathy wanted more than anything else. Oh yes! She must have known the risk, even though you didn't. But Kathy longed for your child. You've got to see that.'

'Who's going to look after it?'

'We've been over and over things until I'm sick and tired. *We* are going to look after her. Yes, you and I.'

He glared at her. 'You've got your own life to live. You haven't slogged your insides out for the past six years only to give up now. Look, Marion, you're still only just twenty years old. You could have stayed on and taken—'

'I was lucky to get a place in that firm,' she interrupted. 'Very lucky indeed. They're the only people I know to specifically employ a few women in their offices. I was taken on as a kid simply because my old headmistress is a relative of the Drews and heard of the opening. She put in a word.' Marion laughed deprecatingly. 'I was her top pupil, you see.'

'I should say you were.' He really smiled at her then. 'A genius, no less.'

'Nonsense. Miss Drew happened to be pleased with my exam results, said they reflected the high standard reached by the pupils of her school. She told old Mr Drew how amazed she was since I was only fourteen, and hoped that I could pass all their tests as well as I had hers. I did, as you know, and I left school and went to them as an apprentice. I was an experiment!'

'All the more reason to stay on and go even higher up the ladder.'

'I don't want to. It hasn't been easy,' she told him. 'I was very definitely made to know my lowly place in the scheme of

20

things. I had been "spoken for" and so I was envied and hated. Jack, there was no love lost at all.'

'But you have reached a good position for all your youth and I can't and won't—'

'I started out as the general dogsbody, Jack. But the more those high-ups put on me, the more determined I got. And Mr Drew took an interest in me – from afar. I learned that from dear old Miss Drew, so I had to make good for her sake. I enjoyed the challenge. I'm a workhorse like you. And in spite of everything, I've managed to make a place for myself, that's all.'

'You're just being modest. You got the job against all the odds, and although you're young you have earned a position of trust. Even better, you have that nice room in the hostel near where you work. You live in a decent area, Marion! I can't and won't allow you to take a step down in the world.'

'I now wish to live here, in Solomon Street,' she flared up at him. 'I want to! For goodness sake, Jack, can't you accept that, and stop making a fuss? Pull yourself together. You haven't even given the baby a name!'

He stuck his chin out at that, glaring at his sister who was as tall and fair and goodlooking as he.

'Bloody hell, Marion, hasn't it sunk in yet? I just don't give a damn. I just don't bloody well care about anything any more.'

'Don't use bad language, Jack! Particularly not now, not in front of the baby. I thought we made a pact all those years ago, to be as much like our parents as possible? To remember that they were lovely decent people, and that we'd try never ever to let them down? Now we must make sure that we never let Kathy's daughter down.'

'It would have been better off in Barnardos.'

'Never! She's here and here she'll stay. She has earned it. After eight weeks touch and go in the hospital, she won her fight for life. Now she needs all of our care and all of our love, just as baby Burza has all of the love and devotion of the Cuttings family. Burza has lost her mother too, in a different way – but the outcome is the same, Jack. You and I had each other to turn to and we were lucky in that respect. All the young need love. Our baby most certainly does.'

He sat there, arms folded. 'I've none to give.'

'Well, at least give her a name. You were going to call the

21

child Jack if you'd had a son, and Kathy for a girl.'

'No!'

'Then what about Lily?' she persisted. 'After our own mother?'

'If you like,' he said, and turned away to stare at the orange heart of the fire.

'Poor Jack,' Marion whispered, deflated, and felt her own aching heart reaching out to him. Tears fell hotly onto her cheeks. The baby stirred uneasily and woke. Marion, looking into the tiny pink face, felt all her maternal instincts rushing to the fore. All the mother love that would never be for her own child, not now. Not without Paul. Paul who had so let her down – whom she should hate, but even so could not get out of her mind. But she still had Jack, and Kathy's child for whom she would fight tooth and claw.

She kissed the downy head and thought of Kathy who had died. Her hair had been silvery-blonde, her eyes large, dark-lashed and deep violet-blue. She had been very pretty, tiny and shy, an orphan whom Jack had immediately taken under his wing on the day he found her being bullied in the huge grey Home they had all shared.

Jack and Kathy had grown up together, had been sweethearts almost from the moment of first meeting. Their marriage had been as inevitable as summer following spring. Now Jack was lost, out on a limb, hardly knowing which way to turn, or what to do. He did not want the baby, but for Kathy's sake, she, Marion, would see to it that Lily would be the little princess Kathy had always hoped for.

Marion had truly loved Kathy like a sister. Who could help it? She had been such a little darling. And number twelve Solomon Street reflected her character. Each room was gentle with the pale clear colours of spring. Lace curtains made swathes of feathery froth against windows. Homemade rag rugs created patches of warm colour glowing on creosote-polished wood floors. The kitchen was as dainty as a doll's house and all forget-me-not blue and white. There was a white painted dresser holding willow-patterned china, each piece having been lovingly collected. As had been everything in the house.

Just then the bells of St Christopher's sang out. The ringers were practising again. Marion stood very still, holding the baby and watching the raw look in her brother's eyes. He was in the depths of despair, having lost someone he loved and who had loved him. She on the other hand had lost someone in such a way that she felt degraded, humiliated and above all hurt. She knew that, like Jack, her life would never be the same again. It had happened months ago, but she had kept it close, and always would.

'It's odd, how people's looks don't portray their true characters, isn't it?' she asked pensively. 'One can never really tell. Don't you agree, Jack?'

'No,' he replied, feeling that she was trying to converse in order to take his mind off things. 'I remember our father being exactly as he seemed. He was tall and strong for all he was a white-collar worker. He had a nice face and gentle hands. Our mother was beautiful and looked the lady she was.'

'I don't remember them,' she told him honestly. 'I was younger than you when they both died in that 'flu epidemic.'

'And you were terrified of fireplaces after that,' he told her. 'No one could understand why.' He smiled briefly. 'I only cottoned on when you heard that someone was coming in to clean the flue. You had nightmares, and then you finally explained that you were scared because the flue above the fire had in some way been responsible for taking our parents away. I spent hours trying to explain about influenza. You couldn't understand at all.'

'Silly me!'

'No. You have imagination. That's what happens when you have the kind of mind you have. You're the brainbox of the family, remember? I'm the dumb chap with very little up top, who got left behind.' He smiled faintly, adding, 'So I just had to get down to brass tacks and use my own bare hands.'

'And made a far better job at things than I. You look what you are, Jack. A fine, strong, no-nonsense man. Do I.- do I look clever, Jack?'

'You look lovely. And you look refined. You have an air about you. Class!' He stared at her, long and very steadily. 'You don't have to, you know – work so hard at trying to get me out of the doldrums. It won't work; it never will. Besides, I can't fathom what all this is about.'

'I knew someone once who looked and acted kind and gentle, but who was in fact hard and cruel and – and greedy.'

'Like old mother Mason who locked you in the cellar? She fooled the authorities all right.'

23

'And you fooled Mrs Mason!' Marion's voice held pride. 'She thought she was fostering a couple of well-behaved simpletons – until she locked me in the cellar because I was crying for my mother. She'd hit me so hard! To teach me a lesson, she said, and I was terrified. Of the dark, and the smell, of all the rats I imagined were down there. You tried to break down the cellar door, didn't you? I heard it all, and you threatened to kill her at the top of your voice. After that you ran off and found a policeman and told him that the woman was torturing me.' She laughed softly, 'And you talk about *my* imagination! I remember when you—'

'Don't!' he cut in roughly. 'Going over things won't work.'

'I know,' she whispered. 'And – I'm sorry, Jack. So very, very sorry.'

'So am I,' he told her and turned his face away.

She tried again.

'When I was out wheeling the pram, I met young Peggy Cuttings. She's the ten-year-old twin sister of Sid. Anyway, Peggy was looking after Burza and little Rosie. I went with them, and – Jack, I have found a park with a children's area. There were swings and ...'

He was looking at her again, his eyes direct and ice cold, then slowly and deliberately he said: 'Ye gods, you're going daft. Hobnobbing with people like the Cuttings when you're a cut above them all. And now you're making plans, searching out things that won't matter for years. Acting as though it's some kind of princess you're handling.'

'She is a princess. Ours! We Londons have pride, remember? That's what you used to drum into me all the time. "You just hold on," you used to say. "We haven't anything in this world yet, except our dignity and pride. We must always fight tooth and nail to hang on to both".'

'Now what are you going on about?' he grated.

'Our Lily is going to have everything we can give her. Everything! And one day you'll look at her and see her as the light of your life. You'll see Kathy, because your daughter has her mother's eyes, her face and it looks as though she'll even have her hair. What's more ...'

'Why don't you bloody well shut up?'

Outside the sky became empty of the sound of bells. There was an air of waiting, of hush. Even the street seemed to be holding its breath.

Marion suddenly changed, looking more furious than he had ever seen her. She inhaled sharply, and for the first time in her life spoke to her brother in a voice of steel.

'It won't do, Jack. This can't go on and I'm not going to allow it to. You have obligations now, things you can't get out of. You have a daughter, for heaven's sake.'

'Codswallop!' he grated. 'Can't you give it up? For two pins—'

At that moment Lily awoke and began to cry. Marion stood up. He jumped up too, glaring. But she was fiercer than he. She was looking almost as though she hated him and he was shocked.

'Here!' she snapped. 'She's Kathy's baby. Yes, *Kathy's* since you seem to want to disown her. Her name is Lily and she's beautiful – and going to be the spitting image of her mother. *Take her!*'

She all but shoved the baby at him. He had either to hold her or let her fall. His arms held her safe. Comforted, she became quiet. Then he turned and walked stiffly into the front room, Kathy's favourite place. He looked unseeingly over Aspy's green head. He continued to stare sightlessly at the white lace curtains that Kathy had been so proud of. Hesitantly at first, then confident and clear, the bells of St Christopher's began to chime again.

Jack lowered his head and looked long and intently into Lily's violet-blue eyes. She stared back at him and her hand fluttered like a pink moth, reaching for his face. Jack took a deep, shuddering breath. Tears ran down his weather-worn cheeks.

'Lily,' he whispered hoarsely, 'Hello?'

And outside, over the sooty rooftops and dark alleys, soaring above back yards with their pigeon lofts and rabbit hutches, rubbish piles and stacks of wood, the bells rejoiced.

Inside number six Clara heard the bells and smiled lovingly at Burza who was kicking her feet, waving her fists, and gurgling fit to burst in the warm cosiness of her cot.

'Well, ducks,' Clara told the baby, 'them bells is the song of our lives. The little baby along the road – well, her mum loved the sound, and I think you will too. And know what? You an' the little London child will get to be great mates. You're of an age you are, and I can see it now. Close, you two will be. Real close. Won't that be nice?'

Chapter Three

At last the memories of the war were fading. World economy was prospering so it was said, but nothing much altered in the East End. There were still the not so poor, the poor and the downright wretched. Denizens of Solomon Street mostly shivered behind their curtains and fought to survive. To be employed was to be one of the chosen. Bosses became gods. One kowtowed to superiors for they had power in their hands.

The sack was an ogre with a capital S. Men queued at the docks and prayed for casual work, unloading frozen carcasses for the odd half-crown. Others walked the streets with tins of black paint, offering to make door knockers and letter boxes like new for twopence a time. The desperately hungry roamed the street markets after the stalls had closed. They scavenged through the rubbish for fruit or vegetables, no matter how damaged or bruised. As in Dickensian times, homeless children who had slipped through the do-gooders' nets, huddled against bakers' walls for warmth, while the night glared down with obsidian eyes.

As yet none of that mattered too much in number six Solomon Street. There was an air of excitement as Clara and her children gathered round to gaze with awe at the plate holding six fairy cakes, each with a glacé cherry on top.

'Cor!' Sid said. 'You ain't half clever, Mum. Melt in the mouth your cakes do. They ain't rock hard like ol' Steadman's, an' yours look as good as his hany day.'

'Not bad, are they?' Clara beamed. 'Even better than I made for our Burza, and as you say, at least they're fresh.' She looked fondly over at the rickety pram where Burza was playing with a bone ring that had been handed down to each child in turn.

'Burza's a little corker,' Peggy said, following her mother's gaze. 'She's gonna knock 'em all stone dead when she grows up.'

'And so are you, gel,' Clara replied. 'You'll marry young, like me, and if you get a man as good as mine you'll be in luck all the days of your life.'

'I wanna a bloke just like Dad.'

'When they made him, they broke the mould, ducks. Now, who's gonna take these down to number twelve? I think you better had, Peg. Tell Mar that they're for Lily with our love.'

'Mum,' Betsy's eyes were greedy and fixed on the goodies, 'What about us?'

'What about you?' Clara replied sternly. 'It ain't your day, is it?'

'No, but—'

'Well, mind your own. You've got a sweet tooth like your dad, I know, but greed is greed, and you have to learn to be unselfish in this life.'

'Oh shit!' Sid exploded. 'All we want is one of our own mum's cakes! Lily got one on Burza's day, and we want the same. What's so greedy about that?'

Clara clumped him. 'That's for language, all right? An' you'll have a slice with jam and feel yourselves fortunate. Now get out to the scullery and wash your hands and faces, and comb your hair ready for tea. All of you, you 'orrible little demonts. Go on!'

They scattered. Clara walked over to the pram and smiled down at Burza who had large lovely brown eyes, shiny dark curls, and a generous, rather sensitive mouth. Burza was extremely beautiful, and spoilt, and had a temper when things went wrong.

'Well, Burza Webb,' Clara told her softly, 'you're one of us all right. There's not one of us what wouldn't hang for you, an' I'm only sorry your mum and dad ain't around to see what a little gem you are.' Then over her shoulder she yelled, 'You Peg, 'ave you gorn orf yet? And hurry back, d'yer hear me?'

She heard the front door slam and then her lips twitched and her expression was soft. The kids' tea was already prepared and the large teapot filled, just waiting to be poured. She went to the kitchen cupboard and brought out a plate of bread and jam – and six fairy cakes.

'And that, kids,' she whispered, 'is ter make up for the fact that you'll never get invited to no birthday in Jack London's house. But who cares? I'm sure we don't ... '

It was 30 September and Lily London was one year old. There was a cake with white icing, on which one white candle was held in a central spray of waxen lily-of-the-valley. The edge of the cake was ringed with tiny decorative silver balls. There was a white silver fringe encompassing all. It was a splendid cake, Marion's first ever effort, and Clara had helped her every step of the way. There was raspberry jelly and pink blancmange, and now, thanks to Clara, lovely fresh fairy cakes.

Jack's meal was keeping warm in the range oven. He had promised faithfully to knock off early on this very special occasion, and Marion could hardly wait.

He arrived at last, smiling and getting to be more like his old self every day. He came into the kitchen as Marion lit the candle. He saw Lily, strapped in a chair set before the table. She was waving a spoon and looking intent.

'Happy birthday, Chickybit,' he said and leaned down to kiss her, his breath gusting out. It made the flame flicker and dance. Lily watched, fascinated, then she smiled. A mysterious, wonderful smile that held the reflection of the candleflame in her violet-blue eyes.

Marion laughed and clapped her hands, then gave her offering. Eagerly unwrapping the red crepe-paper wrapped parcel herself, while Lily watched. A white velvet bear with a pink bow round its neck emerged. It had a black nose and eyes and smiling mouth.

'His name is Snowy,' Marion told the wide-eyed child. 'And, my darling, in the winter you will see real snow. Oh, it's such a wonderful world, and you have so much to see and learn and—'

'Oh shut up,' Jack teased. 'Our Chickybit's exactly one. Give her a chance.'

'But Jack!'

'But nothing. That evening blouse of yours has never looked better. I'm sure its makers never guessed that it would turn out like that!'

'You like the bear?'

'You're a clever clogs all right. I can tell you now, when I saw you cutting up that thing of yours, my heart sank. But

28

now, seeing what you've made out of it, and the cake and all, phew! No wonder you reached High School and I never got out of Elementary. I'm a bit sad that you had to cut up your nice clobber though.'

'Since when would I ever wear it in Solomon Street?' she laughed. 'And Clara helped me. She made Burza a grey monkey out of a piece of Army blanket. Burza's birthday was a little while back. The whole Cuttings family adore that baby, and her eyes! Like shiny black grapes they are, and she has masses of dark hair. She's as different from our Lily as chalk from cheese. Just watching the pair of them cooing at each other was such a pretty sight.'

'You took her into the Cuttings' house?' Jack's lips went down at the corners. His tone was sharp.

'Don't worry,' she told him airily. 'It's all clean and decent. We're none of us like the Feathers end, you know. Anyway Clara and I get on, and she's very clever at making ends meet. When I saw that monkey, well! She loved helping me with the bear, and I'm only too delighted that it all turned out so nicely.'

'Look, I don't want Lily to mix with that lot.'

'Oh come on! Now what is your gift going to be?'

He opened a small box and took out a silver chain on which hung a St Christopher pendant.

'Oh,' Marion breathed. 'Kathy's most precious possession!'

'I gave it to her on the day we moved into this house,' Jack told her gruffly. 'Lily's too young to wear it of course, but one day ... And I want her to know when she's old enough, that her mother gave it to her after she had spent one full year on this earth.'

'You old softy,' Marion whispered with tears in her eyes.

'What about you?' he grinned. 'There's no doubt about it, we're both fools, but that won't stop us from making our little chick the real reason for plodding through this life, eh?'

Marion looked at Lily whose feathery silver hair was just beginning to grow.

'She's our own darling angel,' she said. 'Didn't I tell you how proud of her you'd be one day?'

'Yes,' he replied, and beamed.

Burza's earliest memory was of lying in her pram feeling

29

warm, cosy and contented. She felt as if she was bathed in sunlight, while somewhere in the distance dogs barked and there was the ponderous clip-clopping of a horse's hooves. A shadowy face without form or definite line hovered above her for a moment, then receded. Burza closed her eyes. The warm sun tilted against her eyelids, and the noises fell away to a whispering nothingness.

The world grew larger and the pram smaller. Burza's most tangible memory was of being taken to the park. On Aunty Marion's days off it would be with big sister Peg walking alongside the lovely lady who pushed Lily's pram. They would go to the Jubilee Gardens where it was calm and beautiful. There were trees and ornamental bushes and beds of flowers. And little plaques warning people to keep off the grass. There was so much to look at, the birds that Aunty Marion pointed out, the butterflies, and the way the leaves danced in the breeze. And Burza's heart would dance too, and she would smile into solemn little Lily's face and think that the other child looked like one of the fairies in Rosie's prized picture book.

But there were other times, exciting ones, when Peg took them out on her own. First they would go to number twelve and collect Lily. Peg would knock and say pertly, 'Is Uncle Jack gone – and is Lily ready, please?'

Burza could never understand why Peg always asked about Lily's dad. After all, they all knew that he had left. Peg always waited and watched behind the front-room curtains to make sure of it.

'Yes,' Aunty Marion would reply. 'Be very careful, Peg, and watch if you take Lily out – especially if you cross the road. Here's a halfpenny. Don't buy boiled sweets, mind. Promise you won't? Jelly babies or chocolate buttons, but not boiled sweets.'

'It's all right, honest!' Peg would say indignantly. 'I know as how I daresn't do nothing to choke our Lily to death. And I'll mind the road.'

Burza was happy and she would laugh at Lily, and then Lily was happy too. She loved Lily, and Lily loved her, it was as simple as that.

Somehow Burza sensed about secrets. There was excitement in the air as she and Peg waited, hidden by the orange-yellow curtains in the front room. When Aunty Marion was gone,

Peg would sneak back outside with Burza herself now plonked in the bottom of Lily's posh pram. Then it was a whizzing through to the High Road and along it until it went dark because of the railway arch. Then there was a great building that Peg said was called St Christopher's. The church marked the corner where they turned. Round the corner was a splash of green-painted railings guarding a thick privet hedge, and the huge gates that led to the glory of Abbots Park.

The tufty old grass was yellow in patches, and sometimes quite bare. The large space was flanked by a path of little stones and sand. Set before the privet hedge there were seats on which old people sat. Facing them was a high fence. It looked like net, but was made of iron. Showing through this were some tennis courts that had no grass at all.

Upon reaching the glorious freedom of the park, Peg would laugh aloud and kiss Lily in a rough and ready way simply because she'd done the same to Burza before popping a chocolate drop in each of their little mouths. Then it was time for the game they always played. Peg would point to the gloomy-looking shelter and pull a delightfully awful face.

'Eek! There's a nasty old man in there!'

Then Peg was running with all her might and laughing and shouting and calling out rude things to big boys. Burza's breath caught in her throat because the pram was bumping like crazy and going so fast and Lily's eyes would open wide and look like the violets on Clara's one and only hat. Then Burza would laugh out loud as she enjoyed the thrill of fear. A kind of delightful terror of the unknown old man, of the world rushing away, and of actually getting caught! And with all this she experienced the utmost exhilaration.

Without effort it seemed, the pram was discarded. Peg was grown up, and it was Betsy who looked after Lily and Burza, and sometimes Rosie as well. It was all fun, but it was still secret. And Mrs Jessop next door to Lily was in the secret too. And so was Clara. Nowadays Lily was allowed to say 'Aunty Clara' just as Burza did, and both little girls loved the idea. It was easier that way, the grown-ups said.

In number twelve, Lily, quiet and dreamy, had digested and accepted everything they told her. She sometimes wondered

31

why she couldn't call the lovely warm lady 'Mum' like Peg did. It was explained to her that Burza called Mrs Cuttings Aunty because that was what she was. She was also told that if you called a lady 'Aunty', her children were cousins. But over and above all, staying with Aunty Clara was something that her father must not know. It was a secret.

The most incessant warning in Lily's young life was that nothing on this earth must ever destroy Daddy's pride. Aunty Marion told her this at great length. It was all to do with him having pride if nothing else. He had suffered a great loss and he must be protected from being made sad. In the end Lily became actually fearful of upsetting her nice old dad, who called her 'Chickybit' when he was in a good mood, but who could look like steel when cross. Deep down, because of Aunty Marion's warnings, she was afraid of him.

Now, Lily thought as she sat at the table with her crayons, there was a different sort of fear tingling in her head, and utmost excitement. She would be with Burza and so everything would be all right. It was nothing to do with secrets, but everything to do with new happenings. Tomorrow was the day! Lily was five years old and it was to be her first attendance at school. She sat protected and cosy in the kitchen which was her favourite room. Blue was her favourite colour, Burza's, red. Now too the room held Lily's favourite smells. Still, very faintly, of breakfast toast, more strongly of the pearl barley, beef and onion stew that was simmering on the range.

She glanced above her colouring book and saw all the new things. Set out on the far end of the table there was the wide navy-blue velvet ribbon that would hold back her long ash-blonde hair, and a new dress to match the ribbon. It was a lovely dress, dark blue with a white collar and cuffs. There were the new shoes and white socks. New knickers, vest and liberty bodice to wear underneath. There was also a new navy-blue coat to put on over the rest. It was spring term and the weather remained cold.

Mrs Jessop from next door, who to Lily looked very much like a washing dolly with a painted face, glanced at all the finery laid out and sniffed. It was going to be grown-up talk, Lily thought, and let it all waft over her head.

'Crikey, Mar,' Florrie Jessop said. 'It's all luverly, but the other kids won't be done up posh like that. I mean, it's a pound to a penny young Burza'll have the elder girls' hand-me-downs. What's more, I'm sure that old blue coat will have its airing again. Good togs are for best, not for school, and 'sides – kids like to be the same as each other, you know.'

'Lily is not one of the other children,' Marion replied calmly. 'She is Miss Lily London, lady born and bred.'

'In spite of being Miss Brainbox of the year, Mar,' Florrie exploded, 'you ain't half daft – and pig-headed with it. Poor Lily. The others'll knock the stuffing out of her. Kids can be little shits. You mark my words.'

'Oh no, Florrie. I'm merely carrying out Jack's wishes. I have made it my business to see the Headmistress, though.' Marion's gaze held the clear blue of the sky. 'I am certain that the staff understand and agree that it is up to individuals to make the most of themselves. Even more so when their young are concerned. Lily will be left alone.'

'Of course she will. They won't touch her with a bargepole. She'll be Teacher's pet. Strewth, wot's the matter with yer? If she gets by it'll only be 'cause young Burza'll look out for her.'

'Well, really, Florrie, I don't think it will come to that.'

'No? On your own say-so, you needed Jack to look out for you when you was kids. Lily will definitely need Burza. It's a good job your Lily's got such a nice mate, one what's got a bit of grit in her to fight back. Our Lily's the dearest little angel on Gawd's good earth, but ...'

Marion looked hastily over her shoulder. 'Sh!' she cautioned, then glanced smilingly down at Lily. 'Little pitchers have big ears.'

'Blow me, Mar.' Florrie gave up. 'You don't never change, do yer?'

'Not really,' Marion replied and smiled her golden smile.

When Florrie left, Marion busied herself, trying to clean and get a better colour on the old stone sink. As she did so she began remembering how it had been five years previously. She knew that even now, though managing was hard, and indeed the situation was worsening every day, she would have nothing different. Not really. There was love in her life, from Lily and Jack, and she knew that she needed love more than anything in the world.

A swift picture flashed into her mind of Paul Drew, her

33

boss's son, pushing her onto that bed, his knees trying to nudge her legs apart, his fierce demand for her submission, her desperate tears, her own breathtakingly fiery reaction ... She hastily shuddered the memory away.

Marion thought back to her final arrival, with her tail well and truly between her legs, in Solomon Street. She remembered how determined she had been all those years ago, to become part and parcel of her brother's life. She had set about becoming fully accepted in Solomon Street. It was Florrie from next door who had really started the ball rolling.

Marion had been pushing the pram backwards and forwards outside in the yard, intent on getting Baby to sleep. She was looking pensively at the flat projecting roof of the outside lavatory. Yes! There could be a small extra bedroom built on top of that. Obviously, unlike most of the folk round here, Lily the little princess must have a room of her own. She would talk to Jack about it. And to get him in a mellow mood she would reiterate how right Kathy had been to choose this dear little house. Actually number twelve Solomon Street would do. It really would!

''Ello!' a voice had said, and there was Florrie Jessop from next door peering over the wall. All that could be seen of her was her head, weaving on top of a long neck. For the umpteenth time Marion thought the lady's face looked like a balloon with a face painted on it.

Florrie's straight greasy black hair was parted in the middle and pulled like wings to each side. Her eyebrows looked as though they had been drawn on, though they were not. Her nose was triangular, her mouth small, her eyes seemed too close together, but they were friendly for all that.

'Hello,' Marion replied and smiled.

'You're still 'ere then?'

'Yes, and I'll stay until Jack tells me to go.'

''E won't do that, ducks. Fond of you, 'e is. Kathy told me as how 'e dotes on you and always has.'

'He's a wonderful brother.'

'Yers, and a husband. Give ol' Kathy a good send-off, didn't he? The black horses with them great big ostrich feathers and everything. And the flowers, real luverly.'

Florrie Jessop's long arms reached up and she rested her elbows comfortably on the wall. Clearly, Marion thought,

34

they were in for quite a session. The lady continued.

''S'funny ter think we all thought Jack an' his missus was stuck-up at first. "'E's a right snotty bastard," my Bill said. Well, for once even he's agreed he was wrong. My life he did!' Her voice had changed, became softer and was most sincere. 'Shame about young Kath. I liked her a lot. We sort of got on.'

'I know,' Marion had replied in kind. 'She told me.'

'We always passed the time of day. Used to share a pot regular we did.'

'It's strange you should say that,' Marion had quickly replied. 'The kettle's boiling and I was just thinking that now Lily's asleep, I would make tea.'

'Kath used to make toast.'

'Really? I was going to have a biscuit or two. Strawberry wafers or milk chocolate.'

'Ooh, nice. Posh, but ever so nice.'

'If you'd care to join me, Mrs Jessop?'

'Florrie – and ta. See you in a tick then, all right?'

Within seconds Florrie had plonked herself down in Jack's chair. She was beaming.

''Ello again.'

'Hello, Florrie. Sugar?'

'Cor, the way you said that, all posh! Just like Kath said it an' all. I'll 'ave two.'

'I'm not posh,' Marion told her firmly. 'I'm Jack's sister and I was brought up in an orphanage the same as he and Kathy. Please help yourself to the biscuits.'

A long thin hand stretched out and selected a pink wafer biscuit.

'Ta! Luverly. I buy broken biscuits up Binky's. Mike, her ol' man, sells just about everything. You wanter go up Binky's, Ma. Their prices are cheap and cheerful, if you know what I mean.'

'Cheaper even than the market?'

'About the same, but you don't use up your shoe leather, plodding all the way to the Baker's Arms, do yer? Nor 'ave to lug it all back neither.' Florrie leaned closer. ''Ere, while we're at it, if yer need 'elp, either with shopping or housework, I'm only next door. I ain't brilliant at nothink, but I've got a good pair of hands.'

'Thank you,' Marion told her, adding, 'Kathy told me how

good a friend you were. You stuck by her right up to the last, didn't you?'

'Who wouldn't? Little sweetheart, she was. 'Ere, can I 'ave a proper look at 'er baby?'

They went back into the yard and Florrie looked at Lily and said Ooh! and Ah! and lots of very complimentary things in a most satisfactory way. Then she eyed the line full of washing, which was mainly composed of napkins. She nudged Marion in the ribs and laughed.

'Talk abart Lily! Gawd, what a joke. Wait till you can't keep up wiv your little flower's wee-wees. Then it won't be no Lily, it'll be your little piddle-the-bed. You'll wish you called her Dandelion.'

'Dandy for short, eh?' Marion laughed back. 'How Mrs Cuttings manages with all of her young ones, I'll never know.'

Florrie's expression changed drastically. 'Gawd! Don't mention her name. She ain't forgiven me yet, or rather my Bill. Opened his big gob about tribes of kids, he did, and ol' Clar got to hear about it. Strewth! She don't realise how envious Bill is. We've tried, but no nippers ever come our way. What he said caused ructions. You don't want ter ever get on the wrong side of her! Mind you, she's a goodhearted soul. 'Elps out everyone what needs her and she'd give her last farthing away.'

Marion smiled to herself, still busy with her thoughts. These days the two ladies had buried the hatchet and Clara, Florrie and Marion were the best of friends, their mutual secret holding them close. Her mind went back again to that first time she and Florrie had spoken, had come together as 'mates' as they put it locally ...

'This yard is awful,' Marion had said, looking round. 'I hope Jack will do some digging. I want there to be flowers growing here.'

'Like what I've got.' Florrie's tone held utmost satisfaction. 'Mind you, nothing's decent this time of year, but Bill likes his dahlias and chrysanths, and they'll do till the first frost. Everythink's raggy and dying now.'

'And I want another room built onto the house,' Marion had said slowly, dismissing the subject of dying dahlias. Florrie stopped in her tracks.

'Do what?' The older woman's small eyes got busy in her

36

face as she looked back at the grey building behind them. 'I don't get you. It's painted up and looks a bloody sight better than ours. 'Sides, building rooms on top of these places 'ud look like pimples on haystacks.'

'Not on top! And it is possible, really,' Marion enthused. 'See? Over the roof of the lavatory. I'm sure it can be done.'

'Blow me, Mar. You gorn mad?'

'A little pink nursery.' Marion was fired with even more enthusiasm. 'And later on it will have a single bed. Lily shall have her very own place – or I'll take the new one, if Jack says. Or she can have the back where I am now, if that works better. But it doesn't get the sun and—'

Florrie snorted. 'You're as nutty as a fruitcake, Mar.'

'We'll see,' Marion had replied and laughed out loud.

And the room had materialised. No expense had been spared. Set out in rose pink with a paper frieze of lily-of-the-valley and bluebell design, it was Lily's very own place. It had cost more than Marion and Jack had dreamed, but really sold on the idea now, Jack had gone ahead.

Brooking no interference, he had seen to all the business side of things. He had put down the deposit and paid so much a month, barely looking at the agreement; his attitude had been the same when purchasing the house. Jack was, Marion often told him fondly, just like a bull in a china shop. He was only interested in the end result, not in bits of paper. These days it took all of Jack's time to pay the interest. The actual debts never seemed to come down.

'I don't seem to have made even the slightest pin-prick in our actual house payments,' he said ruefully on more than one occasion. 'At this rate I'll be in debt up to my eyebrows for the rest of my life.'

'Cheer up,' she had comforted him. 'Things must get better soon.'

'Things are getting shaky,' Jack told her and ran his hand through his fair curly hair. 'And I'm feeling like a bloody old man.'

'Yet you look young and very handsome,' she teased. Then because of his impatient snort, she added, 'If things get really bad, dear, perhaps you'll let me try to look after all the business side of things? I manage the house-keeping very well, don't I?'

'You're the cat's whiskers at making one penny do the work of two,' he admitted. 'Good for you, old girl.'

After that, for all Jack strived, he was still only managing to pay back the interest. The situation became worse all round and Jack gave in at last. He accepted Marion's offer to take over all the business affairs, happily handing over his takings and leaving the rest up to her.

It had taken Marion less than an hour to realise that there simply wasn't enough coming in. Seeing how strained and ill Jack was beginning to look, knowing it was all her fault because of her grandiose ideas, Marion felt sick with guilt. She was at her wits' end. Jack was losing money all round no matter how hard he tried.

As always, the poor were getting poorer, but even the better-off were having to tighten their belts. The people in the larger houses seemed to be suffering the most, for like Jack, they had their pride. It was so essential to keep up appearances. Now their windows were either cleaned not so regularly, or else by staff, and even on some rare occasions, very surreptitiously by themselves. All of which meant Jack's takings went down.

In number twelve Solomon Street, fresh debts began to pile up. Then out of the blue, Marion had seen the advertisement in the newspaper, for an experienced office worker in Drew Wholesalers, the Keens Estate branch. Not the main office where she had worked with Paul, but a subsidiary. Strange, she had thought, that the old firm was still holding its head above water. But then, Drews had their fingers in so many pies. They made deals – and arranged things. She should know!

A knife-like agony seared through her. She could not, would not even entertain the idea of working for the Drews again. It would be hell on earth – and one day ... Oh, dear heaven, one day she might even bump into Paul!

Her face had gone red. Her old sense of shame and despair rose to the fore. She felt as though she was choking to death. But the advert in the paper seemed to be leaping from the page. The money would save them. It would save Jack from terrible shame. They had threatened to summons him if his repayments did not pick up. He could lose the house. God forbid! That, on top of everything else, would just about kill him.

It was all her fault! She should never have talked him round. Never all but practically tied his hands behind his back about having the extra room built on. He had always given in to her, his little sister. And now look at the trouble they were in!

'Clara,' she had said the following day, having just returned triumphant from Keens Estate, 'please can I have a word?'

Then later on, over the garden wall: 'Florrie dear, I have a favour to ask.'

It had taken courage and cunning to work it all out. In spite of Jack's strict instructions that Lily should not mix with the rough and ready element too much, and so copy their ill-bred way of speaking, it all worked out beautifully. Clara or one of her brood minded Lily until Marion came home. This made Lily ecstatic since she and Burza had become closer than sisters. On the other hand, Florrie did the housework and prepared the evening meal. Even though Marion paid them both a few shillings each week, there was enough left to help out all round.

Very slowly and definitely things were growing more easy. Jack continued to work all hours God gave. He accepted that Marion was a brilliant manager, one who by some magic was able to make the money go round, and he never questioned how.

'You're a marvel, Sis,' he told her more than once. 'I never knew you were capable of bringing about miracles.'

'We both are,' she had laughed back at him, thanking all the gods that he thought her as above-board as his own honest and upright self. He would never guess she was working, and letting the one jewel in his crown run free with Clara and her kind. No, never in a million years.

From the moment Marion had taken the job at Drews' Keens office she had ceaselessly reminded Lily how she must speak nicely, forever correcting her if she so much as dared copy Burza.

'Remember your aitches, dear. Hat, H. – H. That's right *H* – at!'

On other occasions: 'Darling, please don't speak like Burza, and I know that Aunty Clara says blooming, but you must not! Sounding like Aunty Clara would upset Daddy and we must not have that, must we?'

'But we love Aunty Clara, don't we?' Lily had whispered in her young, prettily husky voice. 'Don't we, Aunty Marion?'

'Of course we do. It's all to do with your daddy's pride, darling,' Marion would reply, and her tone was so desperate, so meaningful, that from her earliest age, Lily, a quiet adaptable child, had done her best to obey. She even told Burza how things were in her shy way and Burza, though not fully understanding, happily complied.

Unaware of anything except her excitement, Lily continued with her picture. She was wishing the time away. She was going to be a big girl like Betsy and Rosie. Not all grown-up of course like Peg. Peg, as well as Sid, gladly grabbed casual labour in Hymen's Market, mostly helping out old Ma Hutchins on her veggy stall. Lily carefully drew an apple and a banana, and thought how good it was to be a big girl. Aunty Clara had said that she would make her a newspaper parcel holding bread and jam just like Burza's. And she, Lily, would just love school because Aunty Marion said that it was wonderful to learn things. That she would enjoy everything just as had Aunty Marion – who had been Teacher's pet.

Daddy had laughed and said that was more than he had been. Quite the reverse in fact. But Aunty Marion had put her fingers to her lips and said that Lily was going to be exactly like her. So it was going to be fun. It was going to be wonderful. It was so exciting to be a big girl ...

At ten-fifteen the following day Lily, a diminutive downcast five-year-old with cheeks the colour of fire, faced the classroom wall in disgrace. Her shoulders drooped and quivered beneath the new dress. She had been smacked. Actually smacked!

Miss Wetheral said that she had lied. That there was no place in her class for people who wilfully told untruths.

Inside of her, Lily's heart was swollen with hurt and wild despair and utter disillusionment. She hated school. She hated Aunty Clara, and all aunties, and she hated fathers who must never be shamed. Apart from Burza, she hated the whole wide world. The pain of her shock and disbelief was so deep that it would never go away. She wished she was in St Christopher's lying next to the unknown mummy who had loved her so greatly that she had died. She longed to be with the mummy who would cuddle her close and tell her that everything would be all right – just as Aunty Clara did when things went wrong. Aunty Clara ... No, that was wrong, wrong, wrong!

Two tears glistened like crystals on the end of dark lashes, then fell silently to the wood-beamed floor.

40

Chapter Four

Both tiny, pensive and vulnerable, Lily and Burza walked along Solomon Street hand in hand. It was dinnertime and the rough cobblestones teemed with children who, until two o'clock, were blessedly free of school. Some were swinging on ropes looped over lamp-post bars, others kicked footballs made from rolled-up paper tied with string. The really lucky ones had whips and tops, or glass marbles that rolled along like so many prize gems.

From the Feathers end, the rougher element shouted and scuffled. Scruffy girls with their drawers hanging down watched a group of lads playing footer. They were convulsed with high-pitched giggles. This following each filthy comment on the sizes of the team's private parts. The largest lad, ragged and ill-kempt, who had been accused of having a 'winkle wot wouldn't do nuffink for no one' leapt towards them at last. He was redfaced and furious, his fist raised. Skinny girls flew, screaming with joy.

There was nothing unusual about the scene. Lily walked alongside Burza, crushed and dazed, aware only of feeling the comfort and security of her friend's hand. Burza was equally confused, but she felt defiant and furious and deep down sad – for Lily. Lily was not the sweet smiling, gentle little girl who had always been so calm and sure of things. Lily was lost and bewildered and terribly afraid. She seemed all squeezed up, misshapen, like a balloon that had been let down.

Burza wanted to yell and scream and call out bad things, but she knew that Lily needed her to be quiet and still. Burza was uncaring that the noonday sun was intensifying, heedless of

41

the indiscriminate smells of Solomon Street – of kippers, herrings, of boiled cabbage, and of the horse dung being shovelled up by one of the older Frazer boys. It was common knowledge that Bill Jessop would pay a halfpenny for a bucket full of the stuff, a penny with luck. He was crackers on gardening. The whole world knew that!

Sometimes the big boys were not around and Rosie would kid Burza up.

'Go on. Go an' get it! Then we'll buy some sweets up Allenby's.'

'I don't want to!'

'If you don't do it, gippo, I'll tell everyone how your mum and dad dumped you on our doorstep. That you ain't never been wanted, not even by us. That you're a – a foundling.'

And even though Burza gave back as good as she got, even though she knew that none of that talk was true, she was afraid of lies going round school. Rotten lousy lies begun by Rosie who had never forgiven her for usurping her place as the baby of the house. It was Rosie who had thrown Moo-Moo under a steamroller. The poor old grey monkey that Clara had made, even though mended as well as possible, had never been the same. Burza and Lily had wept together over poor Moo-Moo. Then in sympathy, when the chance came, Lily had rubbed soot all over Bo-Bo her beloved white velvet bear.

As much as she loathed collecting horse dung, Burza loved being asked by the chimney sweep to go outside in the road and tell him when his brush appeared above the chimney pot. She had wanted to cry when his soot had made such a mess of Bo-Bo though. Cry with love for Lily who had made such a terrible sacrifice.

Now, as they walked home together, Burza was wishing that she had been allowed to take Moo-Moo on her first day at school, and that Lily had Bo-Bo to cuddle. The two raggy animals were dearly loved friends and they both smelled faintly of Rinso because they had been washed so much. Instead, there was the strong stink of cats' pee wafting on the air. This from the evil-eyed ginger tom who lived in the long-suffering Em Bede's house.

Em's husband, ol' Fatty Bede, who was deaf but told everyone he wasn't, thought he was a very funny man. Burza hated

Art Bede because he had ginger eyelashes and red-rimmed eyes, and a face under carroty hair that looked just like the pig's head that was placed in the butcher's window. Burza also hated their grown-up daughter Minnie who took after Art.

Minnie lived upstairs to her parents and in her turn had four very young steps and stairs all of whom had her features and colouring – which was as well since they all had different dads.

Lily barely knew that either the man or his family were alive. She knew only to be nice and not hurt the feelings of her dad and to obey the lovely Aunty Marion. Burza forgot Lily long enough to dwell on thoughts of Marion. So tall, so beautiful, so refined.

'You try and be like Lily's aunt,' Clara would say. 'You can't go far wrong then, Burza. She's a lady, an' that's what you wanna be.'

Burza pulled herself together. This was not the day to think of nice things. This was a time when you had to hate grown-ups, or some of them, and Art Bede was very hateable indeed. Burza's open dislike had been born on the day Art had said rude personal sorts of things to big sister Peg. Peg had given back as good as she got, yelling, 'Up yer arse!' Then she'd walked away, warning her younger sisters: 'You be careful of 'im. Bloody careful! 'E's a filfy, wicked, evil ol' man!'

Burza heard a suppressed, breathless sob and was instantly not thinking of any dirty rotten grown-ups just then. Burza, shiny dark curls bobbing, lips pursed with concern, was scared for her dearly beloved friend. Burza suddenly and very desperately needed Clara and knew that Lily did too. Lily looked ill, she was too quiet, too remote even for her. Her violet-blue eyes were huge in her face.

'Lily?' she asked. 'You all right?'

Lily shook her head, her straight fair hair floating like silk in the air. She wanted to tell Burza how she felt, but did not have the right words. How could she explain that the sense of Aunty Marion's betrayal remained strong? This even though she was now in this street which was her world? She accepted its river of life, went along with it because it was what she knew. She had recognised it from her first awakenings on this earth. It was her own place. Her family and friends were here.

It was as familiar to her as was her bounden duty not to be like any of its inhabitants. And to remember to always and for ever be a good girl – for her father's sake.

Now, on this, the most important of days, she had not been good at all. It had not been wonderful as Aunty Marion had promised. It had been frightening – and she hated school. Hated it!

Lily took in a deep sobbing breath. She had been very wicked. She did not know why. All she was sure of was her ocean-deep sense of guilt. She had betrayed her father in an unfathomable way. She had been smacked! Oh, a featherlight touch to be sure, but the humiliation, the shock, and sense of adult treachery had seared through her in an immense and awful manner. And her new dress, the one Aunty Marion had slaved to get, was ruined and Aunty Marion would get all tight-lipped. She always did when upset.

The new dress had been torn by a big fat girl named Josie Briggs. Josie had shouted, 'Snotty moo!' as she viciously pulled at the material and split the seam. The front of the dress was a mess, stained because Andy Beldon of Dunton Street, the road next to her own, hated her being sat beside him. This had been her punishment, but it had turned out to be his punishment too. He had uttered, 'Bitch!' as she, timid and trembling, had taken her place at his side.

Unbelievably, Miss Wetheral had announced in a cold, crystal clear way, that people who told falsehoods would never be allowed to sit next to their friends. So Andy's best mate, slum kid Richard Wray, had been made to sit next to Burza. Absolutely furious, Andy had waited until Teacher's back was turned, then he had thrown the contents of his slate-cleaning jar directly at Lily. Traumatised, she had sat frozen as the sopping wet, chalky rag fell from her chest and onto the floor. Too terrified of being noticed by Miss Wetheral again, she never uttered a sound. Andy, tow-headed, baby-faced, went red with shame. He drew in his lips, frowned savagely, and waited for her outcry and the ensuing punishment. Neither came.

At playtime, Burza, who had not missed a trick, saw Andy and Richard moodily kicking a deflated ball about. Yelling like a miniature banshee, she weighed in, arms and legs

44

weaving like a windmill, punching and kicking at both boys. Intimidated, Andy Beldon and scruffy black-haired, good-looking Richard Wray had fallen back. Neither attempted to defend himself.

Angular, steel-eyed Miss Tooks, who had playground duty, came over and put a stop to it. Quite unrepentant, Burza still managed to yell at the top of her voice to the rapidly receding Josie Briggs: 'I'd rather be a snot than a big fat ugly old cow!'

Lily and Burza were shamed before the class, Lily lightly but reprovingly slapped for the second time. Belittled, crumpled, utterly confused, she stood before the staring pupils, eyes down. In a kind of dream she heard her dearest friend receive her punishment, and Burza's mutinous, 'Didn't 'urt!'

Burza and Lily were then made to look at the wall in opposite corners of the room. They were, they were told, troublemakers. Behind Miss Wetheral's back Burza pulled a face and poked out her tongue. This raised a ripple of frightened sniggers, which snapped silent at the Teacher's returning glare.

All Lily needed over and above all, was to go home.

Now, after what had seemed to be an interminable morning, it was twelve o'clock and her wish was coming true.

'You have to say "I don't care!"' Burza told Lily in a firm little-girl way. Her luminous dark eyes were seriousness itself. 'Go on. Say it!'

'I don't care,' Lily whispered unconvincingly, knowing that she did.

Then it was in number six and being surrounded by the Cuttings family and big warm mother Clara, saying brightly: ''Ello, me darlings.' Then, 'An' how did my gels get on?'

'We were smacked,' Burza said importantly, aping the way Lily spoke. 'And we were stood in the corner because we were two very naughty girls.'

'Oh? Smacked was yer, on your very first morning?' Clara's smile faded and the twinkle was replaced by a nasty glint in her eyes. 'How come, luv?'

Burza explained as best as she could. Clara looked grim.

'Well,' she said, sniffing furiously, 'we'll 'ave ter see about hall this, won't we?' She stroked Lily's long silver-fair hair. 'Never mind, gel. Guess what? Your Aunty Marion made a special journey 'ome just for this once. She's been thinking about you all the time. Come on, young Lil, orf we go and see her, eh?'

'Can I come?' Burza asked.

'No. You just stay 'ere while I—'

'Ow, ow, ow!' Burza wailed, and since a very real storm looked like brewing, especially as Lily had walked over to her bosom-buddy and they were holding hands again, Clara gave in.

'Proper Babes in the Wood you two are,' she said. 'I dunno, what am I going ter do with the pair of yer.' And since her feathers were well and truly ruffled, she added sharply, 'Come on then, and don't either of yer perishing-well dawdle! D'yer hear?'

The two youngsters were marched along to number twelve where Marion waited, her greeting smile fading when she saw the state Lily was in. She looked from the ashen-faced child, at the red-faced Burza, and then helplessly at the very angry Mrs Cuttings.

'Come in, Clara,' Marion said quietly. 'What has happened?'

'I'll tell yer,' Clara said, her voice tight as she bustled along the cream wall-papered passage and into the blue and white kitchen. 'Lily don't understand it – and I'm sure I don't, since we're s'posed to be dealin' with clever people what should know better. But what's clear is, Lil was smacked – in the first place, mind you – for making a plain an' simple mistake! The second time—'

'Smacked?' Marion's head jerked up. 'For the first time? And a second? Explain, Clara. Please!'

'She was given a fourpenny one for trying to be polite, an' for being, what she thought, as honest as the day. She believed Burza 'ere was her cousin, yer see. Easy done since she calls me "Aunty", know what I mean? We've all gorn along with that, ain't we?'

'Yes, Clara, of course we have. Just as Burza calls me "Aunty". I told Lily to call you "Aunty" since she's in your house as much if not more than her own."

'It ain't young Lil's fault that it's a cruel and heartless world. Yes, an' with cruel an' heartless old cows in it.'

46

Clara's voice grew even more indignant. 'It seems as how Miss Wetheral asked if anyone had a relation in class. So Lil put up her 'and and says that Burza's her cousin.' Clara looked down at Lily's face, saw the expression in her eyes and exploded, 'Gawd 'elp us! The pore little mite looks like she thinks the world's come to an end.'

Further heated remarks followed and Marion said quietly at the end of it all, 'I'll get my coat.'

'What for?' Clara was openly surprised.

'I am going to see Miss Wetheral.' Marion was icily cool. 'And I am going to—'

'You won't get no joy up the school,' Clara cut in. 'Not till after two o'clock. Them teachers all buzz orf dinnertimes, or say they do. It's certain they won't talk to no mothers during their break. It might addle their brains! 'Sides, you've gotta be back at your job before that.'

'No.' Marion was dangerously quiet. 'Oh no! No one smacks Lily. I will not tolerate it.'

'All you'll do is get the sack from your job if you're not back on time,' Clara said dismissively, pointing out the hard facts of life. 'And that'd mean me and old Florrie will be out of pocket too.'

'I am sorry, but—'

'No! My Burza's in this little lot as well, Mar. That's right, my young Burza – just because she done the right thing an' stuck up for her mate.' Clara nodded her head in an intimidating way. 'You just leave all the mouthing orf ter me! You can write a stiff letter to the Head. Threaten to take it further in your posh way. That's somethink I can't do.'

'But—'

''Ave you ever been up the school?' Clara warmed to her theme. 'Like on the war-path?' Clara's tone became belligerent, yet triumphant at the same time. ''Course you ain't! They'd 'ave your guts for garters, for all your la-di-dah ways. You're still under their thumb because they've got your kid in their clutches. Stuck-up mares! Well, let me tell you, no one gets the better of me when it comes to a bull and cow.'

'I know that you can row with the best,' Marion replied tightly, 'and still come out on top, Clara, but ...'

'I'm going to sort it, believe me.' An unholy gleam came

47

into Clara's eyes. 'I've done it tons of times and – well, they'll know what they're in for when they see me! All right?'

Clara had her way. Marion was given her marching orders in no uncertain terms and hastily made herself ready to catch the tram back to work. The two children were taken off to Clara's house.

Burza and Lily sat with the others and dipped wedges of dry bread into lukewarm onion and potato soup. Lily was merely going through the motions, and only this because of Clara's insistence. She was frightened, and very aware of the grim look she had seen on her Aunty Marion's face. It was all her fault and she still could not fathom why.

When it was time to go back to school, Lily showed her feelings. She pulled her hand away from Clara's warm clasp, dug her toes in, and screamed high and wild.

'Bloody hell!' Clara said to Betsy and Rosie. 'The pore little mite's terrified. You wait till I get hold of that Wetheral. I'll give her what for. Just you wait and see!'

In the end Burza and Lily stayed home while Clara, looking like a warship in full sail, marched to school.

What happened there the children never knew.

But that evening before her father came home from work, Lily was warned not to tell Jack of the upset, but just to mention all the nice things that had happened. There had been nothing nice, Lily thought fearfully, nothing! Wishing to make her escape, she quietly asked, 'Please, can I go out and play with Burza?'

'Yes, dear,' Marion replied lovingly, her heart aching for the small girl who as yet knew so little of the hard-as-nails life outside. 'But you must come in the moment I call you. We must be safely indoors and all washed and clean for Daddy, mustn't we? Oh, an' it's *out*. O-U-T! Not "art". And you mustn't say "Git art of it," either. I heard Burza saying that to Peter Frazer only yesterday. Burza must learn, as must we all.'

'Pete's horrible to her, Aunty Marion,' Lily whispered. 'He hit her!'

'He shouldn't have. Boys should never hit girls. But Burza insists on calling him names, as well as throwing stones, and poking out her tongue.'

'That's because he's lots bigger than her, Aunty Marion.'

48

Here was something she could do, Lily thought wildly. Defend her friend. She answered back, in a small voice, but said her piece just the same. 'Burza says that all the Frazers are bullies and they've got to know that she isn't scared of them. Pete—'

'Peter Frazer, like his brothers, has been taught to stick up for himself, Lily,' Marion said firmly. 'He comes from nice people who train to be boxers. They do not go at things like crazy windmills rolling in gutters. They are not like the uncouth boys who do not speak properly and who, even like some men, can be very cruel at times.'

On her pet hobby horse and forgetting the streetwise Burza, Marion suddenly remembered the pressure of Paul's mouth, the feel of his hand reaching under her skirt, and she had wanted to ... had needed to ... had desired above all else ...

Flustered, she added, 'But that does not mean we must copy them, dear. Clara's boys and girls are in with the swim, but the Frazers are more like us. We ourselves must be upright and correct as is Daddy.'

'Will he be as cross as Aunty Clara?' Lily whispered, her heart in her eyes. 'When he knows I've been naughty at school?'

'You were not naughty, darling. It was a misunderstanding. So there's no need to say anything at all to Daddy.'

So that evening Jack was allowed to keep his pride, while Lily kept her hurt and shame to herself – and her loathing of school, along with her hatred of people in authority, and of horrible boys, and men with red eyelids, and Miss Wetheral, and Miss Took, and Aunty Marion for saying that she had to keep going to school, and even her father who mustn't be told things because of his pride.

That night Lily lay in her room which was pretty and clean and smelled of the Mansion furniture polish, wanting Burza and wishing to be held in Clara's warm, bosomy embrace. She knew that above all the people in the world, second only to Burza, she loved Clara – who was not her Aunty after all ...

In the main, after that traumatic first day, the girls' education went fairly smoothly. Burza, bright and bouncy, ready to fight at the drop of a hat, stuck by Lily at all times. It soon became known that if you yelled at Lil, you got bashed by Burza. In fact, Burza went wild and looked ready to do murder if anyone even hinted at upsetting the quiet fair-haired little girl. So it was that Lily was left severely alone when Burza was around. On the whole, Lily remained silent, obedient, thoughtful, always listening and learning.

Miss Wetheral, who still felt sick with guilt every time she saw Lily, was increasingly conscious of the child's large-eyed steady gaze, and would look away. The woman felt ashamed. A dedicated teacher, she knew that she had been far too harsh. But it had all happened moments after the Head had refused permission for her to marry.

'Out of the question, Miss Wetheral,' Miss Ogleby had told her crisply. 'The policy remains the same, no married teachers. If you go ahead with your plans, I am afraid that we will have to dismiss you.'

Miss Wetheral had lost her dreams on the morning Lily had begun school, and shortly after that, her young man too. Miss Wetheral knew that from now on her life would run on exactly the same lines. She was a spinster with a job – until she was retired, of course. Then who knew? The scrap heap probably. A dreary outlook indeed. But for now there were the children, other people's, but better than none.

'Clearly,' Miss Wetheral told Miss Took one day, 'Lily London is no longer actually afraid of us. I'm glad.'

'She has very soulful eyes,' Miss Took replied. 'Somehow I sense that the child's attitude is quietly dismissive. She is painfully polite. She suffers during playtimes, I sense it, even though I cannot see out of the back of my head. The other children bully her when they dare. The Briggs child pinches her black and blue when Burza's not around. I do my best, but generally speaking, most of my time is spent trying to tame brutal, forever fighting, foul-mouthed little boys. The working classes are so – so disgustingly crude.'

'Lily London does not fit into that category and, sadly, the child cannot win,' Miss Wetheral replied. 'She looks and acts differently to the others in class, which makes her stand out. I can't help thinking that she must pick up the odd bad word or mannerism from the rest, and lets it slip at home. That means she will get into trouble there too. To my mind, the way that young aunt's bringing her up is tantamount to cruelty.'

50

'She has certainly fashioned a square peg in a round hole,' Miss Took agreed. 'But as you have said several times before, still waters tend to run deep, and more's the pity. Lily is an exceedingly pretty, likeable little thing, but have you noticed how boiling kettles eventually have to let off steam?'

'I cannot believe that of Lily. Still, at least she has the Webb girl on her side.'

'Ah!' Miss Took's angular face softened. 'Exotic, extremely beautiful little Burza. You can tell that she's a relative of that awful Cuttings woman. Ready to argue at the drop of a hat, happy to mouth off at the top of her voice. But I like young Burza. She is courageous, and above all, loyal to her friend.'

'I have rather a soft spot for Lily,' Miss Wetheral said unexpectedly. 'I have noticed that she seldom speaks, but when she does, in her quiet way, the others listen.'

'Except Josie Briggs.'

'Exactly,' came the reply. 'Actually I cannot help wondering just what is going to happen to the London child. It does not augur well for her, I'm afraid.'

'What is clear,' came the reply, 'is that come hell or high water, where there's London there will be Webb. Chalk and cheese perhaps, yet to coin another overworked phrase, as thick as thieves. However, we all need friends, don't you agree?'

'I do indeed.'

The two teachers looked at each other and smiled.

Chapter Five

Burza progressed through school terms, living, learning, joining in happily on all the something days. Christmas break-up days were magical and marvellous, with decorated classrooms and everyone buzzing with excitement, for there was the Nativity play to watch. One year Lily played the Holy Mother, and Burza, bearded and fully into the part, played Joseph. A Joseph that drew himself up tall and loudly threatened to ram the innkeeper's teeth down his throat for refusing a room for Mary. The innkeeper just happened to be Josie Briggs.

There was Empire Day, when everyone must wear red, white and blue and give a rousing rendering of 'Land of Hope and Glory' in the assembly hall. Boat Race Day was fun, when little celluloid dolls dressed either in dark or light blue were pinned on lapels. Some of the light-blue boys had pitched battles with the dark if Oxford beat Cambridge and vice versa. Fighting was the thing to do.

Then there was a sad time, Armistice Day when poor old Miss Nurse always cried because she had lost her loved one in the war. Scarlet poppies were everywhere in school, the colour of blood and with the black eye of death in their hearts. Before hometime the poppies were collected and placed with much ceremony under the plaque in the hall where a list of local heroes was displayed. The poppies made a patch of red, just like the flower-bestrewn Flanders fields where so many Tommies had fallen.

It was the same every year. Burza fiercely refusing to give up her own poppy. Defiantly sticking it behind her ear among her dark curls in spite of the contemptuous looks from the rest.

Shocked the first year it happened, then understanding, Lily had gone to St Christopher's with Burza. In the graveyard they had walked to a tiny mound, with a nameplate at its head, saying Violet Cuttings. Before it, a vase holding a single florist's flower. Sticking in the ground beside it there were five Armistice poppies. Burza reverently placed her poppy alongside.

'It's Violet's birthday today,' Burza said quietly, 'and Aunty Clara loved her very much. She would have bought her some more flowers, but Aunty always gives us money for our poppies out of respect for Uncle George's fallen mates. So in our turn, we all give our poppies to Violet.'

Lily started to weep for Clara and the unknown little baby, but seconds after telling the sorry tale, Burza made her laugh about how alone and unaided she had managed to make Josie Briggs drop her farthing chew in some lovely steaming horse-dung.

'That'll serve her right,' Burza said breezily, feeling the familiar burst of unholy joy. 'She said you were a milk-sop and I told her! She hates us and d'you know why? She likes Andy. Over my dead body, she likes Andy!'

By now Andy and Richard had become the girls' champions and friends. They were highly honoured in this since it was generally agreed that Burza and Lily were the prettiest girls in school. The effect of the two contrasting beauties on the rest was clearly defined. The girls in class loathed them and made catty remarks – behind their backs. The boys became redfaced and tonguetied.

Andy Beldon and Richard Wray had been accepted as bosom buddies the day after Burza had tried to kill them both on their first day at school.

The third boy, a little outside the foursome but seemingly always there, was Pete Frazer. All the boys loved fighting and better still boxing. Peter, his brothers and father were all into boxing in a big way. Boxing could be the means to earn a bob or two. It could take a bloke to the heights. Pete often took Andy and Richard on, usually both at the same time, as sparring partners. Always in seriousness at first, but usually ending up with laughter from Andy, since he couldn't fight the skin off a rice pudding. Then Pete would throw back his shaggy head and laugh too. He had the heartiest laugh around. Pete Frazer was big, tough and goodlooking, with eyes the clear colour of golden syrup. He had even white teeth, and deep chestnut-bronze hair. He was a little older than the four, but not as old as Dicky Cuttings. Pete was the spitting image of Vin, his father, and Brian and Ben the two older brothers. All the Frazer men looked very much alike.

Their mother, Rene, had hair the colour of marigolds. She was pretty, small, grey-eyed and as houseproud as they came. Her husband and sons towered over her, obeyed her without question, and adored the ground she walked upon. She read a lot – romantic books that had happy endings. Lily and Burza liked Rene Frazer simply because she seemed to like them. They liked Pete too, but would kill themselves stone dead before admitting it.

Fight and squabble though they all did, young and old alike, there was an innate bond between the people of Solomon Street. It was like a big, raggle-taggle family, all mixed, nice and nasties, held together by the fact that their street was their place, their own patch. It was to be defended at all cost. Solomon Street was also the home of the Firestones Club.

Firestones elders were a matey lot. Their main object, apart from being ardent Orient football supporters, was that of looking after their own. It said a great deal for Andy Beldon that he was allowed to be a junior member of the Firestones for all he lived in another road.

Richard Wray, considered to be one of the very low, curled his lips and was not a member of any club or gang.

'Don't need no trouble,' he told Burza. 'I've got enough to cope with, just with ol' Gippo, and he's a handful all right. Besides,' he added, 'one of these bright fine days there's going to be all-out war and then where will us four stand? Gip's a Matson bloke, see? And I'm with him. Let's face it, I'd never be wanted by your lot.'

'Don't be silly, Richard,' Burza told him, her cheeks suddenly as red as fire. 'And what's the matter with gippos, might I ask?'

'You're a fat-head,' Andy put in, ignoring the talk about gippos. 'You only have to do what I did – and ask!'

Richard shook his head and scowled, which made him look

even more handsome, Burza thought lovingly. Richard was a strong-minded, very clear-cut young man, one who went his own way. He was always welcomed in the Cuttings house, which was one up on Lily since he was frowned upon by Aunty Marion. Burza knew that Lily loved Richard too and had been equally amazed on the day Aunty Marion had said reprovingly: 'You must choose friends that are more fitting, Lily dear, and you also, Burza.'

Burza wanted above all else to be a real lady like Lily's Aunty Marion, but sometimes it was hard. Especially since Aunty Marion's theme was always the same.

'Reach for the highest rung of the ladder, girls, and no matter what happens, hang on!'

Lily had taken it all quietly, merely looked pained. Burza had contented herself by glaring. It had taken her a long time to cultivate her glare. It could be disbelieving, hold contempt, or else downright fury. Today her glare was pained. Surprising, really, since Burza usually agreed wholeheartedly with everything Marion said. Even so she had her own ideas. Some of which would have driven Marion mad.

Burza enjoyed being outrageous; she liked being naughty, but never ever wicked or unkind. She had become wilful over the years and Lily always quietly and determinedly followed in the footsteps of her dearly beloved friend. So it was that they now regularly walked in the slums, going home from school with Richard Wray, Burza openly experiencing the same thrill of daring that she'd had when Peg used to run the pram from the pretending old man in the park.

Both girls knew that Aunty Marion would die the death if she ever found out – and as for Jack! He would hit the roof and never come down. Lily smiled her secret smile; Burza grinned unashamedly.

'It's more fun to live wicked, Lily,' she'd laugh. 'It makes me tingle all over just thinking about what "they'd" say if they knew. Besides, you don't have to be naughty to get punished, do you? We learned that from old bossy-boots Wetheral.'

'If my father ever finds out, he'll ...'

'Give you a fourpenny one? Come on,' Burza teased, 'your dad would cut his right hand off before hurting you.'

'I was going to say that he would be very, very ashamed of

me. At the moment he thinks everything I do is good.'

'Prunes and prisms! Soppy Soft! Gawd, Lily, how does it feel to be choked to death?'

'Pardon me?'

'By having your halo slip down to your throat.'

'Now you're being horrible, Burza.'

'No, but I learned long ago that one might just as well be hung for a sheep as for a lamb.'

'But we're being really and truly disobedient, not going straight home after school. Clara doesn't mind too much, just so long as we're not too long gone, but even she wouldn't like this. As for Aunty Marion!'

'She believes that darling Chickybit is safe only in the posh area of Solomon Street?' Burza scoffed, her eyes dancing, cheeks dimpling. 'I love her, but there are times when I'd like to stick pins into your Aunty Marion. She goes on and on. All about doing the right thing, living the right way, being honest and above board about anything and everything – except her own secret job, of course!'

'That's for my father's peace of mind,' Lily reproved her. 'My aunt is always going on about keeping his pride intact because he really doesn't have much else. Mostly though, I think it's because she hates it when he gets angry. I do too. He goes sort of ice-cold and he's strict, so strict.' Lily's cheeks glowed pink. 'And – and if you dare call me Chickybit in public ever again Burza Webb, I'll hate you all the days of my life.'

'No, you wouldn't. You couldn't! If you did I'd want to die!' Burza struck a melodramatic pose. 'And, cor lumme, you can't half talk posh!'

'Oh, shut up.' Lily's slow, golden smile lit her face. 'And it's Miss Prunes and Prisms again, is it?'

Burza often called Lily Miss Prunes and Prisms, yet it was she who tried to ape Aunty Marion. How silly when she was lucky enough to belong to Clara. Next to Burza, Clara was the love of Lily's life, and both girls knew it.

Life with Clara was warm and noisily merry. A madcap sort of world against the settled orderliness of number twelve. And big, motherly Clara was the very heart and soul of it.

Clara's good deeds were legion, as some of the poorer folk in Solomon Street could bear witness to. Clara would give away her last farthing and think nothing of it. She would nurse old people and do errands for them when they could not do it for themselves. She adored kids. She would help out when needed as a matter of course, and got on with everyone – well, nearly everyone. She was a bit wary of Mrs Jessop still, since her husband was George's boss. And she didn't like Ethel Jacobs of number four much because she drank gin and was thin and a spiteful mischief-maker. Clara's pet hate was Em Bede who nagged morning, noon and night in spite of the fact that her husband was near deaf.

'Like a machine she is,' Clara would say, 'droning on and on. How that fat pig of an' ol' man of hers can stick it, I'll never know. Fair gives me a headache she does. You can hear her carrying on all down the bloody road. And I can't stick that slimy son of hers neither. He's for the hangman one day.'

'Nicky Bede's a slug,' Burza would say. 'Almost as bad as his dad.'

''E'll turn out a damned sight worse than ol' Art,' Clara sniffed. 'You mark my words.'

Burza and Lily always faithfully marked Clara's words – for two seconds at least. Just as they listened carefully to the Sunday School teacher at St Christopher's and completely forgot everything the moment they escaped outside. There were far more interesting things to see and do. Together with Richard and Andy, the girls began to explore the local area.

Beyond Solomon Street there were two other nice streets, namely Dunton where Andy Beldon lived, then Burchel, where Josie Briggs came from. Then there was the high brick wall with its top fringe of broken glass shards that divided the decent sorts of places from the Shattery area.

Shattery, home of the Shatts Gang, who were evil and murderous, was a large estate wherein stood the doss-house and all its down and outs. Then public baths and wash-houses, an assortment of rag and bone yards, stables and a Sally Army-run hostel for fallen women that was, by all accounts, a kind of Psalm-singing hell. There were also some sweatshops that seemed as dark and secretive as their surroundings, and a few indescribably horrible broken-down sheds where methies hung out. Besides the stabled horses there were lots of rats and skinny evil-eyed cats, and dogs running alive with fleas.

57

There were evil-smelling alleyways that linked the Shattery to Matson and then through to Furze Street. The whole place being a veritable warren which enabled all sorts of criminals to make their escape. Here were the slums proper, where hordes of riff-raff slept, slunk or stayed. Ragged children ran wild, Richard Wray among them. He told the others lots of interesting, exciting things as he led them to the smelly one-room hovel in Matson Street that he called home.

'Next to this is Furze Street,' he boasted in the beginning. 'Zoe Zuckerman lives there. She runs the whores. Hymen's Market's beyond that. It's mad down there, with everything going on. The costers have their own royalty, yer know.'

'You!' Lily told him firmly. 'Not "yer".'

'Shut yore marf, Lil,' Andy put in, grinning and deliberately aping a rough and ready style. 'Go on, Richy.'

'They have Pearly kings and queens,' Richard continued. 'Their clothes are all covered in pearl buttons, and the Pearlies go round collecting for charities. They rule the roost they do, and they keep the market safe from outsiders.'

'Tell us about that woman,' Burza egged Richard on, dark eyes dancing. 'You ought to hear the things Aunty Clara says about her.'

'Zoe ain't, I mean isn't so bad. She and her friend Denis Quiller of my street run the Matson Street gang. The Matsons are thieves and rogues, but not cruel and wicked like the Shattery lot.' His handsome face blazed as he grinned, 'Are you sure you're safe down here?'

'Yes!' they all chorused, loving every minute. Richard was an expert at telling colourful yarns. Besides, they were perfectly safe from the stone-faced men who wore chokers, and had ciggies sticking to the corners of their mouths. They were also totally ignored by the women who screeched out filthy things and snorted as they laughed.

Exhilarated because she was doing something she shouldn't, Burza didn't mind these people at all. She felt at one with them, simply because they flouted authority at every chance they got. On top of that, Richard, who was as handsome as a picture she had seen once of *The Laughing Cavalier*, was the apple of her eye.

'They call my Uncle Harry, Piss-arse Wray,' Richard told

her defiantly one day. 'I'm telling you now, so you won't look down your nose if you hear. He ain't posh like Lily, and you copy her a lot, don't you? But she goes all red, don't she? Still, she'd go through fire and water for you. I dunno how she'll take to the fact that my uncle's always drunk.'

'Oh!' Burza breathed. 'Lily would never look down her nose at anyone of yours, Richard.' She turned to the silent Lily, 'Would you?'

Lily shook her head vigorously. Burza went on, quite forcibly now, 'And of course I copy her! I want to be like her Aunt Marion.' Her tone softened, for Richard's face had changed. 'Poor old you! It can't be fun when they call your uncle names. What a shame!'

'Dunno about that,' Richard replied doggedly. 'He's got somethink else to think about. Last time he was up the hospital the doctor said as how he ain't got long. His liver's gorn up the creek, they reckon. When they told him about his mucked-up inside he just shrugged and said, "When you've gotter go, you've gotter go." His mates heard all about it and d'yer know what? They laughed their heads off. They said they didn't believe it because he's a bloody old soak what's too pickled to die.'

'He sounds very brave,' Lily told him, quietly fascinated. 'Does he have lots of friends?'

'Of course he does. He's been in and out of clink so many times everyone admires him. Oh, an' they also call him Gippo Wray, which ain't so bad where you're concerned, Lily. That's because he looks like an old raggle-taggle gipsy-o.'

Burza's expression changed again. Her dark eyes were enormous and momentarily very sad. Lily reached out and took Burza's hand, then she smiled her usual sweet smile and continued the conversation.

'And doesn't your uncle mind being called names, Richard?'

'Course not, Lily. They reckon he could pick the pocket of a copper's nark and not get found out. Lot of bloo – rubbish, that is! When he is caught, he does his time and comes out all ripe and ready to have another swipe at the law. He's a real old devil.'

'He's daft,' Burza cut in loftily, having pulled herself

together. She loved Richard, but would have her teeth pulled before showing it. 'Just plain daft. And don't swear! You know that Lily hates it when we say bad words.'

'Don't get on to him.' Andy – sunny, baby-faced and everyone's favourite – stuck up for Richard just as he always did. 'An' as for ol' Gippo, he's a good bloke for all he's a tea-leaf.'

'He's the only relation I've got,' Richard put in fiercely, 'and he's all right. What's more, I don't want him to conk out on me. If he does, they'll put me in a Home.'

The idea was so horrible that they all fell silent, then Burza said, 'They will not put you in a Home, Richard, because we will all run away. They will never ever catch us.'

'And just how would we live?' Lily the quiet, ever-practical one asked.

'I suppose we could steal food and clothes – and everything.' Burza laughed and felt an impossible delight at the thought. 'I think I would like to be a tea-leaf. It would be such a lark. Oh shit!' she chuckled. 'When I say tea-leaf instead of thief it sounds so soppy! Come on, I'll race you all to Richard's house.'

'Talk about me!' Richard shouted indignantly. 'You swore!'

'Didn't!'

'Did!'

'All four ran, laughing, down Matson Street. Three of them thrilling at the thought of catching a glimpse of the real-life criminal Gippo Wray.

Richard ran with them, but he was feeling ashamed ...

After America's Wall Street Crash in 1929 there had been repercussions all over the world. Now in 1932 matters had grown worse and there were three million unemployed in Great Britain.

Jack's window-cleaning round was shrinking fast. To try and make up for it, always conscious of repayments for the house and the extra room he'd had built, Jack worked further afield and through every hour of daylight that he could. In this way, still blithely ignorant about his sister's job – and believing that Marion was a magician the way she managed, life in number twelve seemed to be on an even keel. There was cash for coal, and for good basic food, and even though they still seemed to be paying interest rates rather than original debts, they still had a roof over their heads.

Shopkeepers reflected the sign of the times and sold everything, tea, margarine, anything at all, in ounces. One pound of potherbs, which amounted to a swede, onion, turnip, and carrot boiled in water, plus a handful of pearl barley and some gravy salt, made a main meal for six. Most folk queued up to buy stale bread.

On 15 October 1929, Fascists held their first mass meeting in Trafalgar Square. Blackshirts!

'Gawd help us!' Clara said.

'Bloody hell!' George Cuttings replied, taking back his newspaper, 'that lot will upset the Reds. I can see trouble brewing – and I wouldn't touch Mosley with a bargepole.'

'Ain't nothing ter do with us, George,' Clara told him. 'Though I reckon as how any strife will be a good excuse for the Shattery lot to join in.'

The following year, in May, Germany's new Chancellor Adolf Hitler claimed that he only wanted peace. Even so, George's newspaper said that the Germans were going all out to make guns and bombs.

'Ain't nothing peaceable-sounding about that,' Clara sniffed, and looked down her nose. 'Thank Gawd that lot live in Germany and not 'ere. Blooming hell. They'll never learn, will they?'

'People are getting edgy, luv,' George remarked. 'Got anything for tea?'

One evening as the fire glowed in the kitchen range in Lily's house, Jack leaned back and relaxed. He sat in his easy chair indolently filling his pipe with the Players Navy Cut that Marion had bought him. Marion was ironing at the table, outwardly as calm as usual. Inside she was in a turmoil and could almost believe that the thudding of her heart was audible.

It had happened at last, this very afternoon, just as she had feared, and yes, hoped that it would. An assistant had ushered HIM into the office and left them to it. He had swept in, upright, even more handsome now his hair was going grey, the son of her employer – Paul Drew, the man who had managed to sweep her off her feet so effortlessly. The one person who had peppered her dreams with out-of-the-world fantasies over all these years. Thoughts of him, thrilling memories, had made her body burn and scream with longing, her mouth go dry, and the blood race through her veins. Paul, for whom she had such an unrelenting obsession from the very second he had entered her life. And now, dear God, there he was! Yes, standing before her, his velvety eyes staring into hers.

He had always hypnotised her – and she had actually believed all the promises he had made. All broken, of course, quite ruthlessly. Yes, every single one. And she had tried to fill the gap losing him had left, with a slavish devotion to Lily and Jack. But the deep and abiding soul wound she had received had refused to heal.

'So it really is you,' he said in his deep, plummy voice. 'I saw your name and I didn't dare hope. Well, I'll be damned! After all these years, Marion. This is a wonderful surprise.'

As of old, her palms grew damp and she was taking deep breaths to calm her nerves. She was fiercely glad that she looked as well-groomed and smart as always. Clothed in her classically cut black suit, she was every inch a lady of management. The two-piece, expensive when first bought, had been carefully preserved. A crisp white blouse, peach-coloured silk stockings and leather shoes polished till they shone like patents completed her ensemble. That, and on her lapel, the little silver anchor set with crystals that Jack had bought for her birthday the previous year.

Its sparkle had momentarily caught Paul's eye. It was small and had been very moderately priced, not in Paul's sphere at all – and momentarily she cared! It was terrible of her, but she wished they were real diamonds. Something at least to give her that little façade of not being a peasant. Then, suddenly she changed her mind. No, she thought fiercely. No, no, no! Being a peasant will do!

How feverishly her mind raced. In that split second she wished to be ruthlessly rough and ready. She wanted to be wicked. Wicked and wanton – whether Jack found out or not. She had the wild desire to be as coarse and common as a Shattery slut, or as immodest and painted as a Matson Street pro. She wanted very desperately to dismiss the shackles of pride and decorum that, for her brother's sake, had so restricted her life. Lily was thirteen years old now. At fourteen she would be leaving school and looking for work.

'I'm still waiting for you to change your mind,' Paul said softly, his dark eyes greedily challenging hers. 'Yes, even after all these years! God, you're beautiful. Your hair is like ripe corn, and as always, your breasts are driving me wild.'

'Please,' she whispered urgently, and began tidying the pencils, replacing her pen on its tray, and straightening papers next to the blotting pad. 'I need this job.'

'Marion, darling,' he was drawing nearer, 'I want you and you want me. Yes, you do! I can see it in your eyes.'

'No! Go away!' She had all but panted out the words. How absurd she had sounded, she thought. How childishly absurd and here she was aged thirty-three! She remembered how dizzy she had felt, just looking at him, smelling his cologne, and the tang of tobacco clinging to his expensive tweed suit. Then she was recalling the ecstasy she had known in days long ago, and was again suddenly imagining things. Wanting and needing and feeling on fire.

'I've never got over you,' he told her huskily, and he was near enough to touch, his gaze searching her face and seeing into her soul. 'Right now I want to take you to bed. I want to kiss you all over, lick you, nibble at you, enjoy! Marion, just looking at you makes me ... '

She shivered and would have given her soul to be able to submit to him. He was holding her now, his arms like bands of steel. He was bending her backwards. She could feel his body, hard and demanding, through the material of her skirt. His lips were searing against hers. His hands began their searching and she was as alive and on fire as she had not been since those times with him long ago.

'Stop it!' she had gasped while her treacherous body was whispering, *No! No! Keep on and on ...*

But she was Miss Marion London, strait-laced and forever walking on the highway to heaven. Always treading the path set for the congregation of St Christopher's Church. Sweet Jesus, she had even read the lesson last week! So she should, *must* continue living as Jack had taught her, to be upright and honest and full of self-pride. Above all, she must remember that she was Lily's Aunty. Dear dainty, very beautiful Lily ...

Marion came back to the present. Lily looks like an angel, she thought, seeing her long-legged niece stretched out on the rug reading a book. And she is an angel, though I don't much care for her reading-matter. She has that same old book, I see. The one she was always diving into.

Marion tried to concentrate on Lily's book, anything rather than give into this wildly racing temptation. What was the title? *Notorious Ladies*? Yes, that was it! One of the true-life characters being a certain Jane Webb who had been hanged by the neck for picking pockets in the year 1740. It had always amazed Lily that the notorious lady in question had enjoyed the same surname as Burza. What a horrible idea.

Lily is growing up so fast, Marion thought. Soon she will be fourteen and leaving school. She is so lovely and how her hair shines. It looks like a waterfall of spun silk ... I must pull myself together. I really must!

For a while the rhythmic ticking of the clock was the only sound in the room. Marion replaced the now cool iron on the range, lifted the other, carefully keeping the padded holder in place. She licked her finger and lightly tapped the iron to see if it were hot enough. It sizzled in a spurting, satisfactory way. She took in a deep breath.

'Jack,' Marion said, lifting her lovely head and staring at her brother whose eyes were the same clear blue as her own, 'would you mind very much if I went out one evening next week? Thursday perhaps?'

'I don't own you body and soul, girl,' he replied and smiled his nice slow smile. 'Though sometimes you act as though you believe I do. Where are you off to, by the way?'

'I don't exactly know. I have a friend at work and it's a birthday function. It's to be a surprise, so ...'

'Ah.' His lips smiled, but his gaze was suddenly wary and searching her face. 'This friend of yours – male or female?'

'A lady of course,' she told him and tried to laugh as she lied. I am as bad as young Burza, she thought. She gets up to mischief and laughs like a drain.

Chapter Six

In spite of dark-haired, wizened Em Bede slaving from dawn to dusk, even though she was unstinting in her use of lavender furniture polish and carbolic soap, her house was noisy and overcrowded. Worse, it stank of pee-wet napkins being dried out for re-use. This was a nasty habit of her daughter Min's – to merely dry out the non-pooeys.

This morning the eldest of Minnie's kids were playing, laughing and yelling, else screaming and falling down the stairs. Em Bede was making pastry at the kitchen table and wielding the rolling pin as if she could kill, kill, kill.

'Gawd help us,' she said to Art and Nicky their son who were hunched up close to the range on their kitchen chairs, 'I think I prefer you two after what I saw last night.'

Unshaven husband and son ignored her. Both had cigarettes dangling from their mouths. Their shirts were clean and ironed, thanks to Em, but their braces were not in place, merely drooping to their waists. Father and son, one fair one dark, were slobs. They were far from pretty sights.

'Last night she had a bloke what said his name was Marcel,' Em explained. 'Some hairdresser he was – an' I don't think! His own thatch looked like a moth-eaten hearth rug – and smell! Like a French brothel he was.'

'You don't know nothing about French brothels,' Art said, and smirked. 'Not like what I do.'

She glared at him. ''Eard that all right, didn't yer? Anything ter do with the other thing and you're away, you dirty ol' sod.' Suddenly there came a piercing scream from halfway up the stairs. 'Gawd!' Em exploded. 'That's young

Priscilla biting Hughey's arse again. It's about time Min got her lazy bloody self up!'

There came another piercing scream and then Minnie was yelling down, threatening to do them all in.

Em marched to the kitchen door and bawled up the stairs. 'Shut up and get up! You still ain't too big to 'ave yer ears boxed, my gel. D'yer hear me?'

'Who d'yer fink you are?' came the reply.

This was like waving a red flag to a bull. Em's black eyes glittered as she bawled out: 'The woman that pays the rent, all right? The woman what will chuck you out bag and baggage without a second thought, and I mean kids an' all. That's who I am. So, Minnie Bede, get bloody up!'

In the ensuing sulky silence Nick, all five feet eight of mean hatefulness, raised his bushy dark brows and snapped: 'Bleedin' hell, I'm off!'

'Gotta cough?' Art's piggy eyes almost disappeared behind his near-white lashes as he joked, 'Wot end?'

'Belt up, you daft old sod,' Nicky told him. 'You ain't funny. You never was, even though you think you have everyone in fits.'

'Min's tits?' Art roared, his two chins wobbling as he laughed. 'Gawd 'elp us, Nick, she's made use of 'em over this last five years, eh? Ain't you proud of all your little nephews and nieces?'

'Like a donkey's arse!'

'Let you pass? Ain't there enough room?' Art pushed his chair back. 'Pub ain't open yet, is it? I'll come wiv—'

'Oh no yer don't,' Em Bede said quickly. 'It's Wednesday an' you promised. D'yer hear me, Art?'

'I ain't a fart.'

Em looked resigned. 'Do what? Oh, it don't matter! It's Wednesday and you promised you'd get me a bag of coal.'

'You're in a hole? What d'yer mean, you're in a hole?'

'Coal. C-O-A-L. D'yer hear me, Art? You promised me! Min needs a fire to air off the kids' washing and—'

'Let Nicky go. Lazy little sod don't ever do nuffink.'

'He's gone, Art. He can't stand the row the kids are making.'

'Do what? What d'yer say?'

'I said, you promised me. It's Wednesday.'

'I know what, Em,' he said, and leered. 'I've just remembered. I promised to get a bag of coal. 'Ere, give us the money. I'm skint.'

'Not too broke to be after going up the Fevvers with our Nicky a minute ago. An' what's more, Art, let me tell you, there's times when I look back and think I was a fool to have took you on.' She slammed the pastry down and the flour flew as she re-dusted the rolling pin, continuing, 'You always was a selfish old sod and I could have done better. My mum always pointed out that I had plenty of strings to me bow. 'Andsome strings what thought I was a little beauty. An' just look at me now! All wore out. Ter think I had me chances! I could 'ave 'ad Tommy Morris, not forgetting Abe Shultz what had his own fish and taters place. Then there was ... '

The door slammed behind big Art Bede. He walked along Solomon Street chuckling to himself. He always buzzed off when she got to Abe. Lucky, bloody old Abe Shultz. Boss-eyed Abe who had now reached the status of that film star what always played the part of a sheikh in the desert. Some bloody sheikh! Still, that was it so far as Em was concerned. He continued to muse as he walked along. Abe ought ter thank the gods that he, Art Bede, had stole Em from right under his nose. Why, the bloke had had a lucky escape if only he knew it.

Art betted to himself that Em wouldn't stop to breathe for at least another half-hour. She weren't half bad, not really, but a right old nagger. Blimey, she could jaw the hind legs off a donkey. P'raps that Jerry shell had done him a favour after all, going orf with such a bloody bang.

All but blew his eardrums out it had, too right. Still he'd kept his ears after all, and all his limbs, and his balls. Gawd, that'd be hell, ter be a real mutilated DSO! Nar, not the brave and honoured kind what was given medals. The other sort. The poor sods what had their dicks shot off. D – icks S – hot O – ff. That was a good 'un. But no joke for the poor bastards it'd happened to. There's been thousands of 'em, by all accounts. Rather have his head blown to smithereens than have had the Krauts do for his nuts and bolts.

He reached the High Road. As usual on Wednesdays Jack

London was there, doing his shop windows. Quite a decent old boy was Jack. Bit of a stiff-necked sod, but with no real harm in him. Of course he would've had a better life if he'd loosened up a bit. After all, he'd spent donkey's years without a woman. Strewth! That'd be enough to drive a bloke barmy. No nooky for years. Not that he hadn't knocked out a little beauty with that young Lil.

Comes to that, Ol' Webby hadn't done too bad neither, with young Burza. Proper little cracker she was. She walked easy, probably took after her gippo mum. And Burza had the kind of wildness in her that would come out one day, no matter what. There was a sort of merry devilment dancing in her eyes even when she was mouthing off. Saucy little mare! For two pins he'd ...

He came to the greengrocers that also sold bundles of firewood and bags of coke and coal, and made his purchase. Then having spent a happy ten minutes exchanging filthy jokes with the chap behind the counter, he swung the small sack onto his shoulder and went outside. He could smell the tar where they were resurfacing the road and decided to cross before rather than after he reached the workmen.

He stepped off the kerb ...

Jack was halfway up the ladder when he saw Art. The man wasn't looking where he was going, the sack he was carrying blocking his view as he stepped off the kerb. And of course, he could not hear the sound of oncoming engines. Ye gods!

Jack leapt down from his ladder and ran. He was in time to shove Art out of the way of the car. It went on, but the charabanc was too near. There was nothing the driver could do. Jack heard the screeching of brakes and then a fierce agony swept through him. Fire seemed to leap up from his feet and rage along his legs and make a huge writhing holocaust in the pit of his stomach. In his mind he was yelling out – for Kathy ...

She could never have come. No, not in a million years. She should have stayed home, back there in Solomon Street and – done what exactly? Go mad?

Pale-faced, her eyes huge in her face, Marion sat opposite Paul in the luxurious Lynndale Club. She held a long-stemmed glass of sweet white wine in her hand. For all that she was in a state of complete shock, she looked poised, the epitome of grace and cool loveliness. She was wearing a blue woollen suit which was completed by a white blouse with a froth of lace at the neck. She wore pearl earrings. Her corn-gold hair swept up in a shining chignon gave her a ladylike air.

'You have the profile of Nefertiti,' Paul told her in his rich plummy voice. 'Your beauty grows by the hour, Marion. I am proud to be sitting here with you.'

'I'm sorry?'

'Darling, I said that you are growing more beautiful every time I see you. I have always loved you. Now even more so. And I have just paid you a compliment and said that you have the profile of Nefertiti.'

'Thank you,' she replied and tried to concentrate. 'Nefertiti?'

'An Egyptian queen of long, long ago. As you turned just then, how you looked, your perfect bone structure, honestly! Darling, it's the way you hold your head. Yes, a beautiful, fair-haired Ancient Egyptian lady of nobility.'

'From Solomon Street?' She tried to smile, not to sound bitter. But it really was too great an effort to put on an act. She felt confused, worried, out on a limb because she felt, above everything else, an awful sense of guilt. This because just being with the man made her heart pound, when it should have felt dead, dead, dead – because of what had happened to Jack.

She should not be here, she thought again, and was distraught. She would not have been, had Lily not been in the bosom of the Cuttings family. Dear old Clara's comforting, Marion thought wryly, had always been so much more necessary to her niece than her own. Clara and Burza, they were the loves of Lily's life. Whereas she, Marion, was probably looked on as the wicked witch of the West.

But didn't Lily understand, not even now, that the nagging and warning, the checking and correcting had all been for Jack's sake? Poor Jack whose soul had died on the day he had lost his Kath. Jack who had worked and slaved, putting everything he had into building up his rounds. Jack whose only concession lately had been to take on a boy to help. Poor Jack who had been so near death's door.

She had wanted to die herself, just seeing him there, so stark and still. On top of that, they had sent Marion away from the hospital. The danger was past, they had said briskly. Jack was still out of this world, but there was absolutely nothing she could do at this stage, although he would need all of the help and encouragement that she could muster for him later on.

So here she was, with Paul whom she had adored, for whom she would have died. With Paul Drew, the boss's son, who had dropped her to marry Melissa Fanshaw-Nugent whose father was worth pots of cash. Paul who would walk out on her again as easily as winking an eye. That fact was clear as day. He was a too-handsome, self-centred and arrogant devil. He was a playboy. She knew it, had always known it, but the awful thing was, she didn't care! She loved him to distraction and always had. She had carried a torch for him for years – and she was a fool!

Why am I here? she asked herself and felt dazed. How dare I be here! Her thoughts were wild, like a trapped animal going round and round in a cage. She was filled with grief and also with fear – for Jack. How could she sit here, opposite an experienced charmer, at a time like this? When poor darling Jack ...

'Oh dear heaven,' she breathed. 'What shall we do, Paul? What on earth shall we do?'

'We?' he asked. 'We don't have to do anything.'

'You don't understand. I'm not talking about us, at least ...'

'Darling, what is it?' he asked, puzzled. 'Calm down.' He leaned nearer to her and took her free hand in his. 'Sweetheart, you're not making yourself clear.'

'Something terrible has happened. I feel I'm going crazy and – and I don't know what to do.'

She looked across the table at him, her eyes huge in her face. She could no longer stop her lips from trembling. The hand holding her wine glass shook.

'Sweetheart,' he told her, 'it's all right. They are discreet here, believe me. There's no need to worry so. Just sit back and enjoy.'

'Paul, I'm not talking about you and me – about being here.

I'm trying to tell you about something terrible that happened yesterday, and – and—'

'Whatever the trouble, there are always ways out, darling,' he cut in reassuringly, and smiled his wonderful crooked smile. 'Surely whatever it is that's bothering you can't be that bad?'

'My brother Jack ... he's had an accident,' she whispered. 'A near fatal one. There was a charabanc edging by – they were resurfacing the opposite side of the road and space was confined. Then there was a car with someone very impatient driving it. He wanted to beat the larger vehicle so he put his foot down. He did not see our neighbour Art Bede crossing the road. Jack pushed Art out of the way of the car, but had his own legs crushed by the oncoming charabanc. They – they had to amputate one of my brother's legs, Paul. Dear God, my poor Jack's life is ruined.'

'Oh Lord!' Paul was all sympathy at once. 'And how is your brother doing now?'

'As well as can be expected, they say. As well as losing his right leg his left is pretty badly smashed up. It will mend, eventually, but will never be the same as before. Oh, dear heaven, my poor, poor Jack.'

'But he's alive, Marion. Thank God for that.'

'He will wish himself dead,' she told him very quietly, and with utter certainty. She felt drained, dreary, accepting this last glaring truth. She went on: 'The one thing that he has lived for is his business. He has built it up from nothing. Why, he was even speaking of taking that boy on permanently. There's so much work, you see. In fact, the boy has been tagging along for quite a little while now. An urchin from Matson Street, no less. But I don't think any of that will apply now.'

'Why?'

'Jack will never climb a ladder again. How can he? And the boy, he's nearly fourteen and won't hesitate to give up school, but Jack only entertained him in the first place because my niece Lily pleaded for him. It seems the uncle is very ill and the boy could be left out on a limb. However, if he can prove he has work of sorts, and keep body and soul together, they'll let him be. It's out of the question, of course.'

'Why?'

'I don't know, really. Jack won't be there to keep an eye on him, and as I have said, he's from Matson Street and I don't think that anyone there can be wholly trustworthy. After all, his uncle is a known criminal.'

'The boy is himself and not his uncle, Marion,' Paul said evenly, 'but that isn't the issue, is it? Let's cut all through the ifs and buts and concentrate on the real facts instead. Explain the situation to me. Everything!'

'I – I can't!'

'Yes, you can. You must. So, what I know so far is that your brother has to all intent and purpose totally lost any chance of employment. But you have a job, haven't you, darling? Surely that should go a long way to help?'

'Jack would kill me if he knew that I breathed this to a living soul,' she faltered, 'but Paul, we are in debt. Terribly in debt. We borrowed money to buy the house, then added to what we already owed when we had an extra room put on. After all these years we seem to be even worse off than before, and—'

'Darling,' he said softly, 'don't you think that perhaps it's time you allowed me to take over the reins?'

She looked at him, her heart in her eyes. 'How exactly, Paul?'

'Your debts, for a start. Bring me the papers – it sounds very much as if your brother has been systematically cheated. I have a darned good set of lawyers. Anyway, allow me to do the worrying in future.'

'And?'

'I'm a married man. Not happily married exactly, but settled. However, it has always been you, and you know it. Marion, darling, let us come to some arrangements, eh? I'll find us a private little hideaway where you will go every day rather than to the job at our estate branch, and I will get to you every moment that I can. It will be our secret and I will take care of everything.'

'In other words I'll be a kept woman? No, Paul, I wouldn't. I couldn't.'

'You want me as much as I want you, admit it.' His voice was vibrant, his expression hungry. 'Darling, it will be so marvellous, so wonderful, just being together. Making love. Let me prove it. I have the keys of a very comfortable room here. It's all been arranged.'

'You were that sure of me?'

'No. I hoped. The mere fact that you're here now has allowed me to indulge in fervent expectancies. Dearest, I have waited so long!'

'Excuse me?' she asked him quietly. 'You have waited? *You*?' She gave a low pained laugh, her eyes bright with unshed tears as she stood up. 'I'm sorry, Paul.'

'Marion!' He was on his feet. 'Marion, darling, no!' He held out a card, his tone urgent. 'Here – my private telephone number. Phone me, darling. Any time of day or night. Precious girl, swear that you'll phone! Darling, I have been so clumsy. I'm an oaf. I ...'

She gave him one long, grave look. Then with quiet dignity, she turned and left him standing there.

In number six Solomon Street Burza sat with her arm round Lily's waist. She was racking her brains, trying to find the right words to comfort her friend, but there were no right words. She found herself wishing that one could run away from all the sorrow in the world, all the fear and nastiness. But when you were fond of people, when you saw the one person in the world you loved like a right arm, so desperately down, it cut deep. You actually suffered. She was suffering for Lily now.

It would be easier not to love, she thought. Yes, much easier all round. Was that why Kiffa her mother had left her high and dry? Because if you liked and loved someone you were tied to them for the rest of your life? Where was the wild and wonderful gipsy lady now?

What must it be like to live happy and free on the open road? To sleep under the stars? To be in places where violets and primroses grew – and bluebells and scenty white may? To listen to the music of the wind, and smell sweet pure air that had never been tainted by a London fog? Perhaps, one day, she and Lily could run away. Could live like the raggle-taggle gipsies, and wear long gold earrings, and flouncy coloured skirts, and millions of bangles and beads. It must be fun to run away!

73

No, she thought then, and tossed her head defiantly, I don't like running. I like fighting back!

'It's going to be all right, Lily,' she whispered. 'Honest.'

'They have cut off his leg,' Lily gasped. 'He will never walk properly again. He will be like Mr Clark, the flower man, and everyone will call my father old Peg-leg London just as they call the flower man Peg-leg Clarky.'

'Don't be such a soppy date,' Burza told her firmly.

But it was true, they did call Mr Clark Peg-leg. He stood on the corner of the street that led into the High Road, next to his barrow that was piled high with cut flowers. He stomped about, his trouser leg tied at the knee, and below it the cup shape that held the stout wooden stick that used to go thump, thump, thump as he walked. He also shouted and swore at the top of his voice about the bastards that had shot off his leg during the war. He was full of hate and they reckoned his family had to tie him down and gag him during the two minutes' silence on Armistice Day. He was not a pleasant man.

'Your dad will have a much nicer leg,' Burza comforted. 'Something heaps better than old Clarky's. And don't bother with all that now, Lily. Just thank goodness that you still have him. By all accounts it was touch and go.'

'If only Mr Bede hadn't stepped off the kerb when he did,' Lily said quietly.

'The world's full of if only's,' Burza said stoutly. 'I mean, I could say if only my dad wasn't a sailor. If only my mum wasn't a gippo. If only my parents had wanted me. Instead they both skidaddled off and left me. I'll never forgive them. Never.'

'But your dad does love you. He sends money towards your keep and if he bothers to do that he—'

'He does that to help Aunt Clara, but he's never been home, has he? All these years and he's never been home. And as for my mother ... well, she might as well be as dead as yours. The only difference between our mums is that you can at least go and visit yours. You can give her some flowers. You can talk to her, like your dad does every Sunday when he visits St Christopher's. To try and talk to my mum would be like whistling on the wind.'

74

'Do you ever wonder about her?' Lily asked gently. 'I mean, I never saw my mother, but Dad has these photographs of her. I'm rather like her in looks.'

'I know what my dad looks like – the spitting image of Aunt Clara. She told me that. They were twins, like Sid and Peg. As for my mother, I wouldn't know. Aunt Clara says that my dad said she was dark and very lovely, and as wild as Nature. But she dumped me and that says it all. At least your dad wants you, and your mum died to have you. They both love you, Lily, yes even your mum in death. That can't be half bad. Both of mine dumped me without a second thought. If it hadn't been for darling Aunt Clara, I would have been thrown on the rubbish dump long ago. At least I'm safe here.'

'I'll never leave you, Burza,' Lily told her. 'I swear I'll never leave you, no matter what.'

'Not even when you're married, like our Peg will be soon? She would have taken her Charlie on donkey's years ago, but wouldn't leave Sid on the shelf. Now he's going to marry his Ivy, it's going to be different. She'll go, and so will Sid and that'll be the start. The whole family will break up. They've all got someone so they'll all vanish, you wait and see.'

'They'll always come back on visits,' Lily pointed out. 'They adore Aunt Clara too much to ever leave her for long. And I'll never leave you. Not when I'm married, nor when you are. That's a promise.'

'That won't be for years yet,' Burza said, her eyes as bright and shining as polished black cherries because she had taken Lily out of her stupor at last. 'Especially as you and me will have to fight each other unto death.'

'We will?'

'We have both decided we're going to marry Richard, so ...'

'Which will leave poor Andy out in the cold.'

'Never!' Burza teased. 'We'll give him to dear old Josie Briggs. She's still after him. And now she's lost all her puppy fat, she's not bad-looking at all. As for Andy, phew! He's going to be even taller than Richard. About six feet one, I'd say. As big as Pete in fact, but lots skinnier of course.'

Both girls fell silent for a moment, then Lily could contain herself no longer.

'Oh dear, Burza, what shall we do?' she gasped. 'I hope we won't have to go for the Means Test.'

'Not while your aunt has got her posh job,' Burza put in quickly. 'She's so brainy, they might even give her a rise. Yes, that's what will happen. You wait and see.'

'Oh, Burza ...'

Burza held her tight until her storm of weeping ceased. And all the while she was praying that something good might happen for Lily. But ...

A most awful thought occurred. What if Aunty Marion had to give up work to look after Jack? It looked quite on the cards. With no money coming in to pay the bills they could lose everything because the vicious Means Test people would see to it that they did. Perhaps, even worse, they would take the house! Then the Londons would be put out on the street. And where would Jack London's pride finish up then?

Chapter Seven

Miss Burza Webb, sweet and neat in her black skirt and red blouse, eyes dancing, dark hair flying, felt as though she was floating on air.

'Free! I am free at last,' Burza sang to herself. 'No more school. I am grown-up. Hooray!'

Suddenly, brilliantly, the whole world was rosy. Not the world that George read about in the newspaper, not the bits about Nazis, or storm-troopers seen stomping across the cinema screens, not even the football and dogs sporting world that men spoke about on street corners, but her world. Solomon Street and all the streets around, the actual people. She liked people, all different sorts, and they liked her for her beaming smile and mischievously twinkling eyes, and the way her curls flew when she tossed her head in her fiery way. She back-answered when necessary, and dug her toes in. She wanted to take up the cudgels for all the underdogs.

She had driven poor Clara mad taking abandoned kittens home. And had actually physically leapt at a man, fists flailing, for beating his bony, near-blind horse. George had been roped in to help out on that one. Half of Solomon Street had joined in, paying up like the Trojans they were, adding to Burza's collection even to a farthing a time.

Finally, re-christened Firestone, the poor old horse was found a good home near Chingford Mount in Essex. There, retired for life, he had loving care from a Miss Allthorpe, a nice rich old lady, who had a long aquiline nose and faded, heavily hooded eyes. She had a penchant for skull caps, black beaded capes from another age, and looked a thousand years old. They said she was eccentric, and had a suspiciously murky past. She was stiff-necked, and had been known to swear and carry on in a most unladylike way. She liked animals better than most people, which was why she found Firestone a warm stable and a field full of juicy green grass.

It was Burza and Lily's greatest pleasure to take the bus at weekends and visit old Firestone and Miss Allthorpe too. Miss Allthorpe liked Lily a lot and thought her quietly wise, chuckled at all of Burza's witty remarks, and admired her for her courageous heart, and confessed to not liking church people very much. Church people, according to Miss Allthorpe, were usually trying to buy themselves tickets into heaven. A heaven for their own sort, of course; certainly no lesser beings could get a look in. Animals? Goodness, were you mad? And over and above all, certainly not gipsies!

According to these holy high-minded folk, so said Miss Allthorpe, gipsies were thieves and rogues and devils' spawn. They had looked down their noses, she told the girls in her high scratchy way, and said so, many times. They had even gone so far as to ask her to put up a notice saying PRIVATE, TRESPASSERS WILL BE PROSECUTED on her private meadowland. She had refused, very colourfully, of course. She had cackled in the telling of this tale, adding, 'Don't think half of 'em knew what the names I called 'em meant?'

Miss Allthorpe admitted to liking jam tarts very much, apple pies, and Dickybirds ice cream. Last but not least, rabbit stew. Rabbit stew, she claimed, was the mainstay of the gipsies who sometimes stayed in one of her meadows. They never stole chickens, never! They just worked hard making clothes pegs, and pretty paper flowers to wire onto sprigs of privet, and they sold things like lucky charms and told fortunes and such. It was clear that the old lady liked and respected gipsies.

For this Burza not only liked, but passionately loved Miss Allthorpe. One day, she hoped devoutly, when she visited their rich old ladyfriend, the gipsies would be there. She wanted to walk with them, talk with them, ask them if they knew the whereabouts of a lady named Kiffa. Yes, Kiffa Webb – if that was still her mother's name.

But today, this very special day, the most marvellous thing was that she, Burza, was now free to do as she pleased – well, as Clara pleased. Wonderful, wonderful, wonderful! To have, at long last, reached fourteen years old. She had had to wait for those interminable weeks until the end of school term, and now the whole span of existence was hers to use and to choose and enjoy.

'I'm only a bird in a gilded cage,' Burza carolled and smiled and waved across the road to miserable, ratty old Ethel Jacobs, moaner and mischief-maker whose favourite sentence was, 'My Gawd! Wot a life for a crust!' Lily, quiet and serene, who thought everyone nice, had once actually admitted to, 'Not caring for Mrs Jacobs very much.'

Poor Lily had to wait until the summer holidays before she too was home for good. Would it be so wonderful for her? Sweet adorable Lily who listened a lot, spoke only when she thought it necessary, and when that happened she would hang on like a limpet to an idea. She had actually brought about a miracle for dearest Richard. Had got Aunt Marion on her side and then, blow me down, Richard was in work! This made him safe, safe, safe! She, Burza, would love Lily for ever for that alone. What an angel she was.

Burza frowned, remembering how Lily spent nearly all of her free time with her father. Quietly ministering to his every need. Spoiling him as best she could, accepting his moods, understanding, as patient as a saint. Jack, always the proud irascible man who ruled with a rod of iron from his wheel-chair. The leg they had healed was twisted and withered. In fact, it turned out to be more nuisance than the one they had cut off and thrown away.

Burza shuddered, thinking of a bit of human leg tossed off and into a hospital dustbin somewhere. Ugh! Horrible. But there had been the brighter side of things. Jack against all the odds, had kept his window-cleaning round. And it had all been worked out wonderfully well – by Marion and Clara. Of course Clara's intuition about Marion getting a rise had been right, and what was more, the extra money had indeed worked miracles.

Marion had, since Jack's accident, become a changed person. Bright-eyed, positive, almost aggressively happy sometimes, she had insisted on the girls dispensing with the title of 'Aunty'.

'It does make me sound so staid, my dear,' she had told Lily. 'Almost old, and I am not ready to be old. Not by a million years.'

She had gone pink at Lily's grave-eyed stare.

'Don't you understand, love,' she continued, 'the lesson I have learned? What happened to your dad, right out of the blue like that, has made me realise that we must live life to the full while we can. Really live, Lily.' Her colour deepened as she added, 'Correct and pure at all times, of course! We must not forget that. Not that you would ever do anything to break your father's faith and pride in you.'

Oh yes, Burza thought with deep admiration, Marion was thriving on the challenges her brother's invalidity had brought about. She was making such an amazingly good fist of everything she did these days. What a wonderful, sweet and pure person she was. A real lady. And if she, Burza had anything to do with it, she would be a lady too. But it was hard work.

Burza, all ears, had heard when Marion had explained to Clara: 'It's a marvellous opportunity, Clara, and one I dare not miss. I have been offered longer working hours, and now poor Jack is as he is, we need the extra cash.'

'It'll be bloody 'ard on yer, gel.'

'I know. Especially as sometimes shipments are late and their cargoes need to be thoroughly documented. That means that I'll be on duty a whole extra day. Yes, Saturdays whereas before they have been totally free.'

'All work and no play ain't good,' Clara had replied. 'An' you're still young and loverly, an' you ought ter look round for someone of your own. Specially now young Lil's off your hands.'

'She will be there, doing everything she can, of course. And darling Clara, I know I can rely on you!'

'Of course yer can, luv,' Clara replied. 'And since I'll be on 'and, you can bet your sweet life ol' Florrie'll want ter push her nose in too.'

'Marvellous!' Marion had replied.

From the time she had taken on the extra work, Marion really had been able to sort things out. Financially and in every other way. The biggest hurdle had been safely negotiated. Marion had told Jack that from the moment she realised that it was a case of survival, she had taken up a well-paid position in Drew's office – the Keens Estate branch, which was conveniently near. It was a great opportunity and she was all but managing the place.

'Codswallop!' he had begun, coldly furious, frustration making him sweat and feel that he wanted to vomit. 'I can't and won't have that!'

'Oh, please don't carry on, dear. You know it makes sense.'

Jack had begun to argue, loudly, but Marion, cool and dignified, had pressed on, adding that she enjoyed every minute of it and he must too, since it would be the end of him worrying himself to death.

Burza and Lily had been sitting, mouse-like, in the scullery when that conversation had occurred. They had known that Marion would have to admit to her job – well, the latest bit about it, at least. Jack couldn't be hoodwinked now that he was home all of the time.

Listening was easy. The walls were very thin. They had heard every word.

'It really is wonderful for me, Jack,' Marion had said. 'I am to get such good money. It is a chance I must take. We will manage very well.'

Jack, thin-lipped, had looked down at the blanket covering his stump and his withered leg. 'Perhaps I can sell my round,' he had replied raggedly. 'It's a good round. A few pounds for all those years' hard work, but still better than nothing.'

'No need to sell anything, Jack. Honestly!'

Burza remembered how she and Lily had stared at each other, both startled at this revelation. Startled and relieved since the thought of the detestable and humiliating Means Test had been such a nightmarish idea.

'Better sell than have it all going to waste.' Jack had tried not to sound bitter.

'Nothing is going to waste – indeed, quite the reverse, Jack.' Marion's voice had risen. 'Listen to me. Please don't give me that icy glare of yours and just listen! Young Richard Wray has been marvellous and made a huge effort right from the start. He has been working round the clock trying to keep things going for you, a mammoth task for one so young. Then Clara's son, Sid, stepped in to help and between them everything is going smoothly. The High Road shop windows are still London's.'

'Thanks to the efforts of a Matson Street kid?' Jack's tone was ragged with guilt as he decried the lad who had been such a good all-round worker, and honest and loyal to boot.

'And Sid, Jack. So much so that – that you have employed him too.'

'I have?' The deep voice was even more sour. 'Ye gods!'

'Yes and it has paid off, Jack. Bless Sid's heart, he has even added to the round. London's are now responsible for every window, inside and out of Peacehaven!'

His mouth dropped open at that. 'The rest home in Lindley Court?'

'That's the one. Young Sid's fiancée Ivy works there. When she heard they were looking for a new window-cleaner – I believe the old one didn't bother with corners and also left smears – she told Sid. He went along and hey presto, we were given the job, and wait for it – weekly! Just think, Jack darling, you are a governor! You employ that handsome youngster Richard Wray, and Sid Cuttings who is one of the merriest, nicest and most honest fellows I know.'

'Question,' he barked. 'If Cuttings is working, and Peacehaven's a high property, where'd he get the ladder?'

'We've bought it, Jack. You and I. Us! As well as buckets and scrim and leather, everything! We bought a wonderful ladder, a treble size, three extensions no less. I asked for an advance on my wages from the Drews head office and got it!'

Redcheeked, pole-axed, and feeling he had lost control of the whole of his life, Jack still growled. 'I thought Sid worked at Hymen's Market.'

Jack was still unwilling to give up. Still trying to deny the reality that he would never be able to be like a monkey on a stick, up and down his ladder again. Life was a shit and for the second time in his existence, he wanted to punch the guts out of God.

'You sound ungracious.' Marion's voice held reprimand. 'And, yes, Sid did go to Hymen's. He worked as a casual,

Jack. This way he has a regular job, and so has Richard, which is such a wonderful thing in this day and age. They both have set wages, which they consider to be very fair. I have seen to everything to our mutual agreement. Jack, it really is all under control.'

He grunted deep in his throat. His eyes were icy and suspiciously bright. Understanding him as she did, Marion had gone on.

'And it has been all your own efforts that have achieved it for them. Yours and only yours. Jack, feel proud! It all began with you running alongside old man Minchin, and you've slogged it out for years. Now you have taken a step up in the world, don't you see that? Please try and accept that it's an ill wind that blows no good at all.'

'If it's that good,' Jack had said, fighting to the last, 'why must you go to that damned job? Let Wray and Cuttings get on with it. It's not a woman's place to work.'

'No!' Marion's voice had become quite firm. 'You are not going to make me change my mind about my job, dear. You are a proud and independent man, and I'm cut from the same cloth as you. You don't need me so much now. Lily is all but leaving school and can take care of herself – and of you if you want her before I get home. I love the idea of going out and earning my keep for a change, and I won't allow you to spoil it for me.'

Burza remembered how she and Lily had held their breath, but there had come no argument from the other room.

Jack London managed very well after that. He enjoyed wheeling himself about, following his roundsmen, at least as far as his strength allowed, and praising or bullying as the mood took him. Richard and Sid took it all in good part, doffed their caps and called him guv'nor, for all they accepted that Miss Marion was the real boss. Then one day Jack found a new interest. This was in a way due to Bill Jessop, a quiet all over grey man whose love in life was his foreman's job at the railway and growing prize chrysanthemums.

Florrie Jessop had been leaning over the garden wall boasting about her Bill's flowers at the top of her voice, and it had given Clara an idea. She had been shopping for Marion and had put the purchases away in the pretty blue and white kitchen, then she walked outside and stood next to Jack.

'Young Marion's made a nice little patch out 'ere, Jack,' she said in her bright and breezy way. 'Got green fingers, ain't she? Why don't you 'ave a go?'

'Why indeed?' he asked stiffly, not liking her air of familiarity. Frustrated, he gripped the arms of his wheelchair.

'Feeling sorry for ourself, are we?' the irrepressible Clara asked. 'Blow me, it ain't all that bad! 'Ere, tell you what. I'll ask my George to have a word with the bloke up the Feathers. See if he's got some old barrels.'

'My dear Mrs Cuttings,' Jack had said pithily, 'I'm not quite sure that I understand.'

'You can buy some off him, can't yer, and start! No bending down then, eh? You could make this old back yard into a real picture. Young Marion's got things nice, but too low and flat. I've seen lovely shows of flowers up Hainault, where I work. They have fancy bowls an' things, and urns made out of marble and stone and stuff. Real luverly, some of them are. But them good ol' barrels are deep. You could get some real colour up the walls. Hops and nasturtiums, sweet-peas, even roses could climb all over if you care to shell out for a decent plant or two. My George will help.'

'Thank you,' Jack told her. 'I will think about it, Clara.'

And he had, Burza thought, hugging herself. Wonderful, brilliant, down-to-earth Clara. And tall, ladylike, brainy Marion, both so different, but equally clever in their ways. She adored them both. Lily was with her about Clara, but surprisingly, was not so forthcoming where her aunt was concerned. On the other hand Lily seemed to think that Jack London was God. This even though it had taken a while for him to even pass the time of day with Richard and Sid.

Burza carried on along the street and came to a halt outside number twelve. Lily would be back from getting her dad some Players Navy Cut tobacco any minute now, and she had some exciting news to tell her friend.

84

Chapter Eight

'Never!' Lily's eyes widened with surprise. 'I can hardly believe it.'

'And you don't mind?'

'Why should I?'

'Well, you're so quiet and your family have always been—'

'Lonely?'

'Not lonely exactly. I meant ones to keep themselves to themselves.'

'Lonely!' Lily spoke with unusual firmness, then she smiled. Burza, as always, was entranced. When Lily smiled it lit up her face and curved up her lips and danced like a million crystals in her very blue eyes.

'Burza!' Lily gasped. 'With Peg next door perhaps our place won't be so quiet from now on.'

'Not with Peg it won't. I can remember when she used to back-answer all the boys in the park. Our Peg can be as good as Clara when it all boils down to it. Still, that don't matter much. By the way, your dad knows all about it.'

'He never said a word. Oh Burza, I'll be one of the first to see the baby.' Lily's eyes widened as the idea caught on, marched forward and grew to delightful proportions. 'Good heavens, perhaps I'll be allowed to babysit and help all round, and it will be so nice.' She glowed even more as the thought took hold, really taking her fancy. 'Perhaps our house might even turn out to be a little more like yours. I mean, we will at least be able to hear, the walls are so thin! What with our place, and Florrie next door always being so silent, it has been like living in a tomb. Perhaps Dad has felt the same but never

85

said anything. Oh, I'm so glad he's going to be all right about things.'

Burza smiled to herself. Darling Lily, she thought. She should know there's a method in the stuffy old devil's madness. She remembered the conversation held in number six early the previous evening. George had just got up, washed and shaved and joined Burza and Sid at the table. Clara was busily dishing up beef and onion stew.

'Others out?' George asked. 'Pictures for the girls, and Dicky's in the library I suppose.' He looked quizzically at Sid. 'But you at home? How come?'

'You won't believe it, Dad,' Sid was chuckling and beaming and looking very pleased with himself, and Burza who adored him had felt her own heart swell as he went on. 'Me and Ive have got ourselves a home we fancy at last. A little flat it'll be. I'll make it a palace.'

'Bloody hell! Where?'

'The two rooms upstairs in the Elliots'. They're happy to live in the two rooms down. You know, the Elliots! Opposite in number seven.'

'Not old Bob the Parkkeep?'

'The very same.'

George whistled and grinned, absolutely delighted, then exploded. 'I've always said as how Bob's a lucky sod. House to himself – with June his missus, of course. A lifelong job with the Council as park-keeper up Jubilee Gardens. Above all happy, knowing his only kid's married well to a bloke up north. And now to cap the blooming lot, he's going to have my son under his roof. My son!'

'You ain't heard it all, Dad. Listen! Peg and Charlie've got a place too. They're to have the upstairs in the Jessops'.'

'Bloody hell!' George whistled again. 'They're actually going to live in snobby ol' Florrie's house? What 'appened to bring about that little bolt from the blue?'

'My Ive,' Sid had sounded proud, 'and Mum, of course.' He grinned and winked. 'Wouldn't be right if Mum didn't 'ave an 'and in it somewhere, eh? There ain't a thing she don't know the rights of. Yer see, Mrs Pinkerton, the lady what owns Peacehaven knows the boss of Farrows.'

'The big office block on the corner of James's Street.'

''Sright. And their winders are bloody awful. Mrs Pinkerton, through my Ive, wanted to know if London's was a big enough firm to tackle the job. Me and Ive mentioned it to Mum and she told us—'

'To 'ave a go on your own?' George asked, knowing his Clara very well. Her lovely melon-seed-shaped eyes almost disappeared behind her beaming smile. She put an extra potato on his plate to mash in with his gravy.

'Ta, mate,' he said. 'Go on, Sid.'

''Sright, Mum did say something of the sort, but me and Ive agreed that I don't want ter do that.'

'Why?'

'Ain't the kind, am I? I don't like responsibility, Dad, and you know it. And I'd 'ave to buy ladders and everythink – big 'uns, and they cost! It's going to take me and Ive all our time and effort just to start out.'

'I'm going to do your wedding breakfast and all that, seeing young Ivy's lot are all unemployed,' Clara put in. 'And it'll be luverly, I promise yer.'

'Mum! You're an ol' sweetheart, you always was, and me an' Ive can't thank you enough. I'm talking about stuff for our own place, bed and things. Sides, I'd have to get a place where I could put the bloody ladders. I'm not like Jack who now forks out to rent that shed by Abbots Park for his ladders an' fings. No, it's best this way.'

'You could 'ave at least ...' Clara began, but Sid, risking fire and brimstone, interrupted.

'We've had all this out, Mum, and your second idea was so clever. You are a marvel. You know you are.'

'Oi, you lot,' George said. 'I'm the one what's s'posed to be told what's going on. So the pair of yer, get on with it, eh?'

'It's like this, Dad,' Sid continued, 'as you know, me and dear ol' Peg don't want to be too far apart, married or not. You know how it is wiv us twins. She 'urts when I do, an' she don't even get a finger ache wivout I don't know it. Anyway, once Bob said me and Ive can live in, we had to think about Peg. Mum thought of Jack's upstairs front at first, which is empty since he can't climb no stairs.'

'Gawd 'elp us. I've just thought!' Clara cut in, wheezing as she laughed. She raised her brows to the ceiling. 'It don't bear thinking about. How are yer going to be when our Peg ever has her bread-snapper? In blazing agony, I reckon. Us women don't have no picnic, yer know.'

He pulled a face. 'Leave it out, Mum! But putting that aside, being a boss ain't for me. I like coming 'ome, putting me feet up and forgetting all about work.'

'And not forgetting a turn or two at the ol' rumpy pumpy,' George teased. 'Like me where that's concerned, son. I bet—'

'That's enough of that filthy talk,' Clara warned and raised her dishing-up spoon warningly. 'We 'ave our own Burza 'ere what's grown into a young lady like her friend, and I won't 'ave ...'

'All right, mate.' George apologised hastily to Burza. 'Sorry, gel.' His eyes were gleaming like sunlight on grey silk as he winked at her, then he turned back to his son, 'Carry on, Sid.'

Sid's merry face was wreathed in triumph as he continued. 'Then, Mum had this idea and said, "Let old Jack know about Farrows and don't say nothing. Just act like you're thinking of starting up on your own. Then mention casual-like it might be because there's a room to let in James's Street and also one going over the shop next to it what will do for Peg. And that even though you've got the chance of going to live at Bob's, but being away from your twin ..." All that sort of stuff.'

'So that's exactly what you did?' George whistled. 'Phew!'

'All that, and pressed home me point a bit more. I said as how me and my gel wanted a nice place. One as clean and decent as this, the best end of Solomon Street. It worked like a charm. Only I was thinking of his upstairs front what he can't get to no more. But the cunning bastard got round Bill, seeing they're so chummy like with their gardening and all.'

'So me and Mum will keep all our kids near at hand. Luverly grub.' George was really chuffed. Then he pulled a mischievous face. 'Cor, strike a light, Sid! What about ol' Peg living with ear'oles Florrie? All I can say is that when the old rumpy pumpy starts, she'll have to make sure their bed don't creak. Ow!'

Burza chuckled out loud, remembering. George hadn't been expecting Clara to wallop him quite so hard. And with the dishing-up spoon, too. She turned, bright-eyed and laughing, to Lily.

88

'I'm dying to know what Marion will think about all this. 'Specially as the whole world can see that Peg's in the family way. Marion's so lily-white! Still, old moon-face Jessop's a lot worse even than her. She's a terrible snob. Her to have lodgers? My God!'

'Oh, I don't know.' Lily's breathless little chuckle rang on the air. 'Florrie has often pointed out that Peg's Charlie, being a Supervisor at Temple Mills, stands on level peggings with her foreman Bill.'

'Whereas George Cuttings is peasant class?' Burza's dimple came into play. If the Cuttings were peasants, then she'd happily go and eat dirt. Then she said flippantly, 'Anyway, it looks like she's stuck with our Peg. The world's coming to an end.'

'I wonder how it came about? There must have been a jolly good reason behind old Florrie's about face.'

'Don't worry. We'll soon find out.'

They then changed the subject and spoke of Art Bede, who had been so quiet and sheepish since the accident. He was a rough, crude man, but he had a conscience. And his conscience squeezed his guts every time he saw Jack in the wheelchair.

The first time he had seen Jack out of hospital he had walked over to him, his piggy face flushed, his small eyes jerking about like pin-table balls.

'Oi, mate,' he had said. 'I don't know wot ter say. If it hadn't been for you, it'd have been curtains for me. But when I see wot's 'appened to yore legs I feel ...'

'Forget it,' Jack had replied, his eyes like cut glass. 'I did what I had to. That's all.'

And that had been the end of it. But not so far as Em Bede was concerned. She brought the subject up every time she and Art had a row. Nagging and nagging and nagging, fit to jaw the hind leg off a donkey.

'He's hard of hearing,' Burza said, 'so it's not so bad for him, but the rest of us, phew!'

'He will lose his temper with her one day,' Lily said with quiet conviction. 'And then perhaps she will stop using my dad's crippled legs as whipping posts for Art. She doesn't realise that Dad can hear all her gibes. She's a silly woman.'

89

'She's a stupid cow,' Burza replied. 'Oh shit, I'm supposed to be going for a packet of tea. Coming?'

They strolled off, happily talking of Andy and Richard who were both making a good fist of things. Andy was to be gainfully employed by Walls. He was to go round with his freezer on wheels, selling Walls fruit ices. Lovely they were. Three-cornered sticks of strawberry, lemon or orange water-ice. They were enclosed in thin cardboard casings decorated with blue and white squares. A penny each or a ha'penny for half, they were delicious. Strawberry was Burza's favourite. Lily liked Dickybirds ice cream which sold at the same price.

Richard, the special darling of both girls, was now expert at his window-cleaning job. Even better, he and Sid really got on.

The next day Burza and Lily walked together along the High Road, both looking beautiful. Because of Marion's careful teaching, they had style and poise. They dressed simply; each always chose to wear skirts. Lily had several. Her many blouses were in pastel shades. Burza's navy-blue school shirt, threadbare but still with plenty of use, had to do for everyday. Her one good skirt was black. She had three blouses – one red, one peacock blue, and a crisp white one that boasted a frothy lace collar for very best.

By the standards of the area in which they lived, clotheswise both girls were well off. Burza owed her blouses and bits and bobs to the tally man who called once a week. She ran errands for a copper or two, Marion very often thinking up little jobs for Burza to do out of the kindness of her heart. Lily of course had a father and aunt more than willing to see to it that she was never short, and she always endeavoured to share it all with Burza.

Now, on their way to buy chips, they complemented each other in both looks and character. Lily was tall, stately and gentle, and Burza small, quick and vivacious.

Lily put a halfpenny in the cap of an old organ-grinder. He was hunched up standing by the kerb turning the handle so that the mechanical music could spill out. His monkey, wearing a red coat and a little pill-box hat with a gold tassel, stood by the cap, tail weaving. Dray horses pulling a cart loaded with barrels clip-clopped by. They were huge, magnificent animals

90

with reins hung with ribbons and bright brassy bells.

'I love horses,' Burza said, 'and the country. I suppose that's the gippo in me. One day I'll go all out to find my mum. In the meantime, it's Miss Allthorpe's place this weekend, all right? I can't wait to cuddle up to dear old Firestone.'

'I will see if Dad needs me,' Lily replied, then, 'Do you ever want to run away for ever and be a gipsy?'

'I don't know! You might as well ask if I ever want to run away and go to sea like my dad. Sometimes I – I just ache inside. I don't know why.'

'I like things as they are.' Lily's tone was pensive. 'I'd enjoy having a house like Dad's, and marrying Richard, and having babies. Lots of babies who will be fat and happy and able to speak and act just like their friends.'

'Sorry,' Burza teased, 'Richard's mine. But as for this place, I will admit it all goes on round here. And as you say, it's homely like.' She watched a tram trundling by – a large red vehicle captured by its metal tramlines, overhead its rod catching the wires and flashing blue fire, the visible halves of passengers ranged along the window looking for all the world like clothes pegs. Pedestrians milled around on the pavement, busy about their business. Unemployed men wearing raggy clothes, down at heel shoes, caps and chokers, stood in groups on corners. A street singer, voice high and sweet with the Irish brogue, sang for the folk waiting to be served.

They reached the fish-fry at last. The appetising smell of fish and chips made their mouths water.

'I'm starving!' Burza said. 'How long must we wait, d'you think?'

'Ten minutes at most. Oh, and a little titbit to tell! It was Bill's idea, about letting the room.' Lily's lips were upcurved. 'He said that since it was possible for us to have an extra bedroom put on upstairs over the lav, he saw no reason why he couldn't have a small greenhouse built next to his W.C. Florrie played war at the idea. Said that she wouldn't stand for being given less money, and for such nonsense too.'

'She would!'

'But Bill had the last word. When Dad told him about Peg needing a room, he jumped at the chance. The rent money he gets will do for the instalments he will have to pay. Now he

91

and Dad are dreaming about chrysanthemum cuttings and sprouting dahlia tubers, all sorts of things. I overheard them last night. And the cream of the joke is, for being such a mean old thing, Florrie let herself in for that one.'

Lily and Burza looked at each other and doubled up.

'And now,' Burza's happiness was like a golden balloon being blown up, 'you and me's gotta plan for high jinks. We've got to try and get a lovely new dress each. The wedding for the twins is going to be in three weeks' time.'

'A double wedding?'

'Yes. All in one big happy bash. Clara will be in a proper tizzy from now on. There'll be lots to do. There are millions of things to tackle, including fresh wall-paper for the front room. We're going to hire a piano from Turpins, and Minnie Bede can thump out some jolly good tunes for us. Just "Knees up Mother Brown" will be fine. We're going to have lots of food and jellies and stuff – oh, and Clara's going to make some of her special fairy cakes, and ...'

'In only three weeks?'

'A lot can happen in that time.'

Two weeks later George Cuttings fell under an engine that was being shunted back to the yard. He died instantly.

They stood round the hole, watching as George was lowered next to his beloved baby Violet. They all wore deepest black. Peg swayed and clung onto her good-natured Charlie. His face was grey, his brown eyes worried. Peg was taking it all very hard.

'Dad won't never see my baby,' she had wailed the day she had heard the terrible news. 'My dad won't be here no more. Oh God, Charlie! My dad won't never be able to kiss my baby, nor call me his little sweetheart no more! Charlie, Charlie, I can't bear it. I love 'im so!'

She had sunk slowly to the ground, hands covering her eyes, her whole body jerking and being torn apart by grief. She was sobbing now, deep, pain-racked sounds, like a saw trying to cut through hard wood.

Charlie bit his lip and tried to suppress a moan. Blokes didn't howl like two-year-olds. Blokes had to keep their chin up. Blokes had to be bloody hard as nails, and not mind too much when decent chaps like George pegged out. And above all else, blokes had to hang on and be strong for their other halves and future kids.

Sid stood tall, his chin high, but nothing on God's earth could stop his lower lip trembling. He had loved his old man with a fierce devotion that only sons could have for their dads. And the strange thing was, all he could remember was the silver sort of laughter in the old devil's eyes when he teased on about rumpy pumpy. Sid suddenly wanted to reach out and hold on tight to his tiny, no-nonsense-looking Ivy who was now so stricken. He needed to say something comforting to his mum, but there were no words – and she seemed changed. Distant, stone-faced. She ought to cry, ought to! He looked over the grave, unable to bear watching the coffin being lowered, and concentrated on Dicky.

His young brother, very slim, small, angular, had hardly spoken a word since they had all lost their dad. Now he stood between Rosie and Betsy who were both crying and sobbing out their broken hearts. Dicky seemed to be frozen, like a statue, his dark eyes so like Clara's, giving nothing away. No one ever really knew what Dicky was thinking. He had always been there, quiet, dependable, helpful, loyal – and usually overlooked. Even Clara never referred to Dicky as one of her little demons. To Clara, Dicky was the one and only child who had needed to be protected.

As always Burza and Lily stood side by side. They were holding hands, Lily's face like alabaster. Burza was as red as fire, and she was watching, watching, watching. Not the coffin, the flowers, nor the many neighbours who had come to join in the grief. Burza was not taking her eyes off her beloved Clara for an instant. And Sid knew that although his family were, at that moment, aware only of their own gargantuan sorrow, although Burza's grief for George was perhaps the wildest of them all, her concern for Clara was now outweighing everything else. She knows, he thought, ol' Burz knows! And she, more even than me, will help my mum.

He swallowed hard, and his usually merry face was clown-like as he tried to fight his tears. He found that he was feeling akin to Burza. He had accepted her from the moment Clara had taken her in. Frankly, he could either take or leave the kid. Now he felt a strong brotherly love for her. Dear little flamboyant Burza who young Rosie still nastily referred to as 'that gipsy tart wot our uncle dropped like a hot cake'.

'Ashes to ashes,' Reverend Masterson droned. 'Dust to dust . . .'

Suddenly, harshly, Clara's voice rang out. Her face was blank, she was staring into the distance, but her voice was strong, strong, strong.

'Trust you, Georgy Porgy!' she said very clearly. 'I was s'posed to make a wedding breakfast, not 'am sandwiches for terday. But since we're at St Chris's I've gotta say somethink. Gotta! I'm expectin' you to look after me baby Vi. No nonsense now. She's little and weak and she needs all the help she can get. Georgy, you're ter look out for our Vi, d'yer hear me?'

Before Sid could catch her, she dropped like a stone.

Chapter Nine

Life was shockingly, terribly changed in number six Solomon Street. The atmosphere was doom-laden, dour, devastating. Clara had altered. Had become as unlike the buoyant working-class Begum as steam from ice. For a while she became a kind of duplication of the sour-faced, bitter Em Bede. And then, once the quiet phase was over, Clara became angry. Angry at life, angry at everyone around her, above all, angry at George for stepping under that train. And because she was dearly loved, her family, lost and lonely, all but tiptoed in and out of the house.

The double wedding, three weeks later than planned, was carried out in the Baker's Arms Register Office. It was a brief, no-nonsense affair, everyone taking their lead from the blank-faced Clara. Both brides were bereft, both grooms gaunt-faced. All those present wore black, the brides also – mourning clothes rather than the bridal finery that had at one time been so excitingly on their minds. There was not a flower in sight. Flowers had been for the grave, for George and for Violet. No one now liked the idea of flowers.

There was no jollification afterwards. They walked back to the house, like broken-winged birds heading for the rookery. There they had a sandwich or two, a slice of iced cake, made by Ivy's mother, Mrs Worth; fizzy white wine for the ladies (Marion's present), and beer for the men. Then Ivy and Sid went off to number seven, Charlie and Peg to number ten, and that was that.

Clara watched her two firstborn leave. She was dry-eyed, empty, far from the quivering, emotional wreck that she had once believed she would be. In a vague sort of way she felt that she had let Peg and Sid down. That she should have tried to climb over the black mountain that her life had become without George. But indomitable, fearsome, angry, the black mountain had refused to move.

Clara wanted everyone to go, everyone. She needed to lie down on her settee and just look and look at her beloved George. Her Georgy Porgy. Her other half. Her life and soul. He was there, smiling, on the wall. Young and vigorous and with twinkling grey eyes. And with all her heart she was begging and pleading to him, George who was now floating up there somewhere in the sky.

'Don't forget me. Wherever you are, luv, don't forget me ...'

'Phew! I'm glad that's sodding well over,' Betsy said as the door shut behind them. 'Talk about farce. Both brides 'ave been at it for years.'

Before George's death Clara would have risen up like a rattler about to strike. Now she sat on the kitchen chair, seeming deaf, dumb and blind, twisting a handkerchief round and round in her hands. And because her remoteness on this special day was so unnerving, Rosie and Betsy went upstairs to their bedroom, finding Burza already there. She was sitting on the narrow old folding camp bed, never to be used by Peg again. This item was all that could be squeezed in beside the large double bed.

'Bloody good innit?' Rosie said. 'With Peg gone you'd have thought we'd have a bit more space. As it is Dicky's got a whole room to himself and we're still all choked up.' She stared at Burza, her eyes full of hate. 'There's only room for two here, so why don't you buzz off and live with your toffee-nosed Lil?'

'Because I'm going to stay here with Clara, that's why.'

'You ain't wanted. You never was.'

'Neither were you if all I hear's true,' Burza retaliated bitterly. 'How does it feel to be listed as a mistake?'

'Who told you that, you miserable little mare?' Rosie's pale face was working, her dark-grey eyes stone cold. 'Why don't you piss off and eat grass like your gippo mum? Better still, why not drown yourself at sea – 'cos that's wot's gonner happen to your dad one of these bright fine days. He'll be dead, dead, dead – just like mine.'

Rosie threw herself down on the double bed and broke her heart.

'You shouldn't have said that she wasn't wanted, Burze,' Betsy told her, low and fierce. 'That was bleeding unkind.'

'But she can say what she likes to me – is that it?'

'There's times when you act and speak as la-di-dah as Lil,' the usually easygoing Betsy told her. 'It ain't our fault if you don't fit in.'

Hurt, her eyes wide in her face, Burza felt a queer sad pain in her heart. This was the first time ever that Betsy had taken sides with Rosie in her tirade about gippo kids. Up to that moment Burza had believed Betsy to be on her side. Betsy had once even gone so far as to say it was rotten to make Burza always sleep at the bottom of the double bed with no pillow for her head. Had even mentioned the matter to Clara. Clara had come up the stairs like a tornado and wrenched Burza's pillow out of Rosie's hands.

'You selfish little demont,' she had yelled. 'Take her pillow again and I swear I'll tan your arse so hard your eyes'll water.'

'It ain't my fault,' Rosie had back-answered. 'Wiv her stuck at the bottom, my feet get cold because they ain't tucked in.'

'Don't you lip me, madam. 'Sides, your feet won't reach the bottom of the bed for years yet. You just thank your lucky stars you've got a mattress to lie on, an' not a thin bit of canvas like Peg.'

'Peg could come in wiv us.'

'She'd sooner get shot than poisoned,' Clara snapped pithily. 'And don't think I'm deaf, dumb and blind neither. You've been gunning for our Burza from the start, and I won't have it. D'yer hear?'

She had looked so puffed up with fury, her eyes so fierce, that Rosie had lapsed into silence – until Clara had gone stomping back down the stairs. Safe at last, Rosie had sneered, 'So you got a pillow for your head. Your poor rotten gippo head what looks like a manky turnip.'

'And yours looks like a pimple on a haystack. An oozing, pus-y ol' pimple.'

97

Rosie had smirked, getting in the last word: 'At least I'll say this, Burza Webb. I'd sooner 'ave a 'ead what looks like a pimple than a face wot looks like a bucketful of arse'oles.'

'You Rosie,' Betsy told her sharply. 'Shut up!'

And that had been an end to it.

Now Betsy was on Rosie's side and Burza felt deepdown hurt.

'What have I done?' she asked, her voice small and shaky because her throat felt so tight. 'Betsy, why are you looking at me like that?'

'Shut up!' Betsy snapped and promptly burst into tears and threw herself down beside Rosie.

Burza would have none of it. She shook Betsy hard. 'Why?'

'Because you're always held up to us, that's why,' Betsy told her, quietly furious. 'An' because when I was going out with Simpson I was told he was treating me like a tart, and I oughter mind. I've been with him from the time I was fifteen. I would have married him the very minute I was sixteen but the sodding nosy-parkers had to put in their two pennorth.'

'Betsy, I thought all that was over and done with years ago.'

'Well it ain't, and I 'ate ol' mother Frazer. No one knew till she found out and told Mum and Dad. They said he was a thug! And when I said he wasn't, an' that I loved him, the roof all but fell in.'

'They were worried about you, Betsy. It's common knowledge that all the Shatts carry knives!'

'Who cares? Not about bloody neighbours anyway. Look what Minnie Bede gets away with. She don't give a shit, and neither do I, about what people say. I said as much, if you remember. I was told that there was no hope for me – and that I oughter try and be like you, whose best mate was a lady. Like you wos always trying to be a lady too.'

'It was nothing to do with me that you weren't allowed to go out with Simpson,' Burza told her fiercely. 'George put a stop to it because the great big bully punched you.'

'It weren't his fault. He was drunk, that's all. And who told him? You! Why didn't you keep your big bloody trap shut?'

'I didn't have to – the whole world knew. And as for keeping traps shut, who never told how you would have got beaten to death by your darling Simpson after George told him to buzz off? If I hadn't have come up in the nick of time ...'

'You shouldn't have 'it him in the face with that brick,' Betsy yelled, her pale face now whiter than a sheet cruelly accentuated by the black she wore. 'You scarred him for life, and he chucked me – because of you, of what you did, and because you threatened him with the police. It should 'ave been *me* getting married today. Me and my Simpson, but I've lost 'im, and now – now I've lost me dad too. Go away, Burza Webb. Bloody well go away!'

As Burza walked slowly down the stairs she heard Rosie sob, 'I 'ate her! She can 'ave the camp bed. It's cold to lie on. I hope she dies the death. If we didn't have to put up wiv her, we could have our chest of drawers back, instead of having it shoved outside in the passage. I always knock meself on it when I try to get by. I'd like to kill Burza, I really would!'

'For Christ's sake shut up!' Betsy snapped. 'You've been getting at her all your bloody life.'

'You don't understand,' Rosie whimpered.

She buried her face in her hands, tears streaming down her cheeks. It wasn't fair, she thought, remembering how it had all begun. How suddenly, with Burza's coming, there was seldom enough room on Clara's lap for her own yearning self. How it was always Baby Burza who had to come first. She cast her mind back to her own jealous tantrums, and her dear darling old mum who she loved more than life itself, explaining why they must all make an extra fuss of the newcomer.

'Her own mum's gone,' Clara had said. 'Run orf with them raggle-taggle gipsies. Her dad's my very own brother, and he knew I was the only person in the world what he could trust his baby with. So I took her in, don't yer see, Rosie? We've gotta be kind ter the little baby. And this I promise yer: I'll never ever leave my luverly Rosie, nor any of my little demonts. I swear ter this before God.'

But even while her mother was saying these words, young as she was at the time, Rosie had believed she was fighting a losing battle. She had always been first with her mum, just as the sweet-toothed Betsy had always been first with their dad. Peg had Sid and they were like one. Dicky, quiet, self-contained Dicky didn't seem to need anyone at all. But she,

Rosie, needed her mum quite desperately and up until Burza, she, Rosie, had always come first.

As she grew older Rosie had seemed to need her mother even more. Especially when she had lost Simpson, because in her rough, but caring way, Clara had understood about matters of the heart. On top of that Clara made her feel safe. Now in this gargantuan emptiness they had all fallen into since they had no dad, Rosie wanted to make her beloved mum feel protected, precious and warm. But it wasn't to be. Of them all, Clara seemed to be turning more to Burza.

'I'll make the bitch pay,' Rosie sobbed. 'As God is my witness, I will!'

Chapter Ten

'Oh God, no!' Burza wondered if the whole wide world had gone mad.

Miss Allthorpe, sitting on her easy chair in the drawing room, shook her head, her beaded cape glinting in the late afternoon sunlight like so many glass eyes.

'There was nothing we could do. I am afraid he had to have peace and freedom from pain. He had a very good life here – while it lasted.'

'I know,' Burza choked. 'He would have died long ago in the hands of that awful man. But he has had some lovely years, all thanks to you. And he was very old, wasn't he? But I loved him. And he knew me, and – and ...'

'You've lost your uncle, and in some ways, some members of his family also? It happens, dear. Grief makes some folk very bitter. And now the demise of your poor old Firestone ... Life hardly seems worthwhile to you. Isn't that it?'

'Yes.'

'Well, you know the answer, don't you, child? When one love dies, replace it with another.'

'I – I have Lily. She is my dearest friend.'

'True. True. But she is not here with you now, is she? And has not been here for some time. I take it that this is because she is a good daughter as well as being your good friend?'

'Yes.'

'And her father is a stern old devil. Very dyed in the wool, so they say.'

'He is a very proud man, Miss Allthorpe,' Burza replied, springing to Jack London's defence. 'His sister Marion, and

Lily, never forget that! They live on the straight and narrow path according to his values at all times.'

'Wrong!'

'I beg your pardon?'

'They should live as they see fit, not as Jack London wants. Firestone had other visitors from Solomon Street, don't forget, so I do know a little of what goes on. But that is beside the point. We are speaking of you now.'

'I do my best to be like Lily, but sometimes I ...'

'Wonder what is the point of it all? You are feeling unloved – isn't that so? Since that's the case, it's important that you must love and be loved as quickly as possible.' The old lady nodded her head and smiled in a mischievous, old and wrinkled way. Her eyes were sparkling as brightly as her black beads. 'When I lost a lover I would snap my fingers, kick up my heels, and find another beau. There were many to choose from, waiting outside the stage door.'

'Oh, Miss Allthorpe, you were on the stage!' Burza was glowing at the thought. 'How wonderful. You must tell me ...'

'We are talking about you, girl. Now, go and be comforted.'

'Go? I don't understand.'

'To Firestone's stable – and make a fuss of what you find there. Go!'

One always obeyed Miss Allthorpe at once. She had that kind of manner. Burza ran outside. Around the path, through the garden gate to the cobbled yard and the stable. Beyond the stable there was Firestone's field, and that in turn led to open meadowland. Burza ran to the stable and through the half-open door, then:

'Oh, oh, oh!'

Entranced, Burza looked at the cream and chocolate-coloured foal that none other than Pete Frazer was making a fuss of.

'Do you like him?' he asked unnecessarily. His golden-brown eyes were smiling, his even white teeth gleaming. Nearly two years older than Burza, he had grown huge, his athletic body in perfect proportions. Pete Frazer, Burza thought in passing – her eyes on the foal – had become a very handsome young man.

'He's beautiful,' she choked. 'He's not poor beloved old

Firestone, but this baby's a darling.' She was down on her knees beside the friendly little animal. 'What's his name – and how is it that you're here?'

'Miss Allthorpe suggested "Roan". As to how I'm here, I volunteered right from the start, with all the others, to cope with Firestone. Don't you remember? That was in the beginning. Most helpers drifted away once the first enthusiasm faded, but Andy and I kept on. He was as regular a visitor as me before he got the Walls's job. We came weekday evenings, mucking out, everything. Between us we took a lot off old Granger's shoulders. Granger's a brick.'

'I know. He's been with Miss Allthorpe for years. I reckon he's always looked like that, old and crabby. He looks after the house, the garden, and carries out Miss Allthorpe's wishes – moaning at her all the time. I think Granger's the only person on God's earth who'd dare answer her back. I think he loves her very deeply.'

She smiled, then kissed the nuzzling Roan on his nose, but there were tears in her eyes. Pete was watching her, then he said, very gently: 'I – helped when they – Firestone, you know? I was with him to the very last minute. He knew nothing about it, so you don't have to worry on that score.'

'Thank you, Pete.' She tried to suppress a sob.

He went on, 'Miss Allthorpe told me to look out for a foal, providing I gave my word to help care for him. She said she's of an age when taking on pets that could outlive her didn't make sense – unless she knew that there was someone there to look after them. She seems to think that Granger will go with her.' He laughed, a rich deep sound, adding, 'Perhaps he wouldn't dare not to.'

'Don't!'

'Sorry,' he told her, his voice suddenly gruff as he remembered her loss. 'That was stupid, thinking about George and all. Come here, Burz.'

Suddenly, not knowing quite how it happened, Burza found herself enclosed in Pete's masculine embrace. No one had actually cuddled her for years, not since she was five, when Clara had comforted her after that first-day fiasco at school. Oh, she and Lily had held hands, and still did, but this closeness, this warmth was wonderful.

103

She cuddled into Pete and wept until she could weep no more. It felt warm and wonderful in his arms. It was private in the stable, and the straw was soft and comforting. She clung on to Pete, fiercely, never wanting to let go.

Strange emotions were flooding through her. She felt dreamy, yet alive in a different kind of way. And she wanted to stay close to Pete – whom she had never really thought about until now – and wanted him to, yes really and truly wanted ...

His lips sought and found her own. And the sensation was out of this world. She kissed him back, arms round his neck, wanting to let go of her senses, or faint, or fly away high into the sky. She was conscious of a kind of urgency and gasped as his lips pressed harder on hers and his hand moved down to cover her breast.

Afterwards she was not sure of all that Pete did to her. But it was all wonderful, wild and wanton. When it was over she lay close to him, eyes closed, listening to the steady beating of his heart. She felt relaxed, sleepy, and for the first time since Georgy's death, not alone.

Lately, she had been feeling more alone than she had ever been in her life. Lily was becoming more and more under her father's thumb. Lately Rosie kept shouting that Clara was turning to her, Burza, more than anyone else, and was just plain nasty. Clara was on another planet, one that was millions of miles away in space, with George. Burza felt somehow that Clara would never willingly come back. All Clara seemed to want to do these days was sit in the front room and talk to the picture of the young soldier, George, who was smiling into eternity from the wall.

Peg and Charlie, Sid and Ivy were enjoying their own private wedded bliss and were complete. They visited Clara every day but their mother's attitude was such that they were happy to rush away.

Dicky, quietly self-contained, spent more time with his books than people. A whizz at learning, he had gone up to senior High School. Now he was a civil servant no less, working for the Post Office. Starting out as a telegraph boy, he had progressed. Dicky really was, quietly and steadily, going up in the world.

Betsy, now fatherless and with a mother who was seemingly no longer aware of what was going on, had sneaked back to Simpson. She sometimes crept back into the house when the night was all but through. Getting on for twenty, she wanted to marry him, but Simpson was far too slippery a customer for that! So, frustrated and bitter she contented herself with hating Burza.

Now all that no longer mattered. Oh yes, Burza thought dreamily, a little later as she and Pete walked hand in hand along the winding path that led to the large old house, it was good not to feel so alone.

Moonlight and black shadows, the breeze soughing through leaves, gave everything an eerie unreality which was strange and exciting. She wanted the night to never end.

The country, she thought blissfully, is where I began and where part of my blood belongs. For all that Miss Allthorpe's gipsies were suspicious of me and wouldn't talk, for all I sneaked away wishing that I hadn't even tried, I know that in my heart I have a little bit of gipsy in me.

At this moment I am feeling how my mother must have felt. I am a child of open spaces. I believe I was born on a night of moon and magic, when the wind was breathlessly whispering secrets, and my unknown mother held me in her arms and listened to the music of the stars.

She felt Pete's fingers briefly close comfortingly round her own. He released her as they reached the house, and suddenly she wanted to cry out high and wild, hardly knowing whether in grief or joy.

A little later Pete said quietly, 'You don't have to worry, Burza. I never went all the way. And I won't tell anyone what happened.'

'I know,' she replied. 'It's our secret.'

'And will be,' he promised, 'until the day you choose it to be different.'

'Thank you,' she replied and glowed.

Miss Allthorpe's sitting room was alive with candlelight when Burza and Pete went to say goodbye. She looked at them, her eyes wise.

'This is the first time you have visited me together,' she

told them. 'I do hope that it won't be the last.'

'Oh no!' Burza replied, and Pete's smile was wide and all-embracing.

They began the long walk to the bus stop. They were in a beautiful rural district, where there were hedges and trees, and cows were like moving black shadows that looked ghostly somehow. On high, the huge milky moon seemed to float along with them.

'She is very rich, isn't she?' Burza said, for the sake of saying something out loud.

'Yes,' he replied easily. 'She could afford to have the electric put on, let alone gas.'

'She prefers candlelight. It's more gentle, she says. Pete? Peter?'

'Mm?'

'Am I your girl?'

'If you want to be,' he replied with studied casualness.

She thought about it. 'Only if I want to be? Don't you have any thoughts about it at all?'

'I know that you are an innocent little sweetheart for all you try to act as tough as old boots. You are very beautiful, Burz. And because of what's happened I'm a lucky chap all round. It was all sparked off by Miss Allthorpe.'

'Really?' she asked uncertainly.

'She put it in my mind. Said that from what she's heard, you weren't getting treated right these days. That you needed to be comforted. So I comforted you in the best way I knew.' He laughed soft and low. 'God, Burz, I'll repeat the process any time you like. Any time, anywhere. At the drop of a hat, you might say.'

'So you did it out of sympathy?' she said in a small voice.

'I suppose so, Burz – at first.'

'And now?'

'Best night of my life. Especially as – Burz, you've never been with a chap before, have you?'

'No. I – I always thought that – I mean, it's always been Richard in my mind and ...'

'He's making sheep's eyes at Lily these days,' Pete told her in an offhand way. 'He doesn't stand a chance. His guvnor's daughter? Phew! And what a stiff and starchy old devil

London is! No, it's curtains for my old mate, Richard. Even Beldon stands a better chance.'

'Andy?'

'Make no mistake he wants you, mate, and always has. I think even Richard had eyes for you once. So did half the school – yes, even us older blokes. But as for Richard, you stepped back, didn't you – when you saw how Lily looked at him. You always try to please Lily, don't you? She'll turn out to have feet of clay one of these bright fine days, but you won't see it, not even then.'

'You seem to know an awful lot about how I act and feel,' she told him tightly. 'How come?'

'Spent a great deal of my time side-stepping my mother and Lily's aunt, don't I? They seem to have set their hearts on me and Lily getting together. You don't try to weasel out of any situation dealing with Lily without immediately having to include you too. It's common knowledge that you mates are about as close as Peg and Sid.'

'Oh! Really?' She was shocked, jolted out of herself.

He went on complacently, 'But where Lily or anything else is concerned, I have a mind of my own, Burz.'

'No,' she told him coldly. 'You haven't. Not at all. I mean, Miss Allthorpe made your mind up for you a while back, didn't she? You did as she told you – and comforted me!'

He was staring down at her nonplussed. 'Now what have I said?'

'Nothing! Oh, and since you don't shorten Lily's name, I'd prefer it if you call me Burza in future. All right?'

Ahead the dull light over the bus stop gleamed its pallid luminosity. It was a false light, a mimicry of Nature's wonderful moon. The whole love affair, for that was what she had believed was beginning, was false. As phoney as was the gas lamp against the moon. She was right back to square one, feeling abandoned by everyone and hurt beyond measure.

She never wanted to see Pete Frazer again.

Chapter Eleven

Burza shivered as she waited outside Steadmans the baker's shop. It was a chore she had taken on, to help Clara. Buying stale bread was a necessity these days. Without George's wages, money was tight. Clara, whose proud boast had once been, 'There's them as don't like getting on their knees, an' them as don't mind. I'm just thankful I don't mind,' now seemed neither to mind nor care about anything very much.

'Given up, ain't yer?' Rosie had said the previous evening. 'You're worrying me skinny, Mum!'

'Don't be such a daft 'aporth,' Clara had replied stonily. 'It's just that nothing seems to interest me no more, now we ain't got your dad.'

'All the more reason ter pull yourself together, Mum. If you go to pieces we all will.' Rosie pressed home her point, seriously concerned. ''Sides, you'll lose all your people if you keep this up. Me and Bet 'ave scrubbed your doorsteps till our fingers bleed, but we're scared all the time.'

'Of hard work, Rose?' Clara gave a sad smile. 'That's our sort's lot in life, gel.'

'Scared of what'll 'appen if we get found out. You know what a bloody awful lot they are up the Labour Exchange.' Rosie began to get nasty and her eyes glinted sparks. 'And another thing. Where are all them bleeders what held out their hands to you when they were bad off and needed help? Ain't seen nothing of them, have we? Different story now, ain't it? Bleedin' hell! Everyone knows what a soft touch you are and—'

'No call for all this nonsense,' Clara told her evenly. 'And

108

while we're at it, Rose, no one on God's earth'll ever call *you* soft. You've always been a spiteful little demont behind that innocent look you manage to put on. Your dad knew from the moment he heard you getting at Burza and he said ... ' She halted, overcome for a moment, then, 'Oh Gawd! Rose, shut your mouth. I can't stand your whining. I need time to sort meself out. Is that too much to ask?'

Rosie had gone white to the lips at the mention of Burza's name as she replied fiercely, 'We're all cut to ribbons, Mum. We're all changed. Poor ol' Peg and Sid are gutted. Me and Bet want ter die ourselves, and Dicky's gone into his shell more'n ever. But we're trying to go on same as usual. Yes, really and truly trying. It just ain't like you to just sit here staring into space. Mum, you've gotta buck up!'

'Where's Burza?'

'Where you'd expect,' Rosie said, her voice becoming openly hostile. 'With that snobby cow Lily London, that's where.'

'Really?' Burza said, having come downstairs and heard the gist of the conversation. 'I was trying to tidy our room.'

'And that's another thing,' Rosie exploded. 'That room just ain't big enough for—'

'Oh, put a sock in it,' Burza cut in, then on an impulse she kissed Clara who remained sitting there looking as impassive as stone. 'But I'm off now. All right?'

She had gone to call for Lily and tiptoed upstairs with her to her room. Burza had looked round at its neatness, its pale lily-of-the-valley colours now set off with sweetpea pink, and felt relaxed. Lily was so special.

Burza sat on the bed next to her friend, who as always, sensing her mood did not speak. Closer than sisters they gained a sense of security together that was seldom with them when apart. These days they were apart more often than not because of Lily's absolute love and devotion for her father – which had intensified from the moment darling George Cuttings had died. Lily's grief for George had been whole-hearted and sincere.

Burza had begun quietly considering her dearest friend. In most activities of life Lily was inclined to take the middle course and she avoided extremes of any kind when possible.

She constantly craved peace and happy surroundings, and her horror of worry and unpleasantness made her far too accommodating. Because of this, Burza wanted to shake Lily sometimes. She allowed her father Jack to rule the roost to an absurd degree, and of course, Marion's sermonising about gentility, good behaviour, and the straight and narrow path went on endlessly.

Lily seldom allowed her own feelings to interfere. She obeyed her father and accepted all that Marion said without question. Gentle and courteous, Lily did not like making waves. However, having made up her own mind about something, she could be quietly persuasive. She could in fact bend Marion to her will, though she seldom tried. But it had been Lily who for once in her life had dug in her toes and made it possible for Richard to work on the window-cleaning round. A fact that Richard, tall, dark and handsome, and often brusqueness itself, never forgot.

'Are things still as bad for Clara?' Lily asked at last.

'Worse if anything. She's gone into herself, and sometimes I could just strangle Rosie. I admit she tries hard enough, but her nagging doesn't help. And she's still going on about me sharing the bedroom with her and Betsy. Oh shit! You don't want to hear all this.'

'Apart from unnecessary swearing, it's good to get things off your chest, Burza.'

'What chest, Prunes and Prisms?' Burza quipped. Both girls looked down at their own sparse figures – which set them off into rivers of giggles. After that they discussed books and the pictures, and their dreams for the future.

'My dreams are simple,' Lily said. 'I want to get married and have a family that is as large and friendly and jolly as Clara's was.'

'There was a time when every member of the Cuttings family was considered to be fresh-faced, open and nice,' Burza answered. 'Just think how things change. Even Rosie used to be able to hide her hatred of me. As for Betsy ...'

'Is she still sneaking off to meet Simpson?'

'Rotten old Blood-nut? Yes, much to Nick Bede's contempt.'

They had discussed redheaded Blood-nut, as Simpson was

110

called. He was Nick Bede's best mate. The two had been in cahoots since schooldays with their pilfering and downright thieving. Both bad lots, their happy hunting ground was usually Hymen's Market. Burza suddenly remembered a story about Richard and Andy outwitting Blood-nut and Nick in a spirited paperchase run by the senior school. Then, out of the blue they were forgetting tension and grief and laughing out loud.

Jack immediately banged like a maniac on the ceiling with one of his sticks. This stopped their hilarity very sharply indeed. The stick banging meant in no uncertain terms that visiting hours were over. Shortly after that, Burza had left number twelve to return to the silent as the grave number six.

Now, as she waited outside Steadmans to buy stale bread, Burza was thinking of Lily. Wishing that the spare room – once Jack's upstairs front bedroom – would be offered to her own lowly self. She knew it would never happen. Jack London was the worst of all possible people. An out and out working-class snob. He put up with Burza herself, barely, for Lily's sake. However there was no love lost.

The situation had grown worse from the day Burza, helping Lily with sweeping and dusting, had accidentally knocked against the table holding Aspy. The small table holding the aspidistra, now large, could have gone flying. Jack had yelled out stuff about clumsy kids and practically had a heart attack. Marion too, had gone on and on about taking extra care of other people's possessions. Of Aspy being precious because Lily's mother had loved it so.

'Bloody hell,' Burza had sworn coldly and deliberately to the pink-faced Lily, 'now I really have blotted my copy-book. It's a wonder he didn't call me a clumsy cow to my face. And added something like all gippos being born in open fields or barns. I simply ain't in your class, *Chickybit!*'

'Stop it!' Lily had quavered. 'Oh please Burza, don't make me feel even worse.'

Now, remembering the incident, Burza scowled. I don't know why the old sod don't move to a posh street somewhere up Hainault Road way, she thought angrily, then hastily changed her mind, knowing full well that where Jack went, Lily would go too.

111

Well, she mused, if Jack London thought himself God, she could tell him a thing or two about a real gentleman! Dearest George. A picture rose up before her, of twinkling silver-grey eyes and strong hands that had held one safe while obstinate milk teeth were removed and carefully placed under the pillow. The tooth fairy had always left a halfpenny behind. Her dearest, dearest George whom she loved as a father. A fine, warmhearted man who had fought for his country, who had worked like ten tigers, who had above all been devoted to his wife and kids.

She remembered again, all of their faces at the funeral. Of how Sid's shoulders had shaken, and Dicky had almost looked Chinese, his emotions were so tightly held in control. And the girls, breaking their hearts, and poor old Rosie trying to cling to her mother, cold statue-still Clara who seemed to have died herself on that terrible day.

Burza quickly brushed her hand across her eyes and bit her bottom lip hard. She must not make a fool of herself.

'Oh Georgy Porgy,' Burza whispered, using Clara's pet name for the man, 'how I miss you. How we all miss you. Georgy, I don't pray much to God, but I'm praying to you now. Make Clara get over losing you. If she doesn't, I think she'll drive herself mad.'

Suddenly all her grief and misery welled to the fore. As Basil opened his door, he saw that she was crying.

''Ello Burz, me dear,' he said, his round, rosy face full of concern. 'An' just what is the matter with yew?'

'Nothing,' she smiled in a shame-faced watery way. 'Just that life gets you down sometimes. I – I don't usually blub.'

'Yew cry if yew want, luv. Sickness and people popping off out of this world are crying sorts of things. Come to think of it, I wanner bawl me eyes out meself.'

Startled out of her own loss, she asked, 'What is it, Basil? What's wrong?'

'Angel's ill and Lucy's beside 'erself – so am I. The little 'un's very fragile, yew know. So, I'm on me own today.'

'You need someone to serve in the shop all the time, Bas,' she told him quickly. 'I've often thought that. Having help would give your missus a chance.'

'Can't afford to take no one on.'

112

'Not for five bob a week with some stale bread and cake thrown in?'

'Five bob?'

Basil was considering it and Burza's heart leapt high. Five shillings a week would help no end, and as to free bread and cakes, it would save at least a precious twopence a day – one and twopence a week! You could get tons of potherbs for that, or pearl barley, gravy salt, even a bacon bone or two to stew, and that added to five bob would be a godsend. Please George, she felt herself silently praying, make it happen.

'When can yew start?' Basil asked.

'Serve me now, I'll run home and straight back. Oh, Mr Steadman, I ...'

'Mister now, is it?' he teased. 'Nice!'

Chapter Twelve

'My Gawd!' miserable ratty old Ethel Jacobs said. 'Talk abart gettin' in! 'Ere mate, I could 'ave done with that little earner.'

'Thought yew had a job, Ethel,' Basil quipped. 'Cleaning for your lady what's kept you going for years.'

'Dead now, ain't she? Dropped down just like that. Like a bloody fly. And her daughter, wot should've known better, give me the push!'

'In other words, you were caught, Ethel?'

The group of listening ladies laughed raucously. A few added their own remarks.

'Wot 'appened, Eth? Caught yer with yer drawers down, did she?'

'Bet you 'ad your hands where they shouldn't 'ave been, Eth.'

''Ere, Eth, 'ow come you didn't give the stuck-up mare the mouthful you've halways told us yer would? Been charring up there for years, an' 'alf 'inchin' fings wot wos laying raund, ain't yer?'

'Shut your lying mouth, Fanny Lyons.' Ethel was going red.

The pug-nosed lady whose woolly cardigan was full of holes, and had its raggy front button bits stained with egg, raised her brows, asking, 'Then 'ow come you showed me yore ill-gotten gains from that 'ouse, as long ago as the beginning of the war? Offered to sell me some of it an' all.' She turned to the others, grinning all over her face. 'An' wot's more she swore like a trooper when I said as 'ow I hadn't got no change.'

The listening ladies sniggered.

'Shut your gob, Fanny, else I'll shut it for you.' Ethel's eyes were darting about like pinballs. 'An' as for what I got the shove

for, well – all that 'appened was I took a sip of the old gel's gin.'
Ethel smirked as she remembered some of her ex-employer's
more scathing remarks about her cleaning. 'After all, she won't
be drinking nothin' no more, will she?' She turned away to look
again at Basil, getting back to the subject that had started it all.
'I'll do it for four and six. What d'yer say?'

'Sorry,' Basil told her happily. 'Burza has the job.'

'Jesus! Wot a life for a crust,' Ethel moaned, then added
cunningly, 'so, can I have double whack for taking it on the
chin, Bas? Like two loaves an' ...'

'A tin loaf, and a half a cottage for a penny, with two
muffins thrown in. All right?'

'It'll 'ave ter do, won't it?' Ethel curled her lip. 'An' while
we're at it ...'

'For Gawd's sake 'urry up,' Fanny from the Feathers end
said. 'I've gotta get back for the rag man.'

'Well, you won't get no ha'penny for rags,' Ethel said
hastily, ''cos I can see you're bloody well wearing 'em.'

Basil, who had busied himself popping bread and a round of
stale scones into Burza's brown paper carrier bag, winked at
Burza and she winked back.

'Why don't yer tell 'er summink else while you're at it?'
Ethel remarked spitefully, seeing the winking going on. 'Like
how her darling Betsy's up the duff?'

Burza froze and all the women, eyes glinting like avaricious
vultures, held their breath.

'A bit of scandal, luverly!' Fanny said, gloating.

'How dare you!' Burza began, but Ethel had everyone's
attention now, her face full of unholy joy.

'Got a bun in the oven, ain't she? Must 'ave, or else she
visited Ma Freeman to have her toenails cut, eh Burz?'

'No, just to tell her to stick her crochet hook right into your
lying mouth,' Burza retaliated. 'What a hateful old hag you are!'

'Good on yer, gel,' someone yelled, but Burza, shocked,
had run out of Steadmans and dashed hell for leather down
Solomon Street.

She fell into the passageway of number six, chest heaving
and eyes twin brilliants with unshed tears. Shit on all women
with evil tongues, she thought. And how silly of Betsy to go
out with Blood-nut. How stupid not to care whether the whole

115

world knew! All the old girls would wag their tongues, and make up lies, and besides ... Besides, Betsy hadn't been back with Simpson all that long – or had she?

An awful fear overcame her. It was only since Clara had been half out of her mind with grief that Betsy had openly gone her own way.

'Oh George,' Burza prayed, 'please don't let it be true. Please, please, please. It will kill Clara! Oh shit!'

Clara was in the kitchen, sitting in Georgy's chair near the black polished range. The fender, gleaming under its latest rubbing with emery paper, was set before the narrow hearth which had been newly stoned white. Burza felt a great relief and comfort then. Clara was beginning to come back to the real, very cruel world. She had been cleaning in her old enthusiastic way by the looks of things.

Clara had always prided herself on her range for it had central position in the room. It was a joy, she always said, and real 'andsome shining as it did with elbow grease and black polish. Its white hearth and gleaming silver fender were set before it like holy offerings. And no one, not even George, was allowed to rest their feet on the brightest fender in Solomon Street. If coal or ash fell through the bars and on to the hearth it was swiftly brushed up. There was a small metal stand holding shovel, brush and tongs for exactly that purpose. Placed carefully on the right side of the hearth, it was as bright and shining as the rest.

Suddenly, Burza thought tearfully, number six was beginning to feel like home again. The range, with Clara's help, burning bright with coal, was the very soul of the kitchen. It gave comfort, warmth, and cooked food in its side oven. Usually a stewpan holding bacon bones, potherbs, and pearl barley simmered on the top. And near to it an ever-ready kettle of hot water for the odd cuppa. There was always a screw of tea to be had.

'Give me a cuppa an' a fag and I'm in 'eaven,' George used to say.

Clara had seen to it that George was in heaven every day of his life. Now he was up there somewhere in the clouds, Burza told herself wistfully. His eyes as silvery as the stars.

'I have some good news, Clara,' she said carefully. 'I hope you'll be pleased. I have a job.'

Clara turned to look at her brother's child, her expression a

116

little more feeling now.

'One way an' another, you've always done your share, gel,' she replied quietly. 'An' from the time you were first born the money your dad sent for you helped us all. Still does, come to that.'

'He should have tried,' Burza replied unsteadily, voicing her most recent, most hurtful wound, 'to – to come back for – for—'

'For George's funeral? From the other side of the world?' Clara shook her head and smiled in her worldly-wise way. 'No ducks, weren't possible. But he did his best. He sent money – for flowers. It came too late, so I've put it with the rest.'

'With the rest, Clara?'

'Every month I took out what I needed, gel. What was left over I put in the Post Office. You've got over twenty pounds to your name now. So now you're left school and all grown up, you can make your plans.'

'Make my plans?' Burza asked, confused.

'Well, if Rosie gets on your nerves, and these days Betsy ain't no sweet'eart neither, you go and get your own place. We've sponged off you one way an' another for long enough, Burz.'

Wild with grief, Burza threw back her head and glared. 'Let me get this straight. Are you telling me to go?'

'No. I'm just letting you off the hook, that's all.'

'Do you *want* me to go?' Burza's heart was pumping like a steam engine. 'Will it make things easier for you, Clara? I mean, stop Rosie nagging on about the bedroom, and Betsy nagging about me and my loathing of her precious Simpson?'

'It won't make things easier, gel, it'll make them a bloody sight harder,' Clara told her honestly. 'You're like me own flesh and blood what's come out of me and George's loins, as the Bible says. No, I was thinking of you, that's all.' Her tone became strong, firm. 'Make no mistake, while you want ter stay, you stay. I'd like yer to. I mean it. D'yer hear me?'

'Then thank God for that!' Burza was laughing and crying and flung her arms round Clara. 'For a terrible minute, I thought you were throwing me out. And as for being rich enough to keep myself, my wages are to be five shillings a week and stale bread, and any spare cake to hand. But it will help us a lot. We'll manage, won't we? I'm sure we will.'

117

'I think five bob is a nice help all round, Burze,' Clara told her stoutly. 'After all, Betsy cried like a baby when she didn't get a job up Luckhams.'

'I think that was mostly because that sweatshop's on the Shattery Estate,' Burza explained, holding her breath, and wondering whether Clara had any inkling of what was being said. 'You know, very near where Simpson hangs out.'

'That nasty sod!' Clara's tone held contempt. 'I hope as how she's told him to bugger orf for good. And as for Luckhams! Them girls get paid eight shillings a week for slaving over machines from eight to twelve, then again from one to six – and later if the right number of clothes ain't been got out. An' they don't get no extra when it's later neither. Poor little cows!'

'How do you know all this, Clara?'

'Seen 'em with me own eyes. I went up there to get Fanny Lyons's gel's wages when she was took sick. Fanny was scared of going. Posh lot they've got in that office, snobby little bitches. You know, the kippers 'n curtains sort! But I ain't scared of no one, so Fan asked me. And what I saw made me heart bleed. Long lines of 'em, all pasty-faced and scared out of their wits in case they got the sack.'

'So you're not upset that I've not tried the Labour Exchange again?'

'No, gel, you're best off at Steadmans. If you ask me, 'e's been generous to a fault. Five shilling for working in the warm, and with them what are such nice people too. And Angel, what's only got a little bit of understanding, is as sweet as they come.'

'I don't know much about what I've got to do at the shop. Serve everyone I expect, and keep things clean and tidy. Still, I'll know soon enough. I can start as soon as I get back there.'

'Then you'd best buck up. Now, about that Post Office book, I ...'

'I don't want it,' Burza told her quietly. 'And that's God's truth! But you speaking about Angel has given me a wonderful idea. I can tell you what I'd like the money used for – from all of us, mind. I want you to go and buy the best stone Mother Mary, or else one of those winged angels you see at St Christopher's, that you can. I would like one that will look after George and Baby Violet for ever.' She smiled steadily into Clara's hurt, lovely melon-seed-shaped eyes. 'Know what I'd really like,

Clara? A heavenly guardian – that has your face.'

'Oh gel, I ...'

They clung together, weeping. And though she was very sad, Burza was also very happy. Clara wanted her. Unlike her own mum and dad, Clara had actually said she wanted her, Burza, to stay! That was blessing enough, but over and above everything else, Clara was crying. Sobbing as though the floodgates of the world had broken.

Clara was no longer the cold, cut-off creature she had been ever since George had died. Clara was alive and in a raging torrent of grief. She was hurting and gasping, sorrow cutting its way deep into her soul, filling it up, and now overflowing. And Burza knew that now at last, Clara would begin to mend.

And once that had happened, Clara would begin to fight back – for Betsy once she knew the truth. And Dicky would be more himself, and silly, stupid Rosie who thought she was unloved, would get a cuddle or two from her mum. She, Burza, would put in a word.

'I'll get you my best pinafore,' Clara said on a sob. 'You want ter look nice behind the counter. An' – an' Burz? Thanks. For George and little Violet. For everything, ta ever so ...'

It was warm in the shop and it was wonderful, Burza thought. It smelled of baking, crusty loaves, of sugar, and jam and cream. And of course the takings had gone up – at least so far as Lily was concerned. Every time she could slip away, there she was, smiling her gentle smile, buying sugar-coated doughnuts, a chocolate sponge, a fruit flan, any excuse to stand and talk and while away the time she had to spare. School had ended for her at last and there was no talk of employment for Lily. She was to stay at home, to be a companion and helpmate for Jack. She would slip off to Steadmans at the slightest excuse, having a chat with Burza and Basil, else Lucy and her little Mongol-looking girl. Then, looking guilty, off she would hurry, back to her dad.

Jack London was a toff these days. Yes, a blooming toff with an ever-expanding business to run. He had three blokes working for him now. Young Richard Wray, Sid Cuttings, and none other than Andy Beldon. Andy had given up his three-wheeler with ice-box up front like a shot when Sid put in a word. In work, regular, Richard and Andy considered themselves as good as Pete Frazer any day.

All the Frazer men worked at the docks. Oh, Pete! Burza sometimes thought when alone. If only ... Oh, Pete! The longing inside of her refused to go away for all she cold-shouldered him every time he tried to speak. He was *told* to comfort me, she always reminded herself. *Told!* She would force herself to get angry as the mental picture of Pete floated like a golden effigy in her mind. Then she would blink him away, fiercely, unmindful of the tears stinging at the back of her eyes. Life was too short for ifs and buts and maybes.

Sometimes on Sundays, once Burza had achieved her early morning two and half hours' cleaning stint at the bakery, and Lily being free since Marion was home for Jack, the four lifelong friends, Burza, Lily, Andy and Richard, would set out.

On these outings the girls would chip in and take turns to pack sandwiches and cakes and bottles of fizzy lemonade. The boys would bring fruit and sweets. Andy never failed to buy chocolate. Then they would set out on the long everlasting walk to Whipps Cross and the Hollow Ponds. There it was grassland and gorse bushes stretching away, far away to the Eagle Pond with its fairytale white swans and fancy Rising Sun pub that had tables and chairs set in the gardens outside.

But for the foursome, Hollow Pond would do. To its left, oak trees, to its right grazing land for sheep and cows. And then there was the vast pond itself with its rich mud so beloved by frogs, and tall handsome rushes for ducks to play hide and seek. There were tiddlers for children to catch in their penny fishing nets, jam jars filled with murky water ready and waiting on the bank. There were silvery minnows, and always and ever, the sticklebacks darting at bigger fish to take nips out of living flesh.

Above this seething watery world, looking like storm clouds, were the huge shadows of rowing boats. Hired by the hour, or longer if one was rich, this was the supreme joy for the four. To row lazily through sunlit liquid, hearing children's laughter lifting through the air, and seeing mums unpacking bread-and-dripping feasts, setting them carefully on patches of heat-tanned grass. Alternatively one could pull over to the little central island, tie up and drink and talk.

Not for them the fact that news had filtered through of the brutal killings by Heinrich Himmler's SS troops – who were by now subject to few rules except those of their own making. Nor that the German Chancellor Adolf Hitler's name was getting known more and more. That was news to do with the wider world. They were concerned only with the news in and around Solomon Street.

So that Sunday afternoon was filled with the talk of Pete Frazer's latest boxing bout in the Youth Club, which he had won hands down; of Vin and his other two sons' various shenanigans in the ring. Of Fanny's old man, Todd Lyons, getting six months for third offence thieving. The silly old sod had actually thanked the judge! And what about Fanny yelling out, telling the whole court to, 'Eff Orf!'

Then the laughing, and Andy's outrageous flirting with Burza stopped and the serious subjects surfaced. Richard's uncle looked as if he really would be popping off this time.

'Don't take it so badly,' Lily told Richard. 'Just think back. You have been telling us that Gippo's been dying for years.'

'He's a goner this time,' Richard said gruffly. Richard had grown even more good-looking with the years. He seldom smiled, but he had a quiet kind of pride. He was always trying to fashion himself on what he had heard of Jack London in his youth. 'He don't know me these days,' he went on. 'I wanted to stop with him, but they said there was no need.' His dark cheeks went beetroot red. 'I loathe hospitals. They're dying shops. Just places where you go to get finished off for good and all.'

'Oh shut up, Richard,' Burza said quickly, her worried eyes belying her words. 'We've heard all this tommy-rot before.'

'It's different this time,' Richard replied bleakly. 'He looks like a skeleton in that bed, all skin and bone. I don't know how people can get so thin and still live.'

'Don't be silly.' Lily's tone was warm and loving. 'My dad's as thin as a rake, and he's very much alive.' A thought struck her and she turned to Burza. 'I noticed that Betsy's putting on weight. I reckon all those free cakes and things you have off Basil are sticking to her hips.'

'I don't know about Betsy,' Burza replied, trying not to go pink, 'but Peg's like a whale. She's a week overdue, by her reckoning. We can't wait! You ought to see the knitting that Clara's done.'

121

'Hey,' Andy said, and he sounded unusually serious. 'Something's worrying you, Burz, I can tell. What's up?'

'Nothing. Nothing really, except – Oh shit! It's nothing to do with me and ...'

'The way you use that word,' Lily began, 'is quite unnecessary and—'

'Shut up, Prunes and Prisms,' Burza told her easily. 'Besides, you're being very bad-mannered indeed. Correcting people in front of company is quite awful! Hasn't darling Aunty Marion ever told you that?'

Lily went the colour of a peony.

'Twopence you two don't have a bull and cow,' Andy burbled.

'We never row,' Lily told him sweetly, dimple twinkling. 'We have known each other the whole of our fourteen years and we have *never* had a row.'

'Only because you won't say anything back, Soppy Soft!' Burza laughed and put her arm round Lily's waist. 'You just button up your lips and then go your own way. I remember how you refused to call Bo-Bo Snowy like Marion said, just because she thought Bo-Bo was a funny name. And there was a time when ...'

'Don't change the subject,' Andy cut in. 'What's up, Burza? Something's on your mind, I can tell.'

'I can't put my finger on it,' Burza said and frowned, 'but I have been thinking that something's wrong at Steadmans. Old Basil seems pretty put out about things in general, and Lucy's gone quiet – you know what a jolly old soul she usually is. And Angel's really gone in on herself.'

'Being in business for yourself isn't all honey,' Richard told her. 'It can't be. Look at my guv'nor for a start.'

'What do you mean?' This was Lily, raising her brows and looking surprised.

'Sorry.' Richard's high-cheekboned, lean and handsome face now wore an uncomfortable expression. 'I spoke without thinking, that's all.'

'I want you to explain,' Lily told him, quietly serious. 'If you can't be honest with me, Richard, I would be very, very sad. Please tell me what you meant.'

'Only that in spite of all the money he's raking in, all the

122

windows he has, your dad can be an old misery at times.'

'I don't know what you mean, Richard.'

He took in a deep breath and told her what everyone else knew. 'Jack London picks holes in what we do. We all dread it when we see his wheelchair heading our way. I wouldn't mind, but I take as much pride in my work as he used to do.' He flushed an even deeper red. 'And if you tell him what I said it'll be curtains for us for good and all. He's that sort!'

Dark-brown eyes looked into violet-blue and a smile was exchanged. Such a smile that Burza's heart caught in her throat. She felt momentarily lost, left out, afraid. For one glorious moment, way back, she had thought, had believed that she and Pete Frazer would be like Lily and Richard. Oh, nothing had been said openly to the others or even between them. But to all intents and purposes, Richard and Lily were a pair. One day they would both wake up and realise the fact. Just as she, Burza, had for one brief evening believed that she and that hateful Pete ... She hastily pushed the thought away as Andy put his arm round her shoulders and began to sing tunelessly.

'I'll be your sweetheart, if you'll be mine. All my life I'll be your Valentine. Bluebells I'll gather, take them and be true. When I'm a man my plan will be to marry you ...'

'Put a sock in it!' the other three moaned, then laughed and began to scuffle together happily on the grass.

It was Monday evening. Charlie was explaining to Peg how he had heard on a mate's wireless set that the old German, President Hindenburg, had died a while back. They were walking back to Solomon Street having bought themselves a penn'orth of chips each.

'Luverly grub this,' Charlie said, licking vinegar off his fingers. 'It seems to taste better straight out of the newspaper.'

'Oh?' Peg smiled. 'So I ain't such a bloody nuisance after all? I mean, askin' for chips at this time of night? Oo-er!'

'All right, Peg, ol' girl,' he chuckled. 'I know being in the family way lets you get away with murder, but just you wait till our nipper's born.'

'And then?' she laughed up at him, daring him with her eyes.

'I'll love yer just the same, silly narner. Fool, ain't I? Now what was I saying?'

'Some boring news your mate heard on the wireless. Why he still hangs about up Temple Mills I'll never know! Must be barmy, that's all I can say. He should be trying to enjoy his life, not always looking back to when he worked with trains, and then went to war.'

'Peg, he's not like you make him sound.'

'No? Not really?' she jeered. 'But according to you, he's on about something that happened in the world last week! Last week's dead and gone too, don't he know that?'

'Peg, you've got a wasp in your mouth tonight. That's not like you. 'Sides, he's a nice old boy.'

'Couldn't I have summink more important on me mind, Charlie-boy?' she asked edgily, then relented. 'Sorry. You was saying as how old 'Enery really and truly got het up.'

'That's right. Well, he served in the war you see, and he saw the really rotten side of things. Blood and guts and all that, so he hates Krauts. Now this bloke Hitler has announced that he has joined Hindenburg's powers with his own and has the title Führer, which is German for Leader. Get it, Peg? The German army has accepted this Hitler as their Commander-in-Chief and every soldier has to swear an oath of personal loyalty to him.'

'And so? What's wrong with that?'

'That's the bit that's really making Henry's blood boil. But then anything to do with the German army would, since the old boy was at Flanders. Everyone working at Temple Mills knows about it. Henry's got a medal, you know.'

'So you've told me – a million times! Well, I think he's daft to worry about fings wot's happening in another country. The war's over and done with. We have our own lives to look forward to. Like our baby's what's soon to be born. Charlie, that's all that should matter to us.'

'Too right,' Charlie grinned. 'You and me and our own little bread-snapper, eh Peg?'

'Talking about bread, Chas, I dunno whether I should 'ave ate so much today,' Peg grimaced. 'I feel bloated, and I've got a hell of a backache.'

That night baby George Charles Harris was born.

The next morning the kitchen of number six Solomon Street shook under the weight of a terrible row.

Chapter Thirteen

The house smelled lovely. Of warmth, and toast, and something meaty with onions already beginning to stew for later on. There was a hint of floor polish, and the smell of the Phulnana face powder Betsy used. Betsy always wore make-up these days. Powder, Tangee lipstick, and mascara, not forgetting the dab of honeysuckle perfume placed sparingly behind the ears. There was the faint tang of Dicky's cologne in the air, too, and the hair cream he used. It all melted and intermingled. A pot-pourri unique to number six Solomon Street.

Burza smiled, delighted with the world. Oh what wonderful, wonderful news! Mother and child doing well, and Charlie overboard with delight, words tumbling out of his mouth as he'd rushed into the house. 'A boy! It only took her two hours,' he yelled loud enough for the world to hear.

'Never on your life!' Clara had exclaimed, lips wobbling. 'And about time too. Never thought I'd see the day.'

'An' there we was, gorging ourselves on chips! Ma, she'd been having backaches for a night and day already, so it must have been starting then. She ain't even had to have no stitches!'

'That's my Peg. "I'll do it right, I'll do it proper" is what she always says. Now she's given you a son, just what you both wanted.'

'He's our own little George, eh Ma? George just as she hoped, and then Charles after me. Blow me, I'm a dad! Ma, I'm a dad!'

'And I'm a gran at last,' Clara had smilingly replied. 'Good on yer, boy. I can't wait ter see 'im. Give Peg my love.'

Charlie had rushed off to work, beside himself, and Dicky had grinned his quiet but happy grin, accepted the cigar handed to him – which he would never smoke – and gone back to bed. Now he had overslept, just a little, but he was in a rush.

Burza called out goodbye to Dicky as he ran back downstairs and straight out to work. Dicky was fastidious about keeping time.

Having made up her bed, Burza was following Dicky downstairs when she heard the raised voices. She stayed still, listening, lips trembling. The tension between Rosie, Betsy and herself had been mounting. Now it seemed the excitement of a new baby in the family had brought things to a head. She heard Betsy first.

'So this is it, eh Mum?' Betsy snapped nastily. 'Gawd 'elp us!'

'Don't talk to 'er like that.' Rosie was defending her mother. 'Mind yore effin' mouth.'

'Oi, you two!' This was Clara. 'We might be rough an' ready, but Rosie, I'll skin you alive if you ever breathe that F word in my house again.'

'Well!' Rosie exploded. 'When I was stickin' up for yer. There's gratitude!'

'Don't need no one to stick up for me, gel,' Clara said stoutly. 'Never have and never will.'

'What about all that scrubbin' me and Betsy did?' Rosie flared. 'Made our hands bleed. Yes, bleed!'

'Going ter last yer for the rest of your perishin' lives, is it?' Clara sneered. 'The few rotten doorsteps you scrubbed for me while I was grieving? Well, I ain't bloody well sittin' on me arse no more. Now the pair of you shut your mouths or you'll feel the back of me hand, big as you are.'

'Oh yes, yes, yes!' Betsy shouted. 'Bloody good, innit? Mum's come to life at last, and wot's caused it, eh? Baby George! So now you'll be boastin' and droolin' and making the biggest fuss in the world of Peg's kid and—'

'Your very own nephew, Betsy, an' yours too, Rosie. You should be as thrilled as me. My Gawd, talk about miserable little bitches. This is s'posed to be a day of joy.'

'Mine'll be an outcast, ain't that right?' Betsy screamed,

beside herself. 'To be kept quiet about, and hid behind locked doors – and loathed because he's brought shame to this wonderful palace of a house. And—'

'What are you saying, gel?' Clara asked very quietly.

'Bleedin' hell!' Rosie gasped, eyes wide in her face.

Beyond holding anything back now, Betsy yelled, 'And even his name has been stole. He was to be a George.' She laughed harshly, tears tearing down her cheeks. 'But that would 'ave been too bloody awful, wouldn't it? My kid would 'ave tainted Dad's memory, ain't that right? Oh Gawd, I hate you. I hate you all!'

'Well, I don't hate you, gel,' Clara said, suddenly strong and defiant. 'An' I never could and never will. Come 'ere.' She opened her arms and Betsy fell into them, sobbing as if her heart would break.

'That's right!' Rosie snapped, coming out of her shock. 'Too bloody right! Now you've got someone else to mind about, ain't yer, Mum? I'm overlooked again – just for a soddin' change, eh? Don't give a shit about me what don't cause you no trouble, do yer?'

Clara looked over Betsy's head, eyes wise, eyes kind, eyes burning hot with unshed tears.

'The day I don't think the world of my own youngest, Rose,' she replied with clear honesty, 'will be the day I lay down and die. You silly old sausage!'

'I'm sorry,' Rosie choked, seeing the truth of it at last. 'Sorry, sorry, sorry!'

'Like I said,' Clara's voice was now calm and quiet and full of care, 'you're my baby, an' always was. Come 'ere, you little demont. Come 'ere!'

They did not notice Burza creeping out of the house. She closed the door very quietly behind her and made her way to Steadmans.

It was early still and neither the destitute ladies holding bread tickets, nor the women waiting to buy stale, had arrived. An old ragbag of a man with a cardboard notice round his neck that read *Injured Soldier* was huddled against the warm brick of the bakehouse wall. His clothes were threadbare, he was unwashed and his shoulders had the stoop of abject failure. But his boots, even though barely holding together, shone. He stood as near to attention as he could as Burza passed and gave her a salute.

'Good morning, sir,' Burza said as she always did. 'I won't be two ticks.'

She knocked on the side door and Basil opened it at once.

'Early, ain't yew?' he said and looked furtively behind her. 'Anyone about, girly?'

'Only my old soldier.'

'Oh yes. Staff sergeant he was. Poor old devil. Never think he was a young 'un once, would yew? Most of his lot are dead and gone. Killed stone dead, an' with no chance. All old hat now, of course. No one remembers nor cares. I bet he don't give a tinker's cuss about the king and country he fought for so hard. Bet he wonders where the land fit for heroes went.'

Burza had a swift memory of George smiling and teasing, and him saying, 'Everything's all right, eh? I've got a job, and as nice a bunch of kids as ever breathed. Yes, I'm a real lucky chap. And though I've got an ol' woman what scares me to death 'cause she hits so hard, on the good side she's tiptop at making me steak and kidney pud.'

Her lovely almond-shaped eyes twinkling, Clara would give him a wallop, just as he knew she would.

'And you can stop your sauce, George Cuttings.' The threat was always the same. 'If yer don't, it'll be curtains. All right?'

Yes, Burza thought, the dearly beloved George had been lucky indeed.

Outside the old soldier waited. A lonely, forgotten old soul who had never had the good fortune to have someone like Clara. Burza looked at Basil.

'May I give him ...'

''Course yew can. Lucy made him up something to keep him going,' Basil cut in easily. 'Oh, and she put in a bottle of hot sweet tea. It's in the carrier bag over there.' He looked uneasily over Burza's shoulder. 'Yew sure as there was no one following?'

'No, Basil. Should there be?'

'No. Just had some mischief-makers hanging round lately, that's all. They get under Lucy's skin a bit, but everthing's in hand. Now, girly, go and give the old soldier his goody bag.'

'You're one of the kindest men I know,' Burza told him impulsively. 'And if I get my hands on any of them mischief-makers you're on about, I'll let them have what for!'

'Gawd bless my soul,' Basil laughed, his round rosy face losing its strain. 'What a little firecracker yew are. Go on, girly, give the man his bag and then get ready for the morning rush. And pray to God that Ethel Jacobs gives us a miss for once.'

For the rest of the day Burza's mind was in a whirl. With joy for Peg and Charlie, with happiness for Rosie and Betsy who now both knew they had their beloved mum wholeheartedly on their side. And also in a maze of pleasure because now, at last, the two sisters would cease to loathe and detest her own half-gippo self. But amidst all of this there was puzzlement. Who were the unknown mischief-makers that were turning a lovely couple like Basil and Lucy into a bunch of nerves?

Mightn't it be a good idea to knock on the door of number eight and mention the business to Rene Frazer? She would tell Vin, head of the Firestones, and perhaps he and ... Again she saw that picture of Pete, and blinked the idea away. She might bump into Pete, who just might be home from work. Being a big-head, yes surely that since Miss Allthorpe must have made him believe he was some sort of comforting God, he would believe that she was making excuses to see him. Perish the thought!

Suddenly, unbelievably, she wanted to blub like a two-year-old.

Chapter Fourteen

Baby George was now three weeks old. How incredible, Burza was thinking as she knocked on Lily's door and waited. The baby was a wonderfully contented little soul and at this stage even managed to look like his grandad, though his eyes were deep blue, not silvery grey.

'They'll get lighter, Peg,' Clara had said with utmost certainty, and choked through her smile. 'Gawd, it would 'ave been nice if your dad had . . . '

'Mum!' Peg, so like Clara in temperament, had whispered. 'Shut up!'

'Don't say it again,' Burza had pleaded too. 'We all feel the same. You know we do.'

As the days had crept by, it was Clara who said briskly, 'No more thousands of visits, Peg. I'll try and keep out of it for a while. What with all the Harrises and our lot traipsing up 'ere, I reckon poor little Georgy's all but wore out.'

'Don't you never keep away, Mum,' Peg said quickly. 'I need you to keep Florrie at bay. Cow!'

'What's she on about now?'

'Her washing line being stuffed up with napkins and baby clothes.' Peg took in a deep defiant breath and looked fierce. 'My Georgy's going to have the whitest, brightest things agoing. Ain't he the most wonderful little soul, Mum? I'm going to be so good to 'im! I'm a mum like you at last. And like you, I'll do it right an' I'll do it proper.'

'I've got two washing lines out back, remember?' came the reply. 'And as for always doing it right, thanks.' Clara smiled her saucy smile. 'But you wouldn't have thought I'd done so

130

bloody good if you'd 'ave heard the carry on in our house the morning he was born.'

'So I heard – from Betsy herself. She's really sorry, Mum, and she can't keep her hands off Georgy. She keeps on telling him about his new baby cousin wot's coming. I'm glad you've stuck up for her. She ain't a bad kid. She ought ter tell Simpson about 'er state of health, though. What's his real name, by the way? We can't have an Uncle Blood-nut for our Georgy, can we?'

'Dunno his real handle, gel. Betsy always says Simpson.' Clara shook her head then added wisely, 'When kids hide behind their second name it usually means they're ashamed of their first. P'raps he's called Alphonse or summink equally chronic.'

Burza and Peg creased up, and so did Clara. All forgetting their troubles for a while.

Burza's dream of Rosie turning into a happy soul and actually accepting her dad had died a swift death. Not surprising really, Burza thought wryly. Behind Clara's back it was always the same. 'Cuckoo in our nest!' 'Bleedin' gippo!' 'You weren't never wanted by no one.' 'Effin' foundling.' 'That bitch Burza' – this to Betsy who had finally turned round and snapped, 'Rosie, for Christ's sake shut up!'

Burza had wanted to weep with relief at that. Now the truth was out, Betsy was back on an even keel. Had actually stuck up for her, Burza's own unwanted self. But that was wrong! She *was* wanted! Clara wanted her – she had said so in no uncertain terms.

Clara, that fine, indomitable woman who now stalked about her work and local area with her head held high, actually wanted her brother's child. 'Make no mistake about that!' she had said loud and clear.

Clara had taken no time in announcing to the world at large that having wee baby Georgy was the most wonderful present the good God could have given her – and that one day soon, she was to be blessed with a second grandchild. That it was her hope for a little girl. Then with chin up, and her special fiery look, stating, 'An' if it is, I hope and pray my Betsy will call the little 'un Clara!'

'Oh, Mum!' Betsy wept. 'Oh, Mum. Thanks!'

131

Now it was a fine Sunday morning, golden and glorious, and sootladen bricks boasted an orange dew. There was a smell of frying kippers, and from further along, streaky bacon being frizzled, also the whiff of browning toast. It seemed that at least the top of Solomon Street was beginning the day well. Even Clara's place was filled with the atmosphere of yesterday's cold potatoes being fried in beef dripping. These days Betsy couldn't get enough of them and Clara lovingly indulged her. This upset Rosie, of course, and she'd pull a face and carry on about how many spoonfuls of sugar Betsy was putting in her tea.

There was still no reply from Lily and Burza knocked again. Perhaps Jack was out and Lily was in the lav. She must be in the house, otherwise she would have said. Now, as Burza waited on the doorstep of number twelve she wondered what to do, whether she should mention her worries about the Steadmans to Lily. Her friend definitely seemed to be growing away from her these days, becoming more and more under her father's thumb. Not because Jack was stronger willed, but because Lily herself was so full of quiet and gentle love that she wanted, above all, to please her irascible old dad.

Today was a home day, no trips to the Hollow Pond, which was just as well. Marion had to work, which meant that Lily would be tied to Jack's apron strings – and he liked nothing more. Of course, if he could manage it that Lily was without her shadow Burza, all the better. Both girls knew that. It was always Lily who gave way. Tall and graceful, as lovely as her name, she would smile her slow sweet smile, raise one brow in the questioning manner she had – and understanding perfectly, Burza would make her excuses and leave.

On this particular Sunday Richard and Andy were away somewhere. They were cycling mad these days, whereas the girls had neither bikes nor the inclination to ride for miles, trying to keep up with two speed-cracker devils. So, to all intent and purpose Burza had most of this day to herself. But she wanted a chat with Lily, needed to think and plan. Her concern for the Steadmans was growing. She wanted a few minutes alone with her dearest friend to chew the matter over. Lily, the quiet and thoughtful one, usually came up with an answer or two.

The door flew open.

'Burza! We didn't hear you. We were in the garden.' Lily

was so happy, her eyes were like dancing crystals. 'Oh, come in and see what Dad has. All of the very latest things! He's back in his room now. Come in, dear.'

Willy-nilly Burza found herself, not in the blue and white kitchen, but in the downstairs front – an honour if there ever was one – looking at Carters latest catalogue. Carters were famous for invalid furniture, and Jack's original self-propelling chair had cost no less than five pounds fifteen shillings.

Jack, in his wheelchair, a plaid blanket round his waist for all it was warm, looked pleasant enough. In a good mood he was a fine, good-looking man. Usually, though, he hated fate for disabling him, and it showed.

Now he was much richer, Jack was looking at a new selection of illustrations – invalid tricycles of all kinds for sale, their prices upwards from a hefty twenty-four pounds fifteen shillings. Marvellous things! Even Aspy's long dark leaves seemed to be quivering in the speckled glitter-beam of window light. Almost like a reflection of Jack's anticipation and pleasure.

'Tomorrow I'll go along to Great Portland Street and see the whole range personally, Chickybit,' he was saying in his deep voice. 'Nothing like looking at things first hand. I'll get young Cuttings to come along with me. The West End's not like being on the other side of the world, is it? Perhaps we'll make a day of it.'

'How nice,' Lily exclaimed. 'Perhaps we can have a pot of tea and some cakes. I love those scones with strawberry jam and cream.'

'No, dear, this will be a long haul. I don't want Sid to have to worry about getting us both there in one piece. It'll be hard enough managing me. You must stay here like the jewel you are and keep an eye on things.' Jack took out his pipe and began carefully stuffing tobacco into the bowl.

'But what about the window rounds?' Lily queried. 'I'm sure that you and I could manage the journey very well.'

Jack struck a match and lit his pipe, then puffed for a second or two until satisfied. Then he leaned back in his wheelchair and told her briskly, 'Richard and Andy must use a bit of effort for a change. A few dollops of elbow grease, eh? In my day I put that, as well as plenty of guts, into all that I did. Not that the young believe in such principles. These days it's the easiest route that's always taken.' He blew blue smoke from the side of his mouth, then went on, 'Hard work has never killed anyone.'

Lily coloured, but said nothing. She should have stuck up for the boys. Should have! Burza glared. And even though she knew that Jack was deliberately goading in order to get her, Burza, to have a fit of temper and flounce out, she did not turn tail and retreat as usually. Instead she looked at him straight and refused to budge.

'That's a real fact, Mr London,' she told him firmly. 'I agree that only worry kills. It's never plain old-fashioned hard work! And so from what I've seen, Richard and Andy look all set to live very long lives.'

Jack's blue eyes were stone cold. 'What's that? What did you say?'

'I said that from all I've seen, Richard and Andy do their fair share, and what's more, take great pride in all they do.'

'I think you should stick to serving mumpers, my girl,' he told her grandly, 'and not poke your nose into where it's not wanted.'

'Mumpers, is it?' Burza's cheeks began to flame. 'The poor who have to line up for hours to get their measly hand-outs from the Relief Office.'

'Not the Means Test? The Relief Office, is it? Don't you people still usually use the term bunghouse?' he asked sarcastically. 'Either way the outcome's the same. Tickets for a penny or even better, three halfpence for stale bread.' He added grandiosely, 'And if it wasn't for me, my workers would probably be lining up alongside them.'

Filled with contempt, Burza stared at Jack London and tried to remember that he lived with constant pain. That his life, or at least the life he loved, had ended on the day he had lost his leg. That even though he felt he was a cut above all the other people in Solomon Street, he was a prisoner here because memories of his dead wife held him chained. He had even gone so far as to tell Lily once, 'If I left this house, Chickybit, it'd be like leaving your mum. She's here, in the walls. I sense her every time I hear the St Christopher bells.'

Lily had wept on the day she had told Burza of this.

So all Jack London really had left was Marion, who couldn't wait to spend as much time as possible working for Drews. And even more important, there was Lily. But surely Lily would marry and leave him one day. With Pete Frazer, Burza though sourly, if both families had anything to do with it.

Suddenly, for no apparent reason, Burza felt rage mounting. Of course, she seethed, Jack London had his three workers in his pocket, but that's all they were to him. Workers! So what did that leave? Aspy, a stupid old aspidistra plant his wife had liked. He thought more of a bunch of green leaves than he did of three fine young men.

Jack London was a rotten big-headed snob. Burza's fury grew even more as she accepted yet again that Lily was like butter in his hands. She looked at her friend, who was smiling sadly at her father, but saying nothing. It was too much. Really Lily should be ashamed!

'Mr London,' Burza said in a tomb-cold voice, 'if it hadn't been for, firstly Richard, and then Sid, and now Andy of course, you might have been standing in that mumpers line yourself. And do you know something? I'd sooner be one of the deserving poor than anything like mean-minded old you.'

For the first time in her life she swung on her heels, and left her friend to it. Absolutely furious with Lily, she left the squeaky clean, soulless number twelve in a rush. Almost blinded by tears, she bumped straight into Peter.

'What's the hurry?' he asked, his large hands reaching out to steady her.'

'Nothing.'

'Really? If that's the case, would you like to spend today with me?'

His face was like sunlight through a blur of grief. She felt her heart leap and her soul yearning.

'Where?' she quavered. 'Could it – could it be away from here?'

'I'm going to see Roan. He's a beauty and growing apace. You haven't been to see him lately, have you?'

She felt her cheeks burn. He knew why she hadn't been to see Roan, of course he did. He was probably feeling very pleased with himself. Guessing how embarrassed she felt. Knowing how odd he had made her feel. Smug devil! He probably believed he could make her fall into his arms like an overripe cherry. Well, she would show him!

'Thank you,' she told him tremulously. 'I'd like to visit Roan very much. I – I haven't been because I work for an hour or so on Sunday, cleaning at Steadmans.'

'I know. And after that you all go to the Hollow Ponds.'

'Why?' She was feeling better already. 'Have you been spying on us?'

'Living so near it's hard not to know what goes on,' he told her easily. 'I've often envied you.'

'You have?' She raised her brows. 'But you could have come too.'

'Not really. Four's company. Five's a crowd.'

'Don't be silly. We are all good friends, that's all.'

'Are you sure about that?'

'Positive.'

'Better and better,' he teased. 'Hey, there's a Green Line going our way. Run!'

They caught the bus, panting and laughing, and sat beside each other allowing their bodies to rock in unison with the motion of the vehicle.

'I really like our old Chingford lady,' Burza said. 'Did you know that Miss Allthorpe used to sing and dance on the music halls?'

'I did. And that Granger used to be her ex-manager, and has looked after her for donkeys' years.'

'I reckon he loves her, and always has. And she's never truly loved him in return, has she? Oh, how sad.'

'She often treats the poor old devil like dirt,' Pete agreed. 'She was sold on a certain Mr Sheen. He was a stage-door Johnny by all accounts, very married and very rich. In his turn, he was darned keen on her.'

'But not enough to leave his wife?'

'Oh come on!' Pete grinned in a cheeky masculine way, then went on: 'However, when Sheen died, he left her pots of money. God knows what his relatives thought. She didn't give a monkey's though. She bought the house – which was named Manchu, but she calls it her digs. "Let's go back to the digs, dear boy," she says to me. Anyway, Granger followed her there when she retired.'

136

'And how did she get to know about all of us?'

'Easy. Her old gardener was born down Solomon Street. His own son stayed on. The old lady had a bit of a soft spot for the son. She's been a right old goer, you know. The son's name was Jack. That was long before our time. She gave the Firestones, headed by my grandad in those days, cash to look out for Jack's widow, who was a consumptive. The woman didn't last too long after the death of her old man. The whole family's gone now.'

'How do you know all this?'

'From Miss Daisy herself.' Pete winked, his ready smile lighting his face and dancing in his eyes. 'She likes a little tipple. She drinks elderflower wine. Granger makes heaps of the stuff – and won prizes with it on the local village show last year. Anyway, the old gel and I get on. I like her and she likes me. She's fond of you, by the way. And a bit fed up because Lily doesn't visit very often. She's rather forthright when she talks about Jack.'

'Don't mention old Big-head!' Burza said pithily. 'And I suppose you mean that Miss Allthorpe believes Lily kowtows to him?'

'Well, she does, doesn't she?'

'No! Not really.' On the defensive now, Burza went on, 'Lily loves her dad very much and – and she appreciates him even more since we lost George. It made her think. It made us all think – and deep down, to be scared of death.'

'There's a big difference between loving and slaving, mate,' he said in a no-nonsense way. 'And well you know it. What's more, Jack won't rest until he splits you two up. You know that too, don't you?'

'Only death will do that.' Burza's response was swift, then remembering, she pulled a face and added, 'I hope.'

'Ha!' he teased. 'Not so certain about things all of a sudden? Tell me what happened.'

In spite of loathing and detesting Pete Frazer, Burza told him word for word what had happened, finishing up quietly, 'I was so livid that I – I said things I shouldn't have. Lily might never speak to me again.'

'Don't be daft,' he reassured her. 'My dear old Burz, you are young Lily's safety line. One day she'll blow, and when she does, things will never be the same.'

'Now you're being the soppy 'aporth,' Burza told him and

heard herself actually giggle. Pete's grin blazed out and he looked like a picture Burza had seen at school, of a handsome statue.

He took her breath away. He really did. Her legs turned to water. She wanted to faint. Her heart was pounding away. Her mouth was dry. This can't be love, she thought buoyantly. It's more like a disease! But in spite of all that, amazingly, she hadn't felt so happy for years.

They reached their stop and began walking up the lane towards Manchu when Burza said quietly, 'There's something bothering the Steadmans, Pete. Something really rotten – I can sense it.'

'Well, seeing things don't help much,' he told her straight. 'If you're sure about this, find out some facts. Understand? Find out what's what, then let me know.'

'And you'll sort it?'

'For you, dear, anything.'

'Don't – don't tease me, Pete,' she implored, and looked up into his face.

The sun shining behind him made a nimbus of his hair. His eyes were filled with golden twinkles. His lips were gentle and framed his strong even white teeth when he smiled. He was a god, she thought dazedly, a Greek god.

'I'm not teasing,' he told her. 'I mean every word. And when we're alone in the stable, I'll prove it.'

'You don't half go on,' she told him and chuckled richly. 'You really take the biscuit, Pete Frazer.'

'It's more than a biscuit I'm after,' he replied and began to chase after her as she picked up her heels and ran.

That evening they led Roan back inside. They had worked together on arrival, mucking-out and grooming the fine young animal. Roan was no thoroughbred, but he was loved and adored and deserved the best. They had stood, Burza and Pete, hand in hand watching him run free in the field, kicking up his heels and shaking his mane and having the time of his life. Now he was settled.

The stable was warm and smelled of newmown hay. The young horse, that had been due for the knacker's, then cats' meat had Pete not bought him in time, began munching happily. Everything was quiet and peaceful.

Granger came along to tell them that Miss Allthorpe would like to see them at eight o'clock or thereabouts, then left them to it.

'Alone at last,' Pete said firmly. 'Come here!'

She struggled, of course she did. But not hard enough to make him stop. And all the while her heart was racing and the delight was rippling through her veins. How strong and powerful he was. How magnificent a man. And he wanted her. She wanted him, but he must never actually know. Never ever take her for granted. That would never do.

'Kiss me,' he commanded. 'Come on, Burza, kiss me full on the mouth. Like this ...'

And then his lips were on hers and the whole world spun round while she was drowning in his golden-brown eyes. And in spite of all her self-warning, her previous doubts and fears, her arms were reaching up, embracing him, and she was kissing him back with the innocent and joyous abandon of the very young. Then he began whispering in her ear, lovely things, gentle things, exciting things, and she wanted to believe all that he said. Wanted to so fiercely that she threw caution to the winds and did not struggle as he began gently edging her backwards until at last she was lying beside him in the clover-scented hay.

His hands began caressing her, cupping her breasts, slipping under the red blouse she wore. She gasped and breathed his name on a sigh. She knew that she wanted him to go on loving her for ever. That with this fine and powerful person she felt complete. A whole being, rather than the child that had been so wholeheartedly dumped by not one but two parents. Baby Georgy was lucky, she thought blissfully, to be so loved by Charlie and Peg. And now she was experiencing real and true love too.

She clung on to Pete, wildly, determined never to let him go.

Suddenly, like a freezing blast, cold reality returned. As if from a million miles away they heard a voice. A feminine voice that held a kind of firmness for all it sounded lazily amused.

'It might be better to stop that.'

They sprang apart, blinking in the half light.

Framed in the doorway was a slim, striking-looking woman

of thirty-five or so. A fascinating lady, with a wild waterfall of dark hair, large thickly-lashed dark eyes, and a generous mouth. She wore a scarlet skirt and low-necked but full-sleeved, colourfully embroidered white blouse. Large hooped earrings dangled against her cheeks. Rings and bracelets glinted gold. Round her neck were strings of red beads. Fiery-looking and free, she was the epitome of Carmen.

'Buzz off, nosy-parker,' Pete said, shocked and clearly put out. 'Why don't you mind your own business? And while we're at it, you're on private property. Aren't you supposed to be in Middle Meadow camp?'

'I'm supposed to be where I am, at the time I'm there,' she told him, arrogantly tossing her head. Her eyes, very black, now flashing cold fire. 'And by the look of things, I'm in the right place at exactly the right time.' Her glance left Pete's face and she began to carefully study Burza who was now sitting up. Her stomach was churning, and she was wishing the floor would open up and swallow her. Suddenly, blindingly, *she knew.*

She hastily pulled down her blouse and was acutely aware that there was straw in her hair. She felt guilty of every crime in the book and wanted to die the death. Then, because the newcomer's expression held open mockery, Burza's momentary sense of awe and wonder vanished.

'Well,' the woman said, 'I was told eight o'clock, but curiosity got the better of me. So you're Burza.'

'How strange,' Burza told her coolly. 'I had just been thinking of you. So here you are. After all this time! You're my mother, aren't you?'

'And if I am?'

'I don't know.' Burza suddenly wanted to laugh, and she wanted to cry, then she wanted to run away from the mind-kicking, hard and totally unbelievable truth.

After all the years of dreams and plans, and imagined scenes of loving reunion, there was nothing! Instead of all the tearful love-laden mother-daughter scenes she had pictured, there was only a blank wall in her mind.

She felt naught, not a speck, not an ounce, not a single thing. There were no tears. At least, not for this stranger who had chosen the worst possible moment to appear.

140

Burza's mind raced. She found herself searching for the emotions she had expected and hoped, dreamed and prayed for all of her life. The only true sense she now had was one of ... irritation?

The striking-looking woman was an interloper, she thought. A mere intruder who had put a stop to what had looked like being the most wonderful experience of her life. A truly longed-for involvement with Pete.

'The lady of the house,' Kiffa Webb was saying easily, 'invited me at eight so that you and me could talk.' She shrugged. 'But I don't see much point to it. Do you?'

'No,' Burza told her flatly. 'No, I don't.'

'All right, that's it, then. I had to do as I was asked – for the sake of the others that need this camp.' Kiffa swung round, then stopped and looking over her shoulder, asked, 'Steve?'

'I have never met him either,' Burza replied evenly. 'He sends money regularly to Clara. He's not much for words, but he's like clockwork with money – for my keep.'

'Done the honourable thing then, eh?'

'Unlike you,' Burza couldn't help saying.

Her mother ignored this, remarking casually, 'A good old stick is Steve.' She shrugged expressively. 'I take it then, that this is goodbye.'

'Yes.' Burza bit her lip and turned away.

When Kiffa Webb had gone and was safely out of earshot Burza clung blindly to Peter and sobbed her heart out.

He held her tightly and kissed her tear-wet face, her eyelids and her hair. His kisses grew more fiery and she clung to him, her reactions matching his own.

After a while passion took over and they made love. Burza experienced one swift moment of an agony that was also ecstasy. Then everything became wave after wave of a fiery dream. It ended and she drifted down from the clouds, sighed and relaxed in Pete's arms. Then, side by side in the straw, with Burza clinging on to Pete's hand, they slept until Granger came to wake them up.

'Tea and fishpaste sandwiches,' he told them, 'and jam tarts. What could be better eh, kids? You look like your ma, by the way, Burza. Apart from the eyes. Yours are soft and gentle, hers ain't. How'd the meeting go?'

'You knew?'

'Miss Allthorpe's been looking out for your mum for a very long time, love. I saw Mrs Webb walking here and went back and broke the good news. How did it all go?'

'It didn't!'

'Thought so,' Granger grinned. 'Just as I said. I told Dais how it would be, but she wouldn't listen. No gel with your sort of pride could take to a woman that cold-bloodedly ditched her. That's what I said. Miss Allthorpe believed differently. But then, she always does.'

'It was very kind and wonderful of her to even try to patch things up for us,' Burza replied quietly, then she beamed, 'but it didn't matter too much. You see, Pete was there with me, and that's what counts.'

'That's just as I thought,' Granger told her and looked slyly at Pete. 'And you don't seem too hard done by neither, mate.'

'I'm a very happy chap,' Pete told him. 'Oh well, at least I don't have to worry about gippo mums. I've heard they're tough nuts to crack.'

Later, over tea and raspberry tarts, Miss Allthorpe gave her dry habitual little cough and asked to hear about the meeting. She listened carefully, then queried. 'So, you think you've seen the last of her?'

'Why yes,' Burza replied emphatically.

'Tut-tut, child. It might interest you to know that Granger and I have made a little bet. He reckons that today's seen an end to it. But I know, as sure as eggs are eggs, that this is just the beginning.'

'Oh please don't say that, Miss Allthorpe!'

'Kiffa's not of pure blood. A true Romany has his own special code of honour. He will make his way as best he can, and can sometimes be a rascal. But he's loyal to his own. Yes, come hell or high water. But to put it bluntly, the Kiffas of this world are downright tricky. And you've really put your foot in it by telling her that your father sends money.'

'To Clara. Not to me.'

'Makes no difference. Is he still a sailor?'

Burza laughed self-consciously. 'I don't really know. His letters to Clara are all posted in Australia. Clara believes that he may have settled there.'

'The other side of the world mightn't be far enough,' Daisy Allthorpe said and looked like a witch when she laughed. 'And by the cut of her jib I'd say that your mother's no saint. Oh, by the way, I had Granger drive to St Christopher's a week or so back.'

'Really?' Burza was nonplussed.

'Talking about saints reminded me. Does that angel you've had placed there look like your Clara at all? You told me that's what you wanted.'

'It is a beautiful angel,' Burza told her. 'She has a kind and gentle face. But I'm afraid that she doesn't look very much like Clara.'

'Then what made you choose her?'

'I don't really know. I – I think it has something to do with her eyes and her expression.'

'But the angel is looking down and her eyes are half-closed.'

'I know,' Burza said. 'Even so ...'

'When my time comes,' Miss Allthorpe changed the subject. 'I want you to choose an angel for me, dear. I think you have very good taste.' There was a wicked twinkle in the old lady's eyes as she cackled, 'Though I hope and pray that you never find anything that looks like me as I am now.'

Before they left Manchu Miss Allthorpe repeated her warning.

'Granger was right,' she said. 'I should have let sleeping dogs lie, and now I fear that your mother will turn up in Solomon Street. If she even looks like being a nuisance, tell her that she will have to deal with me – and so will all those of her group that camp on my land. All right?'

'Thank you, Miss Allthorpe,' Burza replied politely, instantly dismissing the warning.

All she was truly conscious of as they walked away from the house and back down the lane was the fact that Pete was holding her hand. Delicious thrills were rippling through her body. Burza found herself wishing that they had time to creep back into Roan's stable again. To make wonderful, wonderful love. Instead, she and Pete had to run hell for leather in order to catch the last bus.

143

Chapter Fifteen

'About Blood-nut,' Burza began as they were dressing in their claustrophobic over-crammed bedroom, 'I think—'

'Simpson!' Betsy told her sharply. 'And don't you start. I get enough of that from Rose. Where is she, by the way?'

'She got up early – she's gone cleaning doorsteps with Clara. That bit about bleeding knuckles lasting you and her for the rest of your lives really reached home. Rosie's going all out to prove to Clara that she's a daughter and a half.'

'That's because she always wants to prove things to Mum. You turning up 'ere really put ol' Rose's nose out of joint. Silly bitch! An' in some ways, so are you.'

'Sorry! What's Simpson's real name?'

'Sid, same as big bruv. But Siddy Simpson, can you imagine what that started up? Snakey Siddy Simps for a start. He 'ates snakes. Gawd 'elp us! They started calling 'im all sorts at school. In the end he butted some rotten kid what was twice his size – and got bashed bandy for his pains. There was blood in his red hair and all, so they yelled out "Blood-nut" – which he liked better.' Betsy gave Burza a cool, very direct stare. 'But I call 'im Simpson. All right?'

'Point taken. When are you going to tell him about the baby?'

'Leave orf! I ain't!'

'Why?'

'Mind your own bloody business.'

'Sorry. Don't get so airiated.' She added wistfully, 'I thought you and I were friends, Betsy.'

Betsy leaned over and ruffled Burza's hair. 'We are! Close

as sisters, in fact – and don't you mind Rosie. She's all right, deep down. She might call you all the names under the sun, but she wouldn't have no sod from outside 'aving a go at you. I can bear witness to that.'

'Really?' Burza didn't believe it for a moment.

'But she'd better get over wantin' ter be a mummy's girl. Wot bloke needs a wife that close to his mother-in-law? Did you know that Nick Bede quite fancied her once?' Betsy grinned and winked. 'Now he's after younger stuff. I've seen him looking in your direction – and Lily's.'

'You're tearing out my heart,' Burza replied, shuddered dramatically, and ran downstairs laughing.

Later, still thinking glorious thoughts about wonderful, dishy Pete, she neared Steadmans. Then she saw Nicky Bede leaving the premises. He was holding two large loaves of bread and everything looked normal enough – even though it was before opening time. Basil often obliged chaps leaving early for work – not that Nick worked. As the unshaven, black-eyed Nick walked by Burza he leered at her and tapped the side of his nose in a suggestive way. Chin up, cold-looking, she swept by him. Behind her now, she heard him swear. Filthy-tongued swine!

She pursed her lips. Nick Bede was a mean-spirited, bad lot. In the past he had displayed the most extraordinary cunning. He could be cruel – but didn't dare even look at Gin, the Bedes' cat. The ginger tom was Art Bede's pride and joy. Art had half-killed him once for pulling Gin's tail.

Normally a loner, apart from his mate Simpson who was at least an outrageously open rogue, Nick Bede seemed to be activated by hatred and self-interest. It was Clara's prediction that he would be hanged by the neck till he was dead one fine day. Burza shuddered at the idea.

Basil was bringing in a tray of hot loaves as Burza went into the shop.

'Goo' morning, yew!' He gave her his usual greeting, but his rosy cheeks were beetroot red, and though he smiled, his eyes were strained.

'Nick Bede,' she told him, knowing instinctively that she was right. 'So he's the mischief-maker! Why didn't I guess?'

'I don't know what yew are talking about,' Basil said and looked quickly towards the beaded curtain. This hid the

145

entrance to the downstairs parlour where Lucy was giving little Angela her breakfast. 'Come on, gel, get your skates on.'

'Half a tick,' she laughed. 'Just let me get me pinny on,' but her mind was racing. So – Nick was giving this nice couple a hard time. Well, somehow or the other she would put a stop to that! Or Peter would.

There it was again. The delicious glow at the thought of Pete. The memory of Roan's warm stable and what had happened there made her hug herself inside, and her toes curl with ecstasy. Oh crumbs! Life was so good!

Things became even better. Mrs Frazer came in. Her hair the colour of marigolds, she was a nice lady who enjoyed being a wife and mother. She was house-proud, and just loved romantic novels.

'Hello, dear,' she said to Burza. 'May I have a cottage loaf, please, and six of those currant buns?' Then as Burza handed her the carefully bagged produce and accepted the money, Rene Frazer said, 'Oh! Pete asked me to give you this – a message for Lily, I think. There seems to have been quite a ruckus going on there.'

Burza said, 'Thank you,' politely, her eyes greedily on the sealed envelope Rene Frazer handed over. As soon as she was assured of privacy, she opened the envelope and read Pete's scribbled note.

Burza, I'm up to my neck all week, work-outs and such. But I'll come over every chance I get. Don't forget we're seeing Roan on Sunday no matter what. Yours, Pete.

Burza carefully placed the prized letter in her apron pocket and felt giddy with delight. She was in a seventh heaven and therefore felt she was on wings all day.

That evening, however, all thoughts of Pete, Nick Bede and the Steadmans were banished from her mind.

Lily was waiting for her, had flung open the door even before Burza had reached for the knocker. The young girl was white-faced, shocked and openly distressed.

'Thank goodness you've arrived at last,' she said, her usually sweetly breathless voice harsh and unsteady. 'Come on, Burza, let's go.'

As the door closed behind them Jack roared out, 'Lily, come back here!'

'He sounds in a mood,' Burza said, watching Lily's strained face. 'Didn't things go well at Carters?'

'He never went. Burza, come on!'

'He's calling you.'

'Let him,' Lily said so quietly and firmly that Burza was stunned. 'Oh, do please come *on!*'

'Where are we going, Lily?'

'To Matson Street. Where else?'

'To see Richard? Why – what's happened?'

'I don't know really. Not about Richard, but I know all about Dad.' Lily's tone remained ice-cold. Her eyes were now striking blue fire and Burza, who loved her dearly, was suddenly afraid. Lily was at long last going to explode, just as Pete had said she would.

'Well,' Burza told her urgently, 'you can at least tell me what's got you so het up.'

'Richard did not turn up for work today,' Lily told her. 'Dad was furious. More horrible even than usual since he was all set to make a day of it with Sid. He's been absolutely seething. You know how he goes on! Then just before tea Richard knocked. Dad opened the door and all Richard was allowed to say was, "I'm sorry, Mr London, but ... " when Dad sacked him!'

'What?' Burza was outraged. 'Oh shit!'

'Yes, just like that. On the spot. He wouldn't let Richard say a word. Just huffed and puffed, going on and on about workers' lack of moral fibre. About illiterates letting people down – when everyone knows how marvellous all Richard's marks were at school. But Dad went on and on like a steam-roller, just because he didn't get his own way for a change.'

'Bloody hell,' Burza said, more upset for Lily than anything else. Of all the people in the world, she knew that somehow or the other Richard would always land on his own two feet.

The usually quiet and gentle Lily was still in full flow.

'And suddenly I saw my father in a different light,' she told Burza tightly. 'He was still bleating on when Richard just turned on his heels and left. I – I called after Richard, but he ignored me. His back was rigid! I could tell he was angry enough to kill. I called out some more, but he did not look back.'

'Why didn't you go after him?'

'I was going to, but Dad stopped me. He suddenly groaned,

clutched his chest and said he was ill. He was, in fact. Dr Bishop has often warned him not to lose his calm. Anyway, he soon rallied round once Richard had gone. Began to – to actually boast! It was then I decided to wait for you.'

'I'm glad,' Burza said simply. 'Matson Street for a girl on her own is not a good place. Come on, let's go and find Richard. You've seen nothing of Andy at all?'

'No. They both probably hate me as much' – Lily's voice was suddenly tomb-cold – 'as much as I now hate my father.'

'Oh shut up, Lily,' Burza said, and her concern for her friend grew.

They walked, arm in arm, along the length of Matson Street. It seemed grimmer and more filthy than usual. Kids with running sores, shaven heads, and filthy rags for clothes, teemed in doorways, kerbs, else in the middle of the dung-stinking street. They amused themselves kicking empty tins, flicking cigarette cards, fighting, swearing, then as they passed, screaming insults to the girls. Their mothers lounging against windowsills let their young get on with it.

Old hags, probably grans, evil-eyed, thin-lipped and hating the world, sat on chairs, legs open, booted feet firmly on cracked paving stones. They refused to budge as the girls tried to walk by. Had Burza and Lily been strangers they would not have been allowed a step further. As it was, recognised, they were unmolested as they diverted their steps over the disgusting rubbish-filled kerb to walk in the road.

'Solomon Street's heaven compared to this,' Burza said quietly. 'At least most of us try to keep clean and decent. Even Fanny Lyons cares about her kids.'

'I respect the Fanny Lyons of this world,' Lily said unexpectedly. 'She is what she is. Nothing more, nothing less. She is just Fanny, take it or leave it.'

'Crikey! You've changed your tune. I remember how you looked down your nose and refused to laugh like common old us when you heard that Fanny's told the whole court, "Up yer arse!"'

'Fanny was sticking up for her husband – accepting him, and going along with him no matter what. She was certainly not trying to pretend that he was anything other than a thief.'

'What's up?' Burza asked quietly. 'You really are over the

top, aren't you? You must adore the ground Richard walks on.'

'Of course I do,' Lily told her tonelessly. 'I always have. He doesn't even look at me – at least in that way. But it's not really to do with Richard, as such. My eyes are open at last.'

'Oh all right!' Burza said, swiftly changing the subject because Lily was looking so odd. 'We'll get Richard first, find out what's what, and then have a chinwag, just you and me. All right?'

Gippo Wray's hovel was shut fast. The girls knocked with their knuckles and called out for Richard, but there was no response. Burza even found the nerve to approach a couple of scruffy old men who were lounging about. She asked them where Richard was. As half-expected she received grunts followed by a grim silence. When she persisted, the sour-faced spoken response from a cloth-capped Bill-Bash'em type was a simple, 'Piss orf!'

The girls left.

'I must see Richard,' Lily gasped, heartbroken. 'I must!'

'I wonder where he's got to?' Burza said, frowning. 'Andy's, I expect. He must be home by now. Let's go to Dunton Street.'

'If Richard's as mad as I think, maybe we'd best leave it.' Lily, now ashen-faced, was tentative. 'On the other hand he might need us.'

'I reckon he's sick as a parrot to have lost his job. You know how he is – the strong silent type.' Burza's own worried expression brightened. 'Perhaps when he's cooled down, your dad will get over his tantrum and let him go back to work.'

'It's worth a try, but I can't see Richard ever working for my father again,' Lily replied quietly. 'Richard because he's been treated like dirt, and Dad because he's the most pig-headed man I know. The only one on God's earth my father ever really listens to is my aunt.'

'Then you must get her on our side.'

'Perhaps I'll go to her place of work. It won't be a scrap of use asking her anything in our house. He'll overhear things, the walls are so thin.' Lily's voice held a new bitterness. 'Marion and Dad are twin souls, so narrow, so strait-laced! In fact, those two are as thick as thieves. But I'll chance it and go to Drew's tomorrow ...'

*

149

Richard, long and lean, knee-deep in grief, waited until he was sure the girls had gone. He was crouching down beside the bundle of rags that his uncle had used as a bed, and looking down at a length of sacking covering something that stretched out, having been hidden under the width of three floorboards. Something uncanny was making Richard hold back. He wanted to find out – yet he did not. God only knew why. Perhaps because once he did, it would be like a final goodbye to the little bloke who'd stuck by his own abandoned self through thick and thin.

'Yer in'eritance,' Gippo had gasped many times. 'Git art of this bleedin' 'ole for good an' all. All right? You can piss orf nar if you want.'

'I'll not leave you.' His reply had always been the same. 'You're a wicked old devil, Gips, but you stuck by me when no one else ever did. Gave me a chance and fed me as best you could. Besides . . .' Richard's wide wonderful grin had lit up his face. 'I think I like you – and that shows I've got ruddy bad taste.'

Gippo Wray's choked whispering laugh had sounded like the rustling of dead leaves.

Now the old lag had gone. Expected though it had been for years, it had still come as a shock. He would be missed, Richard thought, and swallowed hard. But Matson Street where Richard had lived for as long as he could remember, would not! Now he'd take up Andy's folks' offer and move in with his mate. Or would he? That decent idea had been all but taken up when he, Richard, had a job. Now? He'd certainly allow no one to carry him! Above all, not the Beldons whom he liked and respected so much.

He frowned as he lifted up the sacking. Long canvas bags? Actually he'd expected nothing. This lot was probably old Gippo's tools of trade. Gips had left him his tools – jemmies and things, when he damned well knew Richard's feelings on the matter? Still, Gips had always been one for a joke. Well, no more of that lark!

Perhaps he, Richard, would just uproot himself and move away, find employment. Perhaps go to Southend. Work in a hotel or something. They catered for the rich down that way. Come to think of it, now he was alone, the world was his oyster.

Some bloody oyster, Richard thought. Not for poor old Gips it wasn't. He had been thieving all his life because it was the only way he'd known. And over the years it had paid off, as he went backwards and forwards, in and out of stir. At least, that's what the old bloke had always said. If that was true, God only knew why the old man had continued to live like a pig. Why on some days they'd all but starved.

Richard reached down and lifted out the first of the bags, then his guts began to churn. Now, rapidly, he opened the canvas bags one by one. Piles of half-crowns, two-bob bits, shillings and sixpences spilled out. Bag after bag of them. Then pound notes, ten bob notes, roll after roll, the paper money held together with elastic bands. It was all spilled out there on the floor. Richard wanted to shout and yell, or vomit? He didn't know. Hell! He was in shock. This vision of splendour was just bloody unreal!

How had his uncle hung on to all this filthy lucre? Kept his secret all the times he'd been sloshed to the sky? How he had kept his mouth shut and his spoils safely hidden, especially in this God-awful area, was a marvel in itself.

Gippo Wray had always told his orphaned nephew about the inheritance. In his turn Richard had always laughed and let the old boy burble on, naturally believing him to be drunk – which nine times out of ten he was. Latterly he had suspected that Gippo had a little nest egg tucked away somewhere. But this!

The merry old reprobate had left his only living relative a fortune.

Money received from stolen goods, of course!

Should he play the white man and give it all to the cops?

'Well, guv,' Richard said quietly to his uncle's spirit, 'you bloody old soak, you knew all the time, didn't you? That I had the makings of a hypocrite!' He smiled sombrely, yet his eyes were beginning to twinkle just the same. 'I'll give a fair old whack to the orphans of St Christopher's, eh? And in that way perhaps save our souls. And after that, I'll work out how best to use our ill-gotten gains.'

He imagined Gippo's laugh rustling like an old man's slippered feet round the room.

151

Chapter Sixteen

It was late and Lily and Burza had seen nothing of either Richard or Andy. According to Mrs Beldon, Andy was at the local swimming baths, but as far as she knew Richard was not with him. This was unusual, seeing that the two youths were as thick as thieves. Defeated at last, Lily and Burza had parted and gone to their respective homes.

Now Lily sat in the kitchen very quiet and still, reading though she had gone over the same paragraph several times without taking in a word. She was in her usual spot, sitting at the table that was covered with a blue chenille cloth.

The London kitchen was not the usual one for homes of that ilk. Its dresser now held the completed set of willow-patterned china, tureens and all. Its mantel over the range held the same white elephants, the central clock, and not a speck of dust. Indeed the whole room gleamed and sparkled, was fresh and clean, and smelled of lavender polish. Here and there were little touches of elegance, like small original water colours entitled *Misty Mountains* and *St Christopher's in Moonlight* on the opaline walls. Painted by a local artist they had cost Marion the earth and were greatly prized.

Jack had refused point blank to have them in the front room. There everything remained exactly as his Kathy had planned it all those years ago. In some respects even the kitchen was no different. It had been redecorated over the years but still remained a pristine blue and white.

Now Marion and Jack were speaking together; Jack still going on about having been so badly let down. Marion went along with him, agreeing in a mechanical sort of way. Lily was sure that her aunt was barely listening.

'There's no self-pride,' Jack was saying. 'The workers today are layabouts. All I asked for was one day. One day, Marion, I ask you! But all I got was the blighter mentally saying "codswallop" and thumbing his nose. I needed a day away!'

'Perhaps you can go tomorrow, dear?'

'Cuttings will have a full load to carry. He's without Wray now.' Jack's tone was testy. 'Haven't you been listening?'

'A storm in a teacup, Jack,' Marion replied soothingly. 'The boy's never let you down before.'

'And he'll never do it again. I start as I mean to go on. You have to nip that sort of thing in the bud. All I know is that I'll never stand by and allow our Lily to get tangled with that sort. Low-class, lazy, unreliable ...'

Lily was used to them speaking over her head. Carrying on as though she was some kind of beloved puppet expected only to move to the pull of their strings. To always unquestioningly obey! All of her life she had attentively taken in all their words of wisdom. Always doing her level best never to make them ashamed of her, or in any way let them down. When she did voice an opinion – as she had to get Richard a job in the first place – they were so surprised they took note.

'Please don't go on, Dad,' she said quietly. 'And try to remember that we are ordinary working-class people ourselves.'

He turned to her, openly outraged. 'No!' he replied forcefully. 'No! We have different sets of values. We make the best of ourselves. Always have and always will.'

'So do most people, Dad. You just don't see it, that's all.'

'You don't know what you're talking about, Chickybit.' He brushed her opinion aside. 'I've lived round here long enough to know—'

Lily's cheeks went pink, and for the first time in her life she actually interrupted her father.

'Please don't call me that silly name. I'm not a baby any more. I've left school! I can actually work for my living, and if I get a job, I think I will. I can actually sort things out for myself, you know.'

'You'll not work!' Jack exploded. 'Perish the thought.'

'No, darling,' Marion put in quickly. 'After all, your duty lies here with your dad. Has it never occurred to you, Lily, that one day I – I might want to – to move on myself?'

'Stop it!' Jack rasped, looking near apoplexy as he clutched at his heart. 'Belt up the pair of you. I'll have no more of this.'

It worked for Marion, but for once in her life, not for Lily.

'I think you are wrong to let Richard go,' she told her father, even-toned. 'You did not wait to hear why he had time off – and knowing him, there must have been a very good reason indeed. Why can't you accept that he has principles, just like you?'

'If he had, he would have at least come here and let me know that he was unable to carry out his job.' Jack's fury grew. 'Not leave it till—'

'Oh!' Lily broke in on his mid-sentence again. 'I think I understand. It must have been something really bad, Dad. His uncle! Yes, his uncle was terribly ill and ... Oh dear!'

'His uncle's a thief. A well-known old lag that—'

'Dad! You're speaking about Richard's only living relative. Someone he loved.'

'I rest my case!' Jack told her pompously. 'A thoroughly bad lot.'

'Please,' Lily said very quietly, 'try not to be so self-righteous, Dad. And above all, remember how you felt when you lost someone dear to you. Would you have cared about who or what my mother was? Wasn't it merely sufficient that you adored her!'

For the first time in his life Jack London sent Lily to her room.

Before she left the kitchen Lily looked into her aunt's eyes. She saw sympathy there, and concern. There and then Lily made up her mind to go to Drews the next day. She simply had to get Marion alone. Wheedle her round until she was fully on Richard's side.

Lily waited in her bedroom until Marion had left for work next morning. She heard her father leave shortly afterwards. He was probably making his way to James Street to have a word with Sid and Andy. To try and spread the working load so that no one lost out. He would have a job to achieve that. Richard was a swift, extremely efficient worker. Also he was very popular indeed.

What was Richard doing right now? Darling Richard!

Lily was certain now that poor old Gippo Wray had died. Now she understood the real reason for Richard and Andy's non-appearance on the Sunday. They had not been bicycling at all. They had probably been at the hospital. Taciturn Richard would not have told anyone other than Andy about the state of affairs. Richard could not stand fuss. He had said more than once that both Burza and Lily tended to make far too much bother over emotional things.

Knowing Richard, he would tell them what had happened only after the funeral and everything else was done and dealt with. That was how Richard thought. His greatest pal was Andy, and a long way after came the girls. Andy was his only true confidant.

Her father, Lily thought, was not the only person in Lily's life who was stiff-necked with pride. Richard was of the same ilk. But the big difference was, Richard would never ever look down on his own kind. Never look down on anyone! Nor would he toady up to anyone, no matter how high and mighty they were. He would starve first.

So, Lily thought, the only person who had a chance of smoothing over troubled waters was Marion. Marion was nice to Richard, had even grown to like him. Marion could, if she so chose, get round Jack to bend sufficiently to do the decent thing. Marion was a stickler for all that was correct and proper. Marion had never ceased to carry on about being honest and upright, that one must tread the straight and narrow path. Marion's whole life had been built round her brother and niece's wants and desires. She worked tirelessly, putting in hours and hours of overtime just to earn extra money for little luxuries. Now she must work towards the luxury of getting Jack to change his mind.

Down the road she heard Burza's cheery, 'Tata you lot,' and then the door of number six slam shut. Lily flew downstairs, out of the house and ran to catch up with her friend.

'It's Gippo, Burza,' she said breathlessly. 'I'm sure of it. But Dad won't budge. I tried, honestly!'

155

'You told him what you thought?' Burza marvelled. 'You actually spilt it all out?'

'Yes, but it was useless. Sometimes I don't like my father at all, not in the least! According to Marion he once used to be a very nice person, even a bit quiet like me. But the way he goes on and on now is beyond belief. A calm, steady, down-to-earth gentleman? Calm and nice? Well, Marion can't believe the same of him now.'

'He's bitter and twisted – right?' Burza said. 'In a way you can't blame him, Lily. He's had more than his share, eh? Oh shit! It's Richard we must think about. What on earth can we do?'

'We can't do anything. Marion might, though. Are you coming with me?'

'I finish early today, so after work, yes. I have a few problems to sort out at Steadmans as well. I need to think.'

'Look – I'll see you when you've finished work. In the meantime I'm off to catch the bus to Baker's Arms, then from there I'll walk through to Keens.'

The penny dropped. Burza's eyes were twinkling. 'Talk about taking the war into enemy camp. Phew! You're off to Drews Estate Branch?'

'Exactly. I need my aunt to be on my side. She's the only one to get Dad to change his mind.'

'Thing is, who will be able to get Richard to change his?' Burza pointed out crisply. 'And I bet you're right. It must be old Gips gone through the Pearlies at last. Why didn't I think about that? Do you know, I honestly thought the Matson lot were right – that Gippo was too pickled to die. Oh damn! Poor old Richard.'

'Which is all the more reason for him to see that he has friends on his side,' Lily told her in a quietly determined way.

Suddenly Burza grinned and hugged her friend. 'Oh my Gawd, Lils,' she teased, 'I swear you've actually come alive! Go on, gel, go get 'em!'

Lily hurried off with Burza's chuckles ringing in her ears.

The office at Drews was smaller than Lily had expected. It was stuffy and smelled of dust, paper and ink, and all sorts of bookish things. There were ledgers on the desk and a pale-faced, bowed-shouldered young man, pen in hand, was sitting there working on them.

'Yes?' he said ungraciously, looking up. Then seeing Lily, pretty as a picture, he smiled politely. 'Can I help you?'

'Please. I wish to speak to Miss Marion London.'

'Miss London? I'm sorry. We have no Miss London here.'

Shocked, puzzled, Lily persisted. 'Forgive me, but she has been here for years. She works very closely with Mr Paul Drew – on the Imports side.'

'I'm sorry. There's no Miss London here.'

'And I'm sorry too,' Lily told him, her voice suddenly holding a hint of steel. 'I am not moving from here until I speak with Miss London. She has been, if you'll pardon the expression, Mr Paul's right-hand man for many years.' Then unable to hide her youth, she added childishly, 'My aunt does not lie.'

A gleam of enlightenment came into the man's eyes. He stood up from his chair saying, 'If you'll excuse me, Miss?' He vanished through a door behind him that was marked *Private* and bore the name *Mr John E. Jewel*. In a very short while a white-haired gentleman came out. He looked over the tops of his pince-nez at Lily and seemed unsure. Then making up his mind, he said, 'Please do come in.'

He stepped to one side and Lily went into his private office. She sat before his wide polished desk as invited. Now with nervously twisting hands in her lap, she waited.

'I take it that this is a personal matter, Miss London?' the man asked.

'Very,' Lily replied.

'So important that you simply must get in touch with Miss London at once – and at all costs?'

'Yes!' Lily's voice, though still quiet, held firm. 'If my aunt can only be disturbed on matters of extreme importance, you may tell her that her niece Lily believes this matter is of utmost concern – and that it simply won't wait!'

'I see.' The old man took a slip of paper out of his desk drawer, and looked down at it, plainly still considering what was best to do. Lily held her breath. Her heart was beating too quickly. She felt confused. And deep at the back of her mind she was testing, testing, testing.

157

What had her aunt always maintained?

'If you ever need me, Lily darling, go to the Drew offices and I will be at your side immediately. If ever your father gets sick, if ever ... Oh well, if ever you need me, that's all.'

Well, her aunt was needed now! But plainly Marion was not here, and could not be at her, Lily's, own palpitating side at once. So her upright, God-fearing aunt had lied. Perhaps had been all along?

Lily's stomach felt like a lift swooshing out of control down a bottomless shaft. Marion a liar? No, this could not be!

Mr John Jewel made up his mind. He handed the slip of paper to Lily.

'You will find Miss London there.' He hesitated then added, 'And I would be grateful if you would explain to your aunt that you gave me no option, Miss London.'

'I will say that getting this piece of paper was as hard as breaking into the Tower, Mr Jewel,' she promised and although her voice was calmness itself, her mind was racing.

She thanked the old man and left. Outside, having made enquiries from a passer-by, she made her way to what was obviously a rather snazzy private address.

She found the number at last, discreetly carved on oak: *2, Warner Mews*. She pressed the brightly shining bell.

'Paul – darling? Oh!'

'Marion?'

'Oh dear God!'

Lily stood there staring.

This was an aunt she had never seen in her life before.

Chapter Seventeen

Marion stood helplessly to one side as Lily, still-faced, tall and regal-looking, swept by her and into a quietly tasteful sitting room. But there was nothing quietly tasteful about Marion herself. Lily's aunt's eyes were surrounded by black mascara, her eyelashes stiff and thick with paint. Her lips were rouged as well as her cheeks. Over and above sheer lacy underclothes, Marion wore the latest most modern dressing robe of shantung silk. Clinging to her figure, it was open at the front, leaving tantalising glimpses of her cleavage.

Marion was, openly and outrageously, a vamp, a come-on girl!

Marion, the stiff, the upright, the holier than thou, was here parading as a temptress. She had been waiting for a Paul – no doubt the employer she was always on about. Employer! Not in the office it seemed, but here in a style good enough even for darling Aunty. Marion was a rich man's whore. It screamed it, with her make-up, her hair, her clothes and her heady perfume.

How on earth had she managed to get rid of all this paint and powder and return to steady, upright old Marion every night of the week, Lily wondered wildly. Especially the scent! What lies she must have told in the past. The supposedly straight as a die Marion. The two-faced woman who had in fact been as slippery as one of Joe Baker's live eels!

The silence and stillness between aunt and niece grew. Only the ticking of the beautiful marble clock seemed to be busy with the day. Then: 'I'm sorry,' Marion whispered at last. 'Oh darling, I'm so sorry!'

Lily merely sat looking at the woman who had shaped and moulded her so carefully over the years. Who had ruthlessly turned her into a very square peg in a round hole. Who had been instrumental in the torture at school, where she had been habitually scorned, teased, kicked, spat on, or poked fun at simply for being a goody-goody, a prunes and prisms, a lady shit! Who had her hair pulled, her clothes torn, who was beaten black and blue for not being one of the gang – when Burza was not around, of course! But Burza, with the best will in the world, had hardly been able to guard her frigid friend every minute of the day.

School lavs had been the worst ever. Oh, how she, Lily, had waited and waited until she had had to run, unable to hang on a moment longer. There they were, mean-minded, pimply girls full of hate, or even more dangerous, gloating over what was to come.

Strangely, as she had grown older, her main tormentor, Josie Briggs had not been one of the enemy. In fact had turned out to be pretty and quite nice.

School the best days of her life? Never! Rather a harrowing hell where bullies abounded. She had never admitted to anyone, least of all Burza, how she really felt. She had kept the stiff upper lip her father was always on about. Had suffered in silence when she really needed to scream and yell, as Burza did when it was warranted; and fight back tooth and claw, and not be the little lady at all.

In reality a shivering coward, she had wanted to die a thousand times each day – and all because of a snobby aunt, and all for the sake of one man's pride. A miserable bitter old devil trapped in a wheelchair. A hard as nails old swine, yes swine, who honestly believed all the lies his sister had been dishing out! This because his ego would have it no other way.

'Well, well,' Lily said in a tight, clay-cold voice, 'it's a correct assumption that truth will out – eventually. How much does my father owe this sugar daddy of yours?' She shrugged, coolly contemptuous. 'Oh, I can see now where the ladders came from, and all the things that money was found for, even when the cleaners' takings were down. Now I can understand how it is that we never went short even when it had been raining for days, and ...'

'And the workers never went short either, Lily.' Marion's tone was humble. 'Please grant me that.'

'How is it that you were able to convince him? What did you say?'

Lily's tone held such loathing that Marion's cheeks flushed and tears came to her eyes. Then, pulling herself together, she took refuge in defence. No apologies now!

'My dear girl,' she drawled, 'it was easy. I told him that the inside windows of all the Drew office blocks were ours.'

'So! He accepted your word simply because he wanted to. Drew office blocks! What a marvellous expansion. More reason for self-pride. What a fine pair you are! And I suppose that even Richard, Andy and Sid know that you are a habitual liar?'

'They were told nothing. Never! Only that they were to receive basic pay regardless of weather. That they would be expected to work harder when the rain cleared and so make things up. They went along with that, of course.' Marion's eyes were as icy as Lily's now. 'And they were tremendously grateful, I might add.'

'Even so ...'

Marion pressed home her advantage. 'But you have been happy enough to live the good life, my girl, haven't you? You have never seen fit to question.'

'I never knew there was the need. Unlike my father I never had sight of the books,' Lily replied, still keeping her glacial calm. 'I feel that—'

She stopped as the ringing of the doorbell rang out clear and crisp and demanding. Marion leapt up and fled to answer it. She came back with a man. A tall, lion-like handsome man in the peak of condition, and who was filthy rich by the look of his clothes. His lips were smiling but his eyes were wary.

'I say,' he said easily, 'the cat's out of the bag, eh? We are caught out at last.'

Lily did not answer him, her eyes having now returned to her aunt's chagrined face. Marion licked her dry lips and faltered, 'Lily dear, what – what are you going to do?'

'I don't honestly know,' Lily told her. 'But I now see the two people I have tried to obey all of my life for exactly what they are. So it makes me think I'll have to do something just for me for a change.'

'Sweetheart, I ...'

'I was going to beg you to approach my father, to join me in attempting to wangle round him to take Richard back, but ...'

'I swear I'll get Richard's job back for him,' Marion said eagerly. 'Truly I will, dear.'

'You must do as you think best,' Lily told her offhandedly, 'but I want no part of it – now.' She stood up, looking remote. 'Oh, before I forget, I gave your Mr Jewel no option. I let him assume that this visit was a matter of life and death. Now I see it is a matter of life – or rather *your* way of life!'

'Sweetheart, let me explain!'

'I can't stay here! Goodbye.'

As she hurried towards the door she heard Paul Drew rasp, 'Ye gods, this could mean trouble. If my wife ever finds out, there'll be hell to pay. I told you not to—'

Still in a daze, Lily made her way back to Baker's Arms. As she waited for the bus back home her sense of unreality was gradually being replaced with a new feeling. It was an emotion far stronger than the fear she had lived with every living day at school. Far greater than even her gnawing grief when they had lost darling George. It was cutting, stinging, sharp. Indeed, so snappy and bitter that it gradually grew hot! Her cheeks flamed and she felt a blazing anger. So strong indeed that it felt fit enough to choke.

All these years! she marvelled. My whole life I have lived in the belief that my father and aunt were wonderful. I have had to behave as they decreed, and not at all like everyone else I mixed with. My father and aunt have made me an outsider all of my life. I'll never forgive them, never!

If it hadn't been for Burza and Clara I would have given up years ago. Given up like my mother must have, and probably, like her, would have died. It wouldn't be my heart, oh no! It would have been through my naked fear of letting either of my two beloveds down. Beloveds? That's a laugh for a start. Cruel wicked beasts. Father and Marion are nothing more than hypocrites, and as far as Dad's concerned, also spiteful and spoiled. I can't and won't live with them any more. And somehow or the other I'll pay them back. I'll get even if it's the last thing I do ...

*

In spite of all her careful hints and veiled questioning, Burza could get no joy from either Basil or Lucy. Whatever the hold Nick Bede had over them – Burza was sure of this now – they were too afraid to speak.

At last Basil had said very firmly, 'Yew can stop your prying into my affairs, Burz. D'yew hear me? Bede comes here to get his mother's bread and that's all. Do yew understand?'

''Course I do, Bas. If that's what you want.'

'I insist! Now get on off home. And keep a still tongue in your head. And if yew don't, gel, I'll have to let yew go.'

'Cor! That'll cause it,' she bantered, not believing him for an instant. 'Well, I'll be off. Does Lucy want anything at the shops? It don't take five minutes to run errands, you know.'

'Very kind, I'm sure. Very kind! But we're all right for now. Ah!' His round and rosy face beamed as he saw Lucy stepping through the beaded curtain holding Angela by the hand. 'Wave to my littel angel, Burz.'

Burza waved to Lucy and to the happy Mongol child, her heart going out to these very nice people. Both Lucy and Basil would go through fire and water for their daughter, she thought. And who wouldn't? Little angel aptly described the child. And rotten Nick Bede was up to something. Somehow she, Burza, would find out just what was what – then let old Beady watch out!

Burza went straight to number twelve to call for Lily and received no reply. Where could Lily be? Perhaps her friend was out looking for Richard. Surely she wouldn't have chanced going along to Matson Street on her own? Oh shit! Burza thought. I'd best go down there myself, just to see. I could kill Lily, I really could. They'll make mincemeat of her down there.

Lily was nowhere to be seen in Matson Street, though, and Richard's home was still tightly closed. It was such a small, tatty lop-sided building, with smoke-blackened bricks, yellowed newspaper at the windows, peeling paintwork and an extremely poverty-stricken air. It stood at the very end of the street, its back-yard wall against Shattery's doss-house court, this being a very cobbled area that was as miserably forbidding as the hostel itself. At the far end of this area, alongside the building, there stood an alleyway leading into Shattery itself.

163

This had been grist to old Gippo Wray's mill, having afforded him many an escape from the law. All he had to do was leap over his back-yard wall, across the doss-house yard, into the alley and he was free. Richard did not belong in such a place.

All I hope is, Burza thought, that Richard goes and holes up with Andy. They've been chums for years and anything, anything at all, must be better than this.

As she began making her way home she bumped into Bloodnut. Big-shouldered, tough, a scar down one side of his face, another across his nose where she, Burza, had bashed him with a brick, he looked a regular bruiser.

'Ah!' Burza said. 'Just the one I want to see.'

'Push orf!'

'Not till I'm good and ready. Where's Richard?'

''Ow should I know?'

'All right. Well, what's Beady up to?'

He scowled and Burza wondered what the devil Betsy saw in him. Ugly-looking devil!

'Do what?' he asked rudely. ''Ave you flipped yore lid?'

'You know,' she glared back at him. 'Beady. Your mate! God, Simps, I'd have thought even you would have been a cut above the Nick Bedes of this world.'

'He lives 'is life, mate. I live mine.'

'And what a life, eh? Like frightening old ladies and beating up girlfriends. And I—'

'Oi! Shut your gob. I've never touched no ol' gels, and if Bet 'adn't ...'

'Hadn't what?' Burza sneered, hating him with her eyes. 'Dared to stick up for herself – is that it?'

He was ferociously screwing up his face now, fighting mad. Burza knew that she had gone too far. If he wanted to hit her, indeed pound her into the ground, no one in Matson Street would dream of sticking up for her. She wanted to turn tail and run hell for leather down the street, but pride held her where she was. Chin, up, glaring, defiant.

'Don't you know what it was all abart?' he grated then. 'She didn't say? Didn't come art wiv it? Didn't tell yer what she'd been and gorn and done?'

'She didn't do anything,' Burza snapped. 'All I saw was you doing everything – with your fist.'

'Bet Cuttings murdered my kid. That's wot she did!'

Burza felt herself going hot and cold. Her fury at the man before her oozed away and she felt drained.

'I – I beg your pardon?' she stammered. 'Simps, what are you saying?'

'That the wicked little mare went to Ma Freeman and my nipper was flushed down the old gel's drain, or something as 'orrible. I tell yer! My little bread-snapper wot would 'ave been! Punch her? I wanted to bleeding well wring her neck. Make her as dead as mutton, or six foot under like pore soddin' Gippo. I forgive 'er in the end, but it still 'urts. Nar she's gorn all funny on me. Women!'

'Gone funny, Simps?'

'Yers. Paying me back, ain't she? After all this time too. So Burza Webb mind yore own soddin' business and shove bloody orf!'

'So, let me get this straight. You would have liked to have a child?'

''Course! Kids is wot make the world go raund, know wot I mean? Make a bloke pull 'isself up by the shirt-tails an' that. Get on wiv fings!'

Burza reached out and squeezed Blood-nut's thick, full-muscled arm. 'I'm sorry,' she told him. 'I didn't understand.'

'No one ever bloody does,' he snarled. 'Nar piss orf!'

Her mind in a whirl, Burza made her way home. The whole world is full of secrets, she thought. How on earth had Betsy hidden from everyone, even Clara, that she had had an abortion? Had in fact almost gone in for another of the same? Everyone knew this because ratty old mother Jacobs had seen her leaving Ma Freeman's place. And why had she got rid of the first one? A child that would have been dearly loved by its rough and ready old man? Dear God, what on earth had Betsy been thinking of?

Clara was in the kitchen, with Rosie.

'Hello, luv,' Clara said, smiling. 'Rosie's just made a cuppa.'

'Thanks,' Burza replied. 'Where's Bet?'

'Havin' a little lay down. You know how it is, gel. Sit down and 'ave a cuppa char with us.'

'In a minute. I'll just go up and see if Bet's asleep. See if

165

she wants a cup of tea too. All right?' Not waiting for a reply Burza hared upstairs.

Betsy was sitting up in bed, listlessly looking at the previous day's newspaper. Dicky never went without his *Daily Mirror*. He was a fan of Jane, the blonde cartoon character who was always in a state of undress. She looked up and smiled bleakly at Burza's entrance.

'Sorry for ourselves, are we?' Burza said crisply. 'Why didn't you tell me the truth?'

'Now what are you going on about?'

'Why didn't you tell me just why Simps was bashing you bandy?'

'None of your business.'

'No? Not when I hammered him with a brick in your defence? Give over, Bets. He had just cause.'

'Do what?' Betsy's jaw was hanging loose.

'I know about your visit to Ma Freeman's. And he wanted to kill you because you ...'

'I got meself in the family way,' Betsy cut in, her cheeks going red. 'Well, I did what he wanted, then when I went and told 'im, he still went bloody berserk. So now, this time ...'

'Yes?'

Betsy lifted her chin and glared. 'I love 'im and that's a fact, but I'll never do that again, not for no one! I killed a little livin' thing for 'im, an' I'll never forgive meself, never! This one I've got is going to live its little life and be spoiled rotten, and no one's goin' to make me change my mind.'

Betsy, now in floods of tears, grabbed a pillow, held it against her chest and began rocking herself to and fro.

'Oh Bets!' Burza's heart went out to her. 'Let me get this straight. You had an abortion because you believed that was the only way you could keep Simps?'

'Yes. And I'll never forgive meself, nor 'im. Not now, not never.' She let the pillow go and brushed her hand angrily across her eyes. 'Oh sod it, Burz! Life's a real shit. I still got a bashing for me pains!'

Burza was kneeling on the bed, loving Betsy with her eyes.

'You soppy old thing,' she told her. 'Why didn't you talk to him before you did anything? I've just been speaking to him

166

and he lost his temper because you'd got rid of his baby. He
wanted it!'

'Do what?' Betsy's tears had stopped. Her eyes were wide
and searching as Burza leaned over to push her fair hair away
from her tear-swollen face. 'You mean he would have liked a
little 'un?' She bit her lip, then asked, 'When you saw 'im, I
mean – did you mention 'ow fings are with me now?'

'Never breathed a word,' Burz told her cheerily. 'I left all
that up to you. So what are you waiting for? Go get him, Bets.
Oh – and a plain gold ring while you're at it, eh?'

She sat on the bed watching Betsy rapidly tidying herself.
Betsy's eyes were alight, all signs of lethargy now gone. They
went downstairs together, Betsy not stopping for anything.
Smiling mischievously Burza went to join Clara and Rosie in
the kitchen.

'I could do with a cuppa,' she said joyously. 'I think we're
going to have a happy ending.'

'What's that, gel?' Clara asked as she busied herself
pouring out tea and making it as Burza liked it – hot, strong
and sweet. 'What sort of happy ending?'

'I think that Betsy and Simps are about to make things up.
Who knows, there might be a wedding in the air.'

'Oh my Gawd!' Clara replied angrily. 'I bloody well hope
not!'

'Pardon?' Burza was taken aback. 'You don't want Betsy to
be happily married, Clara?'

'Not to sodding Simpson I don't. He's a Matson Street pig.
He's Nick Bede's mate, so say no more. He tried to bash our
Betsy up, and he would 'ave if you hadn't stepped in. She's
better orf with us. Oh my gel, I 'ope as how you're wrong.'

'But he said – Betsy said – I thought I was doing the right
thing!'

Suddenly Clara was rearing up like a turkey cock ready to
fight. Her lovely slanty eyes had become hard, cold, like the
glass eyes on Marion's best fox-fur.

'Do what?' Clara said very edgily indeed. 'Burza, I 'ope
you never had no hand in this. The man's an oaf. A brutal
spiteful swine what my George would 'ave strangled before
... Burza, yer didn't! You ain't! Don't you know my gel's too
good for the likes of that gutter rat?'

167

That's caused it, Burza thought and choked into silence. She couldn't tell Clara why Simpson had wanted to kill Betsy. So, as far as Clara was concerned, she, Burza had poked her nose in where it wasn't wanted, and she had done it all wrong.

'Don't tell me,' Rosie drawled, 'that pushy old you ain't had more'n a hand in all this?' She turned to her mother. 'I told yer as how she's a troublemaker, Mum. Takes after all that toffee-nosed London lot. I wonder if she would 'ave been so anxious at pairing orf dear ol' snotty Lil with someone like Blood-nut?'

Clara did not reply, but the suddenly wary look she gave Burza told its own tale. Burza, shocked, tail between her legs, left them to it.

Betsy never came home, which made Clara look very angry indeed. The strained atmosphere at the breakfast table deepened when Dicky came down to join them. Right out of the blue he announced that he'd be leaving at the end of the following week.

'It's a promotion, Ma,' he told the suddenly ashen-faced Clara. 'A good one, at a large main Essex branch. I put in for it ages ago.'

'When?' Clara's question rapped out.

'Well, there's a need for more space, eh? The girls are all cramped up like sardines, and there was me lording it with a room to myself – and you on the couch in the front room.'

'But no one ever dreamed you'd take all that wranglin' to heart, Dicky,' Clara objected. 'The girls 'ave always enjoyed a cat-fight. And room or no room won't alter that.'

'Perhaps.' Dicky smiled his slow private smile. 'But with me out of the way, perhaps Rose will stop her continual sniping at Burza?'

Oh shit! Burza thought, my name's come into things again. Clara'll start thinking that it's all my fault. Everything! She'll never forgive me over Betsy, and now this! Suddenly, very desperately, she wanted to cry.

'Promotion, eh? Good on yer, son,' Clara said, then very genuinely, 'you make me feel proud. I only wish your dad was here to see. But what about digs and that?'

'All arranged. And a Green Line coach will get you there

any time, and bring me back home. I'll send you some cash regularly, and we'll visit, Ma.'

'Yers!' Clara said stoutly, but they all knew she'd never go. And it was doubtful if quiet, self-contained, a cut above the rest, Dicky would ever come back. After all, he had made his escape from Solomon Street!

'Dicky, congrats!' Burza said, and jumped up to run round the table to kiss him. 'Now I've got to go. I mustn't be late. You know what a stickler old Basil is.'

But there was another shock to come.

'I'm sorry, Burz,' Basil said, 'but I've got to let yew go.'

'Why?' Burza whispered. 'What have I done wrong?'

'Nothing, gel. I just can't afford to keep yew, that's all.'

'Is that really all?' She stepped towards him, her expression fierce. 'Are you sure that's all, Bas?'

His round and rosy face now held unease and yes, an open dislike. 'That an' the fact that yew are stirring up trouble,' he told her. 'And more trouble is what me an' Lucy can ill afford.'

'But Basil, I ...'

'I'm sorry,' he said, 'but my mind is made up. I'll pay in lieu of notice, and p'raps yew'll go now!'

Chapter Eighteen

Burza, her eyes blurred by angry tears, clutching tight onto the pound note Basil had given her, walked out of Steadmans. Under her arm there were tucked two large new-baked loaves. The baker had been generous to the last, but there had been naked fear in his eyes. I reckon he thinks a quid and a bit of bread's worth it, she grieved, just to get rid of me. Troublemaker, eh?

Nick Bede's learned I'm after him, or guessed that I've got the wind up my tail, she thought. Well, I won't be put off. Even more so now. Beady's a rotten evil swine!

The appetising smell of the loaves made her feel her loss even more. She had loved her job, loved it! The hard scrubbing in the actual bake-house, when Basil had looked like Old Father Time dusted all over as he was with flour, and the clearing of the great oven's ashes, all had been grist to Burza's mill. As well as the housework, the shop serving, the running of errands, even sometimes the great honour of caring for the baker's 'little angel' – all this had kept her busy every minute of the day. And chirpy, bright-eyed, always ready for a laugh and a joke, she had enjoyed it all.

'Yew are the best ever,' Basil had often said, and meant it. But that hadn't made him change his mind at all, had it? A huge tear dropped from her lashes and fell onto her cheek. She drew in a long shaky sob. Basil must have done something terrible to be so deeply in Nick Bede's power. What? Murder? Something awful enough to make the poor man pay and pay and pay. Would it be best to let sleeping dogs lie, just as Basil wanted? Perhaps in this case there was nothing more ugly than the truth.

She made her way slowly back down Solomon Street. She heard raised voices and was shocked to see not only Marion but also Jack London on the step of number six. Confronting them, arms folded, was Clara. All three swung round to face Burza who hesitated, wondering wildly what else could be wrong. She knew instinctively there was trouble. Somehow or the other it involved her. These days it always did.

'Come on, gel,' Clara said calmly enough. 'Tell these good people,' she underlined the word *good*, 'what they want ter hear.'

'Excuse me?' Burza asked. 'What do they want to know?'

'Where Lily is?'

'Lily?' A terrible fear clutched at Burza then. 'Lily?'

'She ain't been 'ome all night.' Clara's voice hardened. 'Like someone else I know, eh Burz? And this lot from twelve reckon as 'ow you know what's what.'

'All I can tell you,' she replied, in a tight strangled way, 'is that when I knocked for Lily yesterday there was no reply.'

'And yer didn't 'ang about to find where she'd gorn?' Clara questioned, eyebrows raised. 'Odd!'

'No,' Burza flared. 'I wouldn't, would I?' She spun round and glared at Jack. 'After all, you don't like us peasants hanging about round your doorstep, do you?'

'Peasants?' he replied coldly. 'I have never used the term. That's beside the point. Where is Lily?'

'I don't know.'

'You must. She has turned to you every inch of the way. If she were in trouble ...'

'Trouble?' Burza asked quickly. 'What makes you say that?'

'If she was upset about something! I sacked Webb – I suppose she told you that? I thought so! She's always opened up to you. You know her as well if not better than we do, girl. Could that Webb business make her bolt for it, do you suppose?'

'No.' Burza's tone was quite certain. She went on, 'She would fight for Richard, in her own sweet way.' Burza was now thinking out loud. She turned to Lily's aunt. 'I know that she was intending to see you, Marion. To try to get you on her side.'

The colour flared into Marion's cheeks. Hm! Burza thought

171

desperately, I've put my foot in it again. I've come out with it that sometimes Lily and her aunt go in league to get round the old devil. Oh shit!

'Burza,' Marion told her, almost humbly which was something of a shock from such a hoity toity miss, 'something awful must have happened to her and I'm scared out of my wits. Think! For God's sake put your mind to it. Lily never came home last night at all. She has packed no clothes, not even taken Bo, and you know how she has always clung to that old bear of hers. We're frantic.'

'Have you been to the police?' Burza was feeling panicky herself now.

'Not yet. We hoped that you ... That perhaps even Richard? Burza, I suppose you know how upset Lily is about Richard losing his job? I – I have been there to speak to him, to beg him to come back to us, but there was no reply.' Marion could barely suppress a shudder. 'How on earth people can live in such disgusting hovels, I'll never know. I mean, it wouldn't take two minutes to – to at least take newspaper from windows and have a general clean up. Richard could have at least ...'

'The job's his,' Jack cut in harshly. 'For life if he wants it. Tell her that, girl.'

'If I see her, I will,' Burza said, biting her lips and feeling ill. Lily simply couldn't cope on her own, she thought pessimistically. And no, she would never be with her beloved Richard. He was the sort that even if she had turned up on his doorstep, he would have brought her straight back home. But he might just know where she had gone. Know exactly what was the matter. The next step must be to find Richard.

'I mean it,' Jack pressed home his point. 'For life!'

'I'm sorry,' she told Jack. 'Right now your guess is as good as mine. I would like to know one thing, though. Has she any money?'

'I've always seen her all right where that's concerned,' Jack replied. 'And Marion has too. She also has a Post Office savings account.'

'That's good,' Burza told them. 'We at least know that she can afford lodgings. And to buy food. So for a while at least ...'

172

'The police?'

'No. I'd let sleeping dogs lie, Jack. Give me a chance to think. I'll find her, I know I will.' She stared at him straight. 'And it'd be such a blow to your pride, wouldn't it? Having your daughter taken by the scruff of her neck to a cop-shop!'

He blinked, unable to reply. Truth bloody well hurts then, Burza thought. Point one to me. Rotten old sod. Doesn't he know the dance he's led poor Lily? Strict, selfish old swine! Dear God, what's happened to Lily? What's gone wrong? Should the police be notified? No! her instinct screamed. *No!*

Jack was now frustrated and coldly, bitterly angry.

'Nothing will convince me that you don't know about this,' he told Burza sharply, his expression giving his true feelings about her away. 'Lily doesn't breathe without telling you about it. I could never understand why. She is above all else, a lady.'

'And I'm a liar? Is that it?'

'You said it. I didn't.'

'Now it's my turn,' Clara put in fiercely. 'Shove off, Jack. I don't like your tone. And for what it's worth, the pore kid's probably got fed up with you – because from the word go you've been nothing but a pain in the arse!'

'Mrs Cuttings! Clara!' the now scarlet-faced Marion began, but Clara had had enough. She could say what she liked to Burz, but Burz was hers to treat how she liked. But sod any outsiders, 'specially posh gits like the Londons. She glared at Marion. 'And you, with all them double-dealings of yours through the years, can piss orf too. All right?'

At that, Jack London, spluttering and looking near to apoplexy, and Marion who was so shaken that she could not reply, left.

'Thanks, Clara,' Burza said humbly. 'I reckon I need a friend today.'

'I'm not surprised, the way you go on, gel,' Clara said, all hackles risen. 'What yer got there?'

'Two fresh loaves, a pound note, and my notice,' Burza told her, shamefaced.

'Oh? How come?'

'I'm a troublemaker,' Burza replied simply. 'As you well know. I try to help and it turns out all wrong.'

'Well, get your arse inside and we'll have a talk about that.'

'And a cup of tea – please?' Burza asked humbly.

'It'll be arsenic if my Bets get stuck with that bloke from Matson Street.'

'She loves him!'

'She's mad! I'm hours late already, but I can't do no work till I hear from Bets. Gawd 'elp us, Burz, I could kill you. I really could!'

An hour later Clara looked as though she really meant murders, because Betsy turned up. A Betsy with a face as shiny as a new sixpence. With her, spruced up and as ugly as ever, was Blood-nut.

'We're going to get married, Mum,' Betsy told Clara without preamble. 'Ain't that wonderful?'

Clara sniffed and not even bothering to glance in Blood-nut's direction, asked: 'Where are yer goin' ter live?'

'In Matson Street.'

'You ain't cut out for no Matson Street,' Clara said doggedly.

'I'm cut out ter 'ave an 'usband, and a kid.' Betsy's tone was chokey with happiness. 'And ter live me own life, Mum. Oh come on. Give us your blessing.'

'I wish you all the happiness in the world,' Clara told her, her melon-seed eyes suddenly sad. 'And you'll need it down there, gel.' She looked away from Betsy and gave Burza one of those looks.

Wanting to drop stone dead, Burza crept upstairs to her room feeling sick – even more so seeing Rosie's all-knowing, triumphant grin. Then everything else was forgotten as of no account. There was only that terrible nagging worry over her dearest friend. Where on earth was Lily?

For all that day Burza roamed the streets, going to her and Lily's favourite haunts. To Abbots Park, to Jubilee Gardens, she even hung about outside the Kings Hall picture palace. There was no joy. Then she went back to Dunton Street. Andy was not at home, but, 'Yes,' Mrs Beldon said, 'Richard and Andy have been together.'

'Where are they now?' Burza asked urgently.

'Haring all round on them bikes of theirs,' Mrs Beldon said. 'Shame about Richard losing his job, eh? He don't seem too bothered though. Got a few schemes of his own, he reckons.

My Andy might even go along with him.'

'What? Leave London's?'

'Well, them two's as thick as thieves, just like you and your friend Lily. Where is she, by the way?'

'That's what I'm trying to find out.'

'Gone missing, has she?'

'Yes.'

'Well, Burza, Lily's not the sort to cope on her own. I hope the Londons have called the cops.'

'Yes. I didn't think so at first, but now I'm not so sure. Yes, the police,' Burza agreed, fear making her go weak at the knees. 'I think that perhaps you're right.'

Back in Solomon Street Burza knocked on Pete's door. Mrs Frazer opened it.

'Talk about ruckus,' she said, concerned. 'Is there any news yet? I heard that Jack's been to the police already. This is terrible, terrible!'

'I – I wondered if Pete might have any ideas?' Burza said quietly. 'He's usually so on top of things. I've been everywhere I can think of.'

'Peter doesn't know about any of this, dear. He went straight to Chingford after work. I won't see hide nor hair of him for quite a little while yet.'

'Miss Allthorpe!' Burza gasped. 'Of course!'

Burza ran all the way to the bus stop, then stood there, panting, praying wildly for the vehicle to hurry up. Surely Lily would have gone there, to Miss Allthorpe, to a place out of the area and thus safe – from a father who had so ruthlessly sacked the young man she loved.

Miss Allthorpe looked taken aback when Burza showed up. 'This is a surprise, dear. Granger is just about to bring in tea and some quite delicious little apple tarts. You'll join me?'

'I – I rather want to see Pete, Miss Allthorpe, if that's all right?'

'He's not around, my dear. Gone for a walk. The gipsies are back, you know. He had become rather intrigued with them since he met your mother.'

'Oh! Well, perhaps I'll go along ...'

'No, dear,' Miss Allthorpe said so forcefully that Burza was immediately on the alert. She stared at the old lady straight,

175

saying, 'Pete's with Roan, isn't he?'

'I really don't know,' she replied evasively. 'He may be exactly where I said.'

'Oh, please forgive me,' Burza was almost weeping now. 'But I must go. I must just see Lily – know that she's well. I ...'

Without waiting Burza turned tail and fled.

The stable was dim and warm and comforting. It smelled of horses and clover, of green grass, apples and honey-gold straw. Burza burst in, excited, joyous, wanting to shout aloud her joy. Lily was here, safe, with Pete who was so fine and strong. Then she stopped. Shocked as two figures, hay-spangled, sat up. Lily and Pete? No! her heart screamed. *No, no, no!*

'Wotcher, Burz,' Pete said, sounding disconcerted and defiant at one and the same time. 'How comes you're here, mate? Midweek and all.'

Burza, beyond reply, was staring at Lily whose figure was becoming more clear now that her eyes were more used to the gloom. In spite of her own tearing heartbreak, she had to see for herself that Lily was all in one piece.

'Lily?' she faltered. 'Oh Lily!'

'Give over!' Josie Briggs said.

Even though the police had been notified, two weeks later Lily had still not been found.

Several other things had happened to cause gossip in Solomon Street. One was that Marion London had given up her posh job to look after her worried sick brother. Another was that Andy Beldon had given up his job and had vanished just as had his pal Richard, and Lily. It was assumed they had all gone together, the current belief being that they had all headed for Southend.

The third surprise was that Steadmans was up for sale. Fourth, that Betsy Cuttings was now Blood-nut's wife. This had cut ratty old mother Jacobs' sneering dead in its tracks. Apart from all that, plain as the nose on your face, something real 'orrible bad had happened to young Burz, who was now without her best mate.

The kid was walking about quiet-face, lonely, seeming to want to die the death.

There was one other thing. Art Bede, he of the piggy-face and coarse vulgar ways, had become an upright and dedicated man. He would find young Lil, he swore, if it was the last thing he did. To get back Jack London's kid was the only thing he could think of, to finally atone for making the poor sod lose his leg.

Right out of the blue Betsy came to visit. She waited until she and Burza were now safely alone in Burza's own bedroom. Rosie's prayers had been answered at last. She also slept alone. Clara refused point blank to move out of the front room, preferring to stay close to her George.

'Gawd 'elp us!' Betsy told Burza once they were closeted together in what had been Dicky's domain. 'Mum'll never get over it. First losing Dad, then Dicky off to Essex an' her having to put up with a letter a week. Then there's me and Simps. I mean, I hate coming here now.'

'Then why did you?' Burza asked listlessly.

'To see the old battle-axe, 'cos I love her no matter what. That's why. And to give yer this.' She handed over a sealed envelope. 'A kid give it to Simps. Sidled up he did, like a little snake, and just said, "This is for Burza Webb of Solomon Street. It's important." Then he ran off.'

'Oh!' Burza said, recognising Lily's careful handwriting. 'Oh, oh, oh!'

'Is it real important then?' Betsy asked impatiently. 'Why don't you bloody well open it?'

'Because I recognise the writing,' Burza said, eyes alight. 'And I'll wait to read it, if you don't mind, Bet.'

'A love letter?'

'Yes,' Burza lied, adding carefully, 'but not from Pete.'

'Gorn off 'im?'

'Just say I'm dead off luxuries,' Burza said as carelessly as she could, but inwardly wondering if the pain over Pete would ever lessen.

Once she was alone, Burza tore open the letter.

Darling, she read, *Sorry to have frightened you – I had no way of letting you know my plans before because I never had any. I just went mad! Now things are all sorted out ... And you'll never be able to call me Prunes and Prisms again! Please come to Gippo's house – alone! Make it as soon as you can. I miss you. Don't tell anyone at all. I mean to stay vanished for ever. I mean it! Love, Lily.*

Book Two
1936

Chapter Nineteen

It was Saturday, 6 March 1936. Burza and Lily, all but adults in looks and attitude, were both now streetwise. They were surviving and surviving well. They were sitting opposite each other, reading, in what had been Gippo's dreadfully filthy kitchen. The old drunk's home, once foul and infested, was these days scrupulously clean and bug free. The two rooms and scullery of which it consisted, had been painted white throughout.

The kitchen, facing the street, now had muslin at the window. The material was suitable for letting in light, but sufficient to stop outsiders from looking in. The main room was furnished with a small dark oak second-hand table and chairs. Two small red-covered armchairs added an unusual air of luxury. They stood at either side of a diminutive fireplace in which coals were burning. Before it had been placed a dull red hearthrug on which slept a cat. Big, black and furry, he was beautiful and the girls' belovedest. His name was Boris. They had found him, a kitten, abandoned and half-dead because he'd been so brutally wound round and round with string.

'It's kids!' Burza had gasped, in tears of rage and compassion. 'Bloody cruel kids!'

Now, spoiled rotten, Boris was fed on table scraps and also a penny skewer of horsemeat left by the cat's-meat man each day.

As well as the hearthrug, Boris enjoyed sprawling on the second-hand red carpet that partially covered the stone floor. The room, once so wretched, now had an overall cheerful appearance. Plenty of books stood on a four-foot-long ledge built in the wall. A china encased clock, white with a pattern of green leaves and red roses, held pride of place on the

mantelpiece. This was flanked by a pair of red glass orna-
ments shaped like whales.

The girls loved their home. It was Lily who had gone to
Zoe Zuckerman, the hard-faced black-haired Madam. Zoe had
sorted everything out. The rent for Gippo's old place had gone
up to two shillings and sixpence a week, which Zoe had told
her firmly she could earn easily – either standing, or on her
back. At the time, shocked, loathing her aunt and all that she
stood for, Lily had wanted to curl up, then go along with
anything and everything Zoe had said.

Finally, Lily, now known as Goldie by the gang because of
her hair, had settled for a far more exciting trade. This, she
had told Burza with an air of absolute certainty, adding, 'Oh,
and from now on, you must refer to me as Goldie. It will help
to keep me safe from prying eyes. Isn't all of this fun?'

'If you say so.'

'Don't look at me like that, Burza. I have woken up at last.
Please, please don't get angry. If you don't like me any more
I'll – I'll ...'

'What? Drown yourself in the Thames?' Burza had forced
herself to grin at her own joke. Relieved, Lily had hugged her
and bent her swanlike neck to kiss the top of Burza's curly head.

Burza had found it hard to come to terms with the new Lily.
Her friend had a falsely bright confident air, a kind of don't
give a damn outlook that was glass hard. And like glass, one
sharp tap could shatter it. The state Lily was in now, if broken
into pieces, she would probably never mend again. Burza
accepted this and wondered sadly whether Lily did too.
Because of her fear for the other girl, Burza held her peace.

Burza learned that Lily had moved in at once, spent the
night there, then had begun to scrub and fumigate. In the
meantime she had made some unusually outrageous friends.
Also special contacts with some not very nice people. She
explained that she had known exactly what she was about
before she had written to Burza. Needing, she had said determinedly, to at long last make decisions of her own.

Together the girls had worked like slaves to get everything
nice. For their furniture and everyday things, Hymen's
Market had proved invaluable. So for a while lots of barrows
pulled up at the door of number two Matson Street, and cloth-

capped delivery boys had worked with a will for two such pretty young things.

Now the once empty and disgusting outside scullery was bright and white and useful. A marble wash-stand holding a china basin and jug had been set under the brass water tap projecting from the wall. Beside it, an iron frame with a top shelf on which stood a two-ringed gas cooker. Gippo's cooking, if he had ever bothered, had been achieved on the little fire.

The upstairs bedroom was hardly large enough to hold the three-foot bed which the girls shared. Apparently Richard had slept on a mattress on the floor. Thinking of the cockroaches and mice that had once abounded here still made Burza shudder. Darling, darling Richard. She wondered where he was and how he was getting on. Then her heartbeat quickened as a picture of Pete rose to the fore in her mind. She blinked it away. To the devil with him – and Josie Briggs!

Now Burza, determinedly looking at the evening paper, drew in a deep shuddering breath as she dismissed thoughts of Pete. Then she exploded.

'Bloody hell! Guess what? It says here about a possible air pact between Britain and Germany. I wonder what George would say about that! Especially as the headline is *German Troops Enter Rhineland*. It goes on to say that Hitler proposes to re-enter the League of Nations – on conditions.'

'I don't know why you bother with all that,' Lily replied, eyes twinkling. 'Our world is here. We are at home, Burza. We are rowing our own boat. We are ourselves!'

'Oh shit! You're not going to start going on and on about your aunt and your dad again, are you?'

'You talk about the people in number six.'

'I don't hate them, though. Just the reverse. It's just that they didn't seem to like me very much and I buzzed off for a time. But at least I write!' She bit her lip, adding, 'I've always looked out for you, Lily London, and I can't get out of the habit. All right?'

'More than all right,' Lily replied in her soft husky way. 'I don't know what I'd do without you – even though you keep forgetting to call me Goldie.' She looked at the clock and pulled a face. 'Oh crumbs, is that the time? I'm off.'

'You know you're going to get caught one of these fine days, don't you? Then what will happen? I can see it in all the

183

papers now. Lily London, caught thieving and sent off to prison for years!'

'I only run with them all for a lark.'

'With all the different folk you now know, and all your contacts, you'd think you could meet someone who'd help you find an honest job. Any sort of job. One for me too!'

'Oh leave off, Burza. We're getting rich! I'm off.'

The door slammed behind Lily and Burza tried to concentrate on the newspaper, but her mind was returning to two years before – when her world seemed to have come to an end. Of the time after the police had been informed of Lily's disappearance. She was still probably on the Missing Persons list now. How ghastly everything had been then!

Being heartbroken over Pete had been all but unbearable and at the very moment when she, Burza, had needed all the support she could get, everyone seemed to be against her. One of the most grievous things had been Clara's belief that alone and unaided, she, Burza, had instigated the renewed relationship between Betsy and Blood-nut. Almost as bad on the morning when Dicky had pointed out that Rosie's habitual baiting of Burza had not gone unnoticed. That that was one of the reasons for his going away.

Clara's attitude seemed to have truly altered towards her from then on. Oh, not openly, but it was there, a kind of subtle wariness. Almost as if she believed, like Rosie, that she had taken a young cuckoo into her nest. But then, Clara had never fully changed back to her old self, had she? Oh she tried, and was probably trying still. But with George gone the lovely lady seemed to have lost a fraction of her own fine soul.

Losing her job at the bakery, Burza reasoned, had been yet another bitter pill. Being branded a troublemaker had not helped her own self-image. But over and above all, her grief had been deepest over the rejection of her friend. Lily, who had kicked up her heels and gone without even the courtesy of saying goodbye. Lily had abandoned her! The sense of devastation had been the final and most bitter blow. It had been like losing half of herself – the nicer half.

Things, Burza considered ruefully, had now somewhat altered in that respect!

She smiled pensively. She herself still tried to be a lady, to remember all that Marion had said – no matter that the woman

184

had been found to have feet of clay. Burza remembered how shocked and let down she herself had felt when Lily had blurted it all out. Her strait-laced aunt was nothing less than a whore! However, so far as the girls were concerned, all that remained a private family matter, neither girl wishing to give Marion away.

Whether Marion had herself confessed was another matter. Now neither Lily nor Burza cared. But back in those days Jack had certainly been none the wiser. Especially when, while silently accusing her with his frosty blue eyes, he had been questioning Burza yet again.

Burza's thoughts went back, remembering how lonely and desperate she had felt then. Frustrated because Lily had so easily cast her aside and worried sick about her friend. And loathing the fact that under all the Londons' questions, there was utmost suspicion, along with, as ever, Jack's superior attitude. She had always hated the man's overbearing manner, his dislike and jealousy of friendship with her own lowly self.

'My girl would never go without telling you,' he insisted over and over again, no matter where or when they met. He was saying the same when he almost ran her down in his wheelchair one evening, just as she was turning into Solomon Street. Without apologising he went on: 'She'd hardly breathe without *your* say-so. You know where she is, don't you? And the fact that you're not actually alongside her means that she's with someone else.'

This was a new tack. She had wondered about that herself, but then brushed the thought aside. She was still spluttering when Andy, riding his bicycle, saw them together. He had pulled into the kerb, left his bike and joined them, and then Jack had asked him outright.

'Is my girl with Webb?'

Andy, tow-headed, tall, and now very nice-looking, had put a lie to that particular rumour.

'Richard's gone away to be alone,' he told Jack London very firmly. 'To come to terms with his deep grief. And to sort out other things.'

'So! You're in touch with him?' Jack had asked sharply, his expression more suspicious at once.

'No, Mr London,' had come the easy reply. 'He's in touch with me.'

The tall, sunny-faced young man, who up until that moment

185

had seemed so easygoing, now changed. His tone was cool, his eyes clear and direct. Suddenly Jack looked taken aback, accepting that Andy Beldon had a hint of steel to his make-up that had up until now been totally unsuspected.

Watching them both, Burza wondered why it had taken the older man so long to realise that Andy was just the sort to choose a lifelong friend that he not only liked, but could also greatly respect.

'Let Richard Webb know that he can have his job back.' Jack London suddenly grated out the words almost as though they choked him.

'That's decent of you, sir,' had come the steady reply, 'but he won't come back. Not to London's Windows anyway. He doesn't need them and never will again. That I am sure of.'

'I didn't know about his uncle.'

'Because,' Andy told him even-toned, 'you didn't give him a chance.'

Jack London's face had then flushed a deep beetroot red.

Andy, calm, still, rock-firm, watched and waited for the explosion he was sure would come. Instead, Jack had turned tail and wheeled his chair away.

Burza had said quietly, 'You've got him taped. Andy, I never knew you were so brave.'

'There was a time when you would have laughed your socks off about that,' he told her in his old easy, casual way. 'Cheer up, Burza. Lily wouldn't even dare to die without you.'

'Don't!' she had pleaded. 'I'm scared for Lily.'

'Like your own right arm, isn't she?' he asked understandingly. 'Don't worry. Lily's not the stupid sort. She's the quiet one – in fact, a bit like me. She'll go along midstream for as long as it means a tranquil life. But then, when it comes to the real push, she can strike out for something she badly needs or wants.'

'Just as you have finally felt the need to back-answer Jack?'

'Not back-answer exactly. Just to put the miserable old devil right. London's not so bad once he forgets to hate fate for taking his legs. I can understand him, I think.' His tone changed, became bantering. 'I wish I was as clever with women. However –' Andy's hazel-brown eyes were gently twinkling then – 'I think I can sort out Josie Briggs at long last. Grown into quite a little sweetheart, hasn't she?'

'Oh yes,' Burza had replied, thinking bleakly. Some dear little darling sweetheart! Poor old Andy. He ought to know!

She had stood up on tiptoe to kiss him, suddenly aware of the fact that although not much older than she, he was more of a man than she had ever known. His arms closed round her momentarily, then he grinned a wonderful lopsided grin and let her go.

'Nice,' he told her, 'and much appreciated, matey. Now put your brave face on, eh? It's going to be all right. Honest Injun as they say.'

'Oh you and your Westerns!' she had tried to laugh, tease him the same as ever because of the cowboy comics and books he chose to read. He winked cheekily and went to the kerb and cycled on his way. Then still unable to think of anything else but Pete, and Josie, and of the vanished Lily, Burza had returned to number six, wanting to die.

Not too long after that Betsy had turned up with that wonderful, wonderful note from Lily. That very same evening Rosie had deliberately caused more trouble, and Clara had instinctively taken her own child's side against Burza.

Then and there Burza had decided that if there was half the chance, she too, would disappear for ever from Solomon Street.

Everything was now quite marvellous – apart from the fact that she was still jobless. She smiled to herself. Unless one considered doing all the chores, shopping and everything else in number two a proper job.

Right from the start she had found that it was not difficult to keep her whereabouts secret. Alleys and escape routes into the slums and Shattery's heart were as numerous as warrens. Small backstreet shops abounded, and Hymen's Market was always so crowded that an individual could become lost under its sheer weight of numbers.

She had written regularly to Clara, of course. Lily's friends who never visited the same place twice, posted them for her, near and far. And Betsy had proved no threat at all. She and Blood-nut had not taken up residence in Matson Street after all. Gradually it filtered through that they had taken two rooms in James Street. Burza had come to know this on the day Simpson's father was heard by Lily's friends, carrying on in the Woodpecker. He had been most aggrieved.

'Called my first ever gran'kid Clara, they 'ave! After me

boy's ma-in-law, yer know. Hall right, innit? My choice was
Myrtle after me own ol' woman. But I'm jist the geezer wot
fathered Sid. The stupid git's right under 'is trouble an'
strife's thumb. But you'd 'ave fought 'e'd 'ave listened ter me
for jist this once, wouldn't yer?'

Clara will love that baby, Burza thought wistfully, and Betsy
will be so proud. Of course Rosie will turn green again . . .

Burza came back to the present, her usual worry asserting itself.
Lily, now known as Goldie, was not only running with thieves, but
at times even taking over with her outrageous plans.

Oh please God, Burza thought, help me to understand her.
She thinks that in this way she is paying back her father and
aunt. But she is only hurting herself. Surely, deep down, she
must be ashamed? I wonder exactly what she is thinking now . . .

Lily jumped off the bus, an elegant figure in a baggy but well-
cut tweed coat, a wide-brimmed brown hat that hid her hair
and showed only a little of her lovely face. Her shoes, barred
across the instep, low-heeled and fashioned from brown
leather, were neat and well polished. She looked to be in her
early twenties rather than in her teens. She seemed calm and
purposeful and ladylike.

Inside Lily felt tense, excited, apprehensive and happy.
Yes, happy! She might get into trouble today, tomorrow, or
sometime soon, but for now life was good. It was hers to live,
the rules were hers to flout, the loyalties hers to lever and
mould into bonds too lasting to ever give way. She had infinite
trust in her new friends.

She was Goldie to them. Nothing more, just Goldie, the girl
who had escaped to live.

Charlie Chaplin's latest film was in the news again, *Modern
Times*. In it Chaplin warned how up-to-the-minute factory
work with its greedy, overpowering machines could crush the
human spirit. The man was a genius, Lily thought, but he was
wrong. Machines did not crush people. People did!

As she made her way to the theatre she was remembering
again how her new life had begun. The evening of the day she
found her aunt's secret flat, she had made her way to Furze
Street, her intention to call upon the infamous madam, Zoe
Zuckerman. Lily had not felt in the least afraid when she

knocked on the shabby-looking front door.

Zoe, hair dyed black, wearing lots of mascara and scarlet lipstick, and who had quick, snappy dark eyes, had recognised her at once.

'Richy's friend,' she said in a pseudo-posh voice. 'Don't tell me that now he's gone, you want to be one of my gels?'

'No, Miss. I – I've left home.'

'Then you'd best come in.'

Zoe's house looked rubbishy and poor on the outside. It was meant to. Inside there was every comfort. Zoe, dressed in green, puffed at a cigarette in a jade holder and screwed up her eyes as she stared at Lily through an exhalation of smoke.

'Sit down.' Lily obeyed. 'So! I recognise you, of course. And Richard, one of your best friends, has done a moonlight. And now you're out on a limb. Is that it?'

'I wasn't looking for him, but for you.'

'Oh?' Eyes glinting like glass buttons, Zoe peered at her. 'Not Ma Freeman then?'

'I've never ... ' Lily had gone scarlet with indignation. 'I don't want to ... '

'All right.' Zoe shrugged, not giving a damn. 'Calm down. I just had to make sure. So you are not with child and you don't want to try whoring. What then?'

'I don't know. I haven't anywhere to live for a start, and Richard told me that he believed you'd help anyone in a mess – and I'm in a mess.'

'I can get you number two Matson Street.'

Lily was outraged. 'Gippo Wray's hovel?'

'Ah.' Zoe's face had gone tight and hard, her expression as thunder-black as her over-dyed hair. 'A hovel not good enough for Madame Marmastink, is that it? Not even though there's nowhere else?'

'You don't understand ... '

'Oh yes I do! Don't ever think of doing a hand's turn for yourself, eh? Everything's got to be pincushion bright. Just so long as someone else puts out the tosh, of course.'

'I never said ... I never meant that!'

'You won't ever fit in. My lot, no matter what they do, take the rough with the smooth. They look out for themselves and make a good fist of it too.' Zoe forgot her airs and graces and snapped. 'Christ! Why don't you bloody well sod off?'

'I'm sorry! So sorry!' Then Lily had wept. 'I – I just have to learn things, that's all. I'll try. I swear I will!'

That very night Zoe took Lily to Matson Street. Together they examined the property, holding lighted candles high. The place stank of vermin, damp and dilapidation. Lily had seen bugs herding like ink blots on the shadowed wall. And cockroaches with their flattened oval bodies, long antennae and biting mouth-parts marching across the floor. Above all, Lily remembered the contempt she had seen on Zoe's face. Not only for her own terrified gasp, but also, in spite of her previous remarks about Madam Marmastinks, for the revolting state of the hovel itself. Zoe's place was as neat as Marion's, and as clean as Clara's.

Zoe's unspoken opinion, that she had been right all along, and that Lily could never cope in the real tough-as-boots world had made Lily pull herself together. Instead of doing what she really wanted, which was to run hell for leather back to Burza, just as she had all of her life, Lily lifted her chin and told Zoe that she would stay.

Zoe had left her to it then, and she, Lily, had stood there, in the kitchen, her legs refusing to go back upstairs. Gippo's bed and the room itself had felt evil in the shadows. And the lifted floorboards beside the bed looked like the opening to a black grave. So she had stayed put, in the kitchen, which in spite of all Richard's efforts, was awful. She finally lay, rigidly, on the straw mattress that Richard himself had used.

Lily knew that she would never ever forget that first terrible night in Matson Street.

On the initial outing with the gang the sun was shining. Its light was cool and silver, bleaching old walls. As she walked along, looking at street vendors, mongrels with waggy tails, and urchins with Cheshire Cat grins, Lily felt so happy that she wanted to throw her arms round the world.

She liked the people she was with. They looked ordinary enough. A weedy boy who looked as though he wouldn't say boo to a goose. A man who was silent and snake-thin, but whose friendly black eyes shone like anthracite. Then a plain little woman wearing old clothes and worry, and Lily herself. They were her partners in crime, though a bit cagey until they knew her better. Then they were ready to teach her all they knew.

It seemed that the cardinal principle with thieves was that the one who actually pinched the stuff had to get shot of it as quickly as possible. The youthful Lily was taken along to receive the loot. She stood there, in broad daylight, in a crowded area, ostensibly window-shopping. Seemingly unaware of nimble-fingered passers by who were dropping items into her capacious shopping bag.

The proceeds of that expedition were disposed of for ninety-eight pounds. Lily's share was ten pounds, which she could hardly believe. Ten whole pounds. Some men worked for a month for less.

Suddenly, gloriously, she saw pathways to a magnificent and abundant future. A luxurious life that the beloved Burza would share ...

Lily came back to the present. Theatre-goers provided rich pickings. Zoe was bound to be pleased with what they took tonight – and on top of that Jaime was with them.

Jaime!

Lily smiled her secretive little smile. She had made up her mind.

Jaime was not so serious as Richard had now turned out to be. But then, working all hours and looking after the invalid Gippo had taken a terrible toll. However, the truth was Jaime reminded her of the young and carefree Richard whom she had once likened to The Laughing Cavalier.

Jaime was a charmer. Dark curls, dark eyes, a smile that all but split his face in two, and he wanted her! Just thinking about the saucy things he whispered whenever he had the chance made her go all shivery inside.

Perhaps, if things went well, they would all celebrate later on, in the Woodpecker Inn. Then yes, she would egg Jaime on a little. After all, Burza had done things! Yes, with Pete Frazer of all people. Soppy thing – fancy liking Pete! Jaime now, he was a very different kettle of fish.

Life was so exciting and so wonderfully dangerous. It made her see Solomon Street for the strait-jacket it was. Suddenly, for the very first time, Lily began to not only understand, but to sympathise with Marion. She would forgive her. Must! Then she remembered her own square-peg childhood and pushed the idea away.

Chapter Twenty

Lily took up position by a bus stop, which was also quite close to a taxi rank. Both were near the theatre exit. She was, to all intent and purpose, straining her eyes reading by street gaslight. She had chosen a Penguin thriller by Dorothy Sayers. Paperback books had been launched by publisher Allen Lane the previous year and were priced at sixpence each. Both Lily and Burza were regular shoppers at Woolworths and also avid readers. Penguin books were a boon.

The audience began to leave the theatre. The gang had, as always, timed things well. In quick succession members walked by Lily. The open-mouth bag hanging from her arm was nimbly and surreptitiously fed.

When the bus arrived, Lily was the first passenger aboard and away. This even before many of the unwary had discovered their losses, mostly cigarette cases, lighters, gold fountain pens, purses or items of jewellery.

'Where's your conscience?' Burza had raged time without number. 'Those poor people! How would you like it if some rotten tea-leaf sneaked up and—'

'Oh, don't carry on, Burza!' Lily, always light-hearted these days, teased. 'They are not poor people. I would drop dead before I was party to taking from the poor. Besides, the poor have nothing to take! And ... ' here she had laughed in her light, pretty way, 'how is it that Matson Street is already working so strongly on you? *Tea-leaf?* Since when has thief not been the better word?'

'And how long has it been since I warned you not to keep

correcting me?' Burza snapped. 'I speak as I speak and, Lily, you are a thief. Stop calling the kettle black. You run with people who steal. Your friend is a Madam, and you enjoy jokes with whores. You ... you ...'

'Hypocrite?'

'Yes.' Burza stopped short and looked rueful. 'Oh shit, we're fighting again. That never used to happen.'

'Because once upon a time I let you have all the say.' Lily's eyes were silver spangles as she chuckled. 'And as for being a hypocrite, aren't you? You enjoy the cash I bring home. You eat the food, and wear the clothes, and live under the roof that Zoe's money pays for. And what about the house-keeping?'

'That's it!' Burza had raged only the day before. 'I'll get a job if it's the last thing I do.'

'No!' Lily gasped and, serious now, really meant it. 'Burza, if you weren't here when I came back I – I wouldn't feel safe.'

'Ha! With the people you run with, I don't doubt it.'

But there was more to life than running with the gang, Lily thought. There was a stimulant of a different kind. Jaime Rhodes. Burza had not met him – yet. The mind-picture of him sent an excitement whooshing through Lily, tangling round her veins, making her face flush, and whole body glow. He had been part and parcel of her new life from the beginning. He was a fascinating person. He had fallen for her, or said he had. It had pleased her to keep him at arm's length, but now ...

Jaime! She would see him at their meet tonight, having all carefully kept their distance during working hours. However, as usual they would all get together in the back room of the Woodpecker Inn. There Lily would hand out the payment that she had received from Zoe. Miss Zuckerman could assess a night's loot at a glance. She paid out immediately, and was always fair. She was, according to her girls, the most decent Madam out. She was also known as the best receiver in the business. Zoe had her hand in a number of different pies, she and Denis Quiller, her lifelong friend.

The gang's practice after pay-out had changed hands in the Woodpecker, was to hide it behind a panel in the wall. The various recipients would disperse shortly afterwards and return to collect their ill-gotten gains later, and in their own time. It was always the same. This was the safest and best way.

If only Burza understood the saying 'honour among thieves', Lily thought. Accept that she, Lily, being the 'Safe' of tonight's job would be entrusted with a bag of notes that working-class folk could only dream of. She would hand round individual payments held together by elastic bands and with a name-slip tucked in each. The share-out would be quick, businesslike, and no questions asked ...

The oak-panelled back room of the Woodpecker was private, cosy and warm. Lily was smiling as she, still wearing her coat, paid out the money to her partners in crime. The first three she had ever joined on a job were now known to her, and were her very good friends. The weedy-looking boy had discarded his original guise long since and was now to all intent and purpose a polished young gentleman. His nickname was 'Three'.

The tall, slim man, with sparkling black eyes, standing handsome and upright in theatre attire, was aptly known by his surname, Diver. (He could dive in and out of a pocket quicker than a snake could strike.)

The woman who had once put on a work-weary, very worried face, now seemed much taller. She was done up to the nines. Her face was impeccably made-up, and she had an up-to-the-minute hairstyle. She was known as 'Gee'.

Lily completed their numbers. Late to arrive as usual was Jaime, who refused to be known under any other than his own name. Jaime light-heartedly refused to keep his particulars secret.

'If I'm caught, I'm caught,' he would say. 'Who cares? P'raps my old man will squirm. I hope he bloody well does!'

Thinking of her aunt and her own father made Lily feel like Jaime's twin soul.

Everyone knew that Jaime Rhodes was the son of seemingly respectable parents. His father, Mr Barnaby Rhodes, supposedly a gentleman, was in fact a brute. During Jaime's childhood the father had beaten him so severely that he had often suffered broken bones. Mr Rhodes was also a wife-beater. Outwardly respectable they lived in a nice house in Houndsditch.

194

At thirteen Jaime had been apprenticed in the leather-cutting trade. He went on to a decent job in Stratford. Jaime grew older and larger and the day had finally arrived when he became big and tough enough to retaliate. In defence of his mother, he had finally beaten the living daylights out of his dad. Then, shocked because the woman had turned on him for raising a hand to his father, Jaime had left home.

His first job was house-breaking in Bow, where he got caught. In clink he met a chap who worked for Denis Quiller, boss of the Matson Street gang. Zoe was hand in glove with Quiller. On release Jaime had gone to Zoe. He had been one of her 'gang' for well over a year when he met Lily – and he had taken to her at once.

Jaime's greatest asset, Lily believed, was that he laughed at the world. Also at her own neverending refusals. Well, he won't need to laugh me off tonight! she thought. There were exciting sensations squiggling her toes.

She accepted a fizzy lemonade from Diver and sat with them at one of the polished tables.

Then Jaime came in, bursting through the door like a great gust of fresh air, his white teeth gleaming as he smiled, dark hair flopping onto his handsome forehead, his stance devil-may-care and jaunty. He was dressed for the theatre, silk scarf and all. He was almost too good-looking to be true.

'Hello, Goldie!' he said to Lily and ruffled her hair. 'Gorgeous little gel, aren't you?'

'Cupboard love, that's what it is,' she teased back, and handed him his roll of notes. 'Now you have the cash I suppose you'll love and leave me.'

'Never, darling. Come to my desert tent and I'll show you ...'

'Oh, oh, oh!' She fluttered her eyelashes, playing up to him and making them all laugh with her. 'We have here The Sheikh himself and – Oh!'

''Ello, 'ello, 'ello,' the police sergeant said as he flung open the door and marched in waving a warrant. There were two constables close behind him. 'Wot 'ave we 'ere? A nice little party, eh?'

He was crisp-looking and steely-eyed. Just like old Cop

195

Casey, Lily thought, biting her lip. Casey who used to box truants' ears when he caught them away from school. There was no messing with Casey. You knew exactly where you were with him. Even the toughest of the kids from the Shattery were wary of Casey's great ham hands. The sergeant, closely followed by two constables, was clearly the same breed as Casey. He knew what he was after. Them! No messing. And he needed proof and was going to get it even if it meant physically shaking it out of each individual in turn. He was staring directly at Jaime.

'Ah! I rather thought you'd be here, Rhodes.'

The gang members, unmoving, sat in silence as the three men searched every inch of the room. They missed the panel though. It had been designed for just such an emergency and was well disguised. The sergeant grinned sourly, adding, 'Empty your pockets, now!'

Gee stood up then, seeming far taller than she was in fact, imposing and well-dressed, Woolworth's diamonds in this light flashing and looking like the real thing.

'Officer,' she said in ultra-posh tones as she began walking towards him. 'May I ask why?'

Her dignified progress was such that she momentarily blocked Jaime from the law's view. In a flash his pay-out was passed back to Lily and hidden in her pocket.

'To further our enquiries, Mrs Gordon,' came the calm reply. Firm hands moved her to one side. Gee's mouth shut sharply, like a trap. She was known! He knew her name, her identity. It was a shock.

'Into what exactly?' This was Diver, eyes now empty, like stones.

'Thievery carried out en masse at the theatre tonight, Denis,' came the reply. 'We have reason to believe that all of you, including young Mr Guthrie here, were involved.' His eyes swivelled round to Lily. 'And you, Miss, where do you stand in all this, I wonder? Goldie, isn't it?' His eyes narrowed and were speculative now as he looked at her hair. 'From Solomon Street perhaps?'

Oh God, Lily thought wildly, he's only guessing. He must be! He can't be sure. Otherwise I would have been sent back ages ago. I'll have to ask Zoe just what the position is. I'm self-supporting and ... Has old man Bede found me out? Burza told me he'd made a vow to find out where I am. Her mind was rushing round, tumbling over itself, stunned with frantic thought. This was it! She would have to run away – tonight. This minute, now!

'Strike me!' Jaime laughed. 'You stampede in here and accuse us of—'

'Being at the theatre, sir.' The officers of the law were holding the men now, frisking them. Were being rough. Lily and Gee were at this stage being left severely alone. 'Show us your tickets,' the sergeant ordered. 'Or it'll be worse for you.'

'Tickets?' Jaime looked pained. 'We're not your actual theatre-goers, mate. What d'yer take us for?'

'Don't ask!'

'Why us?'

The officer jerked his head towards the Woodpecker's saloon and public bars, saying, 'Because you're the only persons wearing—'

'Decent togs?' Jaime laughed again, good-naturedly putting up with being frisked and being treated like one of the dregs. Lily wanted to scream, yell, do anything. 'Bloody good, eh?' Jaime went on. 'Come back to the local for a quiet drink after a posh and bloody boring wedding and this is what you get!'

'Take the women,' the sergeant grated, adding, 'to the station where they are to help us with our enquiries.'

They can't do this! Lily's imagination was running wild now, imagining the scenes she had seen at the pictures, of heroes wrongfully sent to unmentionable places. Of iron balls round one's ankles, and chains, and all kinds of terrible things. She had never set foot in a police station before. The idea was too awful to be true. The roll of notes in her bag seemed to be burning as brightly as bonfires.

'You've no right!' Jaime began.

'Shut up!'

'If they go, we all go.'

'Right you are,' the sergeant said sarcastically. 'What made you think otherwise?'

Knowing nothing of the law, sure only that this sergeant would have his way if it killed him, terrified because of Jaime's money, Lily and the others were herded outside.

197

Diver was hustled against her as they were crammed into a Black Maria.

They were driven to Frances Road police station. There they were treated with scant respect. Lily and Gee had the deep indignity of being searched by a hard-faced policewoman in an extraordinarily ugly uniform. Lily, hating it all because it was sordid, felt her heart beating. Her mouth became Sahara dry. She was firstly very afraid of the indignity, then of getting caught with the cash. Then all she wanted was to curl up, cringe, sink through the floor.

Suddenly she pulled herself together. She began to take a leaf out of Jaime's book. She had deliberately chosen this path, so she must take the rough with the smooth.

She inhaled, deeply, shakily, determined not to lose face, but oh, how she wished Burza was there to hold her hand. Burza! Darling, tough-talking, best friend Burza. If she could see me here now, being actually manhandled by this ghastly-looking woman, she'd be ... speechless, Lily thought. My Burza would for once be quite beyond words!

The idea of Burza being struck dumb for a change was suddenly very funny. Lily wanted to laugh and never stop. It was welling up inside her and even if the King had ordered her to stop she would be unable to do so. It was all so ... so incredibly funny.

The search proved fruitless. Looking coldly contemptuous the lady policeman escorted Gee and Lily back to the main interview room where the sergeant was saying in a heavy-handed way, 'Don't be too sure of yourself, Rhodes. There's someone out there gunning for you and your group. Someone who'll bear witness that you were at the scene, that you all returned via the bus that pulled up at the stop at exactly the right time.'

'What scene? And who was the witness?' Jaime asked, brows raised in mocking enquiry.

'Theatre, boy. You know it and so do I. As to the witness, he or she shall remain nameless.'

'We have told you, over and over, Officer, that we haven't been near the theatre.'

'Empty your pockets again,' came the order. 'Here, on the table. Now!'

Looking resigned they did as instructed. Inside, Lily's tummy was churning first with fear, then with relief. Miraculously her bag contained no bank roll. She remembered Diver being pushed against her as they entered the Black Maria. Please, she thought, let Diver have proved even more magic than usual and banished all evidence.

Diver's pockets proved empty. So were bags, waistcoats and even the turn-ups on the men's trousers. Then Lily realised that the officers were not exactly after money or jewels. Tickets would do. Proof of their wrongdoing was needed. Theatre tickets would be proof enough.

Lily was now thanking God that Zoe's instructions had been carried out to the letter. Tickets bought by the gang had been disposed of at once.

Unwilling to give up, late though it was, the police made enquiries by telephone about the wedding they had supposedly attended. They were informed by a disgruntled, half-asleep vicar that yes, a rather decent ceremony had been carried out in St Christopher's that very afternoon. And no, a guest-list was not available.

There was no proof against them. Only suspicion remained. There was nothing to warrant custody. They were let free.

Once outside the station the fugitives melted away into the shadows. Jaime stayed at Lily's side.

'Well, Goldie,' Jaime laughed and tucked her arm through his, 'how does it feel to be a marked woman? They'll be keeping their eyes open for you from now on. And they won't stop until they've ferreted out all of your particulars.'

'I don't care,' she said airily, wanting to cry with relief. Being inside a police station was horrible. 'At least, not at this moment. It's so marvellous to be free!'

'But I care,' Jaime told her. 'Someone's split on us, and I want to know who.'

'None of your own,' Lily replied quietly. 'I'd be prepared to swear to that.'

'Someone's got it in for us, darling,' he told her thoughtfully, the laughter gone from his voice now. 'Probably one of the Shattery mob, but they're not normally bothered with our little jobs. They go for the really big stuff and with no holds barred. This smacks of just plain old-fashioned spite. Now who ...?' He snapped his fingers. 'I bet it's that swine that used to hang about with Blood-nut. Nick Bede! He's never forgiven Blood-nut for gettin' spliced, nor Zoe for refusing to let him come in with us.'

'Oh, that bastard!' Diver said, appearing from the shadows behind them. 'We'll have to look into it, eh? He's real choice! Did you hear about Steadmans – the bakery on the corner of Solomon Street?'

'Don't do that!' Lily gasped. 'You made me jump out of my skin. I thought you'd gone ages ago.'

'Sorry, mate, but I hung round for the same reason as you. And I've been needing to think.'

'Where the hell did you come from?' Jaime asked.

'I back-doubled, mate. The Plod was set fair and square in my path. Watching my house they are – an' I didn't want them barging in, upsetting the other half and kids. And as for what I was saying about my number one suspect, the little bleeder's squeezing the baker dry.'

'But Basil has been moved away from Solomon Street corner for years,' Lily said quietly.

'I know, ol' gel,' Diver told her. 'They went to a bakery up Walthamstow way. Bede found 'em – 'course he soddin' well did. Like a terrier he is, still puttin' in the bite, wearing 'em down even after all but two years. I reckon they'd top themselves if it wasn't for their kid. She's got a screw loose you know, so who'd look after her with them out of it?'

'I wonder what their secret is?' Lily said softly. 'They must have done something terribly wrong to be so afraid.'

'We all know, Goldie,' Diver told her shortly. 'You would, too – it's just that you don't stay around gossiping with us all the time. We always get to know what's what eventually.'

'Most of it being pretty crummy,' Jaime told her. 'You're not the sort to bother your pretty head about things like that.'

'Not that it's any concern of ours, eh?' Diver put in. 'But I'd like Quiller or someone to really drown that lousy rat, Bede. What d'you say, Jaime mate?'

'Diver?' Lily broke in, thinking of Burza's feelings now. Burza had been so passionate about her job at the bakery, so cut up when sacked, and over and above all, she had grieved about being called a troublemaker. Now the real reason for the need for secrecy looked to be coming out. 'Diver, what have Basil and Lucy done that's so bad?'

'They live together as man and wife and they had little Angela.' Diver's tone became self-righteous. He was a father and proud of it. 'All of which is a sin before the eyes of God.'

'Why?'

'They're brother and sister.'

'Oh!'

'Bloody hell,' Diver went on, 'the very idea makes me sick! It's like me bedding my sister Joan, and who'd want ter—'

'Nick Bede makes me feel even more ill,' Lily told them truthfully. 'He's like a blood-sucking bat. He needs stopping.' She knew that she must tell Burza this story. Somehow she felt that Burza would know exactly what to do.

Shortly after that Diver reckoned it was safe to get to his home. Before he did so he remarked casually, 'I lobbed it behind the lamp-post – in the shadows. If you're in luck, it'll still be there. Cheers!'

He went and once again Lily and Jaime began walking together. So closely that she could feel his body moving rhythmically at her side.

'And now,' Lily said, 'I'm not so sure that I ought to go home myself. That sergeant suspected that I was someone else.'

'He was right, wasn't he? Of course you're the plucky young 'un that went missing from Solomon Street. You know it – and so do I simply because I made it my business to find out.'

Young 'un? Lily forgot everything except the wild outcry of her desire to become a woman at last. To achieve what Burza had achieved all that long time ago. What she, Lily, should have achieved – with Richard – had she not been such a stupid little fool. Well, she wouldn't miss the chance with Jaime. She wanted to know how it felt. Whether it was as silky and warm and wonderful as Burza said. Whether she, Lily, would feel for Jaime as Burza still felt for Pete. No, Lily thought sadly, I'll always love Richard, but he just vanished – and I let him go.

'Well, well,' Jaime said, 'alone at last and the cat's got your tongue. So tell me, are you off and away to Matson Street?'

201

'Are you off and away to your room at the Woodpecker?'

'It depends.'

'On what?'

'You. If you're off to Matson Street, I'll see you home.'

'If not to Matson,' she asked him breathlessly, 'where else should I go?'

'To the Woodpecker – with me.'

'That might be ... nice.' There was open invitation in her voice.

He was laughing softly, then, 'Come on, gel. Let's go!'

Chapter Twenty-One

'I'm off to the bathroom,' Jaime said, 'I won't be a tick.'

He left Lily standing there, waiting.

Alone, she had the courage to look round. Jaime's room was luxurious and it smelled pleasantly of musk. The wallpaper was dramatic, patterned strongly in red and gold. There was red carpeting on the floor, the furniture was carved Victorian. The bed cover was of dark red chenille.

Now it had come to it, Lily felt numb with fear. She was beginning to make vague excuses to herself. Finding all sorts of reasons to cut and run. The best and truest being that Burza would be mad with worry for her by now – even more so if she stayed out all night!

Burza, her dearest friend, continued to try and look after her. Was still not accepting how the once quiet, shadow-person she used to know had changed. Worse – much, much worse – Burza was beginning to lose all respect for her friend, someone who actually enjoyed consorting with thieves, and doing wild and reckless things. Though she still tried – God, how she tried! Becoming a right old fishwife, in fact. She kept accusing her elegant-looking pal of playing a stupid game, never ever accepting that so far as she, Lily, was concerned the street-life was for real. A carefully considered choice.

Burza would turn her back and walk away one day. Lily knew it . . . and deep down Burza must know it too.

Suddenly Lily felt alone. Utterly! Physically frozen. Thoughts were splinters in her mind, shards with no real shape, no form, merely isolated bits and pieces. Memories were shooting stars, glimpsed momentarily, then gone. Sparks unconnected with earth, unimportant, of no account.

The picture of a fat woman sitting on the seat in front of her in the escape bus floated before her. It had been her hat that had demanded attention. A black concoction with white buckram daisies on it. The daisies were dirty, Lily remembered, and found the idea of dirty daisies obscene. She – who was sitting there holding a bag full of swag! She, a criminal whose chosen name was Goldie. The very person who might any day now be discovered as Miss Lily London – by the police no less ...

Then all of the bits and pieces in her mind froze, gelled together in a blank white light as Jaime came back into the room. He was wearing a snazzy navy-blue dressing gown over pyjamas. Clearly he had been properly brought up. In a vague way she found it comforting that he was not the sort to retire in vest and pants, even worse a shirt and nothing else. He looked like someone on the films. He belonged on the screen in the Kings Hall picture house. He was, she thought unsteadily, not part and parcel of this strange rag-tag sort of life she was now in.

She half-turned to run, but he caught her and held her fast.

Lily found herself hypnotised by the smell of him. It was a faintly spicy smell. Was it shaving soap or hair oil? It didn't matter really because it was – nice. Almost edible, in fact. She knew then that she wanted to take in great mouthfuls of that perfume. Drown in it. Die!

He was smiling into her eyes, beginning to take off her clothes. She felt helpless, incapable of trying to stop him. Then she was flustering and fluttering, her hands like pale moths against his chest as he lowered her palpitating body onto red chenille. He bent over her, his lips cool and sweet. His mouth enclosed her nipples in turn. She felt his tongue. She was filled with exquisite sensations.

She heard a sigh from far away. The sigh was her own and it seemed to float through the window, flying high above London's chimney pots. Even further, to where a cloud opened its silvered flanks and gave birth to the moon ...

'Jaime,' she whispered. 'Oh Jaime, my dearest dear!'

'Don't speak,' he told her gently, his mouth against her

204

heart. 'Just feel. Let yourself go, sweetheart. Give yourself up to the experiences we are about to share.'

She entered a dreamworld of passion.

Heaven was the colour of apricots and rich country cream. The morning lay low and lazy in the sky, glowing against old grey walls. The ground beneath began to wake up and grow warm. Daybreak seeped through sooty grey tiles, wrapped itself round roofs, and filtered through the window where before Lily, alive as she had never been, had seen the lunar ballerina. Watched her silvery pirouette.

Lily was now happily serene. She had gloried in Jaime's lovemaking. She had experienced the final upwards surge when every nerve within her had raced towards to a suspended eternity. She had cried out to Jaime, clung to him, knowing that Burza had not lied.

Now calm, relaxed and happy, sitting beside him in the bed, she answered Jaime with honesty. He was deeply interested in her. He wanted to know everything – her background, where she had been brought up, about Jack and her aunt. He was particularly interested in old Miss Allthorpe and her isolated place near Chingford Mount. Without thinking, Lily found herself telling him things as they were, not falling back on the pat little fictional yarns she had used to impress Zoe and members of the gang. She had never before admitted to having been a frightened mouse who had hidden behind Burza's skirts for years. Pretended in fact that she had always been nerveless, cool, calm and sophisticated. They believed her! Now she told Jaime nothing but the truth. He listened intently, smiling into her eyes. Understanding.

'I'd like to meet your friend,' he said at last.

'No, you would not.'

'Why?'

'She is very forthright and – and she would tell you what she thinks of our unlawful ways. She is very honest and upright, you know.'

'She sounds a prig.'

'Stop it, Jaime!' Lily was put out, shocked, and it showed. 'Burza is the kindest, most wonderful person I know. She is more to me than a sister. I would cheerfully place my life in her hands.'

He laughed softly and tangled his fingers in her shiny hair. 'Sweetheart,' he told her, 'you already have – didn't you know? From the moment she arrived in number two, in fact. And now you must tell your Burza that it's time to move on.'

'Why? I don't understand.'

'The police have more or less found you out, haven't they? And until you're twenty-one you must do as you're told. Your father will want you back and ...'

'Oh I don't think so,' she told him gravely. 'He would be too ashamed to even know me now.'

'You're being too hard on him,' Jaime told her. 'But that's neither here nor there. It's the police we must worry about, and it won't take them long to know they're on the right track if they catch even a glimpse of your friend. On your own say-so, the pair of you have been lifelong twin souls. Neighbours and relatives will have pointed that out.'

'But no one from Solomon Street knows we're in Matson,' she objected.

'That's beside the point so far as the bobbies are concerned. They know that all of us here last night work hand in glove with Zoe Zuckerman. That means the law will be combing Furze, Matson and the Shattery areas again. One whisper and they'll find your gaff. Your hair is gorgeous, like spun silk, sweetheart, and very distinctive. The sergeant suspected you, didn't he? Even more so when they made you take off your hat and other clothes to be searched. So don't you think it's time for us all to mizzle, my love?'

'All of us? Together?'

'No, sweetheart.' He held her tight against him. 'You and me because I'm never going to let you go. But you and your friend must face the parting of the ways.'

'No!'

'Yes! For both your sakes. If they go calling on her she'll automatically become a suspect, innocent or not. So, Lily, yes I must call you by the name that suits you so well, you and I must make tracks.'

'When?' she faltered, now afraid for Burza who was blameless of all things. 'Oh dear heaven, what a mess I've made of everything.'

'Not from where I'm standing,' he told her. 'Come here!'

Much later, shadows merrily danced and flickered from the points of their feet as they walked. The dizzy shapes shrank, grew tall, whizzed outwards and up the wall. And pensively watching them, Lily saw their actions as being as erratic as the beating of her heart.

Jaime held her hand as they made their way back to number two Matson Street.

Burza, ashen-faced, hearing their footsteps had leapt to open the door, had put her arms round Lily's shoulders and was leading her to the chair by the fire. Then Lily was weeping and begging Burza's forgiveness and trying to explain things all at one and the same time. She fell silent at last, looking woefully from Burza to Jaime who were both standing before her. Burza was staring at Lily, her velvet-dark eyes huge in her face.

'Prison?' she asked again. 'You were actually taken to prison? They searched you.'

'That doesn't matter,' Lily choked. 'What does is the fact that you mustn't get caught up in any of this – and you will if the police come here. Jaime and I thought ...'

'Don't tell me he actually *thinks*!' Burza began nastily, her fear giving way to anger. 'He kept you out all bloody night, didn't he?'

'Stop swearing!' Lily quavered out of habit more than anything else.

'I will – if you stop pinching,' came the swift retort.

'I don't. I never. I only—'

'Stand there like a Christmas tree waiting for the decorations?' Burza was all sarcasm now. 'You stand on the edge even of your wickedness, don't you? You've never dived head first into anything. Know something?' She stepped forward furiously. 'You're worse than they are. Yes you are, because you should know better.'

'Lily and I think it might be a good idea if you went to Chingford,' Jaime interrupted smoothly.

Burza swung round to face him. '*We?* You're both arranging my life for me now, are you?' Her tone altered, became

207

crisp, brittle. 'Thanks a million! Well, me old cock sparrer, *you* can mind your own business for a start.'

'Burza,' Lily faltered, 'please don't lose your temper with us, dear. We – I love Jaime, you see, and—'

'Love? Don't talk rubbish. Face the facts. You'll get two years in approved school for stealing at the very least, you stupid little devil.'

'But Burza, I – we—'

Burza raged on, giving full vent to her feelings at last. 'And to think there was a time when your dad actually looked down on Richard, who's as honest as they come. And he was absolutely contemptuous of Gippo, wasn't he? The same old boy whose shoes you've stepped into, by the look of things. You think your father's like God. Ha!'

'Burza, why are you carrying on like this? My dad is a reasonable man when the chips are down and I don't understand why ...'

'Why? I've told you over and over again that the police won't listen respectfully to your dad like Sid and Andy do. That's if he wanted to stick up for you – which I very much doubt! You'll be out on a limb with no help from anyone. You're a law-breaker and if you carry on like this you'll finish up just like old Gippo. Is that what you want?'

'She'll always have me,' Jaime told Burza firmly. 'And she'll never be alone and out on a limb while I'm in the picture.'

'Jaime,' Lily told him quietly, 'this is between Burza and myself.' She turned to her friend, her eyes now silver frost. 'I want to live my own life. Not my father's, my aunt's nor even yours.'

'I see.' Burza felt stone cold. Cut to the quick, and feeling discarded she stared from one to the other, wanting to cry. Worse, back then, the talk about Chingford had reminded her of the last visit there – when she had seen Pete and Josie Briggs together.

'Oh please, please, please don't be cross.' Lily was retracting now, begging. 'I didn't mean it. You're a brick to put up with me, but ... this is the life I have chosen, Burza. I'm flying free at long last.'

And I feel I'm being strangled, Burza thought despairingly.

I can't take this in. Everyone is abandoning me.

'I'm glad – for you,' she heard herself say. 'Though God knows what you think you're at. Incidentally, I'd drop dead before I'd go to Miss Allthorpe. I'd rather stay here. I can make very quick getaways if and when necessary.' She shrugged, trying to smile. 'And the stepladder against the back wall makes entering the Shattery maze simplicity itself.'

'You can't stay here, Burza,' Lily told her firmly. 'It's too dangerous. I won't let you risk it.'

'I see. Then where shall I go?'

'Back to Clara, of course. You adore her, and she loves you like her own.'

'Really?' Burza tried to laugh and felt that she had received the final betrayal. The one person in the world that she would have sworn she could rely on was actually telling her to return to Solomon Street. To go back to the old life ... if Clara would have her of course. In other words Lily was discarding her, Burza, as effortlessly as she would a worn-out shoe.

'Lily,' she said and felt like a graven image, 'I wish you had never had the gall to say that.' Then her shaken soul gave way to heartbreak and fury. Her cheeks flushed red. 'What are you standing there for? Go on! Buzz off with your fancy man. And I'll never forgive you for this. Not until the day I take my last breath.'

She left them and ran upstairs to the bedroom.

When she came down much later they had gone.

Burza made a cup of tea and sat at the table drinking it. Everything seemed to be too quiet. The gas was buzzing, air plopping occasionally in tiny little spurts through the white mantel. The clock was ticking in a jaunty way. A dog barked somewhere in the distance. Inside the room they had once been so proud of, Burza looked around and felt that her whole life was in shreds.

What to do now? She could hardly just turn up on Clara's doorstep. As for Miss Allthorpe's place – well! She remembered Pete and Josie Briggs, then unbidden, she remembered her fiery-looking, flamboyant mother. An option? She rejected the idea almost as soon as it was born. On the other hand, she could of course stay where she was, but pride reared its head. Lily wanted her out, so be it.

Then she thought of dear old Sid. He would help and advise. He would make a joke out of it all, but he would think of something. He always managed to, and he was the best big brother anyone could have. Yes, he was *her* brother too, no matter what Rose thought about it. Oh my God, Rosie! I can handle her, Burza thought, if it comes to it ... I'll have to. Oh thank you, Lily London. Thank you very much!

She returned to her problem, now seeing Sid as her lifeline. She would find him on his rounds, not call at number seven Solomon Street, where he lived with his wife, Ivy. The Elliots, their landlords, might be home. Certainly nosy neighbours would see. At this moment in time Burza hated the thought of all those wagging tongues. How they would love it ... and the questions they would ask.

I must remember what I put in all of those letters I wrote to Clara, she thought feverishly. And what can I tell her to say to Marion – since I've often sent messages via Clara to say that Lily's all right? Oh dear God, they ought to know what the silly little devil's been and gone and done now!

Burza carefully placed her cup on its saucer. Then with her elbows on the table she hid her face in her hands and cried.

Chapter Twenty-Two

The huge windows, one on either side of the door of the Clothiers, were being cleaned. Opposite each other, high on their respective ladders, Sid and Andy were enjoying a laugh.

''Ere, what d'yer think of this one?' Sid asked. 'All this talk of Hitler an' that's reminded me of somethink me dad told me about the last lot.'

'Go on.' Andy grinned, knowing what was coming.

'Yers! There was this cockney standing on the beach, waiting, tin hat an' all, when this Yank struggles up out of the water. 'Alf drowned he was. An' the cockney, all concerned, says, "Are you all right, mate?" "Yeah!" gasps the Yank. "I came to die – for England." "Ho yus!" says the cockney, all indignant. "Well, you'll jist 'ave ter wait yer turn. I come 'ere yesterdie."'

Andy was still chortling when he saw Burza. He was down the ladder like a monkey, closely followed by Sid. The bear-hugs she received, the huge welcome in their voices made Burza go weak at the knees and her tears flow. She forgot all about the things she had rehearsed and faltered, 'I want to come home.'

'Course yer do,' Sid said. 'Come on me, little cock sparrer, Andy will carry on here and we'll get back and see Mum.'

Feeling fearful, but joyful, Burza walked beside Sid, along the High Road and then at last she turned the corner of Solomon Street. And for all she had tried to convince herself that it had been heaven to make her escape, she knew she was home. And when Sid opened the door of number six with a great flourish and yelled, 'Mum?' Burza wanted to die. Then her cup of happiness was full to overflowing because she was being held close to Clara's ample bosom and the woman was saying joyfully, 'My Gawd. Just look what the cat's dragged in!'

The most amazing thing, Burza thought later, was the fact that Clara did not question her. Oh, that would all come in good time, but for now Clara was so pleased to see her lamb back in the fold that all she could do was press on her numerous cups of tea and offer to make her toast.

'Then – then I may stay?' Burza dared ask once Sid had gone back to his round.

'You try ter move orf my step again, my gel,' Clara retorted, 'and I'll smack your arse so hard your eyes will water.'

'Thank you,' Burza whispered. 'Oh Clara, thank you very much.'

'Where's your things?'

'In my old lodgings, and ... Oh!'

'Now what's up?'

'Boris.'

'Who the hell's Boris?'

'My cat.'

'Strike me pink! I hope as how it's house-trained, gel. Won't the thing run away?'

'I hope not.'

'Well, when you're up to it, we'll go and get your clobber, and the perishing cat.'

'No!' Burza crimsoned under Clara's searching look. Then she whispered, 'Clara, darling, please forgive me, but ... I'd die if you above all people saw that dump. Would it be all right if I asked Andy later on? I mean, a chap's not so fussy about things like drains and – oh, you know! I'd be ashamed if you actually saw the place I've been staying in.'

'All right, gel,' Clara said, having given her a further look. 'Suit yourself. Now let's go upstairs and sort out your room. Oh, by the way, Peg and Charlie's moved out of number ten and into a Warner's flat. Near Abbots Park it is, and real fancy. Peg takes Georgy to the park every day. He walks now and says saucy things, young as he is. And he really does look like his grandad. Thank Gawd Peg's out of Florrie Jessop's clutches at long last.'

212

'I take it that you and Florrie aren't speaking again?'

'No. She's thick with the Londons and they blame—'

'Me for everything to do with Lily?'

'No gel, not just you. All of us. And Florrie sides with them.'

'How is Betsy?'

'Blooming. Her Clara's got the Simpson red hair and she's a high-spirited little devil. Keeps Betsy on her toes, I can tell yer. But she's real lovable if you know what I mean. Her dad lets her get away with murder. He ain't so bad, Burz. Ain't so bad after all.'

'Where's Rosie?'

'Got a job at the Co-op. There's this bloke what's taken a shine to her, but you know Rose. I want her to have a bloke, but she's a tough nut where men are concerned. Still, p'raps she'll take up with Ben Freeman now you've come back. She gets concerned about me, you know.'

'She loves you, Clara.'

'An' I love her. That's why I want her to get on with her own life.'

'Clara,' Burza asked tentatively, 'what of Dicky?'

'Oh, he's all right. Got his job, his books and his learning. Taking lots of steps up the ladder, but he's got a bee in his bonnet about what's happening to Jewish people abroad. Writes real fiery about it all, he does, an' says it's about time we all got our fingers out and did something. Gawd knows what! I get scared sometimes.'

'About Dicky?'

'About him going off and doing something soppy. Like fighting them Krauts like his dad did before him.' Clara's voice lowered, held fear. 'He reckons there's going to be a war, Burza. And if there is, my Dicky will be the first to volunteer.'

Listening to Clara made Burza realise how self-centred life with Lily in Matson Street had been. Old Gippo's house had been like a little island. Once inside the walls, safe from the law and all prying eyes, the general feeling had been that the rest of the world could go hang. She came back to the present sharply when Clara asked, 'Is Lily all right?'

'She was when I last saw her,' Burza replied honestly,

213

adding, 'But I haven't the faintest about where she is now.'

'Thank Gawd for that,' Clara told her. 'Them Londons don't half keep on. You can't blame 'em though. They doted on that girl. They were sure she was murdered until I got that letter from you, the one that said you'd met up with Lil, and that she was all right. That she had told you she had her reasons for staying away – reasons what they would both know about. When I showed them that bit they both went as quiet as the grave. Then they asked me why you had buzzed off.' Clara was watching Burza's face now. 'I explained how it was because of Rosie's bitching. That's right, innit?'

'Partly,' Burza admitted and felt her cheeks flame. 'But there were other things too. Like – like I felt miserable because I'd been jilted by a chap. Oh, you didn't know anything about that. And I couldn't accept that Lily of all people, had run out on me.'

'I can't understand why she went, just like that.'

'Knowing Lily as I do,' Burza replied very carefully, 'I'll say this. She must have had some very good reasons.'

'Like Richard being sacked?'

'Yes.'

'But there was more besides?'

'There must have been,' Burza told her. 'Believe me, Clara, there must have been!'

'Oh well,' Clara said briskly, accepting that so far as Burza was concerned there were things best left unsaid. 'All that's the Londons' business. The Cuttings' latest is that we've got our ol' Burz back home. Come on, gel, let's get some clean sheets to put on your bed.'

When Rosie came home from work that evening she saw Burza and her grey eyes glinted. With spite or pleasure was hard to tell, Burza thought, but she relaxed a little as the other girl's mouth curved up in a faint smile.

'Bleeding hell,' she said, 'you look older and skinnier – and no, I ain't surprised. Sid told Ive, Ive told Peg, and she went round and told Betsy who came into the shop especially to tell me. We all reckon that you've made our mum's day.'

'And you, Rosie?'

'I'll live.'

'I'm glad,' Burza said, and wanted to shout aloud with joy.

Rather later Burza made her way round to Dunton Street and Andy was there, grinning down at her in his lazy lop-sided way.

'Hello,' he said. 'I was going to call, but felt you'd best be alone on the first day. I take it you were treated like the prodigal son?'

'With all flags flying – and it was wonderful. Oh Andy, I'm so pleased to be back!'

'And I'm glad too.' He smiled. 'I've missed you.'

'Oh, you don't know how much I've missed you and Richard and the old days when it was just the four of us. Still, I'm back where I belong and I've come to ask for your help. I must get my things and I have to collect our – my cat.'

'Really? Then you need a strong man. Where are we going?'

Burza went scarlet. 'You can keep a secret, I know. Darling Andy, you will keep quiet about this, won't you?' He raised one brow, as if to say 'need you ask?' Relieved, she admitted, 'Matson Street. In Gippo's old house.'

'Phew!' He whistled long and low at that. 'The last place on earth that anyone would look for a kid as sweet and decent as you. My God, Burza, everyone's searched high and low. Art Bede even followed the gipsies from Miss Allthorpe's place to see if you and Lily had hooked up with them. Oh yes, you and your other half Lily.'

'You guessed?'

'I know you better than most, I think. But Matson Street? Never! Not for you. Lily, now I come to think about it, yes! I always guessed she'd kick over the traces sooner or later. I knew she was steaming inside and that one day it would all spurt out. Then too, there was that secretive little smile she has sometimes. What's more ...'

'Oh, don't go on about it, Andy,' Burza said, chagrined. 'Please? Now you know why I refused Clara's help to get my things. She'd be as horrified as you. Are you coming or not?'

'Of course,' he said, and stepped outside at once, having grabbed his tweed jacket off the hallstand. 'Lead on, MacDuff.'

'Shut up,' she told him unsteadily. 'That's from one of the games we used to play at the Hollow Ponds.' Happy tears flew

215

to her eyes again. 'Oh Andy, it's really and truly good to be back here and with you.'

As they walked together down Matson Street it was as though they were children doing a naughty thing again. They were unmolested, though they received some dark looks from a few Bill Sykes lookalikes, and a mouth full of obscenities from a group of old hags. Then they reached number two and went inside and Andy was whistling again and looking round, astonished, when Burza lit the gas.

'Phew! Talk about the woman's touch. And of course all the hard graft round here has been down to you – we all know that. Burz, I never thought this dump could look like a little palace. Well done!'

'Thank you.'

His eyes had lit on the two threadbare toys sitting on the shelf next to the books.

'So! She's left her white bear behind, or rather what's left of him.' His eyes were searching Burza's face. 'She's grown up at last, eh? Got a chap in tow I bet, and that's hit you below the belt again?'

'Don't be silly,' she flared. 'She had to leave in a hurry, that's all.'

'Sit down, Burz,' he said quietly, 'and tell me the truth. It stands to reason that you and Lily are in cahoots.'

'The same as you and Richard,' she told him directly, certain at last. 'I did wonder, but dismissed it. I don't know why.'

'If I come clean, will you?'

'If you swear never to tell?'

'I swear!'

Burza told him about Lily, and why she had blown up as she had – because of the tight rein she had been on all of her life, held by the hypocritical Marion and dogged old Jack – about Lily and Jaime, and of how they were both now on the run. She did not tell Andy the truth about how she herself had been having an affair with Pete and had caught him and Josie Briggs together in Roan's stable.

Andy was watching her very carefully, then, 'And there's no Jaime type for you?'

'No.'

'So, it's still Richard?'

She smiled at that. 'I had wild dreams about him when I was little – but then so did Lily.'

'But all of that's old hat now?'

'Yes,' she replied gravely. 'It is. Now it's your turn to talk.'

'Gippo left Richard some money,' Andy told her. 'Quite a nice lot, in fact. Being a minor he didn't know how best to use it, so he approached my dad.'

'Who works for Hitchman's Dairy?'

'No. He used to. Remember how good my dad is at mending our bikes, mine and Richard's? Dad's a dab-hand at all sorts of stuff. Well, now he works at Leytonstone, managing a bicycle shop for Richard. He actually bought the shop on Richard's behalf. All signed and sealed and legal it is. Everything! Richard's really pleased. Remember how well he polished that old bike of his, and looked after it like it was the crown jewels?'

'Oh yes.' Burza was astonished, thinking, Richard – wealthy? The slum kid from Matson Street? It was impossible! 'I can't believe what you're telling me, Andy,' she told him. 'And as for the bikes you had, well! Lily and I used to laugh at you two – half killing yourselves cycling for miles. You can't honestly stand there and tell me that Richard has a cycle shop?'

'His shop sells bikes and also, believe it or not, wireless sets. Wireless accumulators are also recharged there and they undertake repairs of both wireless sets and bikes. The previous owner's a whizz at that sort of thing. He's passed all sorts of tests and is fully qualified. Anyway, the brainy devil sold out to Richard and has now moved on to a really large place in the City.'

Burza wanted to laugh and she wanted to cry. So Richard was rich and he had gone all posh! He owned a shop and was therefore, in status, high above the sort of folk who lived in Solomon Street. Even Jack London, self-made man or not, could not now come near him in class. Richard now ranked alongside the Steadmans of the world. No, she thought wildly. Not the Steadmans.

She remembered the rumours she had heard about the poor

old baker and his family. Shocking, yes, but they all loved each other. Wasn't that what counted? Class wasn't so important, after all – apart from the fact that it put Richard out of their sphere. She looked at Andy, liking him even more.

'So Richard's living and working in Leytonstone?' she said carefully. 'Real snazzy now, eh?'

'No, not in Leytonstone yet. He's in the City, with the previous owner of his shop. He's gone there as an apprentice, determined to learn it all, everything. You know how dogged Richard gets once he's made up his mind. But one thing he'll never get is above himself.'

'Then why all the secrecy?'

'Would you want a sizeable inheritance left by Gippo to become common knowledge? There'd be plenty of Bill-bash'em types come calling and putting in their claims. Valid or not, Burz. He wouldn't have stood a chance. Not many would, specially if you're young and come from round here. Another thing, he loathes and detests Jack London. He wants to return not only as a shopowner but also a brilliant craftsman. In fact, he wants to give the two-finger sign to Jack, and who can blame him?'

'In other words, he's pinched his plot from *Wuthering Heights*? The gipsy kid returns a millionaire?'

Andy guffawed at that. 'Trust you. You and your books! Besides, I doubt if Richard would know anything about sissy stuff like women's yarns. *The Count of Monte Cristo* perhaps.'

'And behind it all, Richard also wants to be good enough for Lily?'

'I'd say he's always been that.' Andy became straight-faced and his voice was very firm. 'Yes, always. And from what you've just told me, these days he's a damned sight better.'

'Oh shut up! You know damned well that Lily has her reasons for going wild.'

'And Richard his, for going the other way.'

'Why didn't you go with Richard?' she asked curiously. 'Didn't he offer?'

'Of course he did, but that sort of thing's not for me.' He chuckled and ruffled her hair. 'I'm happy with my windows. If I can't be a train driver, or have a steam-roller, windows will do me.'

218

'A train driver? Oh, you're teasing me,' she objected. 'I can't believe ...'

'Now, no more arguing and let's start getting your things together. By the way, where's the cat?'

'In the scullery, I expect. He sneaks into the washing basket when the fire hasn't been lit.'

Getting Burza's belongings together did not take long. Getting Boris to cooperate was another matter. He seemed to be full of disdain and reproachful stares every time they went near him with the large stiff-lidded straw basket Burza had brought for his removal. Trying to get the animal inside it was an experience full of discovery.

Boris's cuddly, plump body suddenly became like a bag of coiled springs. There was much spitting and swearing, flattened ears and baring of teeth going on. Claws like burning needles shot out of their sheaths. More to the point, Burza's seven and half stones of will was useless against Boris's two pounds of won't.

Boris, she discovered, amazed, who was quite happy to crawl into every left-open drawer, washing basket, an old shoe box used for cottons, even the coal scuttle, wouldn't poke a whisker into that straw basket. Not even with a sardine placed in the bottom of it for encouragement.

Victory at last, with the help of a large towel and a determined indifference to pain, Burza's not Boris's, and finally a bristling black tornado was captured. The straw lid was fastened, then strong string wound over all, just to be on the safe side. Andy was grinning a huge grin and his eyes sparkled like amber.

'You'll have to let Clara bandage your hands. They're scratched to pieces. And you say you love this flea-ridden black creature?'

'He hasn't a single flea, I've seen to that, believe me. And he has been my friend during some very lonely times,' she added gravely. 'I used to stay in a great deal, you see.'

'Doing housework and stuff for Lily?'

'And for me,' she pointed out. 'I'd go mad if I had nothing to do.'

The walk back home was heralded with wild banshee-like howls and screams from the basket. Even the people of

Matson Street looked round, expecting to at least see a child being brutally strangled to death.

'It's my cat,' Burza said to one suspicious-looking old witch.

'Piss orf!' came the reply.

Then as well as Boris's complaining, the redfaced Burza had to put up with Andy laughing all the way back home.

Once they had reached Clara's doorstep, his arms swept round her, cat-basket and all, and he plonked a big beautiful kiss full on her lips.

'That's for being our Burz,' he told her. 'Once you're settled in, perhaps we'll get together and have a chinwag over old times, eh?'

'I'd like that,' she told him. 'I really would. Thanks.'

He left and she was inside number six and there they all were, the whole family – apart from Dicky – come to welcome her back.

Boris was let out of the basket. Stiff-backed and spitting, he was forced by Sid and Charlie to have his paws buttered. Then he was shut in the scullery and left to come to terms with his new home. The men went to the fish-fry and came back with fish, chips, mushy peas and gherkins. The meal was accompanied by lots of cups of strong sweet tea. The children, both gorgeous and cheeky and full of salt and vinegared kisses for their new aunty, were immediately adored. A knock came and then, surprise, a short, stocky chap with a strong face and very short mouse-coloured hair, was led in by Rosie who was practically simpering.

'This is Ben, everyone,' Rosie said. 'He works at the Co-op. He's head of the delivery department.'

'Cor! A boss-type,' Sid laughed and held out his hand. 'I warn yer mate, you'll need to be as tough as a rhino to hold our Rosie down.'

'Rhino's my middle name.' Ben's voice was deep and firm and nice. 'How do?'

Introductions were made all round. Then it was party time, spontaneous, friendly, full of love. And even prickly old Rosie was pink-faced and teasing Burza, and saying she was glad that the lost lamb had returned.

*

The following Sunday afternoon, the fishmonger in the middle of the street was bawling out his wares.

'Winkols, sixpence a pint ... Winkols! Shrimpers ... Get yor winkols an' shrimpers 'ere. Come on then ladies, let's 'ave yer. Winkols ...'

People were getting out their basins and bowls to collect their Sunday tea, which was always enjoyed with celery and bread and butter.

'Take the pudding basin down and get me some winkles, gel,' Clara said to Burza. 'Oh my Gawd, I can't get over you bein' here! You're only to leave this 'ouse ter get married, d'yer hear me?'

'I hear you, Clara,' Burza chuckled and kissed her. 'And since there's not a man in sight, you'll probably be stuck with me for years.'

'Get away with you.'

Burza was returning with the winkles when she found Art Bede blocking her path.

'Jist the girl wot I wanter see,' he told her belligerently. 'Proper sneaky little cow, ain't yer? Where is she, eh? Where's yore best mate?'

'If you're talking about Lily, I don't know.'

'Them lies won't wash wiv me.' His piggy face was red and he smelled of beer. 'You know where Lily London is. You've always known, and now you're goin' ter spill the beans ter me, else I'll know why.'

'Get out of my way, Art,' Burza snapped. 'And mind your own business.' She made to push by him but he barred her way.

They were being watched by a goggle-eyed group of people waiting for their winkles. Art didn't care.

'Oh no you don't!' A podgy finger was poking Burza's chest now. 'It's Jack's business wot I've made mine. So, you're going ter tell me what I want ter know or else!'

'Why don't you look on your own doorstep?' Burza retaliated. 'Finding out about Lily is Jack's business. Finding out about what your Nick's up to, should be yours.'

'Who's talking about whores? What the bleedin' hell are you on about nah?' He was getting more nasty, his piggy eyes were glinting.

'I said yours,' Burza shouted. 'I said that Nick's business should be yours. Y-O-U-R-S. He's a nasty piece of work and he's followed the Steadmans to Walthamstow, and he's bleeding them dry.'

''Em's high?' Piggy eyes were puzzled and blinking through near-white eyelashes.

'Them dry. Your Nick's *bleeding them dry!*'

'Did someone mention my name?' Nick Bede said, coming up. 'I think you'd better shut your marf, Burz.'

'And if I don't?' she asked defiantly.

'I'll shut it for yer.'

'Oh you will, will you?' Furious now, Burza stepped nearer to him, threatening, big as he was. 'Well, let me tell you this, Nick Bede. I'd like you to try! I'll tell you something else, you're a cruel, sneaky devil and a lot of people are scared of you. But *I'm not!* Understand? I'm not afraid of you, I never have been and I never will be.'

Art stepped between them. 'Wot's agoin' on?'

Burza swung round then, uncaring, in that moment knowing that the only person on God's earth that Nick Bede took notice of was his old man.

'I'll tell you what your son's been up to in private,' she shouted.

'I weren't no bleedin' private,' Art yelled back. 'Who the 'ell are you talking down to, eh? I was a corporal an'—'

'*In private!*' came the chorus from the winkle queue. 'She said *in private!*'

'Don't need no yapping in private.' Art's lips were pulled back then. 'If you've got some'ink ter say, spit it art.'

In for a penny, in for a pound, Burza thought. And there and then she told Art that his son was a blackmailer.

'Never in a million years,' Art yelled.

'Ask him about Steadmans. Go to Walthamstow and ask the poor devils themselves.' She took a furious step closer and grabbed Art by his braces. 'And what's more, I'll go with you. And I'll tell you something else. It's common knowledge round here what he gets up to. If Nick won't spill the beans, I will!'

Art was glaring at Nick now, suspicion all over his face. And Burza's heart was thumping like a sledge-hammer in her

222

chest. Then suddenly an easy, laconic voice said from behind her, 'And I believed things were bad in your other place! Welcome back to Solomon Street, Burz.'

'Andy!' She was laughing and crying as he led her away from the two mouthing men.

'I thought Hollow Ponds?' he asked.

On their way back to Clara's they saw Pete. He was alone. He waved cheerily. They waved back and Burza tried to still the palpitations that were now making her insides churn.

Before Burza and Andy left, Clara had to be told about Art's questioning of Lily. Then a ruckus started in number eleven and Art's roar could be heard all down the street.

'You bleedin' little toe-rag. No one's sinking that low in my 'ouse. No one!'

Nick was shouting back, Minnie's name came into it some-where, and bastard kids, and then there were thumps and bumps, bashes and crashes. And Em was screaming blue murder as Art proceeded to beat the living daylights out of Nick.

Clearly the Steadmans would be left to their own devices from now on.

Then, over and above all, Nick's voice, high with vicious-ness and venom, rang all the way down Solomon Street.

'I'll kill that cow Webb. I'll hang for 'er if it's the last thing I do.'

Burza bit her lip and tried not to mind. But in that moment she knew that Nick Bede was her sworn enemy. That he would in fact, somehow, somewhere, attempt to take her life.

223

Chapter Twenty-Three

As Burza and Andy left the bus and began the long walk along Hainault Road to reach the Hollow Ponds, the conversation between them was companionable, easy.

'It's strange,' Burza told him, 'how Matson Street and Lily's goings on seemed to be the whole world to me. Of course I scuttled in and out like a frightened mouse, always scared of getting seen – I hated that! I'm not the sort that usually scuttles!'

'Hold on,' he teased. 'You don't have to explain yourself, least of all to me.'

'I know.' She gave him a cheeky sideways look. 'But it was a relief to get back to my own company. Know what I mean? There was always plenty to do, and I could put my mind on books. There's one out now that I want to get – *Gone With the Wind* – have you heard about it?'

'No. Reading's not my cup of tea. I like the action stuff, footer, cricket, cycling, even tennis. I hope Fred Perry will win at Wimbledon again. Yes, I reckon he'll do it for the third time running. And I'm dead interested in Berlin.'

'Oh I see. Hardly sports! Dicky reckons that the violence towards the Jewish people is out of control over there and—'

'I was talking about the Olympics.'

'Ah!'

'I see what you mean of course.' He grinned down at her. 'I'd like it if a Jewish person won all the gold medals going. It needs something like that to show Hitler's boast about Aryans being the perfect race as so much hot air.'

'Clara reckons there might be a war.'

'Well, I won't think much of our lot if there isn't.'

'Oh!' Burza fell silent, then. 'Would you ... I mean, would you go and fight?'

'Of course I would. I'm a British bloke, and our sort always put on a good show. We did last time, didn't we? A bit of excitement 'ud be like mustard on Sunday beef.'

'I'm sorry you said that,' she told him, her voice suddenly shaky. 'I don't think I could bear it if you vanished out of my life too.'

'You'd survive,' he told her earnestly. 'Just like me. I didn't think I could stand it when you upped and left me to my own devices, Burze. I knew where Richard was of course, but I didn't know where you were at all. That was hard cheddar, mate. I couldn't leave Jack's windows, because in a way that'd be letting Lily down too, even though she'd done a bunk. But I practically lived on the Bedes' doorstep when I heard that Art had gone off after the gippos. There was a rumour that you'd gone off with your mother.'

'Who started that one?'

'Pete. He reckons he met her once.' He looked down at her bowed head, adding, 'And of course you did too. At the same time, I understand?'

'Yes.' Her cheeks flamed. 'Yes, I was there.'

'And?'

'I didn't like her very much. She looked colourful and vibrant, a strong sort of person used to having her own way. A bit hard. She must be. She left my dad, and dumped me, so ...'

'You weren't impressed?'

'No.'

'Well, mate, I bet she was impressed with you.'

Burza was going hot and cold, remembering the time when Kiffa had burst in on her and Pete. She changed the subject.

'I know I shouldn't, but I keep worrying and wondering about where Lily is.'

'Leave it out,' he told her firmly. 'You've got to start concentrating on your own life for a change. Concentrate on what *you* want. Lily will show up when she's good and ready to run back to you for help. In the meantime we'll enjoy today, just you and me, eh?'

'Yes. This is really and truly nice, Andy. Almost like old times.'

'We don't want old times, Burze, we want new! Tomorrow we'll go to the Kings Hall and see that silly thing *Showboat*. I'll put up with that because the second feature's a damned good Western. Oh, and of course the cartoons in between are always good for a laugh.' He ruffled her hair. 'I'll even treat you to a choc-ice in the interval. What do you say?'

'Thank you,' Burza replied.

After that life became warm and cosy and comforting for Burza. Even Rosie stayed pleasant and kept her change of heart. Pete began stopping in the street to chat to Burza. Clearly a ladies' man, he began to flirt with her. Then the day came when he, in all seriousness, asked her for a date. Her ego was restored when she, equally seriously, turned him down. She regretted it five minutes later, but so what? A picture of the gloating Josie sprang up in her mind. Josie was conspicuous for her absence these days. Had she ever got over her adoration of Andy? Burza's thoughts drifted away.

Jack London and Burza came face to face in the High Road for the first time while actually alone. For a while at least, there were no people from Solomon Street to overhear. Burza's mind was on kitchenware. She was elated because she had finally found a job – in the Co-op, like Rosie, as a counterhand selling pots and pans. Ben Freeman had put in a good word and it had worked. Over the moon, Burza was bouncing along when Jack wheeled his chair up from behind and barked at her.

'Where's Lily? Come on, out with it! Where's my girl?'

'I would tell you if I could,' she told him quietly. 'I knew once, but she has gone on her way since then. I haven't heard a word.'

'Rubbish!'

'She promised she would write, but hasn't as yet.'

'Codswallop!'

'Excuse me, Jack,' Burza told him politely, 'but I must hurry back to Clara. I have some good news to tell her.'

'You led my girl astray,' Jack said coldly. 'Yes, you! You taught her your coarse and common ways. The Cuttings' ways! She listened to you and never gave a damn for anyone else. Not me, not her aunt, no one, just you. And now look what's happened. She's a vagabond, a runaway and God knows what else. She's in hiding. My Lily! For reasons known only to herself.'

'You know why she wanted to leave,' Burza told him calmly. 'You understand very well, Jack. You sacked her dearest friend, and she'll never forgive you for that.'

'She's probably in the gutter somewhere,' Jack continued harshly. 'And no doubt with that slum kid, Webb. They don't know where he is either, do they? The police are all damned fools. Dunderheads! They don't deserve their pay. How is it conceivable that two underaged people can just vanish into thin air?' He laughed sourly, his tone bitterness itself. 'Yet I understand from the local station that droves of children disappear. Droves! But my girl's first downward steps in life, of manner, habit and vocabulary were set by you. I blame you!'

Burza felt humiliated. After all her years of learning and trying to be like Marion London, she was still considered to be coarse and common by Lily's arrogant old dad. And the mad thing, it was Lily who was so happily rattling downwards, while she Burza, was trying hard to go the other way and make the best of herself. Just as cunning two-faced old Marion had always told her, in fact!

Standing there, with Jack glaring at her, his blue eyes ice-chips, his knuckles white against the wheels of his chair, she wanted to cry out at the unfairness of it all. Also to think, Damn it to hell! What's the bloody use?

'Yes,' he growled on, frustrated almost beyond endurance, clearly aching with fear for his child, 'Yes you, who's as common as all the Cuttings.'

Then Burza found she didn't care what the man thought after all. She threw back her head and laughed defiantly, her eyes staring down straight into his face. Now she was thinking, All right, Jack, old mate. You've asked for it. In for a penny, in for a pound.

'Oh goodness me,' she said brightly, 'you have to find a scapegoat. Have to! If you don't lump it all onto me you might have to blame yourself, and that would never do, would it?'

'Don't you dare try to sauce me.'

'Just look at yourself, Jack! So puffed up. Think you're

227

Lord Shit, don't you? Well, you're not. You're just a very stupid man who made his only daughter's life a misery.'

'What?' He was taken aback, shocked. 'What did you say?'

'You made Lily's life wretched. She tried to be little Miss Fauntleroy, really tried just to please you! And what did it get her, eh? Bashings at school for being a toffee-nosed little cow. Yes, that's what she got every day of her school life! It was bullying and bitching all the way. If I hadn't fended them off when I could, she would have probably jumped into the Thames by now, just to escape the Josie Briggs of this world.'

'Don't be ridiculous,' he snapped. 'Had it been as you say, she would have told us. Explained. We could have done something about it.'

'Oh you did, you did!' Burza flung at him. 'You told her that she was above us all. That she was destined to go far.' Burza laughed again, 'And she bloody well has, hasn't she? As far away from you and her precious aunt as she can get. You don't know the half of it. Those kids at school were wicked!'

'I never knew. Never guessed.'

'You didn't want to!' The words were spilling out of Burza's mouth now. All of her pent-up frustrations, all her contempt for this man that had been born out of her love for Lily. 'All you wanted was to have a child you could be proud of. One that was like a little princess. But poor Lily wasn't born in Buckingham Palace, was she?' Burza's tone held sarcasm as she aped the middle class as seen on the pictures. 'Wouldn't you know it, old chap? We come from Solomon Street no less. All terribly top-hole, naturally!' She reverted to her usual voice. 'And you and your sister were really successful, weren't you? Yes, in turning your darling into exactly what she was for years. And probably even worse, into what she is now. A very square peg in a round hole.'

'You don't know what you're saying.' Jack was red in the face, angry. Dimly aware for the first time that he was hearing the truth. Aware too that the upstart before him was actually gaining ground in the argument. He began to bluster. 'Lily wanted for nothing,' he told her bitterly. 'We supported her all the way. There wasn't a single thing that we refused her.'

'She needed your care and your understanding. But instead

of comfort from you and her so-called strait-laced aunt, what did she get, eh? Nothing but dawn to dusk naggings for lapsing into the local tongue.'

'Everyone should—'

'Get everlasting tickings-off for wanting and needing friends and belonging in her own neighbourhood? For mingling properly in the environment where she herself had been placed? Oh yes, Jack, I can phrase things quite well for all I'm as common as muck.' She forgot to mind her Ps and Qs now and lapsed into Clara's way as she stepped closer to the glowering man. 'If you loathe and detest everyone in Solomon Street so much, why the bloody hell didn't you buzz off and leave us all to our low and common ways? You sanctimonious old sod!'

'How dare you!'

'Oh, I dare all right!' she flung at him and walked away. Then, as an afterthought, she called over her shoulder, 'Oh and I'd be very, very careful what you say about all of us low creatures. Don't forget that in the beginning you actually owed the survival of your round to the slum kid you think is so low. And that these days you rely absolutely on our Sid. Not forgetting Andy who is my friend and whom I love dearly.'

That's told him! she thought as she went on her way, but she was puzzled and in a way excited too.

Had she meant that? Did she love Andy dearly? She had just said as much to Jack. But then she had merely been stressing a point. Andy was of course her closest friend. The other two were gone. But Andy had always been there. Oh yes! And she wouldn't have it any other way. But what would it be like to be held in his arms? To feel his lips on hers in a seriously intentioned manner? What kind of lover would he be? Would he be like Pete? Could he make her limbs turn to water and her veins fill with running fire? It might be fun to lead him on, to try and see.

The idea took hold and her eyes were dancing as she walked towards home. Andy was so large now, taller than Pete, good-looking, strong and dependable. Had he ever made love to Josie Briggs? Would he ever look at her, Burza, in that special kind of way?

'Now I'm being just plain daft!' she whispered to herself.

Then, pink-faced, she hurried back to Clara to tell her the good news about her job. But at the back of her mind she was still worrying and wondering about her friend. Poor Lily who had Jack for a dad. For the first time in her life Burza began to think herself lucky not to have had a father. Oh my God, she thought, my old man could have been just like him! Poor Lily! I wonder what she's doing now?

It was the fourth of October. Barrow Street, situated in Shadwell, was narrow and full of tenements. It was the home of many families, a few cockneys, a few Poles, but mostly Jews. Lily's home, situated on the outskirts of the Jewish quarter, was one huge room with folding doors, thus dividing the sleeping part from the rest. Jaime never seemed to be short of a penny or two. This even though since their rapid departure from Matson Street, their thieving had stopped. They had not gone without, however. Their home was furnished with quite decent second-hand things, was tasteful, and above all was warm. It was very cold outside.

How long would Jaime be? Lily wondered. He had gone out to order fish since she had told him she fancied a nice piece of haddock. He was lying, of course! But he had promised her faithfully that he would be back before any ruckus started. Another downright lie. The noise, the shouting and confusion was clear enough for the whole world to hear, let alone Lily sitting before the window in her upstairs room. Jaime was down there somewhere helping to put up barricades, getting ready to fight fascists to the bitter end.

Jaime was a popular man and until their meeting had lived a life that Lily knew nothing of. Jaime preferred it that way. He seemed to want Lily to himself, to keep her apart from the rest. Though on the rare occasion Lily was introduced to any of Jaime's closest friends they were all really nice to her. Especially Sophie, dramatically dark and striking in looks. Her roly-poly husband Jacob could not be claimed to be handsome, but his wonderful character, his huge warm heart and beaming smile made up for his lack of height. They were a gorgeous couple and had made Lily feel approved of from the moment they had met. But family and friends to one side, one thing was very clear. Everyone round these parts had been on edge for a long time. Oswald Mosley and his followers had seen to that.

'I want you to swear that you'll not go out alone tomorrow,' Jaime had told Lily the previous evening. 'The streets will be dangerous.'

'But it will be broad daylight and our neighbours know me, and are very friendly,' she objected. 'I have been accepted by everyone and I want them to see that I'm on their side. But I'm not stupid. I'd keep away from any serious trouble.'

'You won't be able to, not as things stand. And in spite of your Aryan looks, you'll have been pointed out as one of us ages ago. It's strangers you'll always have to be wary of round here. They like spying us out, isolating a person, then moving in their bully-boys. No! You are staying put.'

'You're treating me like my father used to,' she told him, feeling despair. 'I'm not to join in; I'm to be the outsider as always. I can't bear it.'

'Everyone who matters will understand, Lily. You know yourself how there's been anti-Semitic meetings on every street corner recently, and the situation's getting worse. It'll probably continue after today if I know this lot, and I'd prefer you to keep well out of it. All right?'

'No it isn't, Jaime. I feel ...'

'This isn't a five-minute wonder, you know, Lily. And you saw for yourself how they cut young Cohen up. Now the Communists are a hundred per cent on our side and ganging up against them! We are growing in number and it's Blackshirts against Redshirts from now on. It's coming to a head with this march. We're heading for all-out war which will start proper tomorrow. That's why you must stay home. I'm a well-known anti-fascist. So, you're tarred with the same brush, dear.'

'Even so ...'

'Mosley's rats are vicious.' Jaime was losing patience. 'They don't care who they hurt. They're cunning bastards and can wriggle around and spy everywhere. Tomorrow it could well be a kill or be killed situation. I don't want them anywhere near you, so stop bloody well arguing!'

'I don't want to be alone, Jaime.' Lily tried hard to put over her point. 'So could I start out very early and spend time with

Sophie? She's a dear and I know Jacob will be with you, so ...'

'I'm not asking you, I'm *telling* you,' he shouted. 'Stay inside!'

He had looked like a stranger, he was so fierce. But then, she thought sadly, he had been like that a lot lately. Even so she had felt shaken at how drastically he had changed. Where was the laughing charmer who had swept her off her feet now? Jaime was far from easy-going these days. Indeed, quite the reverse. Sometimes he frightened her, especially now with his wild talk of actually killing. Surely that was so much hot air? But he certainly hated Mosley and all fascists and it showed.

'Are you Jewish?' she had dared to ask him at last.

'Partly,' he told her, 'but most of my friends are, and their cause is mine. All right?'

'Of course,' she told him, loving him with her eyes. 'Why didn't you tell me?'

'Because it might matter to some. That lot preparing to march through here tomorrow for a start. Are you sure it makes no difference?'

'Does my breed make any difference to you?'

'Breed?' he was laughing at that. 'My blossom, my beautiful Lily a breed? It doesn't sound right at all! We don't actually breed, do we?'

He was back to his old self at last, teasing her and light-heartedly tweaking her nose. They had kissed and made passionate love. The moon through the window had been hard and bright and clear. And Lily had fallen asleep humbly thanking God for her Jaime. But before she closed her eyes she said a special prayer, as always, for Burza her dearest friend.

Now, in the cold light of day, she felt troubled. She had seen through Jaime, of course she had. Haddock would be lovely, the thought of it made her drool. That, or perhaps the old favourite fish and chips? She and Burza had always found themselves waiting with crowds of others outside the fish frier in the Blue Row. Perhaps she should have asked for that instead. Either way Jaime would have made it his business to pass the time of day with his mates on the way to the fishmonger's. Then of course he would down tools and join in. He was always joining in!

232

Fear writhed inside her again. Lily was suddenly, very fervently wishing that Burza was there. She needed her bosom-buddy, needed her to confide in and to tell her that she, Lily, hadn't actually seen that! But, Lily thought, feeling her insides beginning to churn, she hadn't needed eyes in the back of her head to notice Jaime's actions earlier on, to watch him surreptitiously hide a cosh inside his overcoat as he left.

Jaime meant business, as did all the others. Streets were narrow in the area, and warehouses and lock-ups abounded. Huge gates had been forced open, lorries, carts, anything and everything had been dragged out and overturned. Mosley's crowd would not be allowed to pass.

Women were looking down from their windows, just as Lily was staring tearfully down now. But the others were bright-eyed, ready and willing to help the battle along. They would not be there physically beside their men, but they could throw things down!

There was a zing in the air. Young people were defiantly ignoring the warnings of the old.

Stay at home, close your windows, keep out of sight, the *Jewish Chronicle* told them in large letters. The newspaper had gone so far as to use its centre pages to give much the same advice. But all that, the majority thought, was to be profoundly ignored. How could it not be?

It was common knowledge that the fascists were to be reviewed by Mosley in Royal Mint Street. After that they would march contemptuously through the Jewish quarter. Well, Jaime and his mates would be ready for them. Already thousands were there, waiting.

The time went by very slowly for Lily. There was now an even more terrible row going on down below. A cacophony of sound. A hive of activity, preparations, everyone at action stations. Men's attitudes hardening, hostile, waiting for it all to start. They were anxious, eager, alert.

No one was able to get by the barricades. Vehicles were held up, horses and carts turned away. There was a great deal of cussing and swearing going on by those wanting to carry on the normal business of the day. It was something of a let-down that up until now not a single Blackshirt had appeared.

A group of policemen came and ordered the men to take

233

down the barricades. Instructed them to clear the roads. There came a roar of laughter, rude remarks, slogans were yelled, and fiery replies. The street below turned into a seething bedlam, Lily thought. And the crowds writhed, surged forward, fell back, so closely packed together that from her vantage point they looked like a huge fat undulating caterpillar.

The barricades stayed put.

The day dragged on. Inside Lily's home, the ticking clock seemed almost as loud as the beating of her heart. Suddenly she felt nausea rising. She had not been able to get rid of the nerves beating in her stomach all day, fear for Jaime causing it. He wanted to keep her safe, but she needed him to be safe too.

Her head began to swim. She was nervous, the palms of her hand were sweaty, yet she shivered. She was suddenly very afraid of being alone. She thought longingly of Sophie, especially the gentle look in her big brown eyes. If Jaime stayed out much longer she, Lily, would ignore all that he had said. She would risk it and go and sit a while with Sophie. This was England. Home! Where things didn't happen to innocent people.

She went downstairs and outside – a scene from hell. Then stopped, taking a sharp intake of breath. It hadn't seemed so harsh, so vitriolic in the safety of her home far up top. Now it hit her almost like a physical blow. It was awful, the sense of violence and also of frustration all around her. And the ferocious look on the faces in the crowds!

Oh dear heaven, there was a seething mass coming towards her, reaching her, swirling round! She was caught up with them, being swept along. There was nothing she could do against the sheer weight of massed people all heading, from what she could gather, to where the action proper was. It was awesome, unreal. There were thousands and thousands of people.

In a blind panic now Lily found herself being forced along to where the enemy were. But they were not fascists at all. The enemy were the police – the force that had been ordered to clear the streets. Determined policemen were doing their duty. They were charging the barricades – and to the devil with anyone who got in the way.

It was getting out of hand. So the women above were now

234

leaning far out of their windows throwing down things. Missiles of every sort, boiling oil, scalding water, heavy metal, spiked or pointed wood, in some cases the contents of chamber pots. The police as the main adversary were getting the full brunt of it. They fought back, tempers fraying. The attitudes on both sides became even more volatile and uncontrolled.

Terrified, dazed almost to fainting point, Lily was aware that some of the police were now being provocative. Some, especially those with scalded necks and faces, taunted at beyond endurance, even shouted out, 'Heil Hitler!' That in itself was sufficient to drive people mad.

The weaponry from above became more extensive, and some injured policemen began to try and hide in some sheds. Those suffering from burns had had enough. Jeering women flooded down after them then and began battering at the shed doors, screaming out that the police were worse than the fascists if this was what it was going to be. Mouthing on about Hitler and that!

The injured came out finally with their hands in the air. The women laughed like drains, but everyone soon became gracious and laid down their brooms and bricks and back-pedalled in surprise. Coppers giving themselves up? Never on your life! Then the most impudent of the women ran forwards and swept the constables' helmets off their heads, the final and most demeaning insult. Then the cry rose up, 'Shove off!'

Some of the police were taken away by ambulance.

More enforcement, including mounted police, poured into the area. In the mêlée some antagonists went flying through plate-glass windows. Others received broken bones. And the crazy thing was, there wasn't a fascist in sight. Some of the demonstrators, becoming frightened, tried to get out of the way. It was difficult.

There were no holds barred now because, clearly impatient, the law began fighting back, full force, right left and centre. The barricades had to come down and that was that. To that end the mounted police were hitting out with stout laths aiming at men's legs to bring them to their knees. The fight was becoming increasingly vicious; everyone seemed to be whacking away at everyone else.

235

Dicky Cuttings, who had taken time off work especially to travel down and join this fracas, had fought gloriously. Now, in order to try and stop a momentary retreat, he had climbed up a lamp-post. His face was bloody, his eyes alight with fervour, and he was yelling with all his might. His mother would never have recognised him.

'Come on, you lot!' he was shouting. 'Don't give in. These are our streets. Don't let the bastards stop us from defending ourselves!'

A head of shining hair came into his view. Like silk it was, beautiful. Its owner, from where he perched, was unmistakable. As he watched, horrified, he saw Lily being helplessly swept along directly in the path of a pitched battle. Those who were retreating would soon be mixed with those who were pressing forwards. Bricks were flying, stones, glass bottles, on the other side, laths and truncheons.

Dicky leapt down and pushed and shoved his way through the crowd. He reached Lily a moment after a flying brick caught her full on her head. She dropped and would have been crushed to death in the stampede had he not stood over her and tried to shield her with his body. Then a line of police were bearing down on the hordes, pushing them back. There was a gap between adversaries now. The police going forward, the protestors retreating. Lily, still prone, with Dicky trying to protect her, remained where they were, alone, and directly in the advancing party's path.

It looked as though there was to be no reprieve. The foremost policeman had his baton raised. In his own defence Dicky leapt forward and punched him full in the face.

Then high above the noise and confusion, Jaime's voice rang out. 'Lily!'

Suddenly, wild-eyed and bloodied he broke apart from the crowds and was immediately leapt on by the law. He raised his cosh and fought savagely, but was brought down by the sheer weight of numbers. He was arrested, as was Dicky, and a roly-poly little man named Jacob who had left the mob to join his mate. They were carted off.

Lily lay, unconscious, where she was.

The year had been interesting on the whole, Burza thought,

236

and she was as happy as she could be without Lily. But living in Matson Street and knowing all the secret paths in and out of the place had been an experience. She and Andy had been to number two a couple of times, but unlived in, the place was reverting to its old mouldy self, bugs and cockroaches now taking advantage of the place. She and Andy had gone to see Zoe who told them that if Lily did not return within the year, others would take up residence. God help them, Burza thought, seeing how damp had already turned the carpets green.

Of course there was always the nagging worry at the back of Burza's mind about how her friend was getting on. But Jaime had seemed a decent sort, and quiet thoughtful Lily was a good judge of character. Still, it wouldn't have hurt her to write!

On the good side of things, Burza loved her job and the floor manager approved of her bright and cheerful ways. Pete was still trying to get round her, much to her secret delight. Andy's eyes twinkled as he watched them both. His friendship was so greatly valued that Burza had decided not to try and flirt with Andy after all. Well, she had tentatively ogled him just once and he had laughed, ruffled her hair and teased, 'Come off it, Burz!'

Relieved, she had grinned up at him. Quite honestly he was too young for serious romance. Big as he was. Chaps, she thought happily, were never so advanced as girls in that department.

Edward VIII was, though. He had a head on his shoulders all right. All the newspapers were carrying on about his affair with Mrs Simpson. The Prime Minister backed by the Archbishop of Canterbury put in his twopenn'orth, all to no avail. Edward stuck to his guns and on 11 December the King abdicated. It was a terrible shame, the working-class people thought on the whole. He had seemed such a nice down-to-earth man.

Clara and her family were all doing well, and Rosie had fallen hook, line and sinker, and was now wearing Ben Freeman's engagement ring.

Clara worried because she hadn't heard from Dicky, not even a Christmas card. However, she refused point blank to go to his place and visit, fearing she would be accused of poking her nose in.

'He's the quiet sort and he has his reasons,' she said over and over. 'He'll let me know he's alive and kicking all in his own good time.'

Nick Bede was a nuisance though. Out of doors during the dark, winter evenings was bad enough. To be alone was worse. Burza found herself becoming afraid of all dark corners and abyss-like black arches under the railway viaduct. Nick Bede had taken to appearing out of thin air and leering at her like a ghoul. He was biding his time, she knew it. She would tell no one of her fears, and she would sort it all out herself, he knew that too.

Preparing for all eventualities Burza slipped one of Clara's six-inch-long hatpins in her handbag. A lethal weapon like that, she considered, was worth its weight in gold. Even so, it was making her shaky the way Nick Bede was intent on forever stalking her.

Then one morning, when the frost lay thick on the ground, and ice made a glorious fretwork on window panes, the postman brought a letter for Burza. She was on her way to work, rushing not to be late. She took the letter, not recognising the writing on the envelope, and dashed out. It was not until tea-break that she had the chance to read it.

It was from someone named Sophie who had written to say that Lily was ill, alone, and needed help. Would Burza come along and visit at the above address in Barrow Street? Lily would not write herself, but as it had been made clear to Sophie that she, Burza, was Lily's most dearest friend, would she please try to help to put things right ...

Chapter Twenty-Four

Lily opened her eyes and dazedly stared round at the other sleepless forms who, like herself, tried to exist in the streets. High above, the sky was ominous, slug-grey, and there was frozen snow clinging like dirty shaving lather onto shop-window ledges. Icicles hung like glass shooting sticks, and windows bore frosty Paisley designs. Wind with tiny needle-sharp hailstones in its heart swirled the newspaper and cardboard blanket Lily had fought to keep last night, and she clutched at it, inhaling a deep sobbing breath.

There had been a time, when young, that she had prayed to be alone in the world, to be able to please only herself, to walk free! Well, she was alone and free at last. A destitute in a harsh and unfriendly world. Her head and limbs ached, specially her legs. This because so much of her time was spent walking, jumping, skipping anything to keep moving before the extremities of weather put an end to her. Now, huddled in a shop doorway just before the world woke up, she was conscious of hunger. A dreadful gnawing hunger that felt as acute as mortal disease.

She could go back, she thought desperately. To Burza whom she loved. To Burza whom she had so cruelly let down. She remembered her own casual stance when Burza had asked where she must go? And her own monumental arrogance. Had she really said that? 'Why, back to Clara, of course.' Her love for Jaime had made her too selfish to be true. She hadn't even thought of how hurt Burza must have felt. Well, Jaime was gone, hating her still in all probability. And she, Lily, had inherited enough of her father's pride never to run back to Burza with her tail between her legs. Even though Burza of all people would forgive and forget.

'Please God forgive me, Lily thought tearfully and felt utmost self-contempt. Her mind churned on. She could return to her father's fold. Be looked after – smothered! She shuddered the thought away, the idea of Solomon Street as obnoxious to her as the everlasting psalm-pushing was to those refusing Sally Army refuge.

She heard the steady plod of a policeman and the occasional rattle as he tried shop doors. Time to go! She shivered, and attempted to stand, managed at last, and because of an attack of cramp, hobbled desperately across the road. A short, foxy-faced man with a long nose and greasy hair stepped away from a baker's wall. He beckoned to her. Almost beyond caring she joined him. He smelled of stale booze and cheap cigarettes. By the soiled state of his clothes he was recovering from an all-night drinking session.

'Bleeding hell,' he said, 'this is enough to freeze orf your balls. This is the last time I stay out bingeing. Where are you orf to?'

'I don't know,' she replied shakily.

He grinned in a slimy way. 'Like that, is it? I'm Penn, by the way.'

She did not bother replying, just stood there, hands against the warmth of the wall.

'How come you're on the streets, mate?'

'A long story.'

'Ain't they all? Come on, I'll treat you to a cuppa and you can tell me all abart it.'

A hot cup of tea! Worth its weight in gold. She loathed the man, his looks, his smell, his cocky attitude, but for a hot cuppa she would have followed the devil himself.

He took her to a working-men's café and as well as tea he ordered two rounds of dripping toast. She sat at the narrow table opposite him, her hands clasped round her chipped enamel cup.

'Come on then, mate,' he told her. 'A good yarn's like entertainment ter me. Better'n the pictures, eh? What's a pretty thing like you doing on the streets? Yes, pretty, because

240

I reckon you'll scrub up real well. How come you're here with me and not in some house somewhere.'

'I had a nice place – once.'

'Then what happened?'

'I disobeyed my boyfriend and because I did I ... '

'Orders is meant to be ignored.'

'Through me there were a lot of tragedies.'

'Gawd! Piling it on a bit, ain't you?'

'It was in the riot. My boyfriend left the crowd and tried to help me. So did his mate Jacob, and Dicky the cousin of my dearest friend. They were all charged with incitement to riot, carrying dangerous weapons and assaulting the police. They were sentenced to four months' hard labour. If I had stayed at home as instructed and not needed rescuing, they might have all got away with it. Hundreds did.'

'But how come you're here now?'

'Jacob, my boyfriend's mate, was hurt very badly in the struggle. When he was arrested he fought like a tiger they said. Anyway, he received a blow which has blinded him in one eye. Jaime believes they were all fitted up, that bricks and files and stuff were planted on Jacob and also on Dicky. Neither of them would have dreamed of carrying offensive weapons. Jaime did – he had a cosh. But basically, because they refused to run and leave me, they all got caught.'

'So he ain't forgiven yer and has had yer chucked out?'

'He hasn't forgiven me because I was hurt, and shortly after I came to I finished up in General and – and lost his baby. Until that time I never even knew. I didn't realise ... but there it is. Anyway, money ran out, I couldn't pay the rent, and the landlord refused to let me in to get my things. So I lost everything – my baby, Jaime, my happiness and my home. And all for not doing as I was told.' She looked across the table at him with wide tragic blue eyes. 'And do you know something? For many years I tried desperately to do exactly as I was told. Seems I can't win.'

'A pretty girl like you can always make a bob or two.'

Lily knew what he meant. Prostitution. The idea made her sick, but she had reached rock bottom anyway. She sat there, in the scruffy little ditchwater café, drawing cooking-warmth round her like a cloak.

'If you're on,' Penn said and smiled his oily smile, 'I'll get us breakfast. Egg, bacon, bangers 'n' toast. 'Ow'd that do yer?'

'Nicely,' she said.

The streets did not feel quite so cold when they went outside again. A tepid sun was doing its best as she followed Penn to a basement flat. It was an ill-kept place, as far from her and Jaime's home as chalk from cheese, but it was better than the street. Penn led her into a small back room that was situated off the dingy little brown-painted passageway.

The window was filthy and one could not look out at the back yard. There were tired-looking blue curtains hanging at the window. A blue bedspread that was grey with age covered a double bed and there was dark blue linoleum on the floor. The walls were plain washed blue. There was a standing cupboard in one corner and a chest of drawers. Both looked cheap and nasty and were hand-painted blue.

In a panicky kind of way Lily knew that she would hate the colour blue for the rest of her life.

'This bedroom's your'n,' he told her. 'You'll sleep here from now on and I'll look after you. There'll be no rough stuff, bit kinky sometimes, but no rough. Know what I mean? Soap and water's in the bathroom. Get yourself scrubbed up. I'll get yer a comb and some stuff to put on your face, an' some better clobber than them rags you've got on. Soon as you've started earning you can get yourself some real nice toggery. Go high class an' that. All right?'

The door slammed behind him. Lily found the bathroom. The water was freezing, the soap, red carbolic. She almost drooled with pleasure at the clean and wholesome smell of that bar of soap. She scrubbed herself all over, shivering but exulting in feeling clean again. She washed her long tangled hair, then seeing a pair of scissors, began cutting it short. As she continued to rub it dry it flew into golden-glinting curls. She looked at herself in the mirror and wanted to laugh, then cry, then go mad.

Her father would have something to be proud of now, she thought, wonderfully proud! Only this time he'd know the truth. Not have it hidden away like something slimy under a stone. Her reflection, looking back from the mirror, had been

242

Marion's. Yes, they were as alike as two peas. Her lying, cheating, pedantic, darling Aunty Marion!

So be it, Lily thought and felt hysterical laughter bubbling up inside.

Later Penn came back and grinned.

'Knew you'd scrub up good,' he told her. ''Ere, 'ave a go at all this.'

He placed a brown paper carrier bag on the floor and left her to it. There were underclothes, not new exactly, but clean washed. A tight-waisted, slim-fitting black skirt, and a red velvet off the shoulder blouse. In a separate paper bag emblazoned *Bundels Beauty Shop* there was face powder and powder puff, lipstick and mascara.

Suddenly Lily inhaled sharply as she pulled her tummy muscles in to stop their churning. There was no use crying over spilt milk. And she had spilt gallons in her time. She had gone all out to be a thief, hadn't she? She had been the exact opposite of what her father had shaped and moulded her to be. And now, a step forward or backwards according to how one looked at it. She was about to be lower than a tart, or the kept woman her father's sister was.

Now she, Lily London, was about to become an all-out whore. Oh well, she might as well look the part. Just as Marion did while she was in the Warner's flat with Paul Drew.

She began using the make-up liberally, wondered fleetingly how Marion's curls were flattened for her daily returns to Solomon Street. Easy, she thought, having considered the matter as though it was of great importance. A hairbrush heavy with cold water would do the trick every time. Clever old Mal!

Later, while sitting alone in the kitchen drinking yet another cup of hot, sweet tea with condensed milk she heard the street door open. And footsteps shuffling along the small dark passage and into the blue room. She froze, then Penn sidled in.

'He'll pay £2. Go for it, gel.'

Lily shook her head, her courage crumbling. 'I can't,' she sobbed. 'I'm sorry, but I can't!'

'Oh yes yer can, bitch,' he whispered viciously, and his

dirty fingernails dug spitefully into her arm. 'You're going ter pay me back what you owe me at least. Food, clothes, wash 'n' brush up. Ter say nothing abart 'aving a roof over your head. Get in there, d'yer hear? It's on your bleedin' back or else get out on the street an' starve.'

Lily pulled her arm free and took in a deep shuddering breath. She walked out of the kitchen and into the bedroom. A man was perched expectantly on the edge of her bed. He was old, ugly, and there was something nasty about his simian face.

Suddenly she was dying the death, and remembering Burza's withering look when she was really angry, Lily knew she would be glaring now all right. Fit to kill, in fact.

Lily drew herself up tall. Giving Penn a glacier-like stare she curled her lip in contempt. Then, in her best Aunt Marion voice, she told him, 'Don't be so ridiculous!'

She swept by him like a queen. Now the man on the bed was openly gawping. Penn was looking as evil as a cornered ferret.

'You bastard!' The man was jumping up livid-faced and furious. 'You brought up up 'ere, you piss-taker. Give us me money back – or else!'

Lily's last glimpse of the two was Penn trying to fend off a very dissatisfied customer. The last thing she heard was him yelling after her: 'You cow! You owe me! I'll bleeding well get yer for this!'

Suddenly her ladylike act deserted her. Half-demented, Lily flew out of the house, and all the while, deep in her heart, she was crying for Burza.

Burza sat opposite a handsome young woman who lived at the top end of Barrow Street. She had already heard the whole story, or as much as Sophie knew, and was still reeling.

'I didn't think I'd ever forgive her,' Sophie told Burza again. 'My life, I didn't! When I saw her out there, on the street, I remembered how she was once. What a sweet little thing she seemed to be. But that was before, so I just walked away. Still seething, you know. Just left her there, I did. She was begging!'

'Oh damn!' Burza said shakily. 'Damn, damn, damn!'

'I saw this tarted-up old woman actually spit at her. And I wanted to go and face your friend and spit at her too. I was halfway home when it struck me how low I'd sunk myself. I went back but she'd gone. So I turned tail and didn't stop till I got back here. But I couldn't forget the state she was in. Had nightmares, I did.'

'Begging? Lily?' Tears were running down Burza's cheeks. 'And you left her there?'

'I changed my mind – I just told you that. And don't forget my Jacob's doing hard labour!' Sophie flung at her. 'He's injured, lost the sight in one eye and him a tailor, remember? I'll never forgive her, never! Even so, I went to where she used to live, at the far end of this very street, and as a favour I was allowed to go through her things. That's where I found your address.'

'You say they threw her out? That Jaime didn't pay in advance?'

'No, so they said. There's no way of knowing if they lied. Anyway Lily didn't have any cash so she couldn't pay what she owed. Jaime had washed his hands of her when he learned about the baby and —'

'What?' Burza went chalk-white. 'You'd better tell me all this again.'

'It was hardly a baby as such. A couple of months, if that. But that's neither here nor there. Not according to Jaime anyway. She should have done as she was asked and stayed put. I did!'

Burza heard the lot after that. How Jaime and Jacob as well as a chap named Dicky Cuttings had finished up in gaol.

'Dicky Cuttings?' This was the first time the name had entered the conversation. Burza's sense of shock flared into even greater life.

'Yes. Didn't I mention him before?'

'No. You just said this other bloke.'

'He comes from your way.'

'Really?' Burza was holding her breath.

'Jaime knew of him, he reckons. Anyway this Dicky leapt down from a lamp-post to rescue Lily. It was him leaping down from that post that made Jaime look, then he saw Lily on the ground. So my Jacob, Jaime, and this other bloke all got nabbed. Caught because they'd all tried to protect Lily who shouldn't have been there in the first place. Selfish little cow.'

'Something very bad, soul-wounds for want of better words, changed her,' Burza replied chokily. 'Believe me, there was a time when she was the most sweet and obedient person I knew.'

'Well, I'll tell you this,' Sophie said bluntly, 'I hated her. She deserved what she got, to lose out on everything, including the baby. My Jacob's doing time in spite of the fact he's lost the sight of an eye and nerve-wise will never be the same again. I wanted to kill her myself, and was happy to let the streets do it for me. Then – then I saw her and couldn't stand thinking about her, so . . . '

'You sent for me,' Burza said. 'Thank you. Where can I find her?'

'I don't know! How could I? On the main road outside the busiest shops? Perhaps near the bus depot or around the queues outside the pictures, places like that. Usually the tramps and beggars and homeless hang about where there's plenty of passers by. You can never tell exactly, of course.'

Burza jumped up, hand extended. 'Thank you,' she said simply. 'And believe me, I'm very, very sorry about your Jacob.'

'I'll write and tell him you came, shall I? And that you wish to be remembered to Jaime and —'

'My good wishes to Jacob,' Burza cut in hurriedly, 'but nothing to the man who is callous enough to blame someone he is supposed to have loved, for being too scared to stay in on her own! But there is one thing you can do for me. Please? Send a message to Dicky Cuttings. Say that Burza sends her deepest most fondest love, and that his mum misses him very, very much. Ask him, will he please drop his guard for once and write?'

'I'll do that,' Sophie said, taking Burza's hand. Both knowing they would never set eyes on each other again . . .

Amazingly Burza came upon Lily as she was following some church railings guarding the huge grey stone building. The old church, with its spire like a finger pointing to God stood tall

246

and imposing in its frost-bound enclosure. Burza had walked towards this landmark because of blind intuition and because it was just somewhere else to try.

She had been thinking of Lily's little unborn. This in turn reminded her of Baby Violet, who had lived, briefly, and who had been so deeply loved. A picture of St Christopher's had come into her mind, and the holy spot holding Baby Violet and dearest George. As the memories came flooding back, Burza had looked up and seen the church spire. It had seemed to be a pointer somehow. A sign from the Divine.

As she came to the railings and walked along, from ahead a sharp cry rang out. As Burza picked up her heels and raced forwards, she saw a thin, evil-looking man cruelly twisting Lily's arms behind her back.

'I'm going ter beat the livin' daylights out of yer, yer ungrateful little mare!' the man was shouting. Then he let go of Lily long enough to give her a terrible blow to the face.

It was then that Burza, raving mad at the vicious beast, charged.

Clara's hatpin finally saw the light of day.

Penn, hand to face, howling, ran forever out of the two girls' lives.

On the bus home a subdued Lily, now wearing Burza's coat which was much too short for her, listened to Burza's harangue. The side of her face was red and raw, she was tear-stained and shaking. She was looking at Burza as though she was an angel flown down direct from heaven itself. She did not attempt to reply to the things Burza was saying until the very end. Then all she whispered when Burza paused to take breath was, 'Not back to Solomon Street, Burza. Anywhere but there.'

'You can come in with me. Clara would love to —'

'No! Not Solomon Street.' Lily was horrified now. 'Never! If you try to take me back there I shall run again.'

'Where then, Soppy Soft?' Lily visibly relaxed at Burza's childhood term of endearment. Burza went on, 'My God, you're a one, Lily!' She grinned then. 'By the way, he didn't half clump you. You're going to have a wonderful black eye. A real shiner, in fact.'

Lily ignored this, and whispered, 'Back to our place in Matson Street. Please?'

'I'm not leaving Clara's,' Burza told her quietly. 'No, not ever again, Lily. Not for you or for anyone.'

'Not even for Pete?' The old Lily returned momentarily and was smiling shyly out of crystal-blue eyes. 'Get away with you, Burza. You've always been mad on him.'

'I'm keeping him at arm's length,' Burza told her defiantly, though her flaming cheeks gave her away. 'And Matson Street's reverted to style. Bug-ridden, flea-ridden, there's mouse droppings everywhere, the cockroaches are on the march, and the damp's turned the carpet green.'

'It's there or nowhere.'

'I'll tell you what. Let's ask Andy if he has any ideas.'

'Andy?'

'He knows all about it, Lily, and he won't tell a soul.'

'Burza,' Lily whispered humbly, tears slipping down her swollen cheek, 'I'm sorry for all the trouble I've caused. So very, very sorry! And – and whatever happened to our old Boris?'

'He's on top of the world.' Burza hastened to reassure her. 'Clara makes a fool of him and overfeeds him, believe it or not. He has lots of human friends, the kids adore him and are gentleness itself. He has the run of the house, even Rosie's room! Oh, and of the street, of course. Life's full for our old Boris, believe me.'

'I really loved our cat.'

'The Bedes don't.' Burza chuckled full and rich, like chocolate. 'Gin and our Boris have a whale of a time, shrieking and yelling, ears back, all teeth and claws. You know the sort of thing. They're deadly enemies and it's a fair old to-do when they meet up. Almost as bad as Ethel Jacobs and Fanny Lyons coming face to face.' Her eyes were alight and sparkling. 'I think our Boris wins. Yes, he actually beats old Gin by a whisker. By a whisker, Lily! How's that?'

Both girls were smiling and Lily had become more calm as they alighted and walked along the High Road and finally reached Dunton Street. Lily kept to the shadows when Burza knocked on Andy's door. Thank goodness it was Andy himself who came to the door.

'She's here,' Burza said quietly. 'We don't know what to do or where to go, so ...'

248

'It's confab time, eh?' he asked, seeming as calm as if she had just told him what day it was. He turned in an easy, casual way and slipped his coat off the peg. 'Come on, let's go.'

'Where to? Matson Street?' Burza asked, thankful for someone else to shoulder the burden for a change.

'Where else?' he asked, and his teeth gleamed in the lamplight. 'It's a hell hole, but better than freezing to death out here.'

When they walked into the fusty musty filthy number two Matson Street, Lily took in a deep choking breath, sat on the mildewy armchair by the old grey fireplace, and cried.

'Pull yourself together,' Andy told her evenly. 'Howling like a banshee won't help.'

'That does it!' Burza said firmly. 'You're coming back to Clara's. It's dark, no one will see you, and Clara knows how to keep as silent as the grave when necessary. You will stay inside, in my room, until I've had time to sort this lot out. Then when it's warm and clean again, we'll sneak you back here. All right?'

'No!'

'Oh shut up!' Burza said. 'You're going to do as you're told for a change.'

Burza sneaked into number six and found Clara alone. She put her finger to her lips and then vanished outside again. Shielded by Andy, Lily crept into the house.

Clara took one look at Lily's face and held open her arms. And then Lily was warm and safe and sobbing her heart out, while Clara was loving and soothing, and Andy was helping Burza in the scullery, making tea and cutting doorsteps of bread and marge topped with masses of strawberry jam.

'It's to be our secret, Clara,' Burza said. 'Lily doesn't want her father to know a thing about this. I don't know how we'll manage it, especially with all the family, but it's only for one night.'

'And after that, gel?' Clara asked.

The two girls exchanged glances, then Lily admitted, 'Matson Street.'

'Do what?' Clara was outraged. 'Slummy ol' Matson Street? Not on your nellie. No, never!'

And then they told her about where they had lived. And

why. Because Lily had been determined to be the exact opposite of everything her father had relentlessly drummed into her over the years. Lily did not tell Clara about her running with thieves, or the receiving of stolen goods, or her regular habit of being the 'Bank' as they called it, when on jobs. Neither did she mention Penn and the goings-on in that awful blue-grey room.

Clara listened and looked, saying nothing until Lily faltered into silence, then: 'Well, by the look of yer, gel, you've come off the worst of it. Someone's give yer a right ol' bashing – but I'll ask no questions. You look half-starved, and you're wearing nothing but a skirt, and a blouse – what's not even keeping your shoulders warm – under Burza's coat.' She looked at Burza and shook her head. 'I can see you've got your woolly on, but in this freezing weather, and without your coat, you'll go down with pneumonia same as 'er, like as not. Bloody hell, what am I going ter do with the pair of you, eh? Talk about a couple of chumps!'

And all the time she was nagging she was fetching warm water and cotton wool and wiping the tearstains away from Lily's face, and was getting Burza's thick cablestitch jumper off the airer and slipping it over her shoulders, and finding an equally thick jumper of Rosie's and putting it on Lily.

'Now up to bed you go, gel,' she told Lily. 'Burz'll fill me in all in her own good time.' She kissed Lily soundly, squeezed her tight and Lily clung onto her, weeping, and wishing that Clara had been her mum. Then Clara shepherded her upstairs to Burza's bedroom.

When she came down Burza asked carefully, 'Can you stand any more shocks, Clara?'

'I believe I can,' the older woman told her, looking at her straight. 'It's all according, of course.'

'It's about Dicky.'

Clara's eyes went very still, her face became taut, then: 'What about him?'

'He's in prison, Clara. He was in a riot. The Cable Street Riot, the newspapers called it, but it was happening all over. I've only just found out myself. I – I sent our love and have asked him to write.'

It was Clara's turn to cry.

250

Much later that night, when most of the world slept, Burza and Clara slipped out of the house and made their way to Matson Street. They worked and slaved to get the place clean and decent again. Windows were thrown open to give the place an airing. Bugs and other noxious things were given short shrift.

'It'll have ter do for now,' Clara said at last and sniffed, 'but I tell yer what! Since knowing you'll be visiting every day because young Lil's set on staying in this dump, I'm coming here regular-like meself. That's until I'm satisfied it's fit for decent human beings. How'd Lily come by it, by the way?'

'It was Gippo Wray's.'

'Young Richard lived here?'

'Yes.'

'The pore little sod!'

Burza smiled to herself, wondering what darling Clara would have thought, had she seen the place first off.

After that, well before Burza went away to her job in Kitchenware, it was an amazing sight to see Mrs Clara Cuttings stomping down Matson Street. She carried her cleaning things in her hand like weapons, and she had a look on her face that defied any of the old girls to challenge her.

Clara had told Ethel Jacobs that she was taking on a job down Matson Street as a special favour to young Richard. She used the reason they had all agreed on – that Andy had heard from Richard who had said that he wanted the place kept decent. That he was working away as an apprentice in wireless sets and would, sometime in the future, return.

Ethel Jacobs made hay with that one!

Lily, settled in, was a little put out because Burza would not part with Boris. Then she became confident once more. She was delighted that in turn Gee visited her and they enjoyed heaps of feminine gossip, mostly about the gang. Then Three, once so weedy, now filled out and quite a man, came in for a cuppa and a chat. And of course Diver whose black eyes were like chips of shiny black coal was not far behind him. The old excitement filled Lily, and she was anxious to begin work—or her idea of work. After the Penn episode, being with her own gang was like living clean!

251

Burza, nag, rage and carry on though she did, could not change her friend's mind.

In May that year, the German airship *Hindenburg* crashed in New Jersey. Thirty-three passengers and crew died.

'Like vultures feeding on grief, them newspapers are,' Clara sniffed. 'Keep on and on about it all, they do. And that bloody great mass flaring up like a fire rocket with all them poor devils in the basket below – Ooh, 'orrible!' She grabbed up yet another newspaper account and began to look at it all again.

On the jolly side George VI was crowned and his immensely popular wife Elizabeth became Queen. Festive street parties took place in local communities throughout the country. Even the poorest of the poor had their street parties. Solomon Street became a paradise filled with multi-coloured paper roses and Union Jacks.

Now growing more wilful, selfish and outrageous in spite of all Burza's yelling at her, Lily and her old mates made the most of the crowds and stole to their hearts' content.

Now worldly wise, feeling that she knew a thing or two owing to Penn, Lily became friends with the Madam Zoe Zuckerman. Through that woman, Lily learned of Nick Bede's involvement in a 'Shatt's' robbery, which was carried out with violence, at the Baker's Arms Bank. Lily smiled her secret smile.

In ways known only to herself, and Zoe's old pal Quiller who was boss of the Matson Street gang, Lily set out for revenge. She had never got over her loathing of Nick since Burza had told her of his actions. With the help of Quiller, Lily now joyfully shopped him.

When he was sent down for robbery and grievous bodily harm, he received a message via an old lag. The message was:

For Burza and for the Steadmans. Read this and weep!

'So, dear,' Lily told Burza gloating, 'I have battled on your behalf for a change! You won't have to put up with that beast prowling around after you any more. He'll be shut away for years.'

'Thank you, Lily,' Burza told her, heart aching at the change in her friend. 'You have done what you thought best.

I'll let you know what I think about it all – when he gets out!'

'Burza!' Lily's eyes filled with tears. 'I'd die for you, you know that.'

'Die for me, but not change your ways! Lily, you're heading for trouble, you know you are. Know something? As you're going now, I almost prefer your stuffy old dad.'

'And Marion?' Lily asked bitterly. 'Tell me, does she still work regularly – at the firm of Drews?'

'I think so,' Burza had to admit. 'But it's cut to three days a week now, I believe.'

'Oh dearie me!' Lily drawled in her husky voice. 'Her wages of sin must have dropped. What a pity!'

'You're being childish.'

'And you're being a bore. Sometimes I could – could ...'

'What?' Burza asked and glared, and Lily shrugged in her charmingly helpless way.

In spite of everything Lily still adored her very best friend. Burza knew it and remained steadfastly loyal.

In June the American boxer Joe Louis, known as the 'Brown Bomber', became world heavyweight boxing champion. Pete Frazer was full of it.

'Come on, Burz,' he pleaded, 'come and have a drink with me at the Feathers. Give me a break, eh? I promise to behave. Make this a special night for me. Louis did for Braddock in eight rounds and he's won my bet for me. Help me celebrate.'

Of course, she thought, elated. Lily can do her own ironing for a change. I don't care that she's after impressing Zoe Zuckerman by togging up. She's heading for a fall there, I know it. I should be there, to tell her, but ... No, I must and will go out with Pete.

For the first time in her life Burza willingly let Lily get on with her own affairs. She finished up in Pete's arms, just as she knew she would. His kisses set her on fire, they both knew it, but she drew back determined he'd never take advantage of her again.

Regularly keeping Pete Frazer at arm's length became the name of the game. It made life exhilarating, wonderful, and all the time Burza knew that the day would arrive when she would give way. She wanted to, ached to. Thoughts of her golden-god Pete were with her night and day. But he mustn't know that. At least, not yet!

Andy took Josie to the pictures and told Burza afterwards that it was all jolly good fun in the back row. Apart from the bits shown by Pathé News, of course. One had to pay attention then! It had been all about Germany spreading out, like a crab crawling over everything. And the Japs wanting as much of China as they could grab. And about all of Europe's civilians being issued with gas masks because of the talk of war.

'It was all ugly and awful,' Josie wailed to Burza, but she was fluttering her eyelashes at Andy at the same time. 'It frightened me!'

I'll never really like her, Burza thought, but I give her full marks for trying. She's been after Andy from Infant School days. Oh well, she's hooked him now.

'Let's all got to Chingford at the weekend,' Pete suggested, winking at Burza in his shining sort of way. Lily who had joined them for a change, as well as Andy and Josie, declined. So Burza and Pete went on their own.

Miss Allthorpe was out with Granger somewhere, but Roan knew Pete at once, and Burza too after a while.

'Cupboard love,' Burza said softly as Roan nuzzled at her, searching for the apple she held. 'Isn't he a dear? And how marvellously he's grown.'

'Like you, Burz,' he told her, looking at her in that certain way. 'You know I want you to be my girl, don't you? Straight up I do. I want to call at your door in front of everyone in Solomon Street. Let everyone know! What do you say?'

'I'll think about it,' she told him and seemed calm enough, but her heart was dancing a fandango, and she wanted to sing out loud.

Within a very short while Andy and Josie had paired up, also Burza and Pete. Lily ranged wild and free on her own. It was Andy who drew Burza to one side and confided that he had written to Richard and told him about the goings-on.

'Did he write back?'

'Yes, mate, he did.'

'And what did he say about Lily?'

'Nothing. Nothing at all.'

'Then – what?'

254

'We've done everything we can, love,' Andy told her, 'so for now we must let sleeping dogs lie.'

So a pattern was set. Lily becoming part and parcel of Matson Street. Josie Biggs holding on to Andy like grim death. Burza not only keeping her job at the Co-op, but doing very well. Peter keeping up with his boxing and his determined chasing of Burza, much to her delight. And very occasionally news filtered through about Richard, who was passing exams and progressing along all the right lines.

After the uprising Dicky wrote as regularly as he was allowed. On release from prison he had arrived out of the blue, to say goodbye for a while to Clara. He had joined the International Brigade. Two days later he had left to fight in Spain. He had said that Jaime was to do the same, but that Jacob had returned to Barrow Street. According to Dicky, Jaime seemed to have forgotten all about Lily. On the other hand, Burza thought, Lily certainly seemed to be managing very well without him!

Then, right out of the blue it seemed, everyone was getting used to sandbags and underground shelters, and in spite of Neville Chamberlain's promises, there was nothing but the talk of needing to put old Hitler down. There was a new fighter plane in existence. About time too! It was called a Spitfire.

Suddenly, incredibly, Burza was nineteen years old, and war was heading towards becoming a stark reality. It seemed that the whole world was about to go mad.

Chapter Twenty-Five

It was terrible, awful, the day young Georgy and Clara, called Clarry, were evacuated. There they stood, hand in hand, Clarry's hair shining like a halo, her eyes huge in her face. Georgy was solemnity itself because his mum couldn't stop crying, and his aunty was bawling too. The children waited among hundreds of others, tickets with their names and particulars pinned to their jackets, gas masks hung over their shoulders, suitcases holding the barest of necessities in their hands. Two tiny people, bemused at the fuss, half excited, half afraid, and conscious of bewilderment more than anything else.

A harassed-looking teacher was shepherding them in line. With a high, animalistic shriek the huge train roared into the station and pulled up. The noise made Clarry jump and she hid her face behind her free hand and began to cry.

'It's all right,' Georgy told her roughly, his own face white to the lips. 'It's only our train making a fuss.'

Betsy made to grab her child within the safety of her aching arms, but Clarry wouldn't let go of Georgy. The children stood together, both small for their ages, unnerved, sure of only one thing. Nothing and no one would part them. It had been the same from the moment they had been wheeled side by side in their prams.

Carriage doors were swung open, children were herded in by perspiring adults, and after an interminable time, when everything and everyone was sorted, the train huffed and puffed and blew out clouds of steam. At last, seeming slow and disgruntled, it pulled its young and tender, handkerchief-waving load away from the city danger zone.

'Bleedin' Hitler!' Rosie sobbed, 'I'll never forgive 'im. Never!'

'Bastard!' Peg gasped and she too broke into fresh sobs.

They cried all the way back to number six where the grim-faced Clara was waiting for them with cups of hot sweet tea.

On 3 September, war was declared between Britain and Germany. it was a relief for it to be made official at last.

Conscription had been introduced in April, to provide six months' military training for men aged twenty. The National Service Act now made all males aged eighteen to forty-one liable for military duties, unless they were in some vital occupation. Now Clara's womenfolk knew what fear was. All of their men were liable for call-up.

Dicky came home from Spain. He looked older but was unscathed. Clara's joy was shortlived, however, because he immediately enlisted.

Civilians became part and parcel of a National Register, and all forty-six million of them were issued with identity cards. All of course having received gas masks. Clara worried herself stupid over Boris.

'How the soddin' hell's he going ter survive, poor ol' love?' she asked Burza over and over. 'I've tried all I know to get him used to things. But he won't even let me hold a soft damp cloth up against his face.'

'Perhaps he'll manage on his own,' Burza replied hopefully. 'And they do say that cats have nine lives. You should have seen what he managed to overcome when a kitten. Honestly, he was half dead when we found him.'

In a very short time life in Solomon Street had changed. Old enemies forgot ancient slights and instead exchanged derogatory remarks about Lord Haw Haw the swine who was spitting out propaganda on the wireless. Of course ol' Adolf 'Itler was regularly consigned to all the seven hells. Call-up at this stage was slow, but every man of eligible age waited and wondered how soon.

Pete was one of the first to volunteer for the Army. Volunteers had a choice of service – Army, Navy, Air Force. Burza was devastated that Pete was so anxious to leave her, then even more put out. By now he had made a name for himself as a half-decent boxer and had won many bouts. He believed that the Army, rather than putting a stop to his boxing career, would enhance it. Thought of further glory egged him on.

At home Pete had acquired a fan club. Burza had known, of course, but it hadn't seemed to matter. But on the day she scrounged a morning off work and went with him to the station to wish him goodbye, most of Pete's fans managed to be at the station to see him off too. Pete postured, grinned and winked, then gave Burza a huge bear-hug, but it wasn't the same. Not in front of an audience of groaning girls.

'The rotten devil's enjoying this!' Burza told herself. 'And it will be the same wherever he goes.' She watched sadly as the train took her Pete away. Only it didn't feel as though he was hers. It felt as though he belonged to England, and an army of female fans.

That evening, after work, Burza walked disconsolately round to see Lily in number two Matson Street. Lily was sitting in the armchair, reading. She looked up and smiled, but in a weak and watery way.

'He's gone then?' she asked.

'Yes,' Burza replied, thinking the tears were for Pete. 'I expect you would have liked to see him off, too. Still, it wouldn't have meant that much. Half the girls in England were there.'

'And so you're fed up?' Lily's voice was strained. 'In fact, rather like me?'

'You could say that.'

'Let's go to the pictures. Then we can get fish and chips on the way back home.'

'I'd rather stay here and just talk.'

'What about?'

'How all of this is altering our lives.'

'It's not altering mine,' Lily said, picking up. She added firmly, 'I don't intend to let it.'

'How can you sit there and be so smug?' Burza exploded, outraged. 'If anyone had told me you'd turn out a hard person I would never have believed them. Aren't you even afraid that the enemy might come over and smash us to pieces with bombs?'

'Then we'd all be dead. We wouldn't be able to worry

about it or anything else then, would we?' Lily seemed defiant, then she laughed her charming husky laugh, and managed to look bewitching and wicked at one and the same time. 'Oh come on, dear, let's look on the bright side.'

'Has it never occurred to you that your father is hardly in any position to defend himself when the Germans invade us?' Burza flared at her, refusing to look on the bright side for once.

'Who says that's going to happen?' Lily replied, unfazed.

'Just about everyone. And what if they use mustard gas? They did in the last war and it was awful. It burned out men's lungs, their faces, and blistered their throats and tongues. It – Oh dear God, it doesn't bear thinking of!'

'My father,' Lily told her tightly, smile banished, 'will manage very well. Windows or not he must have managed to save himself quite a little nest egg by now. He has always been on the careful side – since Marion took over managing his affairs, in fact. So don't try to make me feel guilty just because you're feeling fed up just now.'

'Your father ...'

'Dad will just sit glaring in his chair and order everyone to behave correctly. And to speak correctly, and to mind their manners! That, whether they're the British Army, the German Army or even the Sally Army. Besides, I don't give a darn about what he thinks.'

'No?' Burza snapped. 'Really? Then what's all this attitude of yours about? All this stealing, and running with thieves? And cocking a snook every way you can at the rules of law?'

'Oh do be quiet, Burza.'

'I'll say my piece whether you want me to or not.' Burza was in full spate now. 'Deep down, it's all about defying your dad, isn't it? Yes, he who you supposedly don't give a damn about! Why are you always trying so hard to do the things that would make him want to curl up? Think! Yes, him and also Marion because of her airs and graces ... which I grant you is a laugh!'

'A hypocrite.' Lily's cheeks went pink. Her eyes glittered cold fire. 'A lying, cheating faker.'

'But better than you!' Burza flung at her.

'What's that supposed to mean?'

'At least she's stuck by your dad. That's in spite of wanting to cut and run to her fancy man for good! Oh yes, that's what she would have chosen had he not lost his leg. I'm sure of it. But you? You want revenge on Marion and your dad and that's all there is to it.'

'I have lived on my wits and I—'

'Don't give a shit about the police, even I know that. You just go on your own sweet way no matter what. In fact, you've got to be that much too cocky just because you've evaded the law for all these years.'

'Oh shut up!'

'No, I won't. And you're not even clever – just bloody cunning the way you can disappear at will. This is the perfect spot for it, isn't it? Now we know why Gippo always clung to this dump. Of course, all your so-called friends have helped you on the downward path too. We mustn't forget that!'

'For heaven's sake, Burza!'

This is getting out of hand, Burza thought wildly. Why am I carrying on in this way? Lily is Lily no matter what. She's got to work out her own salvation, and me mouthing on at her won't help a bit. In fact, it will probably only make her dig her toes in. Lily's years of repression have turned her into this disobedient, stupid person glorying in all the wrong things, and I should be more patient. More understanding. She felt deflated, then reared up again. No! I've been understanding for years and not saying much. Now it's time she was told!

She heard herself continuing fiercely, aggressively, still in a manner she had never used to Lily before.

'But I can see through you, Lily London. You're not a natural wrongdoer for all you think you are. I bet sometimes that all this – this nastiness you're caught up in really goes against the grain. But on you go, wrecking your life. Yes, wrecking it because you're just asking for trouble.'

'Don't take it out on me just because you came second to Pete Frazer's fan club,' Lily drawled. The skin tightened over her cheekbones and gave her face a marble look, cold and clean and as stiff as a statue's. 'As for all the rubbish you've just come out with, you're talking out of the back of your neck.'

'Really?' Burza cut in impatiently. 'Face this fact. You're

260

just living every minute of the day in the manner you think is flying in the face of your poor crippled dad! You ought to feel ashamed.'

'Now you sound just like Clara,' Lily replied and shrugged in a cool expressive way.

'Good! I'd rather sound like her than anyone else I know.'

'My way of life is daring, and dangerous, and fun!'

'Codswallop!'

'Now you sound like my dad.'

'Correction, Lily. I sound just like me!'

'They admire me round here.'

'Really? How spiffing!'

'Now you're descending to sarcasm, Burza.'

'Because that's the only defence I have left,' Burza told her bitterly, throwing in the towel and letting her tears fall. 'And it's you that should shut up, Lily. I came here because I was fed up, not because I want to have a slanging match. But I meant what I said. I don't know how you can live like you do. I don't understand you any more.' Then on a sob, 'I don't feel I even know you.'

'Burza!' The years flew away and they were children again. Lily sprang up from her chair and her arms went round Burza and held her close. 'Burza, you are my best friend. I love you.'

'And I love you, Lily, even though you're no longer my old Soppy Soft,' came the choking reply. 'Oh shit! I hate men!'

'Me too.'

In the ensuing silence Lily began to think about things as they were. Although she was not a person of much feeling these days – Jaime and Penn had seen to that – she inspired a good deal in others. From the time she had returned to Matson Street she had come to be held in admiration and respect by the whole of Zoe Zuckerman's crowd, and also many of Denis Quiller's gang. This had made her feel like a somebody for a change. Even right from the start Jaime had overridden her, she saw that now. Here in Matson Street she was truly accepted, had even received praise.

She had, they told her in their different ways, every quality necessary for success. her natural elegance and her taste for fine clothes, Zoe told her, enabled her to mix with fashionable people without arousing suspicion. A marvellous gift. Lily believed her. It had helped her with one of her earliest exploits which had not been as selfish as Burza believed.

Lily began remembering the day she had got her own back on a crowd of snobs.

One Sunday a church well known for its rich and extremely snobbish congregation was to listen to a sermon on 'Helping The Deserving Poor'. The Deserving Poor curled its lip at the idea. The well-heeled, dressed-up-to-the-nines ladies' help usually amounted to very little in truly useful terms. They held pious little meetings on the vicarage lawn. There they drank scented tea, and ate inch-sized cucumber sandwiches. With perhaps a cream cake or two.

At the end of the bird-pecking and gossiping, a silver plate would go round and money, usually the minimum each individual could get away with, would tinkle into it. From this bounty the cost of aforementioned tea, cakes and sandwiches would be taken to reimburse the vicar's wife. The rest found its meagre way into the nearest Salvation Army collection box, or Dr Barnardos, some other such charitable institution, or even Church Funds.

As it was the snobby types she loathed, Lily set out to become one of them, and to watch and wait. She became particularly angry when a grand-looking woman, clearly afraid she might catch something awful, shuddered visibly. This when a consumptive-looking beggar girl approached. The do-gooder, with wellgloved hand, pushed the girl to one side. Too frail by half, the beggar had stumbled. She was still gasping for breath as the group swept away.

'The old witches!' Lily had said as she helped the girl. 'They're as ignorant as the crones Dickens used to write about. Never mind, dear. You'll go to heaven, and they won't. Not even though they think they're bribing their way through God's gates.'

The girl hadn't fully fathomed the bit about Dickens, but she fully understood the five florins Lily pressed in her hand.

Seething, feeling she was hitting out at Marion in some way, she let it be known that she was a Mrs Smith-Summers and that her husband was in high management of the Drew Importing business. Her fictitious address was that of the large and impressive house standing on the corner of the road where Marion had her flat. In a short time the ladies graciously invited her to one of their special 'do's' for the poor.

Ever helpful, Mrs Smith-Summers served tea and sandwiches and cakes. Charming everyone with her warm husky voice, her courtesy and good manners.

When an animated conversation was at its height – no one agreed that sons of the poor, however gifted, should be allowed into Universities – Lily, unnoticed, took her leave. With her went the contents of some very fat purses. The fattest, she noted, belonging to the most niggardly of the contributors.

Every single penny of that haul was given to the Salvation Army in Shattery, with a special bequest for the soup kitchen brigade. Now, Lily thought, in spite of Burza's nasty remarks, that had been fun! More so than the normal outings, in fact. These had, of course, gone into swelling her own bank balance.

One day, Lily thought, she and Burza would have a cottage in the country and they would smell the perfume of flowers and cut grass rather than horsedung in streets and human urine where filthy men peed up the wall. Burza loved the country, she certainly looked like an exotic sort of gipsy, and her spirit flew wild and free. Just as she Lily felt wild and free running with her thieves. But, going back, she really had relished stealing from those detestable women.

Lily came back to the present, forgetting the past and still remembering everything her dearest friend had said.

'I can take or leave all men now, Burza,' she told her quietly. 'Some of the lessons I've learned have been hard. But even though I'll never forgive my father, I don't honestly think I could bear it if anything awful happened to him.'

'That's a turnup for the book,' Burza told her joyfully, tears gone. 'Sanity at last. There was a time when you wished him stone dead.'

'It's this war business changed my mind, I suppose,' Lily said, back-tracking on her previous 'I don't give a damn' attitude. 'There's too much talk of death and dying. Besides, Andy and Richard ...' She stopped, trying to hide how upset she was from an already heartbroken Burza. But her own sense of shock and hurt was strong, then on top of everying to have Burza going at her too!

'What? There's something wrong, isn't there?' Burza asked sharply, fear suddenly curling inside her stomach at Lily's change of tone.

'They're going,' Lily admitted flatly. 'The pair of them. I heard it from Andy, he came with the message only today.'

'What?'

'Richard and Andy have volunteered. By doing so they had a choice, you see. Richard has been accepted because he's a fully fledged wireless operator and is hoping to continue with that. Andy had no particular trade in mind, but he says he wants to go with Richard, so let's hope they manage to get placed together somewhere.'

'No, no, no!' Burza was wringing her hands. 'Not them! They don't have to go. They're younger than Pete and – Oh, I can't bear it! It's always been us four. Oh God! Lily, tell me it isn't true.'

'I'm afraid it is. And – and something else. Andy also took time out to give me a right old ticking-off!' Lily laughed in a nervous shaky way. 'It was when I started to be upset, and dared to say that without him I'd have no man I trusted to turn to. He's often popped over to see me as you know, and helped me in lots of little ways. But he was angry today. He called me a spoiled brat! Someone who thought only of my own feelings, blah, blah, blah.'

'Andy actually said all that?' Burza was amazed.

'He really went into me hammer and tongs. He told me that I'd turned myself into a character out of a B-grade movie.' She pulled a face. 'An American expression, I believe. Something he's latched onto because of all those second-feature Westerns he sits through. It was a shock, Burza.' Lily's eyes filled with tears. 'I've never seen Andy in a temper before. He looked so stern, so much older, and so contemptuous. To think I actually thought he liked me!'

'He does – always has. perhaps it's the thought of leaving us.'

'He'll have Richard, that's all he cares about. Darling Richard!'

'There was a time when you thought like that too.'

'Richard can go to the devil as far as I'm concerned,' Lily

said defiantly. 'He dropped us as soon as he became rich. He's a shopowner now, and far above even my father. He's never come back to see us, not even once, and only sent messages to you via Andy. In short he has turned out to be as unreliable as Jaime.'

'Don't be so thick!' Burza sprang to Richard's defence. 'He kept away because he learned that you'd left home too. No one knew where you were, even I didn't.' She laughed angrily. 'And apart from you and Andy, he had nothing else to come back for. Certainly not me!'

'Oh? And that couldn't have been because of Pete, could it? Anyway we never acted as though we liked them in that way, did we, Burza? I mean, we've never thought of Andy or Richard as lovers!'

'I gave up thoughts of Richard because you carried a torch for him for years,' Burza flared, knowing that in some way Lily spoke the truth. 'Besides, they were our mates. Our own ages. We shared the same class at school. They were young in thought and attitude, specially Andy. On the other hand, Pete and Jaime were older and more mature by far and ... Well, Pete made me feel as though I had goose bumps all over and ...'

'Oh, do leave off. This conversation is too awful, Burza,' Lily groaned. 'It's not too late to go to the pictures even now.'

Burza obediently fetched her coat off the hook, but her heart was pounding with distress.

'Does Josie know – about Andy, I mean? I can't understand why he didn't tell me his news.'

'He thought you'd be too concerned about Pete's leaving to care about him very much.'

'Lily!' Burza was outraged. 'I'm going round to see him right now, this very minute.'

'He's not there, thank goodness. I don't think I'll ever want to speak to him again. B-grade movie indeed! Oh all right! If you must know, he's gone to stay with Richard. He stomped off saying that he'd washed his hands of me. Damn him! Now, shall we go to the Kings Hall?'

'If you like,' Burza replied, feeling that the bottom was dropping out of her world. How would she cope without her Pete? And now without dearest Andy? And she had never really got over losing Richard. Everything in the world was going haywire. She heard herself adding dispiritedly, 'Though I can't see how going to the pictures will solve anything.'

Lily, usually so patient, tossed her head and her silvery fair hair flew like wings on either side of her face. Her amethyst eyes were the colour in stained-glass windows, beautiful but not of this world.

'I want to see Jeanette MacDonald and Nelson Eddy, Burza,' she said, ice-cool. 'Are you coming with me or not?'

'Of course I am,' Burza replied and wondered why she wanted to cry.

The weepy film she saw, plus hearing that angelic singing voice of Jeanette MacDonald's soaring so high and clear, only added to her feeling of sorrow and wistfulness.

They walked home, Lily pulling her old trilby hat well down over her face which was her usual disguise. Lily was, Burza knew, still seething over the ticking-off she had received from the usually happy-go-lucky Andy. What on earth had been behind all that? What with Andy acting out of character – and Pete so predictably acting his – it had made both girls feel deflated.

On reaching the Blue Row, they joined the crowd at the fish friers and waited to be served. Then, each holding newspaper parcels of well-salted and vinegared rock-eel and chips, they parted, Burza choosing to go straight home for once. Lily would be using the back roads, going nowhere near Solomon Street.

It really was all getting to be like a second-rate picture. Andy was right, Burza thought. Even she suspected that after all this time, there weren't many people interested in the missing Miss Lily London. The police perhaps, and Marion and Jack, but after all, there was a war on!

Burza reached the dark part of the High Road, where the viaduct of railway arches flanked either side. Her footsteps now echoed eerily through the emptiness about her. The gaslights at either end made only the faintest glow, the kind of light one saw in creepy films starring Bela Lugosi. High above was the bridge itself, along which spark-spitting engines raced like fiery dragons. Now the arch stretched vast, and empty, and secretive-looking.

Burza always felt rather uncomfortable in this area. It reminded her of childhood days when Peg used to race the pram away from the imaginary old men, crabbed ancients waiting to grab them from behind the shelter in Abbots Park. Later the frightening suspense had become a reality. Burza remembered how Nick Bede had managed to pounce out from the shadows that lay so thickly under the arches. He hated her and in spite of the brave face she put on, he scared her half to death.

She shivered. Was it her imagination? She could almost feel evil eyes watching her; could sense a presence crouching there, unseen, and waiting.

A nameless terror spread through her. She began to hurry, then to run full pelt, looking neither to left nor right. And then she heard a laugh, low and evil-sounding. There was mockery in the sound and a sense of triumph, and then she knew.

Nick Bede was back! Worse, he had every intention of carrying out his threat.

Richard grinned at Andy in his laconic way then looked round at the cosy room he'd used all during his apprenticeship. When the war was ended he knew he could return to his own premises in Leytonstone. There he would sell bikes and wire-less sets, and also he believed, by that time some of those new-fangled television sets. It was a coming thing all right, and had been growing apace since the BBC had begun operating a service from a corner of Alexandra Palace at the end of 1936.

Now Richard was getting ready to leave his room that had been home to him, and the people he stayed with who had been decent, friendly. He had joined them downstairs for meals and had never experienced such cooking in his life. Beef stew and dumplings, loin of lamb with batter pudding, greens, and roast potatoes sizzled in fat until they were brown. And apple pie and custard afterwards! Before, with Gippo, it had been chips when he was lucky, bread and marge plus jam when his uncle had been in a good mood. Or a couple of saveloys and mushy peas when Gippo had been too drunk to notice Richard helping himself to small change. Yet all the time the old devil had been hoarding away wealth. Just so that he, Richard, had a good start in adult life.

'I wish I'd known what he was up to,' Richard said evenly. 'I used to hate his guts for letting me starve, yet always finding enough cash for his booze. I'd liked to have understood the old boy a bit better.'

Andy watched the light flickering on Richard's face. Richard was a good-looker in a lean and hungry way. He seemed stern and rather distant, this because he did not speak all that often. A strong and silent type, wide-shouldered, thin-hipped, very fit, they both were keen on keeping fit, and his mate was a good specimen all round. No one would dream of how desperately he'd been without as a kid.

Richard did not suffer fools gladly. He was his own man, no matter what, and had always been dedicated in trying to better himself. Lily had set the pattern there, with her, 'You must not swear, Richard!' And: 'You must tuck your shirt in, Richard.' 'That's not the right thing to do, Richard!' And he had stoically taken it all in and tried to comply. Lily of course had been aping either her father or her aunt all of the time. Everyone knew that. Most children poked fun at the girl they thought to be a stuck-up young bitch. But Richard had listened and watched, kept his own counsel, and been determined to be every bit as successful as Lily's dad.

Given half a chance women fell over themselves to get Richard's attention. He took no notice of them; he was always too busy learning his trade. He loved bicycles, but was fascinated with everything to do with wireless. Above all, he found the idea of television so gripping, so exciting and far-reaching that it had come as a blow that they had shut the service down.

It had been decreed that all British television broadcasting was to be closed down until the end of the war. Approaching German bombers would be able to pick up the signals which would have led them to their targets. This would never do. It was a smack in the eye to TV enthusiasts, but wireless was the thing to have, and to listen avidly to.

Over and above all, Richard had come to understand the intricacies of bettering himself.

'When this little lot's over,' his tutor said, 'be like me and remember you must speculate to accumulate. But before that, know what you are doing. Don't leap in the dark. If you do you'll probably land in over your head. So learn all you can in your own special field, aim at being the best, and then go for it, mate.'

Richard listened to all this advice and was determined to live by these rules – for Gippo, for future gainful employment for Andy who had allowed Sid Cuttings the meagre work London's Windows had left, and for himself as a person.

The only females Richard had allowed, up to a point, to gain his confidence and friendship had been Lily and Burza. Andy knew without words that the two girls would always feature in Richard's life. It wouldn't have occurred to him that either Lily or Burza would ever doubt that. He would do what he had to do, then turn up as though nothing out of the blue had happened.

'You know, old son,' Andy told him easily, having considered what his friend had said, 'Gippo didn't need you to tell him anything – and you understood him well enough.'

'He saved my hide, know that?' Richard said, being in an unusually expansive mood. 'He found me in this filthy dump. It was literally a rubbish tip and lived in by a motley crew of down-and-outs, destitutes and dregs, methies, you know the sort I mean? Then there was me, his dead sister's unwanted kid. So he scraped me out from the rest of the waste and took me with him. I belonged somewhere at last. To me Matson Street was Paradise. The whippings stopped, the cruelty. Pain and starvation became things of the past. I actually got to eat bread every day. Dry as a bone sometimes, but bread all the same and always enough! Even better, it hadn't turned mildew-green.'

'Gippo knew you would have died for him.'

'All I hope is that he never knew there was a time when he made me ashamed.'

'Oh come on!'

'Yes. When Lily...'

'Came slumming?' Andy shrugged, now defending the very person he had torn a strip off before. 'She didn't, not in that sense, mate,' he comforted. 'Lily merely prattled on because of Jack. She was too young to know better. Burza now...'

'Burza's in a class of her own,' Richard said flatly and lapsed into silence again.

'And what about Lily?' Andy wouldn't let the subject go.

269

'What do you feel about her?'

'The same as I always have,' came the reply. And with that Andy had to be content.

Within two weeks they were both in the Essex Regiment and thereafter volunteered for the Commandos. Their training commenced.

Burza put the *Daily Herald* down, her hands shaking. People had been trying to dismiss tragedy for a while, but it was always there, specially at sea. The exploits of HM cruisers *Exeter*, *Ajax* and *Achilles* engaging the German warship *Admiral Graf Spee*, had been learned, but now here was the news that should have brought a sense of victory to her, and yet to Burza it did not.

She read that on 18 December, the *Graf Spee* had scuttled herself in the entrace of Montevideo Harbour. Why this brought home the horror of war even more than the cryptic wireless messages, the black headlines, Burza could not tell. Perhaps because Clara had told her once that her father Steve believed ships had living souls. That seamen swore that ships screamed as they foundered and died. But it had always occurred to her that no matter what nationality, English, French, Dutch or even German, all the sailors were someone's sons – and/or fathers.

Her own father, the unknown Steve Webb, had been a seaman all of his adult life. It was unlikely that he was still serving, for he was the same age as Clara. But it could easily have been her father's fate to have been suffocated to death in a sinking ship, else be drowned in angry seas, or burned to a crisp in waters covered with burning oil. It could have happened to the man who, they said, was as like his twin Clara as peas in a pod. Tears slid slowly down Burza's face.

'Gawd Almighty,' Clara said as she came bustling into the kitchen. 'Now what's up?'

'I was thinking of my father. Of what could have happened to him had he still been serving at sea.'

'I dunno, and I don't care to think. But we ain't heard from him for a long time now, 'ave we?'

'I wouldn't know. You don't often mention him, Clara.'

'Too hurt. I s'pose. He's my twin and I love 'im, but I

270

don't think he's ever done right by you. He's sent money and mostly that was it. Just money. He could 'ave come 'ome sometimes, just ter see me an' you. Just to keep in touch an' that. When me an' him was kids we were inseparable. Know what I mean?'

'Did he retire from the sea?'

'Think so. Settled down there somewhere with kangaroos, I reckon. I've never been too sure. A cagey one was our Steve. Some'ink to hide, I reckon.' Clara smiled her slanty smile. 'P'raps he got 'imself another wife and wanted ter keep us lot secret, eh?'

'Oh well, it doesn't matter, does it?'

'No, it bloody well don't. Not any more. Come on, gel, let's 'ave a cuppa and you can tell me all your news. Get any more pots and pans in today?'

'A few. Funny, everyone gave up their aluminium saucepans and things for the war effort, but we're still getting new ones to sell in our shop. I reckon the people up there running things are raving mad!'

'Too right!' Clara said.

Chapter Twenty-Six

'Cor lumme,' Clara said, and beamed. 'You've bought me a wireless, Burza. How d'yer do that?'

'Blew my savings, every farthing, and well worth it I'd say. Now you can hear the news – after the chimes of Big Ben. The BBC tell you the truth. Yes, real facts. Not like all the rumours you get round here. There'll be music, and people like Arthur Askey. ''Big-Hearted Arthur'' they call him. And Tommy Handley, and Flanagan and Allen. They're all ever so good.'

'How d'yer know all about it?'

'Lily has a set. She has all of the latest things. I reckon she's now a damned sight richer than her own dad.' Her expression was gentle as she looked at Clara, loving her for her homeliness, her honesty and her humanity. 'You don't go to see her at all, do you?'

'No, gel, I don't.' Clara's reply was even, considered. 'For one thing I did all I intended when I helped clean the place up when she came back. There ain't nothing else I'd want to do. Specially after the hard-hearted way she's treated the Londons.'

'I thought you liked Lily.'

'Yes I did, a lot. She was such a downtrodden nervous little thing. But her one special sweetness so far as I was concerned, was the way she felt about you. She still does, I know. Like sisters you'll always be, but she's moved on, Burze. She's tougher than you now if the truth was known, and she ain't honest.'

'How do you know that?' Burza asked quickly, feeling panic.

'Didn't. I did what any fool would do and guessed. And your face has just told me I'm right. Anyway, that's not the only reason I've kept away. It's the same as you going all round the 'ouses to go calling on Matson Street. It's bloody nosy parkers, 'specially old Art Bede.'

'Surely he isn't still playing the bloodhound?'

'Too right! He's still going on about finding her – for Jack. Feels he owes the bloke, he does. Art'll feel guilty about that accident till the day he dies. So he's always on the look-out for Lily. Wanders round everywhere, all the wrong places of course. He's practically lived up Chingford Mount. Thinking he knows the gel, an' how she ticks, he'd never dream of going as far as Shattery, let alone Matson Street.'

'Crumbs!' Burza's relief made her eyes turn upwards to the ceiling. 'Bless all angels for their mercy! Miss Prunes and Prisms can thank her lucky stars for that at least.'

'Don't be so smug, you little demont!' Clara was indignant. 'The old sod Bede was following you like a shadow for months.' Clara then gave one of her twinkly Oriental-eyed grins. 'That shook yer, eh? Yes, Art was there, one step behind you all right, till I told him I'd kill him if he didn't leave it out.'

'Thank you – darling!' Burza kissed the woman she adored and was instantly clipped round the ear for her pains. 'Ow!'

'That's for not listening proper. That man was dogging your steps, d'you understand? All thanks to that special friend of yours. If she only knew...'

'I think Nick's taken over.' Burza tried to change the subject, not wanting Clara to question too closely about Lily's 'goings-on'. 'I can sense him creeping up behind me some-times.'

'Then he's chancing his arm, gel, because the MPs are creeping up on *him*!' Clara sniffed with contempt. 'He oughter keep miles away from this area. He's nothin' but a deserter, to add to his sins. Let him out early they did, providing he went in the Army. He didn't last in that lot long, Gawd no! Soldiering's too tough for the likes of 'im.'

'I feel sorry for his mum.'

'What – old Em? Poor cow misses them nippers of Minnie's more than she does her own bloody kids. Cor, talk about the pair of 'em bringing shame to her house. What with Nick, and Minnie's being up the duff four times. Not that Em'd be without little Prissy and Hughey, Pansy and Horry. Though now they're evacuated, their own mum's 'aving the time of her life. She's up at Colchester, a garrison town! What's the betting that number five'll soon be on the way?'

'So now Em only has Art.'

'Yes, and he's going deafer than ever – and potty. Honest, Burza, the poor old sod's up the creek. Em reckons Nick's been the main cause of that. Art half killed him over the Steadman business, even so, Art's always cared most for Nick.'

'Poor old devil. To have a son that has been to prison and has now become a deserter from the Army! I bet Art can't stand the looks he gets in the Feathers now!'

'Em reckons it's just about finished him.' Clara looked at Burza, brows raised. 'So remember, gel, all he's got left is this idea of finding Lily for Jack. Everyone knows how close you two are and that's Art's last chance. Thank God you're adept at giving him the slip through all them alleyways and that. Even so, you watch out! He ain't that daft...'

Right out of the blue, while the Spitfires and other RAF planes were engaged in dog-fights with the German Air Force over Britain, Rosie announced that she was getting married, quietly at the Register Office, she said, with no fuss.

'What d'yer and Ben want?' Clara asked, eyes direct. 'Boy or girl?'

'The way she's eating,' Ben said in his deep voice, his craggy face beaming, 'I reckon one of each since it's gotta be twins!'

So the wedding went ahead as planned and Rosie was gone, living in Ben's flat above the store, and Clara and Burza were on their own.

Now the wireless became the all-important thing. The BBC News, heralded by the booming notes of Big Ben, kept everyone informed.

Burza received a scribbled letter from Pete which told her nothing at all, yet she sensed he was on embarkation leave but chose not to come home. He's having an affair, she thought miserably. I know he is. Rotter! She said as much to Lily,

274

whom she visited regularly every Thursday afternoon which was early closing day. Lily answered by flourishing a letter from Andy.

'He still has the nerve to say he meant every word!' she said indignantly. 'Really, Burza, I never knew what a tough nut he could be. Richard now, he's a different kettle of fish, but he never writes, does he? Then there's Andy!'

'Surely he hasn't always written just about the row you two had?'

Lily's face softened. 'Oh no. Unlike most men, Andy enjoys writing. Read this one for yourself.'

Andy's letter, apart from the opening shots about Lily's behaviour, read in the same happy-go-lucky way he spoke. He ended with sending his love to both Lily and to Burza. This letter, he said, was for them both. Two days later, a letter arrived for Burza alone, from Richard. Cool, calm, friendly and as factual as possible, he signed the letter simply, *Yours*. Burza found that single word immensely important. She put Richard's letter, with its careful writing, alongside Pete's inelegant scrawl in her dressing-table drawer.

'War is terrible,' Burza told Lily thoughtfully on the following Thursday afternoon. 'I'm glad I'm not a man having to go away and fight. You know, risking life and limb.'

'Get away with you! They like it,' Lily jeered in her quietly mischievous way. 'They play soldiers, and Cowboys and Indians, and war games too. And just look at the hours Pete, Andy and Richard used to spend just battling the daylights out of each other – for fun! It's their way.'

'And we women must stay at home and cook and clean and...'

'This woman is going to get rich,' Lily told her firmly. 'Filthy, stinking rich, Burza. So rich that you and I can eat delicious things, and wear exotic things, and do wildly exciting things, and go and live in a house like Miss Allthorpe's one day – which will, of course, be full of lovely things. And I'll buy you –'

'Nothing! Not with dishonest money you won't!' Burza cut her short. 'I don't think you really know me at all, Lily.'

'I do, dear. You think everything can be cut into black or white shapes. You think life can be plain sailing just so long

275

as you stay on the straight and narrow. Well, I'll tell you this. You're riding for a fall, Burza Webb. And when you've hit the ground so hard you're dazed, I'll be there for you.'

'Oh shut up!'

'I will be there to pick you up. Just you wait and see. I'll be rich and powerful and I'll be ready and waiting – just as you've spent all of your life ready and waiting to help me.'

'Right couple of narners, ain't we?' Burza giggled, eyes bright with emotional unshed tears. 'Thank God for friends, eh, Lily?'

The war was progressing in an awful way. British troops were fighting like the blazes in France. British merchant ships were going down like ninepins, sunk by German submarines that seemed to hunt in packs.

Food rationing was in full swing and Lord Woolton was extolling the virtues of the good old-fashioned King Edward spud. Barrage balloons continued to float like inflated silver fish on azure ground. They gleamed like grey silk, sober and serene. Seeming to a pensive Burza to be like ethereal guardians of the nation beneath, just watching. And such odd scenes! Of piled sandbags, of windows criss-crossed with sticky paper, of blacked-out street names, of a people that were determined to carry on as usual no matter what. Of women waiting in line and praying that the sausages never ran out. That there was unrationed offal on sale, that the points system would run to a slice or two of corned beef – that the butcher could stuff his whalemeat right up his arse!

On the whole men and women were busily putting on a brave face, keeping their fears hidden. For fear there was, stalking the streets every minute of every day – one of the greatest terrors being held in the hand of the telegram boy. *We regret to inform you...*

Oh God, who regretted? Burza wondered sadly. The dead man's officers? His mates? His country? No people regretted more deeply than family as telegrams fluttered like dead daisies against broken hearts.

In spite of the 158,000 British troops fighting in France, that country caved in. Britain stood alone.

'A right ol' turn-up,' they said in the Feathers. 'Bleedin' hell!'

Still, September 1940 blazed yellow and gold, an Indian summer they said, and Londoners safe for the moment, paddled in park pools, lakes and fountains. Others tried to decide whether to eat in a British Restaurant, buy chips, or find a cheap and decent café. Anything to save a few ration points for Mum at home.

Then all round the coast small and large ships were alerted. British troops needed to be evacuated from Dunkirk. Churchill, now characterised in newspapers as the man with the bulldog face, was able to boast with the rest of the nation about enjoying a great victory over defeat.

The day after France fell was the beginning of the Blitz.

In those first few nights in the East End, when it was still strange as well as horrible to see streets of houses ripped into fragments, and the midnight sky so lit that one could easily read by the light of the great flames, when the barrage of hollow-sounding ack-ack guns had not yet begun, there seemed to many of the staggered and sleepless people nothing very much before them. Apart from that of sitting and waiting night by night – until they or their homes, or both, were anni-hilated, of course.

'Are you scared?' Burza asked Clara.

'Out of me wits,' came the reply. 'But don't tell no one, eh?'

Now Burza was torn between two loves and loyalties, but that was soon settled.

'Don't worry about me, dear,' Lily told her. 'I've got heaps of hidey-holes with friends. I'm safe and sound.' She laughed in her husky way. 'Darling, I was just going to say I'm as safe as houses! But back to the point, I'll be all right. Besides, there's always plenty to do.'

Relieved, believing that Lily was meaning to continue to help the unfortunates in the Salvation Army hostel – which she had admitted to doing several times before – Burza stayed with Clara. A still spritely Clara who was knitting socks and bala-clava helmets, and squares to be sewn into blankets. Needles click-clacking endlessly, working at anything and everything to help the troops, the homeless, and her own sense of inade-quacy.

'I'd bloody well like to kick 'em up the arse for this, their second go at us,' she snapped. 'But I'm just a stupid old cow that can only sit here helpless, doin' me purl and plain.'

Burza could never tell how many private terrors Clara faced as the bombs whistled down, because they were stifled quietly in the cupboard under the stairs. And when Clara's knitting needles ceased, her strong hands gently stroked Boris who'd stretch and yawn and return to sleep on her lap.

Mornings and the All Clear, and Clara, glad to be alive, smiled and went into the kitchen to make a cuppa, and see to it that Burza ate a mouthful of breakfast before going off to work. Before this the pair of them would go round the house to see how many windows had been damaged by blast.

In number twelve, Jack London shrugged, feigned indifference and turned his back, letting Marion do the walking round.

London's Windows was finished, and had been from the moment glass was being contained by sticky tape. Grim-faced, hardly accepting the fact even now, Jack had lost what amounted to his world. Andy had joined the Army, and only a week later Sid had become a Bevin Boy. He had gone northwards to work in the mines. Ivy continued her caring in the Rest Home but had said that its elderly residents were being prepared for evacuation to Wales. It was Ivy who had tentatively suggested that perhaps Jack would like to join them? As he was in a wheelchair and so on?

His reply, so she wrote to a grinning Sid, had been all but unprintable.

'Pete's coming home, Burze,' Mrs Frazer called out one morning as Burza made her way to work. 'Have you heard from him at all?' Burza shook her head. Pete seldom wrote these days, come to that neither did Richard. Glowing like a poppy in sunlight, Rene went on: 'He was hurt, not too bad he says, but he's been passed fit, and is all right now. And he's coming home. He'll be arriving some time today!'

'Wonderful!' Burza called, eyes sparkling, her own cheeks now going a hot Mexican red. 'Then I'll see you tonight after work – all right?'

'Wonderful!' Rene almost sang the word.

Burza was thinking romantic thoughts all day.

They soon faded and died.

Pete, it turned out, had been one of those safely rescued from the beaches of Dunkirk, after which he had been hospitalised with a shoulder wound. He had not wished his loved ones to be worried, he said, but fine now, he was allowed home on short leave. As well as writing to his mum, he had also written to tell several of his friends in the boxing fraternity.

That evening Burza, heart dancing, went to number eight and, taken aback, found it full to overcrowding. Being something of a hero the girl fans were flocking round her Pete, almost as if he belonged to them. He looked across the Frazers' front room, and caught Burza's eye. She glared back. He gave Burza a chagrined wink, then laughed down at a peroxided blonde who was kissing him.

He looks stupid, Burza thought disgustedly. Daft, and too cocky by half – especially with that lipstick smudge on the side of his mouth. Raspberry pink, that is. I wonder where that stupid bitch got it from. Queued up for hours to get it, I suppose, seeing how everything in the shops is like gold dust these days.

Burza sat mouse-still and watched and waited. Rene Frazer, looking resigned, also stayed in the background.

It was very late before Burza and Pete found themselves alone.

'At last, Burze,' he told her happily. 'Come here!'

He kissed her and she kissed him back, everything forgotten except the charm of him, the masculinity, the heart-wrenching desire to feel him close.

She allowed him to do things to her, and gloried in it. Pete was her man. A hero home safe from the war. He was her lover, his touch was sure. She responded to him and he responded to her. They were a couple and would be for ever and a day. They would get married – perhaps before he went back? She asked him, whispering against his ear. 'Are we to marry, Pete?'

'Forward hussy!' he teased. 'Let's get the war over with first, eh?'

She had to be content with that, but her heart was dancing, simply because he hadn't said no. So, his big brothers, both now called up, would be her in-laws, and Rene and Vin her parents-in-law. There would be babies, lots of them, the way she felt now. And she could think of no greater joy.

From then on Pete found himself knee-deep in flattering fans. He had sex appeal, the reputation of being something of a rascal, he looked like a film star and more often than not acted the part. Aching for him, yearning, wanting to weep. though never for one moment showing the fact, Burza finished up with her head held high. She lied in her teeth and mentioned meaningfully to Pete that she had commitments elsewhere. She finished up visiting Miss Allthorpe and Roan alone for her pains.

She told Miss Allthorpe gravely that it was only recently that she had learned that all the men serving with Pete envied him his mail. He was sent sackloads of letters, so she supposed her own writing was as lost as the proverbial needle in a haystack.

'Dump him, my dear,' Daisy replied bluntly. 'There are millions of our boys out there who all need what only you can give. They've been advertising for people to write to lonely soldiers in papers and magazines. Let him go!'

Burza was so shocked at this idea of saying tata to Pete that she hardly heard the old lady's next words. Daisy Allthorpe was explaining that on Granger's insistence she and Roan and all of her establishment, both human and animal, would be leaving the area for a while. However, should Burza or any of her friends need a roof, Manchu and its grounds would always be available.

'And the same goes for that mother of yours,' Miss Allthorpe added. 'She turns up occasionally. War or no war, life goes on.'

Even on the day Pete returned to duty his mother and Burza were more or less pushed out. A group of people singing 'Wish Me Luck As You Wave Me Goodbye' jostled and pushed on the station platform. Talk about making fools of themselves, Burza thought, unimpressed. Most of them seemed half cut, some of them were actually staggering as they began a mad waving of Union Jacks. Pete loved every minute of it and it showed, but Burza found herself wanting to cringe.

There were other men on the station, in various uniforms,

some wearing bandages too. All heroes of a kind, either returning to or coming from active duty. After all, Burza thought, watching Pete showing off, even Pete had admitted to suffering only a very deep scratch!

I hate him! Burza thought, and felt like the loneliest soul on earth. She wanted to burst into tears. Wanted him to run to her, look at no one else. Needed to be held against his heart and reassured. Wanted to rage and scream and stamp. Instead she stood back, quiet and dignified. Then, just before the train began to move, Pete leapt out of the carriage, through the crowds and swept Burza up into his arms. He kissed her hard, then whispered urgently, 'It'll always be you, Burza. Remember that! I'm enjoying this for what it is. It won't last, you and I know it. But after what I've been through, what I saw happen to some bloody good blokes, a couple of them being my own close mates, I'm just living for the moment. Know what I mean?'

Of course she did! She nodded wordlessly, melting against him, only letting go long enough for Mrs Frazer to kiss him goodbye.

Then the train moved out of the station and life without Pete began again...

It was blackout and the pickings had been good. Lily, still known as Goldie, was wearing her special coat. Long and voluminous, it had many deep pockets sewn in the lining. Gee, Three, Diver, and a chap named Tibbits, had done well. All the loot was now safely hidden and being carried to Zoe in Lily's coat. Later, as was customary, they would all meet in the back room of the Woodpecker Inn. The money Zoe had put in Lily's hand would be paid out.

As she walked, torchbeam held down so that enemy planes could see no light, Lily pulled her trilby hat rakishly lower over one eye. It was brown, matching the colour of her coat, and she loved it. Her father had worn one very much like it for best. He had often worn it on Sundays when taking her to the park. Once he had laughed out loud and stuck a marigold in its wide band, saluted, bowed and called her Princess Chickybit. She had thought him to be the most handsome, most marvellous man in the world.

Afterwards she had become aware that the Princess he had wanted for a child had become impossible to live up to. She had tried so desperately hard, but had never been quite good enough. When had love turned to loathing, to contempt and disgust? And why the devil could she never quite forget his blue, blue eyes, his strong white teeth, the swagger of him when he had walked like a god?

Jack London's values had been impossible well before he had lost one leg and the use of the other. After that he had been infinitely worse. She needed to forget the man, wanted to! He had made her life miserable ... so why the devil couldn't she get him out of her mind?

Burza had been right, of course. But then Burza usually was. Every step she, Lily, took was to make a strike at the dear old Dad.

Regarding her own deliberately chosen profession, 'Goldie's' ascendancy had risen to the fore. Cool, adroit, light-hearted and determined, she showed self-control and constructive ability. It was she who drew up a set of rules, and showed them to Zoe, who gave them the OK. They were (1) No new member was to be admitted without the consent of the whole company. (2) No one should strike out and attempt a job on his or her own account. (3) Any new member should be a month on trial and (4) If any of the gang should be taken prisoner, the rest should swear to anything to help him or her out.

If convicted, cash should be set aside out of common stock so that they might have a nest egg to come out to. One that must be sufficient to tide them over.

Number two Matson Street was now where members received their plan of action. From here they sneaked out in twos, threes or fours to set destinations.

Outrageous robberies were committed, the Docks being their favourite hunting ground. Incoming cargo being worth its weight in gold, warehouses were entered, in spite of armed guards. Matson members were not afraid of guns so much as of dogs. Guards with dogs were given a wide berth. Both Shattery and Matson Street boasted top-class Black Marketeers, so buyers of stolen goods were there aplenty.

Apart from warehouses there were other places to rob.

Homes were left vulnerable and empty while the inhabitants huddled in shelters. Domiciles were left in darkness and usually with doors unlocked. Who cared about locking doors when dawn would in all probability find them torn off their hinges? Or forced open, else leaning drunkenly in someone else's front garden. And who needed doors for entrance when all the windows would be blown out? So the pickings were good, and Lily's itch to become rich was becoming realised as rapidly as a spreading forest fire.

Lily reached Zoe's place and emptied her pockets. Zoe could value an item at a glance. The haul was good. Money changed hands. Lily returned to the Woodpecker and met up with members who accepted their pay-out in a light-hearted casual way. Easy come easy go was the norm. Ill-gotten gains would be quickly spent. Plenty more where that came from.

Some members hid their loot for later pick-up, behind the panel in the wall. Others stuffed notes in their pockets. Drinks were ordered all round and Lily sat back and watched them. Some members she liked, but she trusted them all. The original three she had worked with had become her friends, and so had earthy, sexy, plug-ugly Tibbits. No one knew much about him, nor wanted to. He was there when needed and that was all that counted. All of the Matson people had nimble fingers, were good thieves and were honest in their own special way. Not one would raise a hand, or threaten victims in any way – unlike the Shattery lot.

Gee began laughing full-heartedly at someone's filthy joke, and that set the ball rolling. A singer in the other bar was giving a soulful rendering of 'We'll Meet Again' and the darts team was arguing over a wrongly added score. Things were much the same as usual, but suddenly Lily wanted none of it. She smiled, waved her hand in farewell and turned on her heel and left.

Once alone Lily edged her way through the blackout, finding her way home. She thought she heard ghostly footsteps and was suddenly remembering all the nasty bits in horror films she had seen. She began imagining vampires, demons, and lost souls wailing in the night. It was all awful, exciting, and made one really thankful to reach home where one could put on the light – or a match to a candle if a stray bomb had inconveniently hit the mains.

Indoors at last, Lily divested herself of her outer clothes and knelt before the fire to light it. She heard a knock at the front door and froze. It came again, then a deep, friendly voice called through the letter box, 'It's me!' She hurried to let Tibbits in.

Tibbits was short, rock-solid, square-jawed and tough. He had enormous hands. It was believed that he hailed from a farming community and that he had worked his own poverty-stricken land, with no luck at the end of it all. He had joined a long line of out-of-works and found nothing but contempt from those who considered themselves his betters. He had been on the wrong side of the law from the day he discovered that this was the only way that he could eat decently and survive.

Tibbits liked women and they liked him. He was well-blessed physically and performed splendidly in bed. Lily and Tibbits understood each other very well. They had shared nights together, enjoyed each other with no holds barred, then parted with no strings attached.

As they waited for the kettle to boil they sat one on either side of the fireplace and smiled at each other, well pleased.

'By the way, they got Spud,' Tibbits said. 'Nabbed him with the loot on him. A case full of fags – Army Issue.'

'That means curtains. This will be the fourth time he's been up before the beak. Oh damn! Zoe warned him not to go it alone.'

'He's an old lag, Goldie, and he's probably more at home inside prison than out. Hold on. There she blows!'

They listened as the air-raid warning wailed up and down like a woman in agony. Searchlights began criss-crossing the sky like enormous ice-white wands. Gunbursts exploding alongside tracers were reminiscent of demented firework displays.

Now the droning of planes, and the hollow thunder sounds of distant bombs reaching earth, made Lily strain her ears. Was it getting nearer? Would they make it through the night?

'Live for the day, for tomorrow we die,' Tibbits said meaningfully. 'Well – what do you say?'

'Where?'

'Here.'

She lay on the rug and let him remove her underclothes.

'Open up,' he said. 'Show willing, girl!'

Lily opened her legs wide, feeling wayward, wildly abandoned and without a care in the world. She could hear the kettle steaming, but didn't mind if it boiled dry. She was just waiting for the moment when she became speared to this man. Pinned to his body, crushed by his weight, then moving to the rhythm he set. Riding high, then downwards, as exhilarating as being on the see-saw in childhood days. She was holding onto him, keeping him in, clinging to him, gasping, as he began ferociously beating into her.

This was her final and most utter defiance. It was nothing like the experiences she'd had with Jaime. She had felt love for him. This was the chosen completion of deliberate insubordination. Her final rebellion, a two-finger gesture to a man who lived and breathed pride, and who, if seeing her now, would feel nothing but shame. And the wonderful most marvellous thing was, she herself felt no remorse. She gave herself up to the moment.

Tibbits filled her, his movements powerful and strong. She went with him, finding him immensely satisfying in one way, but in another nothing more than a machine. But who was she to judge? She, Lily London who enjoyed degradation, who was nothing more than a thief? She found herself thinking of Richard's uncle, good old Gippo who probably had a damned sight more self-pride than her. And what of Richard, who had tried so hard, was still trying – and all through her own bossy ways. And then there was Andy. Dear Andy who had always seemed so boyish and nice. Who these days had somehow changed into a kind of distant, critical stranger. Who had looked at her and found her wanting, and worse, had actually told her so!

It was over. Tibbits shuddered then became still. Unbidden tears sprang to her eyes.

'No good?' Tibbits asked bluntly, heaving himself off her and doing up his flies.

'As ever,' she told him, lying. 'And I've known a few.'

'Yet you look so clear-eyed and innocent,' he teased. 'Almost like a child.'

285

'I never want to be a child again,' she told him dispassionately. 'That was when I tried to do as I was told, to act as was expected of me. I tried and tried and tried – so hard in fact that there were times when I couldn't breathe. Now I go my own sweet way, and don't give a twopenny cuss about anything or anyone.'

'Except that lovely dark-haired friend of yours,' he told her. 'She looks as though she could really make a bloke catch fire.'

Lily watched Tibbits and her eyes were like slivers of North Pole ice.

'If you so much as even look at her in that way,' she told him, low and clear, meaning every word, 'I swear I'll kill you.'

He raised his hands above his head, half smiling, half serious. 'I give in. I give in! What is she, some sort of saint?'

'She is the most dear, the most precious person in my life,' Lily told him in a slow and deliberate voice. 'And I swear I'd cheerfully hang for her. Is that clearly understood?'

'Bloody hell,' he told her. 'You mean it!'

'Yes I do,' she said.

Chapter Twenty-Seven

Richard and Andy walked alongside the tangled barbed wire fencing that cut off the beach and sea of Paignton. They were quiet; a companionable silence lay between them, but one that held pride. The kind of pride that hovers in the air as subtly as lingering perfume.

Andy looked across at Richard and said at last, 'Chuffed?'

'It's what we've worked for.'

'We've come a long way together, mate. Not bad, eh?'

'Not bad,' Richard agreed and smiled. 'Have you written to them?'

'Always do. Why don't you down tools and scribble a bit more? After all, now Gippo's gone you've no one else.'

'After you've written about ten pages of bull there's nothing much left for me to say. Besides, you handle it better than me.'

'Why don't you just admit to being a lazy sod?' Andy chipped, and punched his mate playfully on the shoulder.

After that silence fell between them again.

Richard began thinking of the two girls. Lily, tall, fair, lovely, as delicate-looking as an angel. The over-sensitive girl who had been so mentally bruised by the working-class snobbery of her father. Then an extra two-edged sword had been turned inside out all over again. This because of the neverending sniping handed out at school.

It was no wonder that Lily had snapped. Gone over the top, in fact. Now she was thumbing her nose at everyone. Doing anything and everything opposite to what she had been taught. And the awful thing was, the final straw had been Jack sacking him, Richard. A startlingly petty action for someone who so blatantly claimed to have self-pride. Jack had not given a damn that Gippo had died; neither had the rest of mankind. It hadn't even registered that in spite of his roguery, the old man had been buried in St Christopher's holy ground. Yes, alongside so many others, not least being good old George Cuttings. But then George was the sort of bloke who'd give newcomers a damned good welcome. And so, by all accounts, would Kathy London. Yes, Jack's wife! But Jack himself hadn't given a damn that, as Gippo's only relative he, Richard, had actually taken a day off work. This to see his uncle laid to rest in a respectable Christian way.

The injustice of it still made Richard feel tight, angry. Particularly as the hide-bound old man had been the yardstick on which he had chosen to fashion his own life.

Thank God his uncle had seen to it that he, Richard, was beyond worrying about that now. Yet in the beginning his aspirations had been purely to keep up in the estimation of the young goddess with golden hair – Lily, who had got him the job in the first place. And, according to Andy, it had been the loss of that job that had finally been the last straw, the breaking point between father and child, so far as Lily was concerned.

Poor kid, Richard thought. Poor stupid bloody kid! She would never have survived any of life's bitter challenges if it hadn't been for good old Burze, the little dark-haired beauty who stuck by those she cared for through thick and thin. Burza got under one's skin whether one liked it or not.

A picture of Burza floated in the forefront of his mind. Such a fiery little soul, such a loyal, determined young spirit. It was good to have her on one's side. How often had she defended him, slummy old Gippo's nephew? From the moment they made up their squabble on the first day at school, in fact. How young they had been. Young and vulnerable; he'd been open to all the insults handed his way. But the lessons were soon learned. He'd become as tough as old boots, truly leather-skinned. No one now would ever pierce the guard he'd put up.

In the early days, hurt when the big kids had jeered at his lack of boots, he'd grown a backbone of grit and iron. And of course he was always on his dignity, wary of just about everyone, apart from Andy. And without Andy he would never have known, never even guessed how fiercely Burza had fought for him both inside and out of school. But Blabbermouth had told him in the end.

Of all the blokes in the world he, Richard, was lucky to have happy-go-lucky old Blabbermouth as a best mate. More than fortunate to have had the girls on his side, too. They had been like the Musketeers, Andy, Lily, Burza, and himself in there, always clenching his teeth as he accepted Lily's corrections, doing his level best to comply, and just hanging on.

Richard swore under his breath and wanted to confine the Jaimes and Petes to all the seven hells. The girls belonged to him and Andy. The trouble was they didn't know it yet. Ye gods! Were they deaf, dumb and blind?

'What's up?' Andy asked, chuckling. 'You're scowling like a bull with a bullet up its arse.'

'Nothing,' Richard told him. 'Remembering Gippo, and some of the old days, that's all.'

They walked on, both tall, in perfect physical condition, and good advertisements for the green berets they wore. Standards of 'turnout' had to be of the highest in Unit 2, and supreme soldierly bearing was expected at all times.

Richard and Andy, like all the chaps, were utterly and absolutely loyal to their commanding officer Lieutenant-Colonel A.C. Newman. It was well-known that he in turn felt at one with his men. He had been a Territorial officer of the 4th Battalion The Essex Regiment of sixteen years' standing. His normal profession was that of a civil engineering contractor. At the outset of the war he had expressed a wish to have under his command all the lads from Barking and East Ham and outer London.

At the time he was commanding No 2 Commando, one of the twelve that constituted the Special Service Brigade which had been raised specially from picked volunteers.

Richard and Andy had passed the selection procedures with flying colours, and had lapped up their vigorous training. This was aimed at developing the highest reach of physical endurance, an eager fighting spirit, and self-reliance not based on routine battle tactics. In short, to have all the qualities of a highly trained professional soldier, combined with those of the toughest guerrilla. Richard and Andy were immensely proud to wear 2 Commando's badge of a dagger between the letters *SS* – and it showed.

'I'll make a bargain with you,' Andy said. 'I'll write to Lily again – and try to make her see sense – if you'll write to Burze.'

'She don't need to hear from me. She's got Frazer.'

'Faint heart never won—'

'I don't want to win anyone,' Richard said bluntly. 'Forget it.'

Andy shrugged and then kicked the pebbles beneath his feet into gusty little showers.

'You're a bloody pig-headed old sod, Richy, and you act like you don't need anyone, but you do. Just you wait and see.'

'I'm no ladies' man.'

'Then why do they fall over themselves to get you, the lean and hungry-looking type, to look their way. I know it and you do too, you lying old devil. I saw it even when we were in Infants when young Lily spent hours giving you the biggest, bluest sheep's eyes I've ever seen.'

Suddenly Richard was going back to the past, when they were all at the Hollow Ponds and sunlight was shining on the girls' shoulders, and making lights in tangled tresses, one so fair, one so dark. How sweet they were, how lovely, and how far above him they had been. Him, Richard Wray, tear-arsed kid from the slums.

He had sworn then, to work and strive and be like Jack London, and push his way up. It had never amounted to anything so far as Jack was concerned. To Jack he had always been a nothing and a nobody, and would remain so until his dying day. It had cut deep, that sort of contempt. But Lily had not let her father's feelings get in the way of their friendship.

As for Burza, warm-hearted, wonderful young Burza, she was sunny and open, and quite unaware. She had Clara to love, and Lily to love, and Andy and himself as her closest of mates, and for her that had been enough.

The world could be and sometimes was rather cruel for people like Burza. But she seldom let things get her down. She would go in there, all guns blazing, and quite often with twinkly little laughter lights shining in her eyes. When they fashioned Burze they broke the mould, he thought. Must have! Burza was Burza, it was as simple as that. She hadn't even thought of him as a kid from the slums!

And yet, through the despised old man, scruffy, cunning, don't give a damn Gippo, he was now a step above them all! Class-wise that was. Yes, in civvy street, he well and truly outclassed them all. He owned a shop, a good sound one too, and after the war he would buy another. Andy's dad would stay on, managing the original. After the war Andy and his dad would run it jointly. He, Richard, would buy other premises. There was enough money to hand, and plenty of property going begging these days – if the Jerries didn't knock seven bells out of it all first. Perhaps the new venture would be larger, and dealing mostly in television sets. Yes, TV. That would be the up-and-coming thing. Two bloody shops. That would show snotty old ex-window-cleaner London.

Where were window-cleaners in the scheme of things? Not half bad. Good honest blokes beloved by the George Formbys of the world. Friendly, decent, usually with a cheery whistle and a smile. How long had it been since London had actually grinned? Too above himself probably. Never so high as shop-keepers, though.

Shopkeepers were considered way above even the richest stallholders in Hymen's Market, and miles above the sphere of folk in the two-up and two-downers of Solomon Street. Yes, even shopkeepers whose premises all but skulked within the dark, poverty-stricken confines of the Shattery!

So what of the prized London's Windows now? Richard mused. The hateful old sod was finished so far as that lot was concerned.

Richard had the strangest feeling that old Gippo was now rolling round in his grave and laughing his head off at the strange turn of fate.

Out of the blue Richard remembered the day Burza had come to visit them in Matson Street – before they had taken Gippo to hospital, of course. How gently she had cradled his stick-thin aged uncle in her arms, and kissed him, and told him that he wasn't to worry. That everything was going to be all right.

Gippo's yellow face had cracked round his sunken eyes. He had gasped out his appreciation of the chocolates she had taken him. Though unable to eat them, insisting that Richard and Burza should tuck in, the old boy had kept the box – even taking it with him, and placing it on the locker beside his hospital bed. Gippon had treasured that box right up until the last. Now he, Richard, had it. It was kept safe with his own personal things. It had a picture of violets and primroses on it and, so Burza had said, must remind them that after a bad winter there always would be spring.

Again in his mind's eye Richard saw Burza. Her long dark hair blowing away from her face as she had run to greet him. This on the occasion when he had been late turning up at the Hollow Ponds.

Right out of the blue Richard felt that he'd give his right arm to have Burza there with him. Walking at his side. Laughing mischievously, pretending as she often did, to be ticking him off.

'Let's go to the NAAFI,' Richard said abruptly. 'I'm starving. Come on!'

They began walking back to town...

It was after six when Burza walked into the house. Clara looked up from the kitchen range and asked, 'Did you notice if Allenby's was open, gel?'

'Yes, it was. They were still serving. Why?'

'We need our butter ration. I'll never get used to dry bread – if you can call this brown chaff, bread. Never is this a good wholesome loaf. No, not in a million years!'

'For heaven's sake, give me the books,' Burza laughed, 'and I'll run back.'

Clara handed over the ration books and Burza stuffed them into her handbag, not even bothering to snap it shut. She hurried out of the house and back down the road. As she burst into the shop, in one glance she saw studious-looking Mike Allenby out cold on the floor. There was blood at his temple, his spectacles hanging loosely from his ears. His wife, small and dumpy, was cowering against the shelves, her hand across her face, shielding it. At the till, club under one arm, stood a man wearing a balaclava helmet over his face. Hooded or not, Burza knew it was Nick Bede.

In a flash Clara's hat pin was out of the open handbag and in full furious use as she rounded the counter. She began jabbing at the thief's hidden face. All she could see was his staring eyes. He let out a yell as the point struck home on his cheek, and flinched back. Burza went after him; her blood was up. Everyone liked and respected the Allenbys, and this bully had half-killed Mike and terrified Binky, two nice old people who minded their own business and just got on with their lives – so far as the Jerries would let them! Nick Bede was worse than the enemy because he was battening down on his own. He was an out and out evil swine!

'Even dogs don't mess on their own doorstep, Nick Bede,' she panted, beside herself. 'Take that!'

The stunned thug, faced by Burza who seemed to have gone mad, turned and fled empty-handed. He left the Allenbys' day's takings safe where they were. As he went he yelled, 'I'm goin' to get you, Webby. See if I effing-well don't!'

Burza's knees gave way and she sank slowly down, to join poor old Mike. Mrs Allenby, shaking, a bruise already forming on her cheek, was in tears.

'Thank you, Burza,' she was saying over and over again. 'Oh thank you, dear. He was threatening to kill Mike. Me too.'

'Thank God he didn't pinch the butter.' Burza tried to laugh, but it was a shaky sound. 'If he had, Clara would have killed *me*! She hates dry bread, you see.'

She and Mrs Allenby clung to each other then and burst into tears. Mike groaned and tried to open his eyes.

'I'll phone the police,' Burza said, 'And I'll try to forget that Bede'll have yet another strike up against me now. My God, how that man hates me. Just wait until I tell his dad. Not that poor old Art will ever find him now.'

Burza went home with double her ration of butter, and with Binky's promise of anything and everything going – from under the counter – from then on.

'It will be our secret, dear,' Binky said tearfully. 'And I'll never be able to thank you enough. I'm quite sure that man would have beaten me to death before he left with the takings. He knew I recognised him and – oh sodding hell! Did you see his eyes?'

'As deadly and evil as a snake's,' Burza told her. 'Now I'd best be getting back to Clara.'

'But the police said on the phone that they want you to stay!'

'Sorry! I haven't had my tea, and besides Clara will worry herself sick if I'm much longer. If the bobbies want to talk to me I'll be at number six. All right?'

As Burza walked back down Solomon Street, her legs were trembling, her stomach was churning, and she wanted to cry. Suddenly she wanted to have someone defending her for a change. A picture of Pete flashed in her mind. But had Pete been there he would have stayed in the shop and begun posturing, playing the hero for the police. Yes, stopping a thief in his tracks would be just Pete's cup of tea! She thought of Andy, with his nice open face and wide ready smile. Dearest Andy, how reliable he was, steady and strong.

Then she thought of quietly direct, determined Richard who had left so abruptly. Who wrote the briefest of messages, all straight to the point. Richard who had been worldly wise and street-wise from the day he'd started school. Richard who said little, but whose warm grip was firm and strong and said so much.

Suddenly, very desperately, she was wishing Richard was there. Yes Richard, because he was the one to most likely understand why she felt so shaken, so near to tears, so damned down! Richard in his firm, direct way could and would put things in perspective. Calm her. Smile in his serious manner directly into her eyes. But Richard was with his best mate, and far away with the Green Berets. It was up to her, so alone and unaided she must carry on.

She reached home, explaining, and Clara was clucking like an old hen while Burza clung to her, awash with tears.

'I'm so stupid,' she wept. 'I was brave as a lion while it was all going on, it was only afterwards! It was definitely Nick Bede, I'd swear to that, and I have the strangest feeling that one day he'll do for me.'

'Over my dead body, gel!'

'Darling,' Burza smiled through her tears, 'that would be even worse. I don't think I'd want to live without you. You are the centre of my life.'

'Oh, Gawd 'elp us,' Clara groaned and shook her head. 'Talk about spreading it on thick.'

'I mean it! You've always been my lifeline.'

'Shut up, silly cow,' Clara said and clipped Burza's ear.

294

'Now where the bloody hell's that butter?'

A little later a harassed-looking policeman called. He was a Special, wearing a peaked cap, and that was it so far as Burza was concerned. Part-timers, older men, or maybe unfit in some way? One could never be sure. Of course, they were good men, stout-hearted and true, but not used to creeps like Nick, the younger Bede who was as wily, sly, and as cunning as a fox.

'You can write down that I'm prepared to swear in court that it was Nick Bede,' Burza told the constable. 'The same whose parents live at number eleven.'

'Solomon Street?'

'Of course,' she replied, thinking the bloke was either dense or mad. 'You may also like to make a note of the fact that Nick Bede has said on several occasions that he means to kill me. The first time because I instigated him getting a jolly good hiding from his dad. And now because I caught him in the act of trying to steal the Allenbys' takings. How is Mike Allenby, by the way?'

'They'll both live,' the Special constable said dryly. 'Thank you very much, Miss. Good evening to you.'

'And that's the last we'll see of '*im*!' Clara sniffed as the street door closed.

'I'm going to tell Art about his darling son,' Burza said impatiently, 'because I'm fed up with hearing back all the spite he spills out about Lily. He calls her all the names under the sun. A lot he knows! He also says she's alive and well, and that she's up to no good.'

'Well?' Clara asked, eyes twinkling. 'She ain't no little angel, is she?'

'Art doesn't know that. He's only prating on because he feels sorry for Jack. And who is he to talk? What with having two kids like Nick and Minnie I'd think he'd want to keep his trap shut! Lily's out of line, of course she is, but she does a lot for the Sally Army hostel, so she's not downright wicked.'

'Gawd, you'd swear black's white where Lily's concerned. But I think stealing from people taking cover in their shelters is really 'orrible!' Clara was speaking her mind, forthright as always. 'Taking away their precious personal things, p'raps stuff what can't never be replaced. Talk about her being like a

295

rotten little vulture picking over people's bones!' Clara's hands were on her hips now. 'Burza, when the bloody hell are you going to really look and see your best friend?'

'She's never picked over anyone's bones in her life,' Burza protested, eyes bright, cheeks pink. 'You should know better than to say such terrible things. Lily is out on the limb because ... It's the way she was brought up that's made her twisted. She had it tough.'

'No more'n you.'

'She had her very own father, and her own aunt, always going on at her and—'

'You had our Rosie for starters. Cruel she was in them days, bloody cruel. And I know all about your best white blouse getting suddenly burnt right through when she ironed it – an accident, of course! An' there was lots of other times. I know all about the things yelled at you by her and her big mates in school. Like being a foundling, an' unwanted, and a rotten filthy gippo kid. And although I put a stop to it where and when I could, I couldn't be behind her all the time.'

'But that was just Rosie's way.'

'An' Marion and Jack just had their way too. It's made Lily into a nasty piece of work, a tea-leaf, and Gawd knows what else. On the other 'and it's made you into a finer person. An' people would kill for your smile.'

'You've got it all wrong, Clara,' Burza said shakily, 'but do you know something? I'll love you for saying those nice things about me. I'll love you until my dying day.'

'An' soft soap won't get you no extra chips, gel,' Clara grinned. 'An' we've only got two skinny little bangers what you can hardly see, to share. 'Ow's that for living in luxury?'

'Can we have fried onions too?'

'Of course.'

'Wonderful!' Burza said.

Art Bede had come back from the Blue Row, two warm appetising-smelling parcels in his hands. Now he sat in Jack London's kitchen, hungrily unwrapping his meal. The gaslight was dim since the power had been cut drastically by the previous night's bombing. Jack's newspaper-wrapped helping of fish and chips stayed unheeded on his lap, while Art talked

296

and spluttered through mouthfuls of food.

'I put on plenty of salt and vinegar, mate,' Art said. 'Eat up while it's 'ot.'

Jack did not reply. Merely sat there in silence, watching Art, who was fat, sallow, and looking very much his age these days. Art looked round him. The blue and white of the kitchen, that once his old Em had envied so much, now looked dingy and yellowing, at least the white did. The blue now looked a dirty grey. Blackout frames were already placed up against the windows. It was a sombre-looking place. Through bomb-blast the ceiling was cracked and there was an air of dampness over all. Jack still sat quietly, not even seeming to notice the food in his lap.

'D'yer want me to fetch you a knife an' folk?' Art asked at last.

'I don't need to bother – at least while my sister is not here.'

'So yore sister won't be coming back till late again? Always late at nights these days, ain't she?' Art smiled and winked offensively. 'Still doin' that hoffice job of her'n, eh?'

'Codswallop!' Jack said coolly, his voice heavy with sarcasm. 'You found out about the flat she shares with Drew a long time ago. Don't pick over old sores. Either way she doesn't know that she's been found out and I'd prefer to keep it that way.'

'I wos only tryin'—'

'To make me squirm, or be grateful? Come off it, Bede. Either way, I'll do neither. I must say I can't get into that devious mind of yours. I reckon it's like a can of blue-bottle maggots the way it works.'

'Bleeding hell, Mr London, I only arst! I can't make out why yer don't let on to 'er that you know about her goin's-on.'

'Because once she realises I know, she'll be off for good.' he replied dryly. 'Can you imagine me managing without her? No, Marion's tied to me while I want her to be.' His voice became gunmetal grey. 'I had pride once, what a laugh! It was that pride, and dismissing the police's indifference to Lily's whereabouts, that made me accept your offer of help.'

'And I've done my best. I've found out fings wot they couldn't 'ave.'

'I felt that between us we could do so much better than the offi-
cials and I was right, of course.' He laughed sharply, a cold bitter
sound. 'So what did you do, eh? Found out about my sister! Quite
a blow, wouldn't you say, Art? Now you're whispering so much
rubbish about my child I could puke. I've known that she's alive
for quite a while, thanks to you. Not forgetting your son, who
hangs out in that sort of area himself. But if I believed all you've
just told me, I'd have to accept that the only pure thing left in my
life is my wife's memory.' His mind changed tack. He nodded
towards the dresser. 'And those. Have you seen them?'

Art didn't even bother to look. He knew what was there.
Lots of aspidistras, of various ages and sizes, all split from
Aspy over the years. Bleeding hell, Art thought, the silly old
sod's getting worse. Got a screw loose, he has. He sometimes
even talks to the effin' fings. I dunno wot's worse, him up the
creek, or his kid what sleeps around with blokes like Tibbits.

'Yers, Jack,' he said, stuffing the last chips in his mouth and
screwing up the greasy newspaper. 'I 'ave seen 'em all, not
forgetting the first one wot's still a giant. Real luverly. But I like
plants wot 'ave flowers, meself. Tulips an' that. Now, I was
telling yer. My Nick knows all about your Lil. An' he says. . .'

'Take your money and get out!' Jack told him tightly. 'And
don't bother to come back.'

'I don't want yore money. I told yer – I'm a doing of you a
favour.'

'Some favours,' Jack replied in a distant, long-dead voice,
'are worse than the hanging sentence. Clear off out of it
before I—'

'You bloody snotty-nosed old arse'ole!' Art growled, all
sense of obligation to this man finally dissolved. 'Fink you're
summink when you're nuffink, don't yer? You're just a
bleedin' cripple thinking as 'ow you're a cut above the rest of
us. Nuffink could be further from the truth. D'yer hear? Why
don't yer just piss orf art of it!'

He went out and slammed the door.

The air-raid warning went.

The guns and bombs were making a racket even before Art
got home to his Em. High above, the searchlights were long
chill fingers probing the sky.

It was going to be one of those nights. . .

Chapter Twenty-Eight

It was three in the morning and the world was hammering at the night with bombs, guns and incendiaries. Flames were shooting skywards and skeletal outlines of huge constructions shimmered in firelight – bizarre blackened bones left with neither heart nor soul.

Survivors of the mighty whiplash became united in underground Tube stations. There were no convenient caves within city confines, but anything remotely capable of giving cover was used. Anderson shelters abounded, standing four square in back gardens. Iron bedsteads or heavy tables were turned into makeshift dens. Alternatively one could use the cupboard under the stairs.

Gradually, as the weeks of Blitz continued, even fear became deadened before the need to sleep. Otherwise one doggedly stared into the darkness, reached for a Craven A, Players, Woodbine, Weights – or one of them rotten Turkish fags if that was all you could get.

Deep in the Underground, livened by the roar and flashing of through-running trains, a jolly stubbornness gave tongue. Rousing choruses of Roll Out the Barrel, Run Rabbit Run or such goodies as Marezee Doats 'n' Dozee Dotes 'n' Liddlelams Eee Divy. In other words, children were told, Mares Eat Oats and Does Eat Oats And Little Lambs Eat Ivy! After that, there came sentimentality, sung with sincere pathos, with minds winging away to loved ones. We'll Meet Again, There'll Be Bluebirds Over The White Cliffs of Dover, I'll Be Seeing You...

Nice ladies came down to the depths with huge tea-urns and

tasty bits and pieces to eat. Red Cross people kept a weather eye open in case of need. Air Raid Wardens, tin hats pulled down, appeared every now and then. Recognisable blokes, all friendly, all caring, and asking the inevitable question, 'Everything all right?'

'Course, mate,' came the defiant chorus. 'Everyfink's tickety boo!' and, 'Mind you take care yoreself, chum. It's bleeding 'ot stuff up there.' Then all agreeing, 'Yers! We can't do wivout you of hall people, Cocker!'

Amateur entertainers strutted their Fred Astaires, crooned their Bing Crosbys, or raised the roof with opera high notes never heard before. Wide-awake little girls were Shirley Temples without the curls, and no one gave a damn if child or adult fell out of step or tune. Each and every one of them were clapped and cheered for the stars they were. Especially the grandads who'd survived the first lot, and who now came alive with their musical spoons, washboards or rhythm-clicking bones. Grandmas continued with their knitting, or childminding, beaming with pride.

In her cupboard under the stairs in number six Clara prayed. She prayed for her children, their other halves, and the two little dears. She called her grandchildren her 'Precious Luvs'.

Clara did not pray to God, Who lived, she believed, in the sky above her church. She prayed to her George who was teaching Baby Vi to dance to the music of St Christopher's bells.

'Watch 'em, Georgy,' she whispered desperately. 'They ain't and never will be as capable as you. Not our pore Sid down them bleedin' awful mines. They're like tombs! His Ivy's a real nice girl. A bit bossy, but just right for 'im. Sid don't send her so many jokes in his letters these days. Misses his Ive, he does...'

There came a terrible crash that shook the foundations of the house. Burza's even breathing did not falter, and Boris merely yawned and stretched on Clara's lap. Her workworn hand reached out to stroke him.

'Ooer!' she breathed. 'That was a near one, Borry.' She raised her eyes to the unseen slope of the cupboard ceiling, not seeing anything of it, but imagining her Georgy up there, miles above the barrage balloons. She was now visualising him leaning nonchalantly against the side of a cloud, eyes like moonlight twinkling on pearl-grey waters.

'It ain't no laughing matter, George! It must be 'orrible working underground. Our Dicky's Gawd only knows where – you know 'ow secretive he is. And Peg's Charlie's turned up in India! Wot with bein' without him and young Georgy, she ain't hardly stopped crying. Bet's as bad, an' she's missing Clarry rotten, as well as that old man of her'n. Simpson's not in India, but in some other hot country – wot stinks, he says. Well, that's as best as Betsy can understand. The poor sod can't help as how he can hardly write, can he? He's turned into a likable young cuss.'

Suddenly, Clara was jolted out of her prayers. She stiffened and listened again, then leaned over to shake Burza.

'Bloody hell! Burz, wake up. There's someone at the door!'

Clara was scrabbling under the pillow for the handkerchief in which she had wrapped her teeth. No one, but no one saw her without them.

'I might be pore, but I'm vain an' I'm proud wiv it, Burz,' she'd say. 'An' my George bought 'em for me for me birthday. So shut up saying I'm soppy to mind about such things, you little demont! I know people don't care whether they're in or out, but I bloody well do!'

As Burza scrambled sleepily to her feet, and Boris swore and leapt to safety, the wild pounding at the door came again. It had to be bolted these days because blast had set it askew. Not even Clara fancied her house being left open to the world at night.

Burza went along the hall, her mind fanciful, scared in case the caller turned out to be Nick Bede, who she knew would turn up some day. Then she opened the door and was taken aback.

'Rosie!' Burza tried to lead the filthy, smoke-smelling, crying young woman inside, but Clara's youngest seemed unable to move. 'Oh my God!' Burza gasped. 'What's happened? Where's Ben?'

Rosie's voice was high, too high, and she was speaking too quickly. She was shaking and in shock.

'Cuts and bruises like me, but he's all right.' She laughed

and the sound held unbelief. 'He's trying to get through to Headquarters. You know, 'cause of looters! They're up there already – blokes wot are young enough to be in the Army. I've heard about them, deserters and all. It's the Shattery lot again, I know it. Bleeders!'

'Come on, love, calm down. Don't let's just stand here. Rosie, dear...'

But the young woman was not listening. She was gabbling, her eyes distended, 'The store's a washout, the bomb fell out back. Everything's mucked up. Our flat's... Oh soddin' hell!'

'Come on, dear,' Burza tried again, wanting to weep because the girl was in such a state. 'Everything's going to be fine. You and Ben are safe and that's all that matters.'

Rosie was babbling on, her eyes wide and light in the surrounding soot-black of her face. White lines showed up on her cheeks where tears had slid down.

'I refused to go to hospital, Burz. The ambulance brought me here and...' She let out a huge soulful wail '... and I want me mum.'

And then Clara was present, all arms and bosoms and, 'There, there, there, me luv. There, there ...'

The years were gone and Rosie was a kid again and Mum, full of love and comfort, was cradling her youngest daughter to her heart. And all the while she was gently backing along the passage, drawing Rosie with her to the kitchen, where Burza was already getting things ready to make a restorative cup of tea ...

With the Co-op in ruins, Burza was out of a job and so, it turned out, was Ben. As a valued worker there were other openings available for him, but further afield, and he refused to travel away from home. He could not leave his Rosie, whose shattered nerves made her cling to him, and also to her mum, in a neurotically desperate way.

Within two weeks Ben, who was unfit for the services owing to rheumatic fever when young, had found himself a shiftwork job in the local Mica factory. This was situated quite close to Lindley Road where his aged parents lived alone. Their three-bedroomed house could be divided into two flats, the idea of which Rosie had disdained before. Now it was clear that it would be much more sensible for Ben to live in Lindley Road. Rosie refused to either go with him or to let him go.

One morning, having worked the night through, and well before the All Clear, Ben was late getting home. There was a raid going on, ack-ack guns were on the loose, and shrapnel fell like rain. He pressed on regardless until he found the main road cordoned off because of an unexploded bomb. On top of that, incendiaries were raining down in freaky clouds.

'Just like them ruddy Indian arrows you see in Westerns,' Ben yelled pithily to one of the two Wardens on duty. Then, the sheer incongruity of it all struck home and he felt a kind of rebellion. Something he, a quiet and steady man, had never experienced before. Ben let out a whoop and did a war dance. He was grinning even though he was tired out and fed up. The blokes started beating dustbin lids in rhythm with his steps, and had a laugh with him. He shared their cocoa, sweetened with saccharine, smacked his lips appreciatively, and then ran alongside them to help put out several small fires, one actually burning on top of a family's Anderson shelter.

When things had calmed a little, Ben wished everyone cheerio, then he about-faced to trudge the long way home.

This news was passed on piece-meal by a hurriedly passing Warden. Ben had been a bit of all right, so the word went. A real brave and decent chap. He was late because he was coming home via Grove Green, that was all.

All? There was hell on the loose out there, Rosie snapped. Then she swore like a trooper. By now she was in total panic, as she continued jittering about on the doorstep, ignoring the racket going on. All the while she was getting more het-up and refusing point blank to go inside with Clara.

Searchlights crisscrossed the sky like pastry on blackberry tart. Guns stationed round the streets were barking upwards like huge mechanical dogs, streets became peppered with shrapnel, spitefully glinting metal djinns ready to do evil wherever they could. Rosie seemed unaware of this.

Time went by and all the while she was watching and waiting, terrified for her Ben. Gradually the fear inside her head grew too enormous to cope with, and Rosie had hysterics.

Shortly aftewards came the release of floods of tears when Ben finally reached home.

Even so, it took a great deal of patience, and solemn oaths from Clara that she would visit each day, before Rosie agreed to go and live in Lindley Road.

'Gawd's truth!' Clara said to Burza the following Monday. 'Talk about it never rains but it pours. Guess what?'

'I'm guessing they don't need me at the jam factory,' Burza said wryly. 'I would have liked that since it's near home, but I haven't heard at all.'

'We're losing Peg and Betsy.' Clara looked exceptionally po-faced. 'I dunno, I really don't.'

Burza forgot her own troubles and looked at her beloved Clara, perturbed. 'I don't understand.'

'You know they went down to see the kids for a few days, don't you? Well!' Clara's cheeks were now turkey-cock red and her lips twin thin lines. 'They found Clarry and Georgy scared out of their lives, pore little mites.'

Scared?' A picture of vivacious, confident little Clarry came to Burza's mind. Georgy was the more sensitive and quieter of the two, but scared? Never!

'That old cow where they stay said as how she insisted on good behaviour at all times.' Clara's knuckles glowed white as she clenched her fists. 'I could wring her neck as think of her. Bitch! Anyways she went on ter say she believed as how children should be seen and not heard. Peg said, all reasonable like, as 'ow that was fine by her. I arst you! I could—'

'Clara! Go on!'

'The kids were ever so neat and tidy, so Peg and Betsy went along wiv her. They was took aback a bit at first 'cause this posh tart spoke wiv such a big plum in her mouth. On top of that they were in a really swanky house. It was overpowering they said, wiv all stuff in it wot cost the earth. You know the sort of thing! So since Peg believes in doing everythink right and proper herself, she didn't see no fault in her Georgy being clean 'n' decent and having real good manners.'

'And so?'

'But our Bet said she was watching Clarry like a hawk while all the talking was going on. Clarry's such a

304

happy-spirited little soul, but she'd changed somehow, was too quiet, and too obedient, and she seemed to be clinging to Georgy as if scared he'd leave her. Them two's always been close, almost like twins, not cousins at all.'

'Oh yes! As close as Peg and Sid are, in fact.'

'Too right!' Here Clara's tone deepened. 'Betsy saw Clarry go all terrified, and she was cowering away when she spilt some water on the woman's carpet. Then the pore little mite couldn't hold it in no longer. She ran to Betsy sobbing out, "Mummy!" and crying like a wild thing. And she was begging Betsy to take her home and never ever let them make her go back. And then...' Clara stopped, unable to continue for a moment she was so angry.

'What? What then?' Burza was filled with a terrible sense of unease. What horrors had Clara's Precious Luvs been through?

'Clarry was asking Bets to please smack the lady who was always – 'ere, get this! – was always locking her in the black cellar with the rats, for being naughty!'

'Oh my God!' Tears of shock and disbelief flew to Burza's eyes. 'Oh, poor little Clarry, and poor young Georgy too! They're both so small and Georgy Porgy must have been at his wit's end half the time. He's not many months older than Clarry yet he's always been protective of her. He must have been frantic, not knowing what to do.' She turned towards the door, wanting to grab up the two little ones and fuss and spoil them as she used to before they were evacuated. 'I must go and see them. Have they brought them back?'

'No,' Clara said flatly. 'Too many bombs an' that. Betsy's been home first thing this morning and packed some of her and Peg's stuff and gorn back again. They've rented a cottage and will look after the kids themselves, and I tell you what – Gawd help that woman!'

'I bet the fur flew!'

'You can imagine ol' Peg and Bets havin' a go.' Clara smirked in an evilly triumphant way. 'I reckon that ol' mare never knew what hit her. Anyway, it's all in the hands of the authorities now. An' my gels won't let things drop, I can tell yer.'

'I wish I'd been there,' Burza began fiercely, 'I'd have—'

305

'Me too – an' I could 'ave a go at that woman even now if I thought my gels needed any help – which they don't! This cottage they took is, so Bets said, big enough for all of us. So you and me can go to the country wiv 'em if we want.'

'Are you going, Clara?'

'What? And break my promise to Rosie? 'Sides ... '

'Yes?'

'I ain't going to leave my George and Baby Vi all alone in St Christopher's, am I?'

'Of course you're not,' Burza choked. 'And you're not going to leave me either, are you?'

'Then you're staying too?'

'What, and miss the chance of working at the jam factory? There's still late post to come.'

'I forgot about that. They blew the postbox up – the one on the corner of Sedgwick, you know. It's a wonder them blokes get letters collected, the way things are. Still, that's beside the point. Yours should be up the sorting office and in delivery by now. Let's hope you get your job.'

The late post brought two letters of acceptance – from the jam factory, and also from the Mica factory. Burza and Clara were deciding which was the best to go for when Ivy came bustling in.

'Burza,' she said, all bright and brisk and businesslike. 'Your troubles are over.'

'They are indeed,' Burza smiled, 'You see I—'

'Our old ladies and gentlemen have given Wales the thumbs down, and Mrs Pinkerton agrees. They'd feel uprooted they said, and wish to stay put, Hitler or no Hitler. So since we've lost staff because of the proposed move that now isn't going to happen, we need you! When can you start?'

'But I... '

'Course, old people can be difficult at times. But they're lovable, and they like to help where they can. They're all a bit like kids, but helpless in some ways. They'll make rings round soft old you!'

'When do I start?' Burza asked joyously.

'First thing tomorrow morning. All right?'

'Eight o'clock?'

306

Ivy smiled her brisk, efficient smile. 'And the rest! Get there as near six as you can.'

After that the conversation became general. Uppermost being that wicked old bitch who had scared Clara's two precious grandchildren half to death.

The next morning, bright and early, Burza entered the foyer of the huge rather stern-looking Victorian building and knocked on the door prominently marked *Office*. On invitation she went in. She saw a tall slim lady with curly white hair and a pink, girlish face, smiling at her from behind a desk. She stood up and came round to meet Burza.

'My dear, how good to see you. I'm Mrs Pinkerton. Ivy has told you that we need your help?'

'Yes, Mrs Pinkerton. I'll do my level best, but I'm not a nurse, and ...'

'My dear child, we don't need nurses. Our medical staff is more than adequate. And Ivy, who manages most things, including even first aid, and all kinds of donkey work, gets through the chores of at least ten men. She's in charge of the daily cleaners, our stores, seeing to the laundry and all that sort of thing.'

'What will I be doing, Mrs Pinkerton?'

'As for you, dear, we need a helpmate, companion and friend for our people. Someone who will do odd jobs, like holding their skeins of wool, helping them with letters, or in Mr Wrawlings' case, crosswords. He gets himself in a right old tizz.'

'I will. I will!'

'Then there will be running errands for them if necessary, little things left behind in their rooms, that sort of chore. Most of them find it difficult to walk. However, most important of all, is just to talk or even better just sit and listen to them. Above all to be nice to our old darlings. Spare them your time and keep them happy.'

'Oh, I'll do my best. Honestly!'

'Good show. You're as sweetly pretty as our Ivy says, so they're all going to adore making something of a teacher's pet of you. I'll introduce you to everyone later on, but in the meantime would you like to help Cook with setting out the breakfast trays? First meal of the day is usually served in bed.'

'Gladly,' Burza replied, knowing instinctively that this j
was going to be the loveliest ever.

The Blitz continued night and rday. Moaning Minnie wai
her warnings or gave her strident All Clears and became p
of everyone's life.

Post Offices were damaged, pillarboxes smashed. M
from the Forces either did not arrive or was delivered
bundles at a time. Burza had heard nothing from Pete fo
while, and was chagrined to learn that on the other hand o
of the blondes in the boxing fan club had received quite
stack. Sadly she realised that with Pete, it would always be i
same.

She heard from Richard, regularly by contra
Straightforward letters, factual, with no nonsense and
frills. Yet they were heartwarming and deeply appreciate
and somehow just holding the page would conjure up
picture in her mind. His strong cheekbones, his well-shap
mouth, his direct dark eyes. He always added Andy's regar
Andy wrote to Lily, and from the beginning, the patte
between the four friends had been set.

Bus wheels, like the feet of pedestrians, often crunched ov
crackling broken glass. Day after day trains ran late and Cent
buses had to try different routes. The yellow sign *Divers*
hung on its barrier across a growing number of traffic arteri
Bomb craters appeared in roads. Rows of small houses disa
peared, in their places starkly raw empty shells.

All this meant early rising for the clerks, warehouseme
waitresses, shop girls, factory folk and the rest. Early risi
after short broken nights. But the general motto was 'Get
and get going – and bless 'em all!' Keeping to a regu
routine wherever possible helped to face immensely unus
things. Like the nightly noise, the sights of skies blood-r
with flames, of the weird aerial dances of planes fighting
the death miles above.

A certain fatalism was born.

'If it's got your name on it, mate, it'll get yer no mat
what – so sod it!'

Lily, sitting with Burza in the kitchen of number t
Matson Street, felt the same.

'I don't think about it – or not much, Burz,' she said

308

Burza's Sunday afternoon off. 'I get on with all that I have to do and let the war take its course.'

'And you don't mind not helping the war effort?' Burza frowned. 'Not even in the tiniest way?'

'Not really. Anyway, since I'm outside the law my hands are tied.' Momentarily the quiet, shy girl that Burza had once known shone through 'But I can't help thinking I would have loved to have worked in Peacehaven with you. They sound such nice old dears. Now, what *you're* doing really is worthwhile.'

'Thank you,' Burza beamed.

'Andy would agree, I'm sure.' Lily pulled a wry face. 'But then Andy reckons you're the cat's whiskers, Burza. His letters are always full of your praises. He gets so cross about things though. Sometimes I think he hates me. He certainly hates my way of life.'

'And you?'

'I can handle it.'

'Is that all, Lily?'

'Let's just say that cocking a snook at my dad doesn't seem so important these days.'

'Why don't you visit him?' Burza asked eagerly. 'He's making a good fist of things, you know. And he loves his new job. He goes regularly, and works three hours, from nine to twelve noon. He sits and weighs slivers of mica, and ...'

'No! And I still hate Marion.'

'She has to work lots of overtime these days.' Burza laughed richly. 'Honestly, aren't men blind? They see what they want to and nothing else, and your dad's like the rest. As for Pete ...'

'Do you hate him, Burz?'

'Sometimes.' She looked at the clock. 'Blow! I'd best get cracking. Clara will worry, else...'

'If yer can risk it, gel,' Clara said the following weekend, after a particularly heavy daylight raid, 'an' if you've told your nice lady that you don't mind helping out on your afternoon off, you get going.'

'And you really don't mind?'

'Course not. I've got plenty to do. That's if the gas still

works an' Jerry ain't cut the mains again. I want ter do something nice and tasty for Jack's tea, though Gawd knows wot you can do with liver sausage! Still, we're all right for spuds. Marion's out all day again, I understand. Eatin' out, I s'pose.'

'Lily reckons she hates her.'

'Really? Well, I ain't too keen on young Lil.' Clara sniffed, then forgetting about wayward Lily, she added, 'I'll do somethink for ol' Bill Jessop too. Fancy Florrie pissing orf to the country to stay with her sister like that.'

'I expect Bill can do with a rest from her tongue,' Burza said saucily.

Clara gave her wicked, slanty-eyed smile. 'Now why didn't I think about that? An' of course he won't leave his flowers. Not that there's much left of his glasshouse. Took his plants inside, he has – no wonder Florrie left 'ome. Anyway, they need Bill on the railway. But as for ol' Jack London, got guts ain't he?'

'He's always had courage of a kind, Clara, but not so much as you. You've never given up on people, or pulled them to shreds because they don't act as you'd like. No. You accept folk for who they are, not what they are.'

'Even so, he ain't a bad old stick. Who knows how we'd be with no usable legs? Well, he's cracked it. Got himself his own little war effort to think about. Who'd have thought it, eh? Three hours ain't much, but getting that sitting-down job at the Mica place means the world to 'im.'

'He's to be admired and I told Lily so.'

Clara chose not to hear that, and continued, 'Through Ben putting in a word, ol' Jack's got his pride back. Jack needs his pride and that's a fact, gel. Now don't just stand there. Get back and help your little old people.'

'Clara, it's not that I don't want to stay with you,' Burza said earnestly. 'It's Miss Rodale, you see. She's tiny, like a little bird actually, and so fragile and sweet. And of course very, very old. She seems to need me and since she can hardly see ...'

'She's got her head screwed on right if she's taken to you, Burza.' Clara flipped Burza playfully round the ear. 'I sort of took to you myself! Go on, buzz off.'

In spite of it still not being All Clear Burza almost danced

310

all the way to Peacehaven. She loved her job and she loved life, and especially Lily even though she seemed to be like a will-o'-the wisp these days. But Lily was her darling friend no matter what, and she was therefore in a niche all of her own. But over and above all, Burza loved Clara like a mother. Clara, the lovely lady who had been her rock and her staff from the time she could remember ...

Burza had settled Miss Rodale, who was now sleeping in an easychair. The large, comfortable sitting room they all usually shared was on the ground floor. Peacehaven was a strongly built place with thick walls and a sense of stability. Even so, while the warning was on, people were taken below, to the basement. It was fitted out very comfortably indeed. Mrs Pinkerton loved Peacehaven and did a good job in her dead husband's name. Her goal in life was to keep everyone happy.

Burza was endeavouring to help Mr Wrawlings with his crossword puzzle when the guns began again. The old chap began muttering rude things about a chap's Sunday peace and quiet being shattered, and going red in the face. The guns were in the distance still and there seemed no immediate threat. Even so Burza helped bolster him up with cushions and reminded him to bury his face in them should things get sticky. Then she went to the peacefully sleeping Miss Rodale, who looked like a cherub, and made sure things were all right.

The nurses were alert and everything was satisfactory. Even so Burza walked from one to the other of all the twenty old people, smiling and joking, teasing and fussing, and in short beaming out confidence and goodwill. They all turned to her, trusting, looking like old-young dolls with crinkly paper faces and thin blue-veined hands. Burza's heart went out to them. Specially some of the old men whose medals showed how splendidly they had served in the last Great War.

Time went on and now the barrage was getting far louder. An extra hollow-sounding malevolent thump sounding quite near woke Miss Rodale, who began to cry. This set one or two of the other ladies off. Burza quickly got them singing. In a little while they were into If You Were the Only Girl in the World, and I'll Be Your Sweetheart, Just A Song At Twilight and so on. Jolly Nurse Merryweather, a huge roly-poly woman who had a voice like a lark, encouraged them all the way, and it turned out to be almost party-time.

'Please stay a while longer dear,' Miss Rodale pleaded. And all the others joined in.

'Yes, wait for me and we'll go home together,' Ivy, crisp and businesslike in her white overall said. 'Thank Gawd young Georgy and Clarry are out of this lark. I reckon as how bombs are more scary even than dark cellars and huge rats.'

And because the hammering outside was going full blast now, Burza agreed to stay.

Peacehaven was rocked on its foundations several times after that. Clearly there had been near misses. It was not until the All Clear went that Miss Pinkerton felt it was safe to let any of her day staff go.

Ivy and Burza walked side by side, looking round at the scars of war. Windows were blown out, some gutters were smashed through by shrapnel. Chimneys were down. The raid had been heavy. There was smoke and fumes rising above the row of houses behind the park. Then almost in line, there was a dull glow rising from behind the distinctive Feathers chimneypots.

'Ivy,' Burza said tightly – was that strange voice really coming from her own aching throat? 'Ivy, that can't possibly be in Solomon Street, can it?'

They both began to run.

Chapter Twenty-Nine

Burza was numb and cold. Her soul held the same purple-black of darkest night. Her eyes seemed to be stretching out of her head, their roots clinging to her mind. But her brain was taut, and it seemed that any moment now it would leave her head, pulled out on the ends of her eyeballs. Would fly out grey and wriggling, like a kind of crumpled jellyfish. And it would flop against that stupid man's face and cover his lips and stop him saying such terrible things. His words were coming out of his mouth like ghouls escaping the grave. Was that her own head beginning to explode? This was a nightmare. Unreal! A fantasy making jagged shapes in her mind.

As if from a million miles away she heard Ivy moaning. It was a dreadful sound, raw and agonised for all she was fighting for self-control. And Ivy was saying things like, 'Oh God, my poor Sid!' And in a strange way Burza was wanting to laugh. Poor Sid? Not poor Clara?

The thought jerked away, scalded in laceration's white heat, and she was mouthing things, begging and pleading, yet no sound was coming. Only a deep dry croak – but she was trying to call to Clara. Then her mind, that had now escaped from the stalks holding her eyes, was floating above her head. And she herself was caught in a whirlpool, rushing upwards, trying to reach Clara. To stop her dearest darling from going even further away. Clara – Clara – Clara . . .

And then that stupid man was calling to someone else. Pete?

She was in a daze, remembering vaguely that she had explained to Pete as well as to Clara that she had to work. That her old ladies needed her. Oh God! Clara hadn't needed her? But she, Burza, alone and unaided had gone rushing off the Peacehaven. Thinking only of everyone else!

And now here was Pete who had not gone abroad after all, and with him Josie Briggs. And there were others too. Lots of neighbours, all shaken, kind, concerned. And strangers, already working like mad clearing up the mess that Solomon Street had become.

Her stretched gaze saw that the cause of all the ruins around had been a bomb. It had left a crater in the middle of Solomon Street, right opposite number six. Ivy's place above the Elliots' flat was gutted worse than the lower half of the house, though that was a caricature in itself; and the blast had taken numbers three and five, as well as the Allenbys' shop. There were many injured, but Clara ...

The baker's on the corner opposite wasn't too bad, but Ethel Jacobs' place was a heap. Most of the numbers up to and beyond Jack London's were truly messed up; however number six had taken the brunt. It was now just a cracked and broken bit of shell brooding above the miraculously still safe cupboard under the stairs. Yet Clara had been in the kitchen, they said, and Clara was gone. Clara was dead. She had been taken away to the mortuary, and they weren't allowed to go to her for a while. She wanted Clara! Burza's soul was bleeding with need. She needed her sweet, wonderful old Clara, but ... Clara would call her 'little demont', and pretend to box her ears no more.

Mrs Frazer and Pete were trying to lead her back along the road. She could not move. Was frozen. Suddenly she hated Pete.

'Get away,' she gasped and felt numb, void. 'I don't want you, not ever. I want ...'

'We'll go to my mum's,' Ivy said, trying to sound calm, but her white face and tragic eyes told their tale. 'And then I'll have to sort things out. Come on, Burz. We've got to pull ourselves together. We've got to let them all know.'

But Burza wasn't listening. She was looking across the road, to where number five's front step was now nothing more than jagged lumps of broken concrete and stone. She was seeing a half-hidden coat of long black fur. Then she was struggling over bricks and mortar and dusty rubble, the

314

anguish making her throat ache like a hammer-pulse, and her eyes burn like coals. She was tearing at the rubble and freed him at last. Her poor old Borry. Then she was cradling him in her arms. Just crouching there, in the dirt and the dust, rocking him like a baby. Her dear old dead cat whom she and Lily and Clara had so loved.

She refused to move, and in the end Ivy said desperately, 'Here's your mate come to stay with you, Burz. I'll leave you with her. I've got to go home! Sorry, gel, but I need to see my mum.'

She swung round, trying to be crisp and efficient, but her face was working, for the whole family loved Clara, Ivy as deeply as most. Burza hardly noticed her going. Then Lily was there, filthy and utterly distressed. Her eyes were distended, her mouth quivering.

'I ran here the moment I learned about all this,' Lily was saying harshly. 'I've been here ages. He ... he didn't want to know me!' She was faltering now, and crying and stroking Boris's face. 'He ... he looked me up and down as if I was something utterly and absolutely disgusting. And he told me to get out of his sight.'

'Boris,' Burza whispered, her voice sounding strange and far away. 'Our old fluff-ball is dead. And my darling Clara's dead. I want to die too.'

'He also told Marion to go to hell.' Lily seemed to be talking to herself but quickly, babbling almost, beside herself. She was clearly taken aback, facing a situation she had never envisaged before. 'They were both there, staring at me. Then he looked at us both in turn and he was so bitter! Burza, listen to me!'

Burza stayed where she was, cuddling Borry, her face statue-still. Lily continued, like a train getting up speed after leaving the station, her words chugging out in an automatic, husky way.

'And then he glared at Marion, swore at her, and told her to get back to her fancy man – and she has! And he just stayed, sitting there in the mess, on his broken wheelchair. He was holding what was left of Aspy.' She laughed disbelievingly. 'He was ignoring me and talking to that damned plant! And then he looked up at me, and right through me, and – and his

eyes! Burza, he's gone off somewhere with Bill Jessop and ...
he hates me!'

'That makes a change,' Burza whispered, now fighting for
reason, for Lily's sake trying to concentrate. Fighting to make
sense. 'It used to be the other way round, didn't it? But don't
you understand, Lily? About Clara ...'

Lily let go then.

'Of course, you stupid, stupid fool!' Lily's voice had risen
high, and she was choking and gasping, and screwing her hands
together. 'And I've been carrying on about my father just to try
to get that awful look off your face. Burza! Look at me! Think
of something else, anything, but get that look *off your face!*'

'I should have been with her. It was my afternoon off, but
I—'

'You did as you always do,' Lily told her fiercely, 'thought
of other people before yourself. Don't try to turn that into a
crime. I'm the criminal, remember? Our sweetest, darlingest
Clara knew that.'

'I've got to search for her picture of George,' Burza said
desperately. 'It's her most prized possession.'

'There's nothing left. Look at it – all gone. There's nothing
we can do. But that's not my concern, dear.' Lily was kneeling beside Burza, rubble spilling over her knees and onto her
lap. Her eyes were red-rimmed, her face swollen and blotched
with tears. 'You are. Thank God you were at work.'

'I shouldn't have been, Lily. I should have been with
Clara,' she sobbed.

'You're coming home with me,' her friend said firmly.
'You'll never be alone while I'm alive. Don't you understand?
We'll lay Boris to rest very beautifully in the garden, and then
we'll have a ...'

In a dim way Burza became aware of someone shouting and
something of a fresh commotion. It grew louder as Art Bede
and a policeman made their way forwards. People stopped to
watch, curious, because by Bede's face there was something
very much up.

'There she is! I told yer!' he shouted, his face working in a
monstrously ugly way.

Art Bede's clothes were in tatters, his hands raw where he'd
been helping the men – until he'd spotted Lily. Then he'd

316

picked up his heels and run all the way to the police station. Now he was pressing home his point.

'Slippery as a eel she's been,' he roared nastily, his deafness affecting his voice. Then his piggy eyes swivelled round to Boris and his cheeks went dark red. 'I helped get his missus out – a good woman if ever there was one, but it were too late. She wos a bloody decent ol' lady an' so's my old gel, my Em wot's been carted orf to Connaught Hospital – and my cat's gorn too, probably conked out somewhere.' He swung round to face the crowds. 'Decent living fings wot don't harm no one, cop it rotten, don't they? But slimy buggers wot steal from others live to tell the tale. Bleedin' good, innit?'

The constable continued to look calm and was clearly unimpressed by Art's tirade. He cleared his throat.

'Calm down, sir. This isn't helping.' He was taking it all in his official capacity. The damage, the general air of shock, the ranting, fat old devil – the two ashen-faced girls.

Art was working himself up to full pitch now, shouting so that he could hear his own words. His face held venom as he pressed home his point, making it clear for the law.

'An' I've got witnesses as'll tell yer a yarn or two about her goin's-on, Constable. Proof as ter all the thievery she's been up to for years for a start, an' there's men ...'

'Mr Bede,' the constable said evenly, 'beware. There's defamation of character for a start. And surely there's a time and place ...'

Art was in full spate and nothing, and no one was going to stop him. There was a crowd round him, still listening and watching. Burza's wax model, empty-eyed expression remained unchanged. Lily looked like a rabbit caught in a snare.

'Goldie they call 'er,' Art Bede roared to all who cared to listen. 'And I can tell yer where she was last night, an' all. Up to no bloody good, and them in Snaresbrook Road will tell yer that when they come to count their valuables. Seen, she was. Nothing's sacred to her sort.'

'Oh God,' Lily whispered to Burza who remained frozen. 'Nick Bede threatened he'd get at you through me. Knew your soft spot was me, he said. Awful, stinking me! He's learned the lot and more besides, and told his dad.'

317

'Clara will sort it,' Burza whispered back in a small voice, trying hard to concentrate for Lily's sake. 'Clara will—'

'Burza, don't!' Lily said on an ocean-deep sob. 'I'm sorry, so very sorry.' She began weeping and wringing here hands together again. 'Just when you need me.' She gasped in horror as the policeman reached down to take her arm. 'Burza! Burza, please stay with me. I'm afraid ...'

Burza turned very slowly and saw Josie standing there at the edge of the crowd. She was alone, watching them, looking sad and sorry and full of concern.

'Josie? Josie, a favour?' Burza breathed, her heart in her eyes. 'Please?' She held out Boris. 'Would you ask Pete to bury him for me, nicely? Somewhere in Clara's back yard?'

'Of course I will,' Josie replied. 'In fact, I'll do it myself. And Burz, Lil? I'm so very sorry.'

The policeman was leading Lily away and Burza followed like an automaton. And all Burza could see in her mind's eye was Clara's brightly twinkling, slanting melon-seed eyes, and hear her teasing.

'I dunno, gel! Orf to Frances Road cop now, are we? What a little demont you are ...'

Chapter Thirty

The Scottish mountains were shrouded and looked purple-grey. The terrain chosen for training was strong, tough, indomitable. And in vast blue counterpanes, spreading out in stretches of icy blue, the lochs and canals glittered cold, cold, cold. And within the heart of this rugged land, equally rugged men played their war games with verve and skill. Stretching themselves to the limit. Battling against anything and everything the elements and environment could throw at them. Minds were crystal clear, bodies taut, reactions as quick as lightning.

And the Spean Bridge stood staunchly under the weight of numbers and remained remote as men spread across its withers. Men who fanned out in waves, then disappeared in the vast surroundings. Men, always exercising, taming, handling, learning. Coming to terms with the vagaries of Loch Lochy, the idiosyncrasies of the huge Caledonian Canal area, and with the lochs climbing steadily upwards towards the peaks.

Crack platoons, Commandos like so many groups of pigmies against Scotland's immensity, drank in the nation's raw power. Hardy men from all over Britain felt their hearts quicken to the swirl of the pipes and the smiling faces of the bonnie lasses. High-spirited men filled with vitality, working and playing hard, then in the quiet moments, reading and writing letters home.

Under canvas, close as ever, Richard and Andy were silent while Richard read Lily's letter again.

'She's in Borstal now, Rich,' Andy sighed. 'It would have

319

been clink if she'd been over twenty-one. She's learned her lesson at last and says she deserves her punishment. But she's terrified for Burza. Burza's taken it too hard. She stuck by Lily through thick and thin, but once Lily was sent off to Kent, she fell ill. I wish I'd known before. They don't allow much mail at all from that bloody place.'

'She'll come through it,' Richard said flatly. 'She's more courageous than most.'

'The little 'un held up like a Trojan for Clara's funeral, Lily says, and she herself was allowed to attend that – just. She was shocked when she saw Burza. She looked like a corpse, she said. But she wasn't allowed to stay with Burza even for a moment or two afterwards.'

'Typical!'

'Now Burz's gone down with a bang. By all accounts she's sent everyone away, and she's packed Frazer in. So she's alone and without Lily too. Now, no more shilly-shally, eh? It is Burz for you isn't it? Always has been – like it's always been Lily for me.'

Richard did not answer.

'All right, so you're a blockhead,' Andy told him, exasperated. 'Feelings ain't sins, but your attitude to 'em bloody well is. Now for once in your life you've got to do as I ask. You've known about this letter from the second I got it, and now you've got to do something about it. You've got to take your leave for a change and get your backside home!'

'It's all been arranged,' Richard said.

Burza sat quietly in what had once been Roan's stable. The straw was still sweet, the place warm. It was heading towards dusk and shadows were growing on the ground. On high, through the door she could see the Evening Star, a mere smudge yet for it was early still. But Burza loved the Evening Star. That was where Baby Vi used to hang out, according to Clara, and then George went there too. Now, after all these weeks, Clara must have reached them there. She was probably bossing them about, and every so often looking over her shoulder to see what her earthbound lot were up to too.

Thank heaven they were all now doing their normal tasks and fighting to keep grief at bay. Up to now neither Clarry nor

Georgy had been told that their Gran had gone. They were, by all accounts, having the time of their young lives in the country. And even Peg and Betsy were settling down.

Burza smiled tremulously, ignoring the slow trickling of her tears, thinking that Clara had probably been very pleased with them all on her final appearance in the world. And very aware of their love and concern. This whether they had been there at St Christopher's or not on that cold, unreal day. Sid had been there, and Ben. Charlie and Simpson had been not, though Peg and Betsy had. Dicky was absent and he too was miles away. But Rosie and Ivy had been huddling close. Each and every one of them quiet, numb, empty-faced. Trying to act the parts that Clara would have expected. Keeping the stiff upper lip and all that, she'd say in her jocular way.

Strange and wonderful how families cling together in trouble, Burza thought. How closely they had all hunched up together round the grave. Of course they had all given way in the end. Holding on to each other, sobbing, Sid loudest of all, while the girls had clung to him like a clutch of terrified and heartbroken young hens.

From the evening of the bomb residents of Solomon Street who had nowhere else to go had all been accommodated in a small church hall. The WI and the WVS and other groups had supplied food and blankets, toiletries, anything and everything that would help them get by. Burza remembered Rosie especially. She had gone into herself upon losing Clara, and looked dead, dead, dead. And Ben, beside himself with worry, had finally broken down and cried. That had brought Rosie quietly back to the sane world, for she dearly loved her Ben.

After the funeral Rosie, her eyes holding all of the grief in the world, had approached Burza. She had put her arms round her and whispered, 'I've always looked on you as my sister, Burz. Always! Really and truly, deep down. An' now you must come and live with Ben an' me. I want ter try and make up for—'

'She's to come to the country with us,' Peg had put in, quiet and firm. 'Me and Betsy want to look after her. We can't thank her enough for all she's done for Mum, but we can look out for her from now on. We're off soon. Can't leave the kids with Mrs Nicholson no longer, so we've gotta go.'

'She's best off with me,' Rosie objected fiercely.

'This squabbling's not on at this time,' Ivy put in crisply. 'Just leave her alone, gels. She's all done in, just look at her. She's taken up Mrs Pinkerton's offer to live in. Me too when Sid's gone back up there.' She turned to Sid, who seemed to have shrivelled and aged since Clara's death. 'Right, luv?'

'Right,' he said raggedly, adding, 'seeing how neither of you fancy coming up north wiv me.'

'It's our old people,' Ivy pleaded. 'I've been with them for years – some of 'em even longer than I've known you, Sid. I can't leave 'em. And Burza feels the same.'

Strictly speaking that hadn't been true, Burza thought, because she didn't feel the same. In fact, she didn't feel anything – except bereft.

She tried to recall Clara's face as she had seen it in the coffin. She had looked extraordinarily like the stone angel. Well, the angel had still been there guarding Baby Vi and George, and now she was also guarding Clara. They were together. There was a small comfort in that.

A dark shadow blocked out the light from the door and then Kiffa was beside Burza. Small, wiry, smelling of gorse and ferns and dried grass. Her beads jangled and clinked, her dark eyes gleamed, her hands were heavy with rings.

'I know what happened back then. You all right?'

'I'm fine, thank you,' Burza replied politely, unsurprised.

'Of course you are. Like a duck with a broken neck, in fact. Still, time heals so they say.'

'Yes. I know.'

'But you don't believe it?'

'No.'

'Accept that we're like animals, Burz. Animals and birds and fish. All living things. They get their young, rear 'em safe, and then watch them go. An' if the young want to hang about and make a meal of it, they're edged out toot sweet. That's all there is to it.'

'So it's all plain sailing?'

'Should be.'

'And – and when someone dies?'

'Same thing. You have to let them go. Then you have to get on as best you can.'

'And if you can't?'

'No such word.'

'You – you find it easy to leave people, don't you?'

'Not always, but it has to be done.'

'My – my father?'

'He was a decent sort and I loved him, but not as much as I loved being true to my own kind and to myself. I never lied to him about that.'

'And you left him for a man of your own kind?'

Kiffa's laugh was round and soft, like the cooing of baby owls. 'Burza, I left my own gipsy husband for your dad. Your dad didn't know, which was as well seeing how he was. I wanted him, and so I got him regardless. Then I was given the option by my old man, to go back and have the whipping of my life for my sins, or have you both pay.'

'Oh! So you ...'

'I took the whipping. Make no mistake about this, I took it because I wanted to. When Tarny was beating me I came alive. I fought him back like a she-cat and he fought me like a dog. We fight even now. I loved your father in a way, but I couldn't take it. I couldn't stand that cottage, or the way of life – and I couldn't stand Steve treating me like a bit of precious china. I felt strangled all the time.'

'And – and me?'

'You were strangling me too. Besides, you didn't belong with us, me and Tarny. It would have been tough going for you, Tarny would have seen to that. Anyway, Steve insisted that you belonged to him.'

'And so he immediately gave me to Clara!'

'Look, I'm as black as painted. Every bit! Your father on the other hand, always did what he thought best. He was a quiet, straight, upright and honest man. I left before I tried to kill him for being too nice. I am what I am.'

'And my father is a sailor who I've never seen.'

'You never will – now. He died a while back. Oh, we gippos know how to find out a thing or two when we need. I made enquiries after I first set eyes on you.'

'But Clara was never notified.'

'She would have been if he'd stayed at sea, at his job serving on his ship with the Company. But he didn't. Wanted to drop off the edge of the world for some reason we'll never know. And he died, alone in Australia. It's all done and done with. None of it matters any more.'

'How do I know you're telling the truth?'

'You don't.' Kiffa uncurled herself as easily as unrolling silk, and stood up. 'I won't be seeing you for a while. I'll probably meet up with Mrs Woman here some time. I'll tell her and ol' Granger that you're still around.'

'Kiffa, I ...' Burza was speaking to thin air. The gipsy woman had gone.

Burza clasped her arms around herself and began to rock to and fro. Too tired to give a damn about a stranger who had died far away on the other side of the world.

She had decided to spend her days off work here, in the quiet, alone, because of all places, sitting here, staring through the door and up at the sky was the closest she could get to feeling peace. She had dismissed Kiffa the moment she had left. Also the knowledge of her father's death. Natural parents? They were nothing to her, blood or no blood.

It would have helped Lily a great deal if she could have been truly divorced from her dad. As it was she had clung to Clara as a mother figure just as she, Burza had done.

The light was dimming into dusk now. The Evening Star was becoming diamond bright. Suddenly Burza knew that she was not alone.

'I know you're there,' Richard said, appearing in the doorway as if by magic. 'You're in the shadows, but facing the door. I can't see you properly. Stand up, Burza.'

'Oh!' Her heart lurched with surprise, then began a deep, slow pounding filled with pain. 'Richard!'

'Come here.'

'I – oh dear!' She was going to pieces. Her hands were sticky, her mouth had gone dry. 'My legs are shaking. Richard, I ... Why – why don't you come here?'

'Burza!'

She pulled herself up and went to him like a sleepwalker.

'Now,' he said, 'can you see into my eyes?'

'Yes,' she breathed. 'Just. Oh Richard.'

'Kiss me.'

'Richard?'

'I said kiss me.'

Shocked, she stared up into the light blur of his face. This was a ragged taunt from a stranger. But no, it was Richard, her Richard. Larger than she had remembered, fiercer, his face dark and his eyes restless. He looked stern and angry but mostly he looked determined. This was a Richard she had never seen before.

She stood on tiptoe, to do as she was told. Her eyes never left his face, her own gaze being wide and startled. Only as their mouths touched did her lids flicker shut. And the kiss was firm and powerful and it was sending thrills and shivers down her spine.

In a dream she felt him edging her backwards, inside the stable where she had first made love with Pete. Her eyes flew open. She tried to pull away.

'No!' she gasped. 'No!'

He held her away from him, dark eyes intense. 'Why?'

'It doesn't matter.'

'It does to me. Are you turning me down?'

'No,' she faltered. 'Richard, I'm so glad you're here. I – I've been so lonely.'

'Then stop arguing.'

'Richard – not here!'

'Where?'

She thought rapidly. She knew where the key to the house was, but – what had come over Richard? No word of love? Just cold black orders like 'Come here' and 'Kiss me.' What had happened to him – and what had happened to her for even thinking of letting him ...

'The house,' she told him. 'We are allowed into the house. Miss Allthorpe left the key, but ... Why, Richard?'

'You need me – and I need you.'

'Oh!'

They were walking towards the house, along the lane sheltered beneath the hedge. It was quiet here, dark and secretive.

'To hell with the house,' Richard said. 'This will do.'

I'm mad, she thought, yet in spite of her sense of emptiness and loss, she did not fight him.

He kissed her eyelids, her cheeks, her lips, her throat, and all the while his hands were searching her clothes, finding the

325

buttons on her blouse, the fastening of her skirt, undoing them, and she did not stop him. In fact, did not want to. He was powerful, his arms like steel bands.

He was too strong to fight as he lowered her to the ground, or even pretend to try. Then he was exploring her body inch by inch, his kisses were growing longer, more sensuous. His mouth went lower to her throat, lots of nudging, tantalising little kisses that were egging her on. He cupped her breast with his hands, his lips encircled her nipple and began to pull, gently, erotically, sending sparkles of fire and ache and need and absolute desire flooding through her. And all the while his fingers were searching lower, reaching her femininity at last, and beginning to tease and pry and probe. She was aware only of this man now, of what he was doing to her, of how he was making her feel.

'You – you have done this before,' she whispered breathlessly against him.

'Not with you,' he mouthed round her breast. 'And you've done it before too, haven't you?'

'Yes,' she whispered. 'But not with you.'

'Then we'll make it the best ever.'

In a dream she felt his hands were becoming more demanding. She wanted more, more, more.

'Richard!' she whispered fiercely. 'Take me!'

The sky was blotted out as he rose above her, then entered her with such forcefulness it was a shock. She bit her lips, but held him close for all that. He was big, was filling her, stretching her, and his movements were powerful, passionate. She gasped, shuddered, then went with him, matching movement with movement, harder, faster, higher, reaching for the summit of sensations. Finally the white heat of the absolute pinnacle. She hung there poised in space, her whole being taut and hot and tingling as never before. Then it was time to let go, and she flew down, sobbing Richard's name.

Her eyes remained closed and she was holding on to him, feeling that at last she actually did have something to cling to. That the world was suddenly not quite such a frighteningly empty, soul-destroying place. That all the coiled-spring emotions that had held her nerves and sinews so tight had unwound, were relaxed, were let go.

She felt Richard's hands brushing her black hair from off her forehead. He had lifted his weight off her now, she could feel him watching her, but kept her lids closed. She heard him say, 'That was well done, Burz, but just an appetiser, old girl.'

She did not reply, just lay still, feeling the night breezes blowing and stinging against her cheeks, thinking. He does not say he loves me. Yet perhaps he does in his way.

'Kiss me,' he commanded.

She lifted her lips and he was kissing her roughly, his stubble spiteful round her mouth. He needed a shave, she must tell him so. It was like being kissed by one of Clara's pot scourers and that was a fact. She blinked and banished the thought to the back of her mind.

'Well, well,' he said gruffly. 'Who'd have thought it, Burz? You and rough, tough, arse-torn-out-of-his-pants old me. We've actually made it. So what do you say?'

'I think it's been more doing than saying, Richard,' she told him, trying to play the game his way.

He was frowning now, his dark eyes serious. Not sure how to take her.

'Now you're reverting to type and teasing me. It was always the same. You teasing or yelling your head off like a banshee. Then there was Lily lecturing, all prunes and prisms, in her God-awful know-it-all way. The pair of you forever twisting me, an ignorant young urchin, half out of his skin.'

'You're far from a young urchin now,' she told him seriously. 'You're big and tough, and oh so very strong. And you're a Commando and ...'

'I want you again,' he told her hoarsely. 'In fact, I think I could keep on wanting you all night.'

'Not in this hedge, you won't,' she told him, hiding the fact that him being so John Blunt about things was not the sort of healing balm she would actually choose. But his therapy had worked and worked well. She was calm now, more able to cope. Oh yes, therapy! Mrs Pinkerton's word, not hers. She, Burza, knew Richard very well. This was his way of healing her. He believed his shock tactics would go a long way towards helping her in her grief. Well, the shock was working all right. Richard had made her suddenly very aware of him as

327

a man rather than just a close friend. She winced. He had also made her stingingly aware of the nettles under the hedge.

She was certain that so far as Richard was concerned, there was no love. She doubted very much if he would ever feel love as she herself understood it. But then he was a kid from Matson Street. Men and women got on with things down there, and took it all in a matter-of-fact way. Not many endearments around, ever. Wives were referred to as ''Er indoors', or, 'the old woman', else 'the trouble 'n' strife'. In short, someone to sort out the kids, the grub, fetch the beer, and provide the nooky. Or at least that was how it seemed. Perhaps it had been different when the couples had first set out when young.

'What's wrong with this place?' he asked. He was a bit edgy now. Probably, she thought, smiling to herself, he was feeling put out because she hadn't swooned and gone all ga-ga at his terrific lovemaking. She had, of course, secretly. Was wanting to melt, in fact, but she would drop dead before letting him know. Mr Arrogance!

'Because rock-hard lumps of clay, nettles and sharp twigs don't do much for the skin on my bottom,' she replied, trying to act as casually as he had sounded. 'And brambles have scratched the backs of my legs to ribbons.'

'I'm not going to the house,' he told her flatly. 'Let's go to the stable.'

'Yes!' she told him joyously. 'I think it'll be far better there, after all.'

They stayed together all night and Burza became happy and restored. Richard was a part of her life and always had been, and now he was here, making her whole again. They did not speak of Lily or Andy, and had no need to, but they were there, in the backs of their minds, and it would always be so. There was a bond between the four of them. An eternal link. And now I'm being fanciful, Burza thought wistfully, wishing that Richard would say something romantic. Anything, to declare that now he felt something just a little more than there had always been.

As they walked down the lane and breathed in the damp dawn of the country, and saw the sparrows fussing and fretting, and watched cows drifting like brown patches on a cloth of emerald green, the war seemed a million miles away.

'Burza,' Richard said carefully, 'I'm going back to camp straight away, and we'll be moving on from there. I don't know how long it will be before I can contact you again, but I will. All right?'

'Yes,' she said.

'And Burza, something else. I don't know if you realise it, but blokes have to make wills when they go in the Army – or at least fill in this printed form. If anything happens ... I mean, I put your name down.'

'Oh!'

'You're the nearest to family I've got – and back home I still have that chocolate box you gave old Gip. I think you were the only person to ever give him a bit of a cuddle. Thank you for that.'

She did not reply, but she was thinking, Gratitude! Richard is acting out of gratitude. Oh, and I so wish ...

'Don't let's spoil our last little bit of time together,' she told him earnestly. 'It's been wonderful, Richard. And it's me who should be thanking you.'

She felt secure and infinitely comforted as his hand curled round her own.

It was very hard for her to wish him goodbye, but he had to go and orders were orders. It was as simple as that.

He left, large, quiet, intense. A Richard she had never seen before. He was quite something, no longer the youth she remembered so well. Now he was very much Richard the man. Whether he would ever be really hers remained to be seen. But he had taken away her sense of isolation, made her feel more confident and able to fight back. To go on.

Chapter Thirty-One

Lily was on her knees, methodically scrubbing the concrete floor of the dormitory. Her hands were chapped, her nails split, her kneecaps rubbed raw. I could do with Clara's kneeling mat, she thought bleakly. Oh dear Lord, bless and look after dearest Clara. Hold her hand up there. Let her be reunited with George and Baby Vi. I wish ... No! I must press on. That's what Burza would say.

She glanced about her, at the depressing scene. At the tightly closed doors on either side of her. They seemed malevolent somehow. Everywhere up here was silent. Down below, and on the floor above there came occasional short bursts of noise. Hollow, echoing. Sharp notes of official-sounding footsteps, a crisp order, a whistle blown. Everything was grey here. The corridor, the doors, even the air.

I've got three years of this, she thought. I spent my six months on remand, and now Borstal. But I suppose I'm lucky. they were going to put me in an asylum! Thank heaven Burza went and saw my father, told him over and over again. Went on and on at him. So he pulled out all the stops – and it worked because he is so well-respected. Yet he never looked at me once. But I can cope, I can and I must. I promised Burza.

Lily's back ached. Her knucklebones were poking through her skin. She felt despairing and degraded. Her thoughts ran on.

I'm being corrected, but do they have to go out of their way to humiliate and crush us so? I suppose we all deserve it – I know I do. Burza never said so, not towards the last, but she knows I'm being meted out with my just deserts. I became a loose woman – like darling Marion. And I dared to feel contemptuous of *her*! Even worse, I was horrible, truly horrible, taking advantage of ordinary people like that. Yet in the end, to me, it was just like an exciting job. Something to get me lots of money and to make Zoe richer than Croesus too. Oodles and oodles of money for me and Burz. I enjoyed it all.

The first thing was to wait for the warning and I'd search out my chosen house. It'd be completely blacked out, and no street-lighting either. Everyone at home hiding like moles. Men far away at war, women in shelters, police of necessity very, very thin on the ground. It was a doddle. An open sesame for rotters like me. Oh yes!

Lily's sensitive mouth twisted in a bitter smile while she was remembering.

Even mornings were profitable. She, Three, Gee, and Diver would find streets and houses that had been flattened, and look for pickings. Yes, just as Zoe had told them to. And it was all a sort of daring adventure so far as Lily was concerned. But it was looting! Just as Rosie yelled out to her in that spiteful way she had, and then glared at her – like a tigress, Lily thought. But then she had witnessed humanity at its most rapacious when the Co-op was bombed.

Oh damn, she thought. Even though Father never said a word, I could tell what he was thinking. That he wouldn't touch me, his living shame, with a barge-pole.

'Shit!'

Lily lifted her hand to stare at the flowing blood on her knuckles. Without having her mind on the job in hand, she had gone onto a rough patch, concrete that had glass-sharp edges. The rawness across her knuckles was now an open wound spurting blood. She shivered and took her handkerchief out of her knickers' pocket, wrapped it round her hand and got on with her chore, her mind almost on wheels it was so churning in circles. And as always going back to her lifelong friend. Her thoughts so painful that she began whispering to herself.

'Burza gave up lecturing in the end. She even made excuses for me. And I knew I could get away with murder where she was concerned, so I took advantage. I'm despicable – a rotten lousy bitch! Why didn't I see all this before? But I didn't! All

I thought about was how much profit there'd be once the stuff found its way on to the black market. I never gave a tuppenny cuss about Clara's favourite saying, which Burza always quoted, about being poor but honest! But then she was always listening to and quoting Clara. Oh my poor Burza, she must miss that darling lady so.'

An awful thought came then and made Lily feel sick.

Dear God in heaven! I wonder if any of Clara's bits and bobs found their way into a thief's hands? She had that little silver thimble. It only cost peanuts really, but George bought her it for giving him the twins. She loved that. Silver! Her only bit of real class, she said.

No! Please don't let any of her cherished possessions have found their way into some filthy devil's clutches. Oh, why didn't I think of things like that before?

A tear that scalded the unwrapped part of her soda-raw hand made her blink back her grief.

'Put your back into it, London,' a metallic voice snapped from behind her. 'Self-pity doesn't wash here.'

Nothing seemed to wash the women officers with the milk of human kindness, Lily thought drearily. They seemed to go out of their way to use every trick in the trade to put you in the wrong. And you couldn't do a thing in your own defence. All self-confidence was banished because for a start one was dressed like a backward child in a uniform that couldn't be duller or plainer, and usually fitted only where it touched. And the hat! That was the idea. To make a person look as ugly as possible, to feel as inferior as possible, and as down-trodden as the lowest of the low. Hair was cut above the ears, a prison crop all but, and this was held away from the face with one regulation slide. Navy-blue ankle socks and extremely ugly shoes completed the outfit.

Punishments were severe. You could be tied to a chair in the most cruel way and left sometimes for even more than twenty-four hours. And if you wet your drawers, or worse, you were dumped into a freezing cold bath and made to scrub yourself with carbolic soap, under supervision, until you were sore.

Mitch Monahan was always getting that, and it just made her more full of hate, more aggressive, and ready to do murder, given the chance. Everyone kept their lips buttoned when goosy-faced sandy-haired Mitch Monahan was around.

A lighter punishment was to be locked in solitary, a prisoner in a small claustrophobic room with no window. It became scary in the end.

The lightest chastisement was to be put on a diet of bread and water. Not much of a hardship when one considered the bilge usually dished out.

In spite of yearning for freedom, Lily had thought a hundred times that there was no point in trying to escape. The uniform would give you away in an instant, and the Borstal was situated in a strange district miles from anywhere. Of course Mitch Monahan was always going AWOL and on return, there she'd be tied up again, probably hit where it didn't show, and glaring like an animal. She was always threatening to do the Warden in. She would too, given half the chance.

Because Lily was an exemplary prisoner she was allowed the privilege of writing two letters rather than the statutory one a month. These were vetted, of course. She was never sure whether she was allowed to receive more than that. She always heard from Burza. Her friend religiously sent her a letter as instructed, every four weeks. And Burza, bless her, always thought to put in postage stamps. Burza was marvellously thoughtful about things like that.

Letters from Andy were never held up. But then he was in the forces and so his letters were allowed – all having been carefully scrutinised first. That was one of the most hateful things, the lack of privacy. It was awful, realising that those hard-eyed bitches read Andy's letters.

Lily's heart and soul yearned for Andy. He was so open and warm, so happy-go-lucky and uncomplicated. Andy who ticked her off, who told her home-truths in no uncertain way, but who accepted her, even for the evil creature she was. Who winked in that merry way he had when he thought she had said something clever, and threw his head back to chuckle out loud. He would never turn his back on her, or look right through her as her own father had done. Darling Andy who was as staunch and true as her own beloved best friend.

Dear Burza, who was the one Lily felt she had let down

333

most. Not so much because of what she had done, but because the one and only time Burza had needed whole-hearted support, she, Lily, had been carted away by the police.

So, without Clara, without Richard and Andy, and most of the Cuttings family who had been dispersed here there and everywhere, Burza was alone. Not forgetting Pete who'd got Josie Briggs pregnant, according to Burza's letter, and he was heading for a shotgun wedding.

One couldn't count Ivy. Sid's wife had never been the warmly sentimental type. She was of course devoted to Sid, to her own relations, to Mrs Pinkerton and her job. She was very fond of the Cuttings, especially Clara, and to Burza of course, but they weren't her own.

Rosie, these days a bunch of nerves, was trying to be all things to all men, taking her ancient in-laws under her wing, adoring Ben, attempting to wipe the slate clean where Burza was concerned. Trying too hard, of course. Clara always said that Rosie didn't know the difference between scratching herself and tearing off the skin. Still, that was Rosie.

On top of all that, Burza had even lost poor old Boris whom she had loved so much, then Roan, and funny cranky old Miss Allthorpe.

'Please, dear God,' Lily whispered as she dipped her brush into the now freezing soda water and tried to ignore the agony of soda stinging her wounds, 'look after Burza for me, and let Andy write to her. I know Richard seldom does, but then he's the strong, silent type. Andy will help her if he can, so will Richard. Don't let Andy love Burza more than he loves me. He's always adored her, and he's so decent himself he's bound to fall for someone nicer than me. Oh damn! I wonder where the boys are now ...'

A vicious March storm was beating its fury to the north. Lightning was flicking its viper-tongues at the sky. Then above Nature's argument there sounded a shrill warning for humankind. Citizens of the French port of St Nazaire took what precautions they could against the forthcoming RAF raid. The German garrison that so needed the port, took action stations at once.

A cacophony fron enemy guns blazed defiance at the storm,

334

momentarily drowning it. The barrage shook buildings, and even in some instances shattered windows. Searchlights were long chill fingers feeling the sky. Tracers made a raging red and green firework display. St Nazaire was vital to the Nazis and must be defended at all costs.

Busily looking skywards, neither French nor Germans were aware of the flotilla of British ships, including two columns of motor launches, that were heading towards the great Normandie Dock. It was of utmost importance to put St Nazaire out of action. It was the only dock on the Atlantic seaboard to which the Germans' great battleship *Tirpitz* could go for repairs. No repairs and the *Tirpitz* would be crippled. Her operations against British convoy routes would cease.

St Nazaire was so well-guarded and so heavily defended that the enemy believed a raid on the dock to be absolutely impossible. On the other hand, Britain had already proved that she did not accept that particular word.

Only men considered to have the required physical fitness, courage and determination had been chosen to take part in the proposed raid. Richard and Andy, of 2 Commando, were proud to be among them. If the raid, for which all preparations and plans had been kept secret, was successful, St Nazaire would be made useless to every kind of ship for at least the next ten years.

The destroyer *Campbeltown* was the head and front of the whole exercise. Disguised as a German vessel, it was she who was to be rammed on the caisson, blown up and sunk at stern, thus effectively blocking every vessel's path.

'This is essentially a mission of demolition, gentlemen,' Newman told his audience. 'Our job is to blow things up and, as we must do so right among the Jerries, the chaps carrying out the demolitions must be able to work undisturbed. So the military force is to consist of two types – demolition troops, who must get on with the job and are not expected to fight – and fighting troops provided by 2 Commando.

'Fighting troops have two jobs. The first is to assault enemy gun positions and hold a perimeter of bridges until they are blown, against counter-attack from the town side of the docks. These assault parties will be first ashore and have to be pretty slippy. The second job for fighting troops is to provide protection squads for the demolition teams. The parties will be small, only about a dozen in each one, equal numbers in each of the demolition and protection squads. If we do it right, the job will be done before the Jerries realise they've been visited ...'

Half an hour after midnight on 27 March, the small force entered the estuary of the Loire. They would reach their goal in less than an hour. The air raid was already petering out. Stars looked like chips of ice in the sky. Richard and Andy methodically cleaned their weapons for the last time, checked their gear and ammunition, and rehearsed their tasks.

The scaling ladders and ropes for use in the disembarkation were brought out and put into position. Three-inch mortars with which the Commandos were to supplement the fire of ship's weapons were mounted on the fo'c'sle. Aboard an ML in the starboard column Richard and Andy grinned at each other, then;

'One thing,' Richard said casually. 'If you make it and I don't, you'll look after the little 'un?'

'Need you ask?' Andy replied. 'And you'll do the same for the Flower?'

'You haven't called her that for years.'

'I haven't thought of her like that for years, but she still is a flower in spite of everything. Besides, we haven't been in this situation before, have we, Rich? This has been described as the sauciest do since Drake.'

'Alternatively just so many suicide jobs,' Richard replied. 'Strange, but I'm getting a kick out of the idea – beating 'em at their own game, I mean.'

'I'll be grateful if we make a safe landing in Old Entrance,' Andy quipped. 'Me and water don't mix, not really. I'll worry about the rest later.'

They winked at each other, fell silent, becoming tense and expectant.

At a quarter to one, in the vicinity of Le Chatelier Shoal, they had their first glimpse of land, the low line of the northern shore being dimly discernible, smudging a leaden horizon.

The air-raid alert had now stopped. The German searchlights were doused. All was quiet. The ships continued, like phantoms, banking on the element of surprise. The soldiers had prepared themselves well, harnessing in their webbing equipment with their heavy loads of ammunition and grenades, and with their fighting knives strapped to their legs. They wore rubber-soled shoes, necessary for stealth. This would also be added protection against any mix-up in the fracas to come. German troops would be distinguishable by the heavy sound of their boots.

It came at last. The order 'Battle Stations,' was given, and men made ready.

Campbeltown towered at the head of the long columns of ships smoothly moving in formation over the silent water. As huge searchlights lit up the scene, German lamps from signal stations winked out their challenge, even though believing they saw a friend.

A call sign first, and then the delaying signal was sent back in reply. Even so, warning shots were fired. Had the newcomer in fact been German she would have stopped. She did not. But she had gained three or four precious minutes of respite. Now every German gun that could bear focus, had her in its sights. The other vessels behind her were now also centred.

'Hoist battle ensigns,' came the order.

A giant roaring of guns broke out at once – a cacophony of sound, of explosions sending out flying debris, and heat; and the appalling shrieking from men's open mouths. Blood flowed in dirty red streams, and bodies became spreadeagled in death, or jack-knifed with wounds, with dead soldiers floating on waters aflame.

A continuous stream of projectiles of all sorts was now striking the *Campbeltown* herself, but so violent was the sound of the replying fire that the ring of bullets on her hull and the crack of small shells was scarcely noticed.

As the smoke cleared, two huge stone arms with a strip of sea between them appeared: the lock gates at last.

The *Campbeltown* went in like an arrow and rammed home. 'Success!'

The element of surprise had long since ended. The flotilla was well under attack and all hell was let loose. The hulks of burning motor launches glowed red. A pall of black smoke, frustrating the glare of the searchlights, rolled indolently

337

towards the north-west. The section of vessels that were to provide transport for home-going troops was fast disintegrating. Clearly there might be difficulty there, no going back, but for the moment this was of little account.

On land the quayside was brilliantly lit, chequered by the sharp black shadows of warehouse buildings. Beyond, in the dimmer half-light, metal lines, carriage-heavy sidings, platforms of sorts, and all the hugamug of a dockland railway.

Richard and Andy, surviving the holocaust, sprang ashore with the others and went forward at a steady double. The Commandos spread out, well-practised, aware of the jobs they had to do. They fought the enemy as they faced them, advancing, fighting machines, conscious only of the necessity of protecting the men who were steadily advancing with packs of explosives strapped to their backs.

The wounded and dying on both sides grew in numbers, but still the Commandos continued, like wraiths, dispatching those who sought to bar their way. Much more serious to them that the superior numbers of the enemy, was the weight of fire from the fixed gun positions. Also there was a continuous barrage from the minesweepers and harbour defence craft, some of them firing from extremely close quarters. These weapons, particularly those of the ships in the harbour and the hastily mounted machine guns, very soon began to turn their attention away from the motor launches, back to land. Concentrating instead on the parties of men they now saw determinedly darting about in the searchlight beams, more groups rapidly moving among the shadows of buildings, the railway dumps, and alongside tracks.

The guns if possible grew more venomous, their detonations interspersed with sharply murderous crumps from battery shells. A group of soldiers sprang out to do battle with Richard and his mates. They were fought off, despatched, then Richard waved just once to Anmdy who gave him the thumbs-up sign.

All around there was growing uproar and clamour, and enormous discharges causing mayhem on a grand scale. The demolition groups got on with setting their charges, calmly going about their job while all around them there was an abomination of men shouting and screaming, fighting and falling.

It was legalised murder in its most ferocious forms. All taking place against a million death-dealing illuminations. A Dante's *Inferno* with all it implied.

'There's the signal,' Richard yelled. 'Our exercise is completed. Let's go.'

They began the race to return to the building Newman had marked out as his headquarters as a fresh bombardment sent a mountain of flying masonry directly in their path. Richard and Andy were now cut off from the rest. They began running hell for leather towards the safer-looking houses of St Nazaire. Something hit Andy high on the shoulder. He swore and yelled at the top of his voice, staggered, blood spurting as he fell.

'Go on!' he screamed at Richard. 'Get out!'

Something hard hit Richard's helmet; it protected him but knocked him back. For a moment the mayhem of the present was blotted out. Feeling a sense of unreality, Richard went back to the past. He had a swift memory of himself, wretched, ragged, a filthy and friendless slum kid. Apart from the young smiler who sat next to him, no one seemed to like him.

He'd been on his own and kicking a tin around in the road outside the playground. Then it started over again. He was spotted by the usual crowd of bullies. They began their taunts and torturing. Chinese burns, kicks, punches, spitting. He, outnumbered, had fought back, and made a good account of himself. That was until a well-off butcher's kid named Fatso Neilly joined in. Fatso, a huge chap for his age, had twisted Richard's arm behind his back until it cracked, while a few of his pals were kicking their victim on the shins. Unable to keep his balance, Richard had gone down. In agony, his body arching up and down under a fresh storm of blows, he thought his last hour had come.

Then Andy came charging up. He was wielding nothing more lethal than a ping-pong bat, but acting as though he believed it was King Arthur's sword, he had weighed in. A hopeless cause, for in those days Andy was smaller and slimmer even than his urchin pal. But such was his red-cheeked boyish fury, that at first the bully had fallen back. Then just as Fatso, to the accompaniment of his crew's jeers, recovered sufficiently to go in for the kill, a small black-

339

haired tornado, the same girl who'd threatened to punch the socks off him and Andy only the day before, joined the fray. Behind her, supportive if nothing else, came the one Andy now called his Flower ...

The fierce screaming of a shell overhead brought Richard back to the present.

'Hold on, mate!' he said, grinning round the blood splattering his own face. Then, as he swung the angrily spluttering Andy over his shoulder, he added, 'And shut up!'

At headquarters Newman began hearing sounds of resounding success. One by one explosions on his right flank and rear began to tell their tale. First the winding-houses went up in smoke. Then the pump-house shook under a deep underground explosion. There was a deep and resounding boom as the northern caisson's underwaters burst.

Tall flames reached the sky, and debris, and still there rose the unceasing crash and clutter of weapons of all kinds.

Their mission accomplished, since transport home by sea was practically non-existent, the men had to get away fast. But there had been one unexpected delay. There should have been one more explosion to come. It seemed it was not to be.

But suddenly a thunderous explosion lasting several seconds rent the air as the *Campbeltown* erupted with an enormous flash and a titanic column of black smoke, and the great 160-tonne caisson burst open inwards. Fragments of steel debris splashed into the water around the ship. Two tankers were flung against the dock walls. A German destroyer blew too, and with her went many human beings, both those aboard and on shore. Men were cut down and dismembered by that huge blast of death. Pieces of body were flung through the air to hang like old clothes onto wire mesh walls. Over all there was the choking smell of smoke, charred cordite, burning paint – and flesh.

The dock of St Nazaire was effectively done for.

With no escape route by sea open to them, those who were able, attempted to escape by land. Those taken captive, as well as the wounded, resigned themselves to becoming prisoners of war.

A short time later Richard and Andy found refuge of sorts

340

in a small cavity beneath a house in St Nazaire. Andy, his wound staunched as best as Richard could manage, had slipped into unconsciousness. All Richard could now do was watch over him and wait ...

Oh damn, Lily thought. I hate it here. Life is hell! I wonder how they all are in Solomon Street? I can see it, feel it, smell it even now. Rough and ready, smelling of cats sometimes, or wet fish, and even the Feathers' urinals when the wind was in the right direction. Even so, once it was mine and Burza's Paradise. I wish I was there now. She pictured it in her mind's eye.

'Gawd, wot a life!' ratty-faced Ethel Jacobs moaned to Jack as he made his way home from work. 'An' you staying 'ere in Solomon Street an' all! Why, for Gawd's sake? All you've got ter live in is a ruin.'

'Even so, Ethel,' Jack replied easily, 'it's my ruin. Just as next door is Bill's ruin. We have both decided that it'll take more than the Jerries to chase us away. Beside, things can only get better now. Of course, since the Blitz proper ended in '41 things can only progress.'

'Wot if the Krauts try an' invade? There's still every chance, yer know.'

'Codswallop!'

Ethel blinked and her lips went down at the corners. She looked how she felt. Nasty. She wanted to take him down a peg.

'Ow's yore gel gettin' on?' Her small black eyes were beady as she asked the question, but she was disappointed at his lack of reaction.

His expression remained calm as he replied, 'As well as can be expected, I believe.'

'Do you go visiting?'

'Not allowed, Ethel.'

'Oh!' She'd got him, she thought. 'I think you'll find you can go an' see 'er.'

'My health does not allow it, Ethel. The travelling, you know.'

She wouldn't be done. 'Would you, if yer could?'

Jack eyed the woman whose tongue had caused so much

trouble in the past, and looked down his nose. Then with quiet deliberation he began to wheel himself along towards number twelve. He was thinking sourly that Ethel and Fanny Lyons deserved each other. Arch enemies for years, yet scruffy old Fanny had offered Ethel and her Dave a roof in their hour of need. It had been gratefully accepted. Now Ethel had other accommodation of sorts supplied, but she and Fanny had buried the hatchet long since. Ethel visited the Feathers end of Solomon Street at least twice a week.

As he went by number six Jack noted that the young potted aspidistra he'd placed near the spot where Clara had died, and Lily and Burza's cat was now buried, was still holding its own. When the weather broke he'd take it in of course, but he'd made a gesture – for Clara, he'd thought. Yes, Clara more than anyone else. But young Burza had seen it and had flown across the road at him and hugged him and kissed him with tears streaming down her face.

'Mr London,' she had wept. 'You old darling!'

He remembered patting her cheek and clearing his throat and wishing that his Lily had turned out so well. Then he became filled with chagrin, knowing that there had been a time when he had honestly believed young Burza was the troublemaker. That his own Lily was the one whiter than snow. As white in fact as that velvet teddybear her Aunt Marion had made so long ago.

Jack reached his home that had been boarded up, was now as tidy as it could be made, repaired where possible, and indeed quite presentable when one remembered how it was. Bill had worked miracles with his place next door too. The Frazers' place was done for, as was the Jacobs' place – and the Elliots' of course, their neighbours between, and the Bedes'. He never saw Art these days, which was a blessing. The Frazers had moved away. He had been invited to Pete's wedding to Josie. The party afterwards was held in the Briggs' house in Burchel Street, but he hadn't bothered. It was a sour thought, how he'd once earmarked young Pete for his Lily. He doubted whether anyone would have her now. He felt a tightness in his throat.

He wheeled himself inside number twelve, through to the kitchen that now only had part of a wall dividing it from the

342

front room. Still, everywhere possible had been freshly white-washed and repainted a rather decent cornflower blue. Then he froze. Someone was here, in Kathy's house. His fists clenched. Vandals, he thought, bastards! I'll give 'em what for! Then a quiet, well-modulated voice said, 'Jack?'

'Marion?' His mouth began to work, his eyes burned. 'What's up?'

'I – I've been thrown out.'

'Oh?' His voice was polite, but dead.

'His wife – they have worries about their youngest son. He – he's missing at sea. His wife – she's out of her mind with worry and grief. She needs him quite terribly. So he's leaving the flat.'

'And you've got the push?'

'Oh, I can still keep the flat, everything! Actually Paul bought it for me in the end. It will be worth quite a lot of money one day,' she smiled drearily, 'if it doesn't get blown to pieces in the meantime, of course. No, it's just that Paul won't visit the place or me ever again.' She laughed, a tired, defeated sound. 'It seems he thinks God's punishing him for all his wrongdoing. That the sins of the father have been visited on his son. In other words, he has developed a conscience. After all these years, too.'

'I always said he was a swine.'

'So ... Oh, there was one blessing. I'm to have my job back. Executive position no less, in the Keens Estate offices. My salary will be extraordinarily high.'

'A pay-off!'

'Conscience money. the thing is, Jack, I'll enjoy working again. I mean, going to and fro from Bakers Arms. I used always to help Paul a great deal from the flat, you know. Obviously I spent a great deal of my time alone, so I needed something to do. But I can't stand the flat any more. At least not on my own. I was wondering – would you like to come and share it with me? It has every luxury and—'

'No!' He was looking at her, weighing her up, seeing how kindly the years had treated her in the physical sense, but how mentally wounded she was. Broken, in fact. Crushed! He heard himself saying, 'On the other hand, if things get too bad for you in your place, you can always hang your hat up back

343

here. It's not much more than a shell, and God knows where you'll squeeze yourself in, but you'll be welcome.'

'Oh Jack!' She was on her knees, hiding her face in his lap, clinging onto his hand, her body racked with sobs. 'Oh Jack, thank you!'

After a while he said quietly. 'We made a terrible mess of things, didn't we?'

'Yes.'

'I – I can't bear to look at her,' he said gruffly. 'When I think of all that stuff Bede told me, and offered proof too. About her men, her way of life, her thieving ...'

'Jack dear,' Marion told him softly, 'you have truly forgiven me?'

He nodded, his lips trembling.

'There was a time, dear, when you swore you'd never look at me again. You said that my presence here, in her house, desecrated what was tantamount to Kathy's shrine.'

'She was an angel,' he replied gruffly. 'Pure, sweet, perfect. When they made her they broke the mould.'

'Well, remember her, Jack, *really* remember her. Think of how she was, how she thought and how she felt. Then think of her baby. Lily, whom she gave her life to have. Do you think that Kathy would have turned her back on her own darling child? Even had she turned out to be the daughter of the devil himself?'

'For Christ's sake, shut up!'

'Jack, dear, cast your mind back. We had this conversation many years ago – almost word for word, in fact. Remember?'

'I said shut it!'

'Next Sunday let's go and visit Kathy where she's sleeping in St Christopher's. Shall we, please, Jack? And then, after-wards, let's go inside the church and kneel together – and pray.'

Suddenly the years slipped away and brother and sister were children again as they clung to each other and wept.

Chapter Thirty-Two

It was 1943 and old Mr Wrawlings was over the moon because Montgomery had been victorious in El Alamein. On top of that, the world as well as Burza was stunned, barely believing the news that the supposedly invincible German Army was bleeding to death in the streets of Stalingrad. But nearer to home, the government became so confident that the danger of invasion had passed that it lifted the ban on the ringing of church bells.

That first Sunday, Burza was told later, when Jack London heard the pealing music his Kathy had so loved, he broke down and cried.

There were no tears, though, when at the beginning of July the Allied armies invaded Italy. Everyone had laughed either at or with the Eyeties, finding them a personable lot. *Pathé News* was wont to show films of very happy Italian prisoners of war. Usually, having given themselves up, they were walking in long lines, hands clasped behind their heads. More often than not they were singing opera at the tops of their voices. Everyone in the cinema would clap and cheer, not looking on these merry fellows as enemies at all.

The true enemy in Italy, it was felt, was rotten old Mussolini, he who had become too big for his boots. Even the Krauts sniggered at him! Anyway he was soon deposed, and finally done for by his own crowd.

By September Italy surrendered and promptly declared war on Germany.

'One down, two to go,' ancient Mr Wrawlings said in his raspy old voice. 'Still, Wops are nothing to worry about. And I hate Krauts more'n Japs.'

'But they are as bad as each other, by all accounts,' Burza objected.

'Hurumph!' he exploded. 'I suppose you're talkin' the truth, gel. An' the Yanks have every right to go bananas over them sneaky little bastards. Yus! Now I come ter think of it, that was uncommon cowardly, the way they attacked Pearl Harbor in '41. No declaration, no warning, no nuffin. Little shits!'

'Mr Wrawlings,' Ivy chided light-heartedly on passing. 'Mind your language. Mrs Pinkerton will tan your hide else.'

'Had more than me hide tanned at Armentiers,' the old devil cackled. 'Real madame she was. An exciting experience, very. An' great fun too.'

'Mr Wrawlings!' Miss Rodale exclaimed in her high sweet way. 'Please behave yourself. We must consider our young Burza. I am sure you are making her blush.'

'Get away with you, Miss Rodale,' Burza laughed. 'Besides, I know very well that all old soldiers are the same.'

'And sailors and airmen as well as the Tommies,' Mr Wrawlings insisted, determined to ram home his point. 'In fact, all men are the same under the skin.'

'Yes they are,' Burza replied, remembering Pete who now had a little son named Vincent after his grandfather. 'So now be warned, Mr Wrawlings, us ladies will have our day.'

'Gertcha!' the merry old man teased. 'Blokes is blokes an' always will be.'

By now Burza was part and parcel of life in Peacehaven. The residents looked on her as a beloved daughter. In return Burza clung to them and thought of them as her family. In her dealings with them she always first asked herself what Clara would do or say. Clara had been so wise, so wonderful, so kind! She had always seemed to have an instinct for acting exactly right. She tearfully said as much to Ivy one day. Ivy shook her head in a sharp, rather impatient way.

'She was a wonderful woman, Burz,' she said, her manner stern. 'But the way you're going on these days, like you think the sun shone out of her arse, you're setting up trouble for yourself. Clara was Clara, who I was very fond of myself, but you're trying to make out she was an angel of God. Don't do that! You have a wonderful instinct of your own. Your own

346

judgement is brilliant, and you have a heart as big as a melon. Rely on yourself. Let Clara go!'

'Just like you'll let your own mum go when her time comes?' Burza said, affronted. 'Easy as winking, is it?' Her anger grew, her cheeks were red, eyes burning as she snapped, 'Thank you very much!'

Unabashed, Ivy had squeezed Burza's arm. 'Sorry, luv,' she said. 'Spoke out of turn, didn't I? Friends?'

'Of course.' Burza was on an even keel again, though the hurt remained. 'I didn't mean to go over the top. Oh! Excuse me, Miss Rodale is waving in that pathetic, wistful way she has.'

Ivy stepped back, her look indulgent as Burza hurried off. Every one of the staff knew that Miss Rodale was Burza's pet love. The sweet little old lady was featherlight, could scarcely see, was practically helpless and her heart was giving cause for concern, but even so she never complained.

Strangely, one of Miss Rodale's greatest pleasures was to hear Burza reading extracts from Lily's once favourite book. Burza had taken it from the house in Matson Street as well as the few of her own belongings left there. They were now very necessary. When number six Solomon Street had been bombed, Burza had been left with no possessions at all.

Like Lily, Miss Rodale seemed to be most intrigued with Jane Webb. Again because the ancient lady had the same surname as Burza herself.

'She does not sound so very bad, dear,' Miss Rodale said over and over again. 'She seemed to be loyal to her friends. It is so terrible that a young lady should be executed for picking pockets! What a dreadful time to live in. 1740 in London sounds worse than – than –'

'Germany these days?'

'Yes dear, these days! However, I lived in Munich for some years when I was young. I was happy there. It was a nice place, with warm and friendly people. It is not the ordinary folk who begin wars, but oafish creatures like Hitler.'

Something in the charming old lady's voice made Burza ask, 'And was there someone special there, Miss Rodale?'

'Indeed. There was a handsome musician I was fond of. He played the clarinet in a band. I used to go and listen to him

347

every Sunday. They played on the bandstand in the park, you know.' She sighed softly. 'But I was very timid in those days and missed my chance. Never mind, I have enjoyed a very comfortable and very happy life.'

'With no real sadnesses?'

'Dear child, of course everyone experiences grief at some time in their lives. I adored my mother and idolised my father. When you look around and see white-haired people you know that they have all suffered immensely. In the nature of things they must have all lost their parents – and that alone is traumatic enough.'

'I never thought to look at it like that,' Burza replied, her eyes burning, her throat tightening, a picture of Clara floating before her eyes. 'Of course, you're quite right. Every human being in the world suffers in that way.'

'Time passing helps one to cope, dear. It really does. You will come to terms with your loss – eventually. However, one never ever forgets. And I have had some sweet times, Burza, happy times. I have enjoyed my life. And you must too.'

'I'm glad you have good memories, Miss Rodale.'

'Thank you, dear. Now tell me, have you heard from that young man of yours? Richard, isn't it?'

'He is away somewhere, in action I know. His mate Andy is with him. They had a near-escape in action last year, but with the help of some French people, and lots of luck, they made their way to Gibraltar and finally rejoined their regiment. Andy was hurt, but survived, thanks to Richard it seems.'

'Will you marry your Richard?' Miss Rodale asked.

'He's very independent, so I don't think he's the marrying kind,' Burza replied, and felt her heart lurch. 'Besides, I'm happy to stay here. Helping to look after you is something that a lady named Clara was proud to see me do ...'

Jack London re-read his letter, then passed it to Marion.

'Oh!' Marion whispered and choked into silence. 'How wonderful of her, and how brave!'

'We must let young Burza know,' Jack said. 'She'll be here for her usual visit this evening?'

'I think so, Jack. She loves her old people, she is with Ivy, and there's Rosie and Ben of course, but she's lonely, Jack.

348

Truly lonely without Lily. They were always such a pair.'

'Read the letter again.'

And Marion read the typed page, marvelling that this was about the quiet nervous little Lily she had known.

As the story was set out, it seemed rather complicated. Essentially it was about a miscreant named Mitch Monahan attempting to kill the Warden. Lily had been scrubbing the office floor behind the Warden's desk at the time. The door had been flung open and Mitch Monahan, wielding a knife, had leapt in, shouting her intention to do murder. The Warden had been getting the worst of it when Lily leapt up and crowned Mitch with the bucket. End of story. Lily was now hailed as a heroine.

'So they're trying to get her a reprieve from Borstal,' Jack said quietly. 'She'll be found a job helping war victims and serve the rest of her time in that special service. If everything goes well she will have her own clean and decent room in a youth hostel. Marion, she will be free! My girl's a heroine. Oh damn! I'm so bloody proud!'

'We can go and visit her whenever we like, Jack.'

'I suppose so,' he replied, his manner bright. 'She answered my letter, but it seemed very stiff, but she'll come round in the end. I can't wait to tell Burza.'

'Oh, Burza's such a dear! And your kind thought, placing that aspidistra there for Clara, made her love us a little, just as she used to. I look forward to her visits very much.'

'Me too.'

Later Burza read the letter and there was happiness in her eyes.

'We'll be able to go and see her,' she said quietly. 'It will happen as they say, I know it will. Oh Marion, Mr London, we're going to have our Lily back!'

It was dark when Burza left Marion and Jack and she was going to go straight back to Peacehaven, but since it was All Clear for once, she changed her mind.

A little later she crept into the tiny house in Matson Street, turned on the gas and held a lighted match to the mantle. It flared into life with a little plop and then hissed merrily away. Smiling, Burza looked around. Everything had been kept clean and decent, she saw to that! After all, it was the only home

349

that Lily could return to. Even if all had been truly forgiven between father and daughter, number twelve was still not capable of housing three.

Burza looked around at the diminutive living room, at the shelf holding a precious collection of books. And at the far end, side by side, a scruffy white bear looking rather squashed, and an even more dilapidated brown-grey monkey. It had been Burza's fancy to keep them together, side by side, waiting for Lily to come home.

One day, Lily had written once, she and Burza would have a lovely little home together. Somewhere pleasant. In a street where there were trees, and front gardens boasted privet hedges, and some had flowers. They might go so far as to live further out, perhaps even Chingford way.

Pie in the sky! Burza had written back. *You'll probably make sheep's eyes at Andy and he'll forget what a little devil you've been and go on his knees. He will propose ...*

Lily had written back simply, *I wish!*

So where does that leave me? Burza wondered. Mrs Pinkerton reckons I can stay as long as I like, but one day I'd like my own place. I'd like to make it warm and cosy and full of love, just as Clara made good old number six.

She went to the shelf and picked up her raggle-taggle monkey and sank onto a chair. Then she was rocking the toy that Clara had made her all those years ago, and weeping as if her heart would break.

She did not hear Nick Bede sneaking into the scullery via the back door that had been forced. Did not know that he was grinning round his pointy, decaying teeth and licking his lips in an evil way. He had watched and waited for a very long time and now Burza Webb was about to pay. She would suffer first, just as he wanted to make her suffer for years, mouthy little cow. He'd do her till she cried for mercy; he felt like a stallion at the thought of it. He would keep her at it for a very long time. And then – curtains! She'd be blacked out for good. Just like that. Serve the mare right ...

Burza felt his grip on her shoulders and though he was behind her, she knew immediately who it was. Nick Bede had come to carry out his threat!

She twisted round and tried to spring up and face him, but

he had the advantage. In the ensuing struggle the chair toppled over and she was on the floor. He was kneeing at her, and his hands seemed to be everywhere. Finally her arms were forced above her head and held there. She tried to bite his face and he butted her with brutal severity. She felt her nose spurt blood and her eyes water. But this was nothing to the horror she felt as his knees brutally forced her legs apart.

He was covering her, his fly-buttons having already been undone. He was on heat, she could feel him, ramrod stiff. He was trying to force himself inside her. She felt sick. His breath was foul, his body stank. She was screaming in her heart and soul for someone to save her. To God for help, only God had Richard's face. To the Holy Mother, who looked like Clara. To anyone. Anyone at all.

Nick's strength was overpowering now. He was holding her wrists with one hand. With the other he was tearing at her knickers and in spite of her frenzied struggles, ripping them off. She could feel his penis, hot and rigid, pushing against the flesh on the inside of her thighs. She opened her mouth and screamed high and wild, knowing that if this animal entered her she would want to die. Nausea was flooding her now; she hated the stench of the man, the feel of him, the very idea of his putridness.

Dear God in heaven, she was losing the battle. Dear God save her from this living hell!

Suddenly Nick Bede grunted, and his head was whipped back. Someone had grabbed him by his long lank greasy black hair. His ferrety face was snarling now. He was yanked away, unable to fight the viciousness of the grip that was pulling back his scalp and tightening the skin on his face. And in that moment his father was the stronger of the two and if anything his piggy face was the more vicious.

Sobbing and gasping for breath Burza pulled herself up and replaced her knickers. Her hands were shaking, her legs were so wobbly it was hard to stand. Then, as the two men began struggling together making it impossible for her to get to the door and escape, she cowered against the wall. She grabbed her toy monkey, holding him tight against her pounding chest. She was wondering wildly if she were living in a terrible nightmare, and began praying that she might please wake up.

The two men were grunting and swearing and there was something terrible in the struggle. They wanted to kill each other, they really did! Heartsick and terrified, Burza watched, transfixed by the awfulness of it all.

There came a gleam of metal and unbelievably Nick Bede had a jack-knife in his hand. He raised it in readiness. Sweet Jesus, he was going to kill his own dad! But Art was a dab hand at such things, as an old Army man, and he moved at the right time, unbalancing his son who fell with a thud – on top of his own knife.

Nick Bede gave a hollow grunt, a gasp, his body shuddered then lay still.

Nick Bede was dead.

Art was kneeling over him, his piggy face ashen.

'He went an' saw his Ma in hospital,' he said in an empty sort of voice. 'She was at death's door at the time – I fought she was goin' to join yore Clara, it was that close. An' *he–*' he jerked his head towards the corpse 'he went an' saw 'er. Made out he fought the world of her.'

'I remember. She was hurt when the bomb dropped, Art.' Burza was whispering, and wondering why she felt she hardly dare breathe. She was feeling faint, wanted to be sick, but knew she had to hold on – at least for this poor man's sake. Art was like a jelly, but part of him seemed to be as dead as his son. 'Don't talk about it any more, Art.' Her voice sounded quiet, tinny, unnatural. 'We've got to think about what we must do.'

Art was not listening. He was speaking, needing to say his piece.

'He actually put his arm round her and kissed 'er,' he said bleakly. 'Something I don't think he'd ever done in 'is life before. An' then when 'e left, know something? Her purse went wiv him! He took every penny she 'ad – an' her little silver cross wot she so loved. 'Ow he got it orf her neck wivout her knowing I'll never understand. He was a bleedin' rotter, Burz, and now I'll hang for 'im. Yers, just as I said I would on the day I wos told wot he'd done. Only thing is, don' let my Em know.'

'I don't see how ...'

'She's up Colchester with Min, and still not strong. Min's

doin' a good job an' looking after her Ma for a change. Burz, don't let me ol' gel know!'

'You stay here,' Burza told him. 'And don't move.'

'Goin' for the perlice?'

'To see Zoe Zuckerman. She might be able to help. So just you hang on!'

'I'll do that, mate. Hang. Just like I promised when I found my pore ol' gel in tears. Not because she give a damn about her purse, not even the cross, but because he could do it to 'er.'

As she slipped out of the house she heard the awful sound of Art Bede's sobs.

Zoe squinted up her eyes, and stared at Burza hard.

'I knew somebody would do that bastard in, in the end,' she said. 'He's crossed everyone. Even had a go at the Shatts and they were just waiting to slit his throat. So – p'raps it'll be an idea if the young git's found on their patch.' She snapped her fingers and smiled a Gorgon smile. 'They'll have some explaining to do, eh? That'll larn 'em for trying to cross my Quill.'

'Will – will Mr Quiller go along with it, Zoe?'

'He'll go through fire an' water for me, gel, so don't you worry.'

'Then what shall we do?'

'You and Bede's old man must piss off out of there. Get out of it fast an' leave the rest to us.'

'What do we owe you, Zoe?'

'Nothing. It's us what's owing. Goldie never opened her gate, know that? She never said a dicky-bird, an' we know they grilled her like she was a raw steak. She might have got away with a great deal if she'd spilled the beans, so we're glad to oblige. So, go on my girl, buzz off and leave the rest to Quil an' me.'

Gang Murder, the local rag's headline screamed, *committed by person or persons unknown. No clues, say the police.*

Burza, wanting to die herself, screwed up the newspaper and threw it away. Art Bede never read it at all. He was, she believed, staying at Colchester for good with his naggy old Em.

*

353

Life went on, the war continued and Penicillin was widely used for the first time. The comedian Tommy Trinder continued to jut out his over-long chin and call his audiences 'You lucky people!' The entire nation listened to the imaginary people Colonel Chinstrap, Mona Lot, Funf and Mrs Mopp. Everyone repeated their signature phrases: 'I don't mind if I do,' 'Don't forget the diver', and 'Can I do you now, sir?' Everyone reckoned that Tommy Handley's radio show *It's That Man Again* with its lampoons of the enemy was wonderful, and that Tommy himself deserved a place of honour in Westminster Abbey. He was a hero to cheer up a nation so. Just as Vera Lynn, the Forces' Sweetheart, was the accepted heroine.

Going to the pictures was the most exciting thing out. And *Pathé News* was where one actually saw how things were going on – which of course always gave the lie to that burbling prat Lord Haw Haw. He'd been silent lately, thank God. Rumours were thick in the air.

In London the overwhelming majority of people were confident enough to go back to sleeping in their own beds. This was lovely for folk like Miss Rodale, who hated being closed in downstairs. It felt, she said, like being entombed.

By summer 1944 people really were beginning to believe that Churchill, Roosevelt and Stalin had worked things out very well during their high-profile meeting of the previous year. For at that time they got their heads together to plan the final overthrow of Germany. Now things really looked as though they were to come to fruition at last.

To most people the Blitz seemed remote enough for them to believe that death from the air was no longer a serious threat. The British had weathered the storm and had triumphantly lived through what Churchill said was their 'Finest Hour'.

Tomatoes, lettuces and other salady things growing in what had once been Peacehaven's flower gardens, were cropping well. In Solomon Street Jack London and Bill Jessop were in friendly competition with their scarlet runners and green peas. Over the garden wall they would discuss the news about young Dicky Cuttings.

'Invalided out of the Army he was, poor sod,' Jack observed.

'Or lucky bastard, depending how you look at it.'

'He's back in his old place, working for the Post Office, and doing well for himself. Bit of a firebrand these days. Going in for politics he is, and shouting it from the rooftops. Brainy devil and all.' Jack grinned sourly. 'To think I thought him thick! Never got a word out of him in the old days.'

'He's a staunch Labour man.' Bill's grey head was nodding approval. 'He'll give the other toffee-nosed gits a run for their money, I reckon. Of course, it was plain as the nose on your face that a Labour landslide's on the cards.'

'Did you see Clara's old place?' Jack asked, changing the subject. 'It's going to be even more of a picture later on. It'll throw its own seeds, of course.'

The two old gardeners then fell to wondering. How did Nature do it? Somehow or the other, against all the odds, the wild flower called London Pride was blooming in profusion among the ruins where houses had once stood.

Hope was in the air.

And then, right out of the blue, in broad daylight, strange things called flying bombs arrived. Look-outs were puzzled. this was something new. Its engine had an ominous two-tone sound. When this cut, the rocket descended. There were moments of awful silence, then a terrible crump as this new German weapon landed and violently exploded.

Others followed. Nicknamed 'doodlebugs', they came crashing down on London streets, hospitals, schools, on shops and factories and on the rows of terraced houses. The carnage was horrifying. There was no known defence against these pilotless planes. Sometimes there was not even time to sound the warning siren, so swiftly did the viciously inhuman things arrive. Their ominous engines purring, then stopping, while the people below threw themselves down, shielding their heads, holding their breath and praying that this particular bugger never had their name on it. Then would come the God-awful bang.

One sounded as if it had fallen too near. Heart pounding, Burza ran all the way to Solomon Street and found Jack sitting there, safe and sound, having just come back from work.

'You all right, Jack?' she panted. 'Do you feel safe left

355

here? Won't Marion be coming back yet?'

'Bloody hell,' Jack said, and suddenly his very blue eyes were twinkling as brightly as they used to in the happier olden days. 'It was worth hearing that wallop just to have you come running in like that. Thank you for your concern, Burza. Now I know why Lily has always idolised you.'

'What a load of old toffee,' she gibed. 'I'll just make you a cuppa and then I'm off back. My old lady is shivering like an aspen leaf. Scary days again, eh?'

'Our mob will finish them all off before too long, love, you mark my words. Now you run along to your old people. I'm really all right. Their need is greater than mine.'

Before she left Burza kissed Jack London who was, she considered, a fine man who still had dignity as well as his pride.

The population of London and the south-east took a deep breath and prepared to face it out once again. The V-1s, nicknamed buzz-bombs as well as doodlebugs and other extremely unmentionable things, continued their deadly flights with a vengeance. This was the Blitz returned, but in a more frightening form.

Victims, shocked and injured, helped as always by courageous wardens, struggled to their feet. They were dazed, anguished, hardly able to grasp the enormity of the madness going on around them.

The damage caused by these new and in some ways very eerie raiders was extensive. Each V-1 was capable of devastating two blocks of houses, uprooting trees and blowing residents limb from limb.

Miss Rodale, now quaking as were most of the aged ladies in Peacehaven, was again residing below stairs. Mr Wrawlings defiantly stayed where he was, saying if the staff had to carry on as usual, who was he to scuttle like a crab delving in mud?

'Don't you worry,' Burza told Miss Rodale determinedly, 'the Allied armies are advancing by leaps and bounds. It won't be long now before all the bases of the flying bombs will be captured and destroyed. Just you wait and see.'

'Such deadly contraptions,' Miss Rodale whispered, clutching her chest. 'They must have been dreamed up in the mind of a devil from hell.'

356

By the end of August, eighty per cent of the flying bombs which came over were being thwarted. Thousands were shot down by fighter planes or destroyed by gunfire.

On 7 September it was announced on the wireless that the Minister had claimed, 'The Battle of London is over.'

'Fatuous pig!' Burza said vehemently, looking at Miss Rodale's tight little doll-like face. 'I won't believe it until they actually declare peace.'

The very next day a new threat became apparent. London became subject to rocket attacks – V-2s, against which there was no defence at all. The ladies stayed where they were, below.

The irresistible ease with which the rockets were able to penetrate all defences was such that plans were made to evacuate London town. In the meantime life had to go on. Yes, it must, Burza told herself, even though neither she nor Lily had heard from the boys at all.

It was morning and Burza was spoon-feeding Miss Rodale with porridge oats when several things happened at once. She did not hear the actual rocket explode, but rather the aftermath – an indescribable noise, something like a colossal growl which was accompanied by a tornado of rushing air. The blast caused an excruciating pain in her ears, which seemed to go up high and finished in a loud singing noise. She felt consciousness fading, but then thought she heard Clara calling fiercely through the holocaust, 'Hang on, gel. Don't let yourself go!'

Burza saw how Miss Rodale had keeled over and was lying on the floor, looking like a puppet with no body inside. Her eyes were closed, her lips had turned blue. The sight of the dear little lady's situation rallied Burza, and summoning all her willpower and energy, she succeeded in forcing herself into a crouching position with her knees and elbows on the ground, her body arching in a protective way over Miss Rodale.

The blast still seemed to be coming at her in successive waves, and the pain in her ears grew rather than lessened. The wall was falling, coming down on them, like a huge wave of plaster and brick. Strangely it was all happening in slow motion.

In a wild, unreasoning way she tried to stretch herself further, to shelter Miss Rodale's china-doll face. And she was calling throughout eternity – to Clara in heaven, and to Richard who was probably dead too. Then she received a heavy blow on her back, another on her skull. Her head seemed to implode. She knew no more ...

It was 1945 and spring already. Again there was a surge of excitement in the air. Smiles came readily to people's lips. Everyone listened avidly to the news. Men on leave felt that it would not be many months before they were returned to civvy street again.

'There she is,' Andy said softly. 'Well, I'll be damned!'

He whistled softly and he and Richard stopped side by side to watch. He wondered what she was thinking as she worked. Whether she ever thought about him.

The lovely silver-blonde girl was spooning out soup to a shuffling line of the homeless – men and women, a child or two. Some of the males looked like roughneck vagabonds. Most were unfortunates for whom the war had been more than unkind.

Lily, wearing a blue overall and with her hair caught up in a blue snood, carefully doled out the free food. For each person she served there was a sunny smile and a few words of encouragement. Next to Lily, a woman member of the Salvation Army was handing out a baked potato and a doorstep of bread to each person in turn.

'Goldie' of Matson Street, whose attempt to kick over the traces had been her undoing, had come down to earth with a bump, Lily thought to herself. This was pay-back time, and she was glad. It was marvellous to think that she was finally doing something worthwhile. She knew that she was at last feeling a fully rounded person, safe and secure. Her unending fear and heartbreak though, was for Burza, her beloved best friend. And as for the other two! There was another kind of fear too awful to think about.

As part of her new lifestyle, the once wild and rebellious 'Goldie' was now happily reunited with her aunt and her dad. She went round to dinner with them regularly and told them all about her life in the young ladies' hostel. She must stay there, she told them, until she could properly plan what to do. She had worked out her time, and could have returned to Matson Street should she so choose, but had decided against it. Her father and aunt had told her eagerly that they could make room in number twelve. It would be a squeeze, but ...

Before they had completed their sentence, Lily remembered how she had shaken her head. Kindly, of course. They had persisted. Repairs were slow, they told her, but things were getting better all the time. She gently refused, saying that the hostel was warm and friendly and against Borstal it was Paradise. That she had to hold her horses and think and plan. There was Burza to think of. She had nowhere to go now Peacehaven was gone. And until she herself was no longer needed in her job, she must continue where she was.

With each passing week she, her father and Marion became more close. There was forgiveness all round, and growing love. And they all shared a very real sense of missing the one other person who had always been part of their lives. Dear sweet Burza. As for the boys, darling Andy – Lily bit her lip again and wondered for the millionth time where he was.

Suddenly she heard him say, 'Hello, Flower.'

Her face became a rosy sunrise as she spun round. 'Andy!' she gasped, then: 'Richard!'

'Hello, you.' Richard gave her a warm and friendly hug, then: 'Where is she, Lily? I don't want to waste time.'

The queue was getting restless. The Salvation Army lady smiled in a wise understanding way.

'I'll take over here, Lily,' she said. 'Be as quick as you can, please. We have a great deal to get through today.'

'Thank you!' Lily's smile held heaven as she was looking not at the woman, but at Andy who was watching her so closely. Then she answered Richard's question.

'They sent her to a different place. No one knew it was going to happen quite so quickly. She's now in a lovely convalescent home. I heard from her only this morning. The place is called "Coniston" and it's situated in an Essex beauty spot called Langdon Hills. Here,' she hastily took her handbag from under the bench, opened it and tore off the top of the letter. 'Here's the address. Oh Richard, be careful. She's very frail still and she's grieving ...'

But Lily was talking to thin air.

'What about me? Don't I warrant some attention?' Andy asked in his teasing way.

'A lifetime full!' she breathed, glory in her eyes. 'But – but do you really and truly trust me, Andy?'

'I don't have to worry too much on that score,' he told her, his voice bland.

'Why?' She was taken aback. 'Don't you care about what I might get up to? My track record is disgusting as I'm sure you'll learn. And ...'

'Well, the Army doesn't breed angels either, Flower,' he cut in, dismissing her words. 'Same thing applies. I mean, what if I revert to my previous evil ways?'

'You mean –'

'Perhaps.'

'Andy!' She was openly upset and outraged.

'Just so we know where we stand,' he told her easily. Then he wanted to whistle and shout out loud with joy. He was realising that his luck was in. His golden-haired Flower was well and truly his at last ...

Burza sat alone on a green-painted seat situated on the brow of a hill. Set before her, stretching to infinity it seemed, was the lush spring greenery of the Essex countryside. It was all so quiet, so beautiful. But she felt so desolate, so lonely and so incredibly sad. And the most miserable thing was, these days she found it just too damned easy to cry. Nerves, they said, due to too many shocks. Eventually it would all pass. She must just give things time.

Above her the branches of trees met and mingled together, making a leafy arch. Nature's church. In its way, to Burza, it was more beautiful than the interior of St Christopher's. She had gone there, to speak to Clara, but it hadn't been any good. Clara wasn't there, she knew it. Clara was flying free, high above, she knew that too. As for time, it was indeed passing. Lots of it, a hiatus filled with agony and sorrow. She had been hurt, her spine, and also there had been a heavy blow on her head. They'd put in a number of stitches on her scalp too. But she was better now, healed, and with no scars that showed. Even better, her hair had grown.

It was 1945 and there was talk of peace. But peace would come too late for some.

She looked up, at the patch of celestial blue sky shimmering through the tracery of green. There was one soul who wasn't anywhere near there. Nick Bede was probably eating coals somewhere far below. But Ivy was up there, briskly bossing angels about. Or was she with Clara and George and Baby Vi? And was Cook looking out for Miss Rodale and Mr Wrawlings? What of dear Mrs Pinkerton? That lady had probably found Mr Pinkerton already, and was having to explain how it was that his beloved Peacehaven was no more.

It was certainly getting crowded up there in heaven. And probably poor darling Sid was wishing he was up there too. He had said as much when he had come to see her that time. He had held her close, called her his Little Sis, and he had cried. She felt that she would never hear him telling his jokes again. Sometimes she herself wished ... Oh, why did all the good people have to suffer so? And why were the wicked devils allowed even to be born?

'Ye gods, girl,' someone said from behind her, the voice so gruff and tender that her tears began to flow. She was dreaming, she must be. She dared not even try to turn her head. Then the voice continued: 'There isn't a ha'porth of you! Oh my dear!'

And then Richard was there, kneeling before her, his arms enclosing her so tenderly, so carefully, almost as though he feared she'd break.

'Richard,' she whispered shakily. 'Is it really you? You're truly here?'

'I'm here,' he told her quietly. 'And I'm going to see to it that you're never alone again.'

'Richard,' she said again, still hardly able to take this amazing miracle in. 'I wish ...'

'Yes, little 'un?' His voice held all the concern in the world.

'If I'd known you were coming,' she was floundering now, uncertain. 'I would have tried to make myself look a bit fatter. I'm sorry there isn't a ha'porth of me, but ...'

'Burz,' he told her quietly. 'Please shut up – and kiss me.'

Her arms crept up to meet behind the back of his head. She

361

was nervous, unsure, suddenly feeling inferior because he had as good as said she was too thin. She wished she had worn lipstick, had at least ...

'Kiss me!' he told her again.

Trembling, she lifted her lips to meet his and he was holding her against his heart, his mouth firm and sweet against hers.

'I lie awake at nights going mad with wanting and needing you,' he said against her cheek, his voice deep with feeling. 'And it's always been that way. No matter what kind of mess I've been in, I've known I'd get back. I had to, to find and keep you.' His voice was low, intense, holding all the devotion in the world.

'Oh.' She was quietly weeping, but they were healing tears. She continued to cling to him in a weak and helpless way.

'I've loved you always,' he went on. 'Yes, scruffy slum-kid old me who wasn't supposed to know anything about human emotions. I did though, had them stronger inside me than you'll ever know. But because I don't show my thoughts, because I don't say too much – Damn, I was dumb! But I've known from Infants' class that I had to be near you, and be with you.'

'I – I thought it was Lily ... '

'I tried to copy Lily's rules because you were so besotted with them yourself. And I wanted to try to make you my wife one day. I've always wanted you to belong to me for ever.'

'Richard. Oh Richard, I ... ' She faltered into silence, still hardly daring to believe, to hope.

'I want to devote my life to taking care of you,' he told her earnestly. 'I want to ... ' He stopped short, then, 'Burz!'

'What is it?' For the life of her, she couldn't stop the tiny bubble of happiness beginning to well up inside. This really was happening. Yes, truly. Just as she had dreamed.

'I'm no Clark Gable,' he told her fiercely. 'I don't have a way with words. So for the Lord's sake let me off the hook and say something!'

'I love you.' The words came out like a song, then became a breathless command. 'So please, Richard Wray, stop wasting time and kiss me.'

As his arms went round her. Burza blissfully realized that she had reached safe harbour at last. Had in fact come home.

362